Don't miss the next exciting, thought-provoking novel by Matteson . . .

If I Should Wake Before I Die

Coming in Spring 2003!

Please check the web site,
www.montrealstarvingartist.com, for more
information.

A NOVEL BY

MATTESON

$LIDE

Published by the author.
For information on future publications or to inquire about purchasing additional copies of this title, please contact the author by e-mail at: **matteson_in_montreal @ yahoo.com**

First Edition
Cover concept by Matteson; design by Ken Desgagné
Edited by Sandy Cytrynbaum
Printed in Canada by Transcontinental Printing, Inc.

Canadian Cataloguing in Publication Data
Matteson 1969—
          Slide
ISBN: 0-9730473-0-5
          I. Title.
PS8576.A85967S54 2002   C813'.6   C2002-901765-3
PR9199.4.M38S54 2002

This is dedicated to those compassionate people in my life who courageously chose to sacrifice rather than demand, enhearten rather than dispirit, love rather than resent. I am a very lucky man.

One night, a woman was carrying water in an old pail bound in bamboo. She watched the full moon reflected in the pail's water as she walked. Suddenly, the bamboo broke, the pail fell apart... and the woman was enlightened.

Afterward, she wrote a verse. It goes: "In this way and that, I tried to keep the old pail together. Hoping the weak bamboo would never break. Suddenly the bottom fell out. No more water; no more moon in the water–emptiness in my hand."

–Zen koan

Part 1

Chapter 1

Hurry!

The memory of that night. Speeding east along the Massachusetts Turnpike. Past exit one...

Two...

Three...

They won't come fast enough, dammit!

Oncoming cars. Their headlights penetrate the windshield, spotlighting the intimate horror show inside.

I don't want to see! I don't want to deal with it!

A shriveled monkey paw grasps Dean's shoulder with surprising strength. Moldy yellow nails press into his flesh, threatening to pierce.

Hurry!

A wheezing sound slithers around the car seats like a choking snake, making Dean sick with fright. Amid cresting waves of nausea, Dean feels impelled to wrench the steering wheel towards one of the light poles blurring by, ending everyone's misery.

Exit four...

Five...

The wet, gurgling wheeze that never stops slithering, that never—

That wet...

—felt so close—

gurgling...

— so much a part of him.

wheeeeeeeeeeze.

The monkey paw quivers, then drops from Dean's shoulder, slapping against the seat. The wheeze dissolves into the night like salt into water.

Was it over? Had the door to Dean's life-long cage just swung wide open, finally setting him free?

Influenced by the movies, Dean expects an unseen orchestra to begin playing sweet melodies. He anticipates the sun will rise and spread its golden wings to the horizon's edge, signaling both a new day and new beginning. He cracks open his window. The car's thick, hot, pasty air sweeps across his face, lashing his cheeks with its stagnant tail as it's sucked outside. A cooler, lighter atmosphere rushes in to fill the void, drying the droplets of sweat on his neck as it swirls past.

Dean pulls his foot off the accelerator. The engine winds down. Within the headlight's glow, passing objects become more defined—a sense of security restored. He shudders as the tension starts to drain from his body. His heart flops somersaults as it wrestles with the Juggernaut of mixed emotions staking claim to his soul. He takes his eyes off the road in order to look at his companion, to stare death in its contorted, cancerous face. To maybe even laugh—

The wet, gurgling wheeze bursts from the darkness like a swarm of bats. Dean recoils as the cage door crashes into *his face, pushing him through the threshold and back inside—*

Noooooooooooo!

—but not before the monkey's paw flicks forth, stabbing a moldy, yellow-nailed, rigor-mortised finger into his ear canal.

The ravaged voice of the once mighty governor of the gridiron returns, reinvigorated with the will to torment.

Hurry! it slurs.

I can't! Dean yells, trying to crush the gas pedal through the car floor. I'm doing all I can! I can't do anymore!

Hurrrreeeeeee!

I can't! I just... can't! Dean insists, as the world outside the windshield once again turns to blur, definitions to dust.

******

Dean Barret shivered as he stuffed the memory of *that night* down into the basement of his mind. He leaned his head against the front window inside his restaurant and followed with his fingertip a half-frozen raindrop that slid from top to bottom. He admired the way its tear-shaped body, with the tiny, spinning, sparkling, merri-go-round piece of ice in its center, either barreled through the other droplets that stood in its way as if it were a running back carrying the ball straight up the middle, or absorbed them, making itself bigger, stronger, faster than any other single drop on the pane glass playing field.

An unstoppable, indisputable force all its own.

He watched the drop take on a splotch of wet snow twice its size—and win. Maybe the icy sliver at the drop's center contributed to its character so it could face its fears head-on, Dean thought. Or then again, maybe it was just the way fate had intended it to be, winners on one side of the line of scrimmage and losers on the other.

Now whose team do you think fate picked you *to play on, boy?*

Dean's mind, which too often bucked like a wild, uncontrollable bronco, kicked up a dusty, oft-heard answer.

It was fourth and goal on the five, with one minute, eighteen seconds left in the Sugar Bowl. Dean's Syracuse Orangemen were down by four to the Missouri Tigers.

With the football firmly tucked under his arm, running back Barret exploded towards the middle, where his father's called-in play—a Fullback Trap—had him crashing through a wall of writhing bodies on the back of the three-hundred-ten-pound left guard, Danny Buchwald—AKA "Peanut Pecker."

On the football field, there was rarely ever any difference between the play called and the play run. But this time something inside Dean made him change direction, made him change, in one mutinous moment, the course given to him by the captain. Something inside made him cut away from the tiny, ever-shrinking black hole beside Peanut Pecker, away from the grumbling tree grinder of flailing arms and legs that the play had him exploding through, and instead take the ball on his own, with no blockers leading the way, on a swinging, defiant arc to the outside, running ten, twenty, one hundred yards, it seemed, toward the orange pilon at the edge of the goal line.

Pump, pump, pump. His tree-trunk-thick legs thrust up and down so hard they could have crushed rocks beneath his feet. *Pump, pump, pump.* He was all alone. *Pump, pump, pump.* The field looked as empty and innocuous as a green grazing pasture. *Pump, pump, pump.* He thought he'd tricked the world.

But his feet couldn't move fast enough.

Move feet move! Faster feet faster!

He could hear the blood-thirsty Tigers closing in, their claws scraping sparks out of the artificial turf.

Arriba, arriba! Come on!

Only five yards. Fifteen feet.

Legs, don't fail me now!

One hundred-eighty inches.

Inches! He only had to run *inches* to the orange pilon and into the worry-free, leisurely life of a legend that could be or do *nothing* wrong! The life that everyone had imagined for him.

Pump, pump, pump.

The Tigers roared and raged at him, eager to rip him to shreds.

He was almost there! No one could stop him!

But someone did. A scrappy, freshman, sonofabitch safety—a rookie—named Horace Green, who had replaced Missouri's injured all-star safety, Barry Malloy, in the third quarter.

Green's first game. Green's first tackle.

The eighteen-year-old took on the six-two, two-hundred twenty pound freight train of a running back, launched his five-ten, one-hundred-eighty-pound-when-soaking-wet body straight at Dean like a missile, striking him in the shoulder and chest, stopping him short of the goal line and knocking him three yards out of bounds into a trombone player who fell and jammed the trombone's slide into Dean's crotch—a highlight that made all the sportscaster's funniest bloopers clips for the year.

At the time, Dean didn't know what had hit him. He was left lying out of bounds in a pain-soaked, semi-conscious daze, the mostly Missouri-loving crowd's cheers crashing down from the stadium stands like waves of burning acid.

"MIS — SOUR — RI! MIS — SOUR — RI!" they shouted, fists pumping in the air.

It sounded like they were yelling 'misery,' huh, boy? Your misery!

Eventually—sometimes he thought unfortunately—Dean's mind cleared.

And then came the long, hobbled walk across the field to his team's sideline where his father stood like a cold marble statue, glaring at him the entire way with bunched fists on hips, his upper lip completely swallowed by the lower, eyes compressed down to black sinister specks, his brain maniacally manufacturing the venom that turned into a "winners and losers" speech that would forever stain Dean's heart.

Winners and losers, boy! Winners and losers! You really showed me today who you want to play for! Thought you could do it all yourself, huh? Goddamn disgrace you are to everyone on these sidelines and in those stands and watching through those television cameras over there who was stupid enough to believe in you! And me—you made me the biggest goddamn fool of them all! I'm ashamed to have my blood pumping through your veins. The only thing I got left to say is don't come crawling and crying home to me ten years from now when you get tired of always coming up short in life cuz, mark my words, I will not take a breath before reminding you how pathetically unsuccessful you were when you did things your way and then slamming the door in your stupid, fricking, puckered-up pussy face!

It wasn't simply *what* his father had said, but *when* he'd said it—when only unconditional support could have salved Dean's guilt-ravaged heart. The fact that it was in front of every lip-reading college football fan across the TV-viewing nation, too, helped rip ragged holes of humiliation into his soul.

The following days made a bad situation worse, as the self-proclaimed pundits of the pigskin put forth their prettily-packaged theories about what went wrong in those final seconds with a team as successful with the run as the Orangemen. And most of their cliché-riddled conjectures pounded squarely on Dean's crumbling shoulders like sledgehammers. Everything from ad-nauseam replays of the game, illustrating why a player with the ball should *never* run away from his blockers, to armchair psychoanalyses of Dean's probable state-of-mind at the time the ball was hiked and whether or not his run was a great big middle finger to an historically overbearing coach who just happened to be his daddy.

Well, was it?

As usual, the motor-mouthed, presumptuous prognosticators reached no conclusions, came to no agreements, and a sinister sort of frat-boy fun was had by all in-studio. It was a fittingly cluttered and confusing cap to a dark period in Dean's life in which he saw his self-confidence all but annihilated. And with it, his desire to try and do anything to restore it to its previous smoke-and-mirrors glory.

He'd disappointed everyone.

He was finished.

Horace Green, the fearless madman, went on to be a Pro Bowl player for the San Diego Chargers. Dean Barret quit football for good after the Sugar Bowl game and, after graduating with a degree in business, "ran away to hide his pathetic head in the snow," as his father had put it, to Montreal, Canada. There, he purchased a franchised, fast food restaurant with the small bundle of money his mother had squirreled away for him over the years.

Dean felt safe in Montreal those first years, knowing his father, who remained in Syracuse after his mother divorced him, would never set foot in a land whose people didn't "pledge allegiance to the ol' stars and stripes" or "*habla ingles.*"

Dean had come to Canada with the intention of starting over, of clean-slating his life and drawing a new design for it that entailed the bare minimum of head-on hits, annoying tacklers, and one perfidious coach. But the nagging doubts and fears, along with self-perpetuated images of a life never reaching expectations—both others' and his own—had infected him like a virus long ago, only to be carried, unbeknownst to anyone in Canadian Immigration and Customs, over the border, and in need of only the slightest provocation for symptoms to reappear.

The recent arrival of Dean's younger brother, Peter, upon their mother's death, provided more than the requisite rub.

Dean looked past the drop once it completed its long journey to the bottom of the window and noticed something very unusual happening on the typically busy Cote-des-Neiges street out front.

Nothing.

The street was *never* that quiet, *never* that dead. Dean's restaurant was empty, too, except for the three employees there with him, still waiting for the post-*Hockey Night in Canada* rush.

He stopped himself from tearing away a painful hangnail as his fingers fidgeted in frightened response to the anomaly before him.

Dean heard the weather forecast the previous night, when they were saying the city was *possibly* in for a *potentially* nasty winter storm. But he found it hard to believe that such a vague prediction like that would keep people shut up in their homes on a Saturday night.

Montrealers were, by nature, partyers, and by necessity, a hearty bunch when it came to winter difficulties and discomforts. Why would they start fearing the elements now while ignoring the call of the thousand- and-one bars and brasseries that normally helped the *Quebecois* keep the winter blues at bay? And especially when all that Dean saw falling from the pitch blackness above, passing through the pale yellow glow of a nearby street lamp to land on the ground no harder than a feather, was a mix of some harmless looking, oversized snow flakes and a light sprinkle of icy-hearted rain drops.

Unless the forecast had since changed into something more defined and threatening.

The snow and sleet combination covered the surface of Cote-des-Neiges with an untread-upon, milky, translucent sheet, giving the street the peaceful appearance of a Hallmark Christmas card rather than an asphalt killing field.

Dean wanted desperately to believe it was just another winter night.

But a familiar, vindictive voice inside called him a pathetic fool for doing so.

Chapter 2

Silent night. Holy night.

Alain slammed his foot down on the brake pedal. The car swerved left and right along the thickening ice, its lumbering body coming unstuck.

And with it went Alain and his already slippery grip on reality.

All is calm, all is bright.

Both Alain and his buddy, Bruno, rejoiced as the vehicle squirted past a series of shops and restaurants. The thirty-year-olds sounded like the innocent, thrill-seeking kids who used to sneak out of their houses in the early morning hours, craving excitement after a snow storm—and finding a temporary but satisfying fix as they sledded head-first down the car-lined chute of Westmount's Clarke Avenue, where the brontosaurus-back-sized hill descended through several blocks of the affluent neighborhood, and the threat of a tire or bumper jumping out of the shadows speeding by and pummeling their faces to the consistency of ketchup-covered mashed potatoes was always but a nose's width away.

Life never seemed so deliciously dangerous nor as thourougly satisfying to Alain as then. Why did it have to end?

Holy infant so tender and mild.

Time had eroded away the innocence, but had done little to lessen the persistence of the nagging cravings.

Sleep in heavenly peace.

Now, much older, and with as many arousing experiences behind him as a porn starlet, the cravings still throbbed in Alain's body like cranky, starving parasites. And they demanded satisfaction.

Shepherds quake at the sight.

Most of Alain's life revolved around trying to recapture those same Clarke Avenue experiences of youth, which once were as natural and life-enriching as the blood that pumped through his veins, and recurring as boyhood bruises. But something had happened along the way of growing up and becoming wiser to life's ways. Something inside him had soured.

Silent night. Holy night.

It wasn't right. Where was the unencumbered joy that

he'd felt as a young boy?

Son of God, love's pure light.

How many more insignificant obsessions was he going to use to try and fill the perverse emptiness inside?

Radiant beams from thy holy face.

Was he doomed to be desperate and miserable like every other aging, know-it-all adult in the world?

With the dawn of redeeming grace.

Not if he could help it.

He wasn't sure when it happened, but another shift had taken place inside himself more recently, providing him with a solution of sorts. Actually, it was the only way he could think of to try and slow the cancerous cravings gnawing away at his already hollow soul. Food hadn't done the job, sex hadn't done the job, drugs, booze, money, and power hadn't done it for him either.

So, as the fat joint he smoked and the smooth sensation of the car sliding down the street soaked into his head, Alain grasped for the only choice he saw remaining.

Alain came fully and completely undone.

Or so he wanted to believe.

Silent night. Holy night.
All is calm, all is bright.

He loved that part. The words were pregnant with possibilities.

Christmas music made him happy. It always had. He didn't know why. He listened to it year round. It also played a large part in Alain's in-head music videos—his mind films. These consisted of a flourish of shaky-cam shots, jump-cut edits and nauseating images, all choreographed to his favorite holy music. Once, there was never any limit to the brutality committed in his holiday-flavored flicks, nor any apparent end to the begotten satisfaction.

Until the satisfaction inevitably ended.

That's when Alain saw the sense it made to bring his mind films to life during his campaign for insanity and the unbounded bliss it promised.

In the back seat of the car sat a large, portable stereo he'd had Bruno pick up for him at Wal-Mart. It played a CD made by Alain from downloaded music. *Silent Night* faded away and *The Grinch's Song* began.

Alain bobbed his head up and down to the song's rhythm for a while before asking Bruno, in French, "I'm so crazy, huh?"

"You're nuts, man."

"Insane, huh?"

But Bruno didn't respond.

The car slid to a stop underneath a train overpass, where the freezing rain and snow had yet to grow a slick second skin on the road.

"All right! That was longer than the first time by ten feet, at least!" Bruno shouted, steering the subject away from Alain's sanity question.

The two friends high-fived and sucked on their joints.

"You like that, huh?" Alain said, holding the smoke in his lungs while pulling a U-turn in the middle of the deserted road and heading back in the opposite direction. "I got more where that came from."

"Oh, you *are* insane, man," Bruno said. "We gonna do it again?"

"No. I got something *better*."

"Better than *that*? No way! How? What do you mean? What is it? Tell me!" Bruno shouted, like a two year old. He rocked back and forth in his seat and clapped his hands in time to the song's denunciation of mean old Mr. Grinch. "Tell me what you've got planned!"

This song's about me, Alain thought, listening to the lyrics. I'm *already* famous—and I've yet to direct my first real movie. Just wait...

He closed his eyes and saw a series of kinetic, frenetic shots for his movie: first shot showed him fighting the steering wheel; the second showed the front tires locked, with ice spraying out from behind them; the third showed Alain fighting the steering wheel again and grinning and laughing madly; the fourth was a long shot of the car going into a spin; the fifth was a tight shot of Alain's eyes, looking insane, bloodthirsty, bottomless...

Alain tore his attention away from his mind film and laid it on Bruno. He watched Bruno rocking back and forth to the music and smiling in anticipation of the coming surprise. He liked it when the big dummy got excited. He felt as though he were a dog owner teasing his pooch by showing it a treat—but not giving it—then hiding the treat and sitting back and watching the mutt scurry about searching for it, vacuuming the house with its nose and licking the drool from its lips in anticipation of finding and devouring the tasty treasure. Alain showed Bruno the treat by telling him he had something better planned. Something *more*. Now he wanted to keep him in suspense while enjoying watching the nose sniff and the drool flow.

Man's best friend, indeed, Mr. Grinch.

Chapter 3

Dean's stomach hugged his spine as he stared out at the empty street for any signs of life. What he saw reminded him of all the people that had recently left him—his mother, his father, his uncle George, who was such an inspiration, his last girlfriend, Annie, who he once thought loved him unconditionally.

Listen to you! If you had just done what I always told you to do, you wouldn't be such a pathetic basket case, his father's voice, strained and wheezing from the ravages of lung cancer, said in his head. It sounded so real, Dean moved his hand to brush at his shoulder, to push the twisted, wrinkled fingers he imagined grabbing it from the deep shadows of his memory.

I'll always be with you to guide you, boy, you know that, the voice said, before ducking behind a passing thought.

Dean shivered.

An old, blue Buick Regal slowly passed by under the

streetlight outside, heading north up the hill, reassuring Dean that at least *one* person—one *real* person—in the world would be there the next day.

He breathed more easily.

And then he was reassured of another companion.

"Hey ugly, we gonna close up here or what? If we have to stay here any longer, I'm gonna have to deliver that baby of Linda's with one of them burger spatulas and a pair of fry tongs."

Dean turned around and saw Peter walking towards him, frowning. The wrinkled bottom of his work shirt sat outside his pants, untucked, and he'd "lost" his hat again.

"Look at you. You're a model of professionalism," Dean said. "I'd better be careful or some blue-suited CEO is gonna come in here and steal you away."

"Hey, what can I say? You expect me to walk proud in a brown and orange monkey costume?" Peter said in that quick, jittery-styled speech of his while looking at his reflection in a nearby mirror and fixing his perpetually messy hair.

He always checked out his reflection in something—a mirror, a window, the shiny metal side of the stove, the oil in the fryer. He certainly wasn't ugly or anything: he was over six feet tall and broad shouldered, with a still-hardening, hearty, L.L. Bean catalog model look, complete with small, mysterious brown eyes, and a chin that had a crew of unseen sculptors chiseling away at it daily. Facially, no one would mistake him for anyone but Dean's brother. But unlike Dean, he lacked any bulging, gym-born muscles—opting for a more wiry, indolence-inspired look instead. He liked to wear his brown hair down past his ears, messy and uncombed, and capriciously hand-swept to the left or right or straight back to match the rest of his seemingly unstable personality—a definite departure from Dean's short cropped do.

Because Peter checked his appearance so frequently, Dean often wondered if something was wrong with him. But then Dean remembered how insecure he had felt as a teenager—a natural phase of maturation further exacerbated, in his own case, by the monster with whom he had shared a home for so many years.

"You sweat the small shit so much, boy," Peter said, after he was reassured that everything about him looked as good as could be—until the next urge to check arose. "Nobody cares. And besides, nobody's coming in here. Look at it outside. It's shittier than a shit farm."

The curse words went straight under Dean's skin like splinters.

"You know, if I'm *ever* gonna feel confident enough to let you be the third key in this place, you're gonna have to convince me you're someone who's got some self control."

"Give me a break."

"You get used to swearing in here when the place is empty, it's easier to slip-up and swear when the place is full, understand? And tuck in your shirt and find your hat. I don't need your kind of bad publicity."

"Yeah, right, I'm starting to see what you *do* need," Peter mumbled, taking the straightened pointer finger of his right hand and sliding it in and out of a circle formed by the pointer finger and thumb of his left.

"What was that?"

"Sir, nothing, sir!" Peter shouted, giving a military salute.

"Did you take care of all the closing procedures I gave you?" Dean said, turning away from Peter and looking out the window. He could see the reflection in the window of Peter dancing around behind him, waving his arms up and down with both middle fingers extended.

"Why?" Peter said, keeping his voice calm despite his

antics.

"Everything?"

"Why?"

"Enough. Because."

"Why?"

"Shut up, shithead."

"Ah-ah! No swearing. Bad words are gonna sour the monkey meat you serve in here."

Punk.

"Did you do everything? Just answer me."

"Yes, your royal ass-burn, sir!" Peter said, bending over and mooning the back of Dean's head.

"We've still got to go do a deposit."

"Why?"

"Don't start, okay? It hasn't been a good night."

"Well, what are we waiting for, boy?"

Boy. In an ironic twist, what had began as their father's convenient and uninspired pet-name for both his sons, over the years became a word Dean and Peter adopted and used with each other. For them, it had been the closest thing to an expression of affection for one another they would allow themselves to speak; a sort of code word that fell comfortably from their lips much easier than "I care about you"—or, God forbid, "I love you."

"Shit, boy, look at it out there!" Peter said, gazing out the window. "The sky's leaking harder than a trucker after six coffees. I guess they wasn't lying this morning when they said we was in for plum-fucker of an ice storm."

Hearing only the bad language, Dean turned and glared at his brother. Peter grinned in return as if he were daring Dean to run after him and give him noogies or claw his stomach like when they were kids. That beaming, cocky, toothy grin of his had recently saved him from more brotherly

SLIDE

beatings than Dean cared to count.

That, and the fact that every winter the Canadian cold brought an almost unbearable ache to Dean's tortured knees, making quick movements sheer agony.

"Go ask Linda to show you how to close out the registers," Dean said. "I don't trust you with anything else; I don't know *why* I should trust you with the money."

"All right! The register, baby! Hawaii, here I come!" Peter shouted, letting out a whoop, spinning around, and then slapping the back of every chair he could reach on his way to the counter as he sang aloud.

The punk was a perpetual motion machine, Dean thought. Never stopped. Always moving, always making noise. Always impatient, always bored, always saying outrageous things in that rapid fire speech of his, and then finding an outrageous action to match... It seemed he'd play whatever role it took to get the spotlight shone on him.

And it was this often abrasive, often offensive tactic to gain the world's attention—either of the positive sort or negative—that Dean feared would eventually get his kid brother hurt.

But maybe that was just the overprotective father in him talking.

Overprotective mother, you mean! At least the boy's got some balls! He's no chicken-shit control freak like yourself— he likes to live a little! So what!

Dean tried his best to ignore that familiar voice in his head.

He gazed out the window again. It *was* getting shittier out there—the kid was right. Dean looked up at the street lamp and saw that the intensity of the snow and icy rain had significantly increased in only the past few minutes.

Maybe everybody was right in staying home tonight, he

thought. And maybe we should join them. ASAP.

Dean noticed the same old, blue Buick Regal slowly passing by—sliding by, really—heading south, down Cote-des-Neiges, in the opposite direction as before.

Must have just run out for milk or something at the depanneur up the street, Dean thought. Risking their lives for milk—go figure. Hope they make it back home safe.

Safe... Safe... You sound like your frigging mother, boy, always talking about being safe.

"Hope we all do," Dean said out loud, trying to drown out the voice, the virus, whose symptoms were so difficult to find solace from these days.

Chapter 4

Joy to the world! The Lord is come:
Let earth receive her King!
Let every heart prepare him room,
and heaven and nature sing.

Alain contrived his humdinger of a plan as they slid down the street out of control. The *Joy to the World* song helped personalize the plan as it took form. Alain liked to think the song was about him. The fact that it contradicted the Mr. Grinch self-image didn't matter in the least. That's what crazy people did: contradict. Lapses in logic were expected from his kind.

The demons Alain imagined talking in his head played an important part in the plan's creation as well. (If people only knew how much careful scheming this being-insane business required! He was *sure* he'd be admired for the boundlessness of his resolve.) Alain felt the sense of lunacy strongest inside of him whenever the demons spoke. "You are so *insssssssssssssssssssane*," their chorus of voices hissed and crackled in his head as if the sound were coming over a cheap walkie-talkie. "Insane, insane, insane, *insssssssssssane* in the brain."

The evil spirits, Alain believed, pointed a way for him to head more directly into the depths of insanity. The plan they dictated was intended to keep the itch of his unsatisfied cravings from driving him... well, insane—but an insanity of a definite *inferior* variety, or so Alain told himself. It was a plan, the demons insisted in their own testy manner, which would best be carried out on this night, in this weather, when the city was so frozen and dead and not a cop nor witness was to be found.

That is, if Bruno, the big, dumb ox who was frightened of his own farts, didn't ruin it.

> *No more let sins and sorrows grow,*
> *nor thorns infest the ground.*
> *He comes to make his blessings flow*
> *far as the curse is found.*

Spontaneity was one key in controlling Bruno; the others being drugs—especially cocaine— and his innate, dog-like desire to please. Those three keys alone had kept the acrophobic Bruno trapped high in the branches of the devil's tree with Alain for years now. Alain was always careful, though, to keep Bruno a few branches below himself. It was perfect for Alain that way. Bruno always needed someone to look up to. And Alain needed someone to break his fall.

Alain, the son of a heart surgeon at Royal Victoria Hospital. Bruno, the son of a corporate lawyer for Bell Canada. Both residents of the upper-class neighborhood of

Westmount. Together, they worked harder to *not* follow in their fathers' footsteps than they would have if they'd gone to the best Ivy League schools and come home with a wall full of degrees and accolades.

Being a bum was hard work when you all ready had it all.

"What's the plan?" Bruno asked Alain again.

"You'll know soon enough."

Bruno pouted while he sucked on his joint.

The car struggled as it tried to climb back up Cote-des-Neiges. More often than not, its tires spun and whined as the car slowed to a crawl, desperate for traction. The ice grew thicker on the road. It collected in the corners of the windshield even as the car's heater huffed and puffed like an asthmatic sprinter. In the middle of the windshield, the wipers smeared everything until it seemed Vaseline, not frozen rain, was falling from the sky. It left the world outside a blur.

In these conditions, chaos seemed a hair-trigger slip and slide away.

The 1990 Buick Regal they drove didn't help their situation.

Alain considered complaining to Bruno about the car he had hot wired earlier that night on his own and had come to pick him up in—a non-descriptive car for their night out was Alain's order. But not *this* non-descriptive.

Several foot-long rips stretched across the light tan, vinyl upholstery, which smelled of pizza, stale beer and cigarettes. The Buick had no traction whatsoever in this weather, thanks to a careless owner who had failed to put on any snow tires. The heater blew air that felt more like an autumn breeze than a furnace blast. No wipers on the back windshield, either, which was crusted over in a white, impenetrable, icy shell.

Nothing like Alain's BMW convertible parked at home.

Alain kept his complaints about the crappy car to himself. He didn't want to give Bruno any excuse not to be a cooperative canine. At least he had his music to help melt away the remnants of his sanity.

Winter Wonderland played on the portable stereo.

He pulled the Regal into the large parking lot of a giant Maxi grocery store on the corner of Cote-des-Neiges and Bedford and parked it at the front corner of the lot, facing north, looking across Bedford.

"We're here," Alain said, putting the car in neutral and turning its headlights off, but leaving the engine running so as not to extinguish at least the semblance of warmth the heater breathed on them.

"What are we going to do here?" Bruno asked, craning his neck so he could look past Alain at the grocery store off in the distance. The facade of Maxi lay behind deep shadows and the blurring effect of the bad weather. "Uh... I hate to tell you this, Alain, but I think it's closed."

"I know, stupid. That's not what we're here for. What we're interested in is right over there." He pointed across Bedford to a restaurant.

"Oh," Bruno said, not hiding too well the disappointed tone in his voice. "So you just wanted to grab something to eat, huh? That was the plan?"

"Something like that, yeah. Is that all right with you?" Alain said, not caring if it was or not. He studied the restaurant for movement inside. "Do something, huh, and go grab that back-pack I threw in the trunk. It's got everything we'll need."

Bruno jumped outside before Alain finished speaking. He went to the trunk, fished around in it for a moment, and then came back with a dark green nylon backpack.

"I never realized how much trunk space these big cars

have," Bruno said as he climbed back into the passenger seat. "You could fit a dead horse back there, I swear."

After having been outside for only thirty seconds, Bruno's down-filled winter coat sparkled with little drops of ice, which reflected the light of a nearby street lamp.

Alain couldn't care less about the car's trunk space. He closed his eyes and listened to the music while feeling every cell membrane in his body pulsating like a tiny drum.

Insane, insane, insane, insssssssssssssane...

"What's in the bag? Your debit card or something?" Bruno asked, interrupting Alain's thoughts.

"You could say that," Alain said, unzipping the top of the back and gently emptying its contents on the front seat.

As *Winter Wonderland* ended, neither Alain nor Bruno said a word. The sound of the car's engine and the heater struggling to warm their close surroundings seemed distant, almost unnoticeable. Only the sound of the frozen rain hitting the car's roof stood out. It hissed and crackled as if the Buick had been submerged inside the ceaseless snow on a television set.

Two matte black, 9mm Glock pistols, ten feet of white, nylon rope, a 13 1/2 inch Shark Bowie knife, a roll of silver duct tape, and a small hatchet with a chipped head lay on the seat.

And beside all of that lay a digital camcorder.

The rippling shadows of the steaming ice droplets sliding down the Buick's heated windshield cast themselves on the weapons' bodies, making it look like they were melting.

Or weeping—in a winter wonderland.

Chapter 5

"Have you always been this stupid or is the lead in the city water rotting your brain?" Dean said to Peter after he watched his brother put his hand down the back of his brown polyester pants, scratch, then pull it out and smell his fingers. "Are you trying to ruin me?"

Peter could only grin at being caught. But this time his shiny white teeth didn't soften his brother's reaction as they'd done before, and Dean let into him.

"Are you two fighting again?" Linda said as she wiped down the milkshake machine. Dean and Peter immediately stopped their bickering. "Because if you are, I'm going to spank you both."

The brothers' mouths dropped open like nutcrackers.

"Sorry," Linda said, shrugging her shoulders and blushing. "I've got to practice sounding like a tough parent *somehow.*"

Linda was the only one who didn't have to wear the

franchise's brown and orange uniform. But it wasn't because she was higher ranking or better in any measurable sort of way. Only bigger. It seemed the wizards at corporate headquarters hadn't thought to make uniforms for industrious, balloon-bellied mothers in their third trimester of pregnancy.

So instead, Linda wore an oatmeal cotton turtle-neck with a light blue Caridigan sweater on top—a very cozy-looking outfit which, along with her wire-rimmed glasses and calm, soft spokeness, gave her an aura of wisdom and serenity that very few other twenty-four year olds possessed.

Peter liked her—a lot. But they were as compatible as hip-hop beats in a violin concerto.

Where Peter would try and impress Linda by rattling off the *many* titles of all the movies he'd seen last month, Linda would unpretentiously talk about the *one* movie she'd seen with such loving and positive attention to its details—its acting, its costumes, its cinematography. Where Peter would tell Linda that he'd recently picked up and started studying a Teach-Yourself-Japanese workbook—a clumsy means to try and appeal to her Asian heritage—before he'd even learned how to count to one hundred in the intensive French classes he had only just *started* taking, Linda would carefully and beautifully quote him some lines from Baudelaire in French, which he would soak up with a smile at as if he understood every syllable.

It was in these awkwardly self-conscious moments that Peter would understand that something was amiss in himself, in the way that he *did* so much, yet, unlike Linda, knew and appreciated so little. But rather than lash out at Linda in a fit of envy and intimidation as many men might have done, he chose to see this beautiful beacon to his own faults as his savior. The one who could deliver him from his "superficial-itis" affliction. The one who could help him become calmer, more patient, more learned, more in love with the world and all its details, as she herself so obviously was.

She *was* the one.

Peter put on his navy blue Gore-Tex/down winter coat, walked over to Linda and, speaking slowly and in a gentle tone of voice requiring much conscious effort, asked her if she needed any help with her clean-up. She smiled and then politely refused, looking him straight in his small brown eyes the whole time—something Peter found few people could do.

He loved the soft, relaxed smile that fell across her full, red lips, as well as her sympathetic, somewhat feline, light brown eyes. To look into her eyes and see her smile made him literally *ache* in his heart to be closer to her, to be enveloped by her and the many types of refuge she represented to him.

The other employee, Joseph, was a very quiet, very religious, middle-aged Hindu man who had three degrees from the University of Montreal, but who was currently on a spiritual quest, practicing Advaita meditation techniques so as to destroy the illusion of self and to, as he once put it, "escape into emptiness."

Despite his education, Joseph chose to work in a place where he could do his job and then leave it behind, stress free and worry free, so he could go home and study Sri Nisargadatta Maharaj's spiritual classic, *I Am That*, and meditate for hours, dispassionately witnessing the various events of his body and mind.

"Look inside yourself and see that you are not your body," Joseph instructed Peter one time in a rare attempt to overtly teach. "See for yourself that you are not your thoughts nor your emotions nor your memories nor your dreams nor the voice speaking in your head. Okay? So what are you, if you are none of these things?"

"Crazy?" Peter had answered.

"Yes, that's true," Joseph said calmly. "But you will see that your are so much more after understanding that you are so much less. Peter, tell yourself, 'I am the untouchable witness of all these things. *I am now.* I am not a moment before nor a moment to come nor life nor death. I am emptiness. Eternally. It always has been and always will be. This is the only absolute truth. The only truth that will make a difference in your life. The only truth worth fighting for.'

"Ultimately, of course, you are neither the witness or the concept of *I am now*, but it's a useful tool when starting. If you are able to reduce your sense of self down to at least this one concept, this one experience of the present moment, of nowness, it will then be easier for you to take the next step, which is to recognize the truth and escape life's suffering. "

Coming from a small, New England town, where religion and spiritual salvation were reserved for one-hour sermons on Sundays and holidays, Peter at first found this lifestyle and philosophy of Joseph's the strangest thing he'd ever heard. He often had to choke back the laughter, ridicule, and over-the-top parodies that came so naturally to him.

I am now.

Meditate in order to clear the mind of thought? Didn't everything in life *depend* on thought? How could somebody take a test or flirt with a girl or put together a damn trio of burger, fries and a soft drink without thought? Well, the trio thingy didn't require *that* much thought. But who in his right mind would *choose* to work in a fast food joint? And especially, why would you work here when you had *three* degrees already?

I am now.

And who could find any joy in sitting for five hours on a pillow with your legs twisted into a pretzel while "watching" your own corn-chip-and-Cola-stinking breath enter and leave your body when there were so many beautiful babes with tight butts and bouncy breasts to meditate on and lose yourself in?

I am now.

And why was a dark-skinned, Hindu man named *Joseph*?

These were questions Peter had no answer to as of yet. But he knew he'd be lying if he said he wasn't interested.

Peter found it impossible *not* to like Joseph. The guy was just too damn easy-going *not* to like. And even easier to make do some of Peter's dirty work around the kitchen; Joseph was sometimes too passive for his own good. But Joseph never preached, never criticized, never judged, never looked down upon people like Peter, who, when he arrived in Montreal, had as much a genuine sense of spirituality or understanding of himself being nothing but *now* as he had knowledge of the French language. He just let Peter be Peter—which was a lot more than Peter could say for his big bro.

So instead of discussing Nisargadatta, Peter and Joseph spent most of their time stretched over the grill and under the hot lamps talking hockey stats and arguing whether Joseph's Canadiens were going to take the season series against Peter's Bruins or vice-versa—the perfect prescription, in tandem with Linda's lovely presence, to help sooth a grieving teenager's heart.

"Let's get out of here," Dean said to Peter, zipping up his own navy blue, Gore-Tex/ down winter coat—the same as Peter's—and pulling the hood up over his head. The brothers often argued which of them had been first to buy the coat and who was trying to be more like whom, although Peter knew the *right* answer to both of those questions.

Dean stuck a blue bank deposit bag into his right pocket where it couldn't be seen. It was barely a third full, thanks to the weather. "I'm taking the weasel here with me so he doesn't harass you, Linda. Hold down the fort for me until we get back, okay?"

"No problem," Linda said, chuckling at Dean's weasel reference. "I just want to mop up here behind the counter before I go."

Peter scowled at Dean. Although he loved to hear Linda's laugh, he didn't think it sounded nearly as nice when it was at his expense. And what Dildo Dean said wasn't even funny!

Peter decided to give his brother a lesson in what being funny was all about. He positioned himself behind Linda as she mopped, made eye contact with Dean and began blinking in Morse Code—a trick the two had learned and developed as kids when they wanted to communicate silently and discreetly with each other at the supper table or in the back seat of the car when their father was present and petulant. Each quick blink stood for a dot, each long blink, a dash.

I D-A-D, Peter signaled to Dean in a sort of shorthand syntax as he grinned and motioned towards the pregnant Linda.

Dean rolled his eyes and said, "Keep dreaming."

"I'm sorry?" Linda said.

"Nothing," Dean said. "I was talking to our resident rat, sorry. You know, the one that's been eating ten *times* his quota of burgers since he made a home here."

Again, Linda laughed.

"I thought it was a weasel," Peter muttered.

"Well, I'm surprised we haven't found any of whatever-it-is's droppings."

Long blink, blink, blink, blink... I S-T-A-R-T, Peter said with his eyes, signaling out the series of letters as if he spelled them aloud, while pretending to unbuckle his pants. He didn't stop there, though; he continued trying to instigate: P-U-T-Z

"Is something wrong with your eyes, Peter?" Linda said, walking up to him to take a closer look.

Dean stifled a laugh, making it sound more like a cough.

Peter had been so focused on sending his loving message to his brother that he hadn't noticed Linda watching him.

"They were blinking a mile a minute," she said. "Do you have something caught in them? Here, let me see."

"I don't know. Maybe," Peter said, looking nervous, but playing along to avoid further embarrassment—and also to see how far Linda's concern would go. "They just got itchy all of a sudden."

Peter leaned forward and let Linda look at them. She gently spread each one apart and told Peter to look first towards his nose and then towards his ear. He inhaled the mix of her fragrant perfume, the herbal shampoo, and the indescribably delicious smell of her skin as he followed her orders. He thought he detected the smell of baby powder, too. Everything about her was so fresh, so clean, so perfect. He wished her turtleneck was, instead, a low cut blouse, over which her large, swollen breasts flowed... and into his waiting, trembling, horny hands.

Peter was glad his winter coat came to his mid-thigh. It hid any of the goings-on below the belt.

"No redness, that's odd. You sure you didn't scratch your eyes with your hands?" she said. "Because if they're dirty..."

"Oh, there's little in, on, or around Peter that *isn't* dirty," Dean said.

Peter hoped Dean didn't tell Linda he'd earlier caught

him with his hand down his pants.

"Do you think I'll go blind and need a beautiful caretaker to bathe and powder me every morning and night?" Peter said, leaning closer to Linda's face while hoping, wishing, waiting for her to reciprocate.

She smelled *so* good.

"Ooops, careful," she said, bringing her thumb up to her tongue and giving it a quick lick. She put it up to the edge of Peter's eye. "You have an eyelash about to fall in. That might be the problem. Careful, I'll try and get it."

To Peter, the cool wetness of her finger sliding against his skin was the epitome of sensuality. He braced himself against the counter as his knees buckled.

"There you go," Linda said, pulling her thumb away and showing Peter the tiny black twig lying across it. "You can make a wish with it," she said, grabbing one of Peter's hands, turning it palm-side up, and carefully letting the lash drop.

Peter closed his eyes and thought of Linda...

"Come on, Romeo," Dean said.

Thought of her naked body pressed against him...

"Let's go."

Oh, yes, he imagined her shouting. *Yes! Yes! Give it to me, you nasty monkey!*

"Hey! We gotta get going!" Dean said, yanking Peter out of his decadent dreamland.

He opened his eyes to Linda's concerned face. Although it made for a great fantasy, he couldn't see anything in her eyes that told him she even *once* called her lover a "nasty monkey."

"If that keeps bothering you, you should get it checked out by a doctor," Linda said.

She spoke so softly. Almost... almost seductively, Peter believed.

Peter wanted to swoon into Linda's warm, fragrant, soft, sweatered arms.

Linda suddenly turned away from Peter to go ask Dean a question.

Dean, Dean, always Dean! What about me and my injured eyes? I could be going blind here! Just when I'm getting my chance to score, along comes Dean to ruin it—again!

He wanted to feel hate for his brother, but the only thing even close that ever came bubbling up from the depths of his heart and onto the back of his tongue was a thick, pasty, bitter-tasting envy.

The strength and taste of that envy towards his brother had been somewhat different, a bit more powerful, one evening a few weeks earlier, when he was left alone at home feeling especially low after Dean had scored a cheap blow to his ego before slipping out the door for work. His frustration sent him searching through his brother's belongings for something to embarrass him with when he returned later that night—a dirty magazine, a sex toy, at the very least some severely stained underpants. Unfortunately for Peter, he found nothing of the sort.

Instead, in Dean's dresser drawer, Peter came across a leather bound Bible their father had given Dean as one of his high school graduation gifts. On the inside cover was written in their father's stiff and jagged handwriting, "As high as I know you're going to rise above the rest of the world, Dean, remember that the Lord is always just above; there to guide you and offer his hand whenever you ask."

For the longest time, Peter had known that Dean was the favorite in the family. Their Mr. Golden Boy. And at some level he'd come to accept and, at times, revel in and even benefit from that fact. But on this night, after Mr. Golden

Boy had tactfully hit so low in order to end up the victor in an ordinary domestic dispute, the words of their father and the idea of Dean as always having been the favorite hurt and humiliated like a slap across the face.

Mr. Golden Boy, my ass!

Peter never had anything written or even said to him by their father—not in a letter, a birthday card, a Bible, nothing. Granted Peter was never as good as Dean in anything obvious, but still... didn't their father think *he* would *eventually* find his way and go far too, finishing second only to the Lord himself?

Obviously not.

And why should he have? Peter never played football, never did well in school, never dated beautiful women, never seemed to do anything quite right. And, of course—the biggy—he never left his home to care for their dying daddy like Dean had—can't *ever* forget that. How's *that* for a big ol' chocolatey brownie point for Golden Boy!

Peter had sulked and cursed and thumbed through the dog-eared pages of the Bible that night to pass the time, stopping every fifty pages or so to see if anything interesting was going on or being said. He eventually came across a part he liked. It was Luke 5, verses 20-26. The passages spoke about Jesus blessing those who were poor and hungry and hated, and promising them that things were going to get *much* better, while at the same time warning those that were rich and satisfied and respected that things were going to get *much* worse.

Peter found great solace in those passages, in the idea that if he could never outdo his picture-perfect, lucky-ass big brother in anything, he and his new powerful pal, Jesus—who, according to their father, always stood *above* Golden Boy—would have the last laugh in the end.

Jesus and I are going to spike your football-playing ass to hell, Mr. Golden Boy!

"What do you want me to do if someone shows up looking for food?" Linda asked Dean, her sweet voice snapping Peter out of his religious-flavored reverie of revenge.

"I don't think that's gonna happen," Dean said. "The roads have been dead for the past hour. Only a fool would go out for burgers."

"Or go walk to the bank," Peter added, trying to get a laugh out of Linda.

Silence.

"Besides, funnyboy here locked the front door—didn't you?" Dean said, slapping Peter in the back and making him drop his yet-to-be-wished-with eyelash.

Goddamn Mr. Golden Boy!

Linda laughed.

"You wanna know what I think—" Peter started to say.

But Dean talked over him, his powerful voice commanding attention. "If anyone knocks on the door, don't open it. Just politely tell them that they can come back and get one of our *delicious* burgers tomorrow."

The sarcasm in Dean's voice when he said the word "delicious" was unmistakable, and, for some reason, surprised Peter. Since coming to Montreal, Peter had discovered a few surprises about his brother, the main one being how much more *boring* Dean's life was than he had imagined. No celebrities stopping by to say hello and to leave their autographed picture on his restaurant wall, no revolving door on Dean's apartment with big-boobed lingerie models coming in and out all day to "pay tribute" on their knees to the former Syracuse sports star, no non-stop keg and dope parties that had to be broken up by the cops every other night—nothing juicy and jazzed.

Mr. Golden Boy's real life seemed to be reducible to only two elements: television and work.

"Let's go, boy!"

Make that *three* elements—causing Peter headache and heartache being the third.

"Have fun out there you two—no fighting," Linda said.

"We will," Peter said, turning to smile back at her as they walked through the kitchen. They said goodbye to Joseph, who was mopping up in the employee bathroom—number four on Peter's "to do list"—and then pushed and punched and finally kicked open the frozen-shut back door by which Dean usually left with the night deposit so he wouldn't be as easily spotted by felonious eyes.

A stiff, ice pellet-loaded wind lashed their faces as they stood in the doorway looking out at a parking lot behind the restaurant seemingly no bigger than the kitchen they had just walked through. It was barely large enough for the three cars parked in it: Dean's Toyota Rav-4, Linda's Honda Civic, and Joseph's Ford Taurus. All of them were crusted from antenna to wheel, bumper to bumper, in a solid coat of beautiful, shimmering white. It looked as if someone had stolen the real cars and put in each of their places a detailed, life-sized ice and snow sculpture of their make and model.

The air was cold, but not nearly as gelid as Peter would have imagined. He heard none of the usual sounds of traffic or sirens that typically clogged the Saturday night air, but instead, only the crackle and hiss of the frozen rain falling upon the milky terrain outside. It sounded like sizzling bacon.

Peter turned around again to see if Linda was watching. She was. She smiled. Peter smiled back. He felt his heart race and his stomach twist and turn like an excited puppy at the thought of her watching him... liking him... maybe even *wanting* him.

But maybe she's watching Dean and I'm only getting in the way.

He chased away that ugly idea and, instead, focused on Linda simply standing there, in her purest form, separate from the sully of his thoughts. Linda, his savior.

He waved and smiled at her soft, radiant body, which stood well inside the kitchen, away from the cold air coming in through the door. Then he turned, feeling good, feeling he'd done the right thing by waving and smiling, feeling he'd ended this chapter of their relationship with the promise of much more to come, put one foot outside the threshold into the beautiful world awaiting, and abruptly crashed to the ground on his rear end.

Lightning bolts of pain shot up his spine, boiling away every last drop of the bath of beauty in which he'd just been awash, as both Linda and Dean shared a chuckle.

The image of Jesus and Nisargadatta teaming up to break some major golden balls quickly came to mind.

Chapter 6

"W- W- W- What do you plan on doing with those?" Bruno sputtered, looking down at the pile of weapons and the camera on the front seat. They looked so harmless sitting there, like toys.

But Bruno knew better. From experience.

Alain didn't answer. He had his eyes fixed on a restaurant across the street. Bruno could see the muscles beneath the skin on the side of Alain's jaw tensing and relaxing in time with the car's windshield wipers. Alain took deep, controlled breaths and then released them slowly, his stuffed nose whistling as the air left his body.

Bruno knew this breathing technique to be part of a series of relaxation exercises Alain had learned during his brief stint with a shrink a few years prior. Alain breathed deeply these days, though, not as a means to help *stop* himself from doing bad things, as the shrink had prescribed them for, but instead as a tool, a focusing and concentration technique, to help himself do bad things *well.* And to meet the demands of the voices Alain said he heard in his head telling him to...

Au-delà de soi-même.

"Go beyond myself. That's what they command me to do," Alain confided to Bruno one time. "Always go beyond myself, they say, and I'll—I mean *we'll*, have it all."

We. That was the only part that really mattered to Bruno; that one little word, we. *Oui* to we, Bruno would want to yell out to Alain, to the world, to the stars and galaxies above. *Oui* to we. But a thin thread of dread over the obscure intention of Alain to "go beyond himself" kept his lips sewn shut.

Bruno never knew exactly what *going beyond* meant other than something bad was going to happen. In the past it had meant such things as mailboxes being blown up in the country or car tires being slashed in the city. But those shenanigans were like an ever-shrinking drop of water in his memory, evaporated to where it was now nothing more than a muddy stain on his sense of self.

The day with the cows, though, was different.

During the day with the cows, Bruno faithfully followed Alain south-east of Montreal, on route 133, to some tiny, flatland farm town, where he found himself in a drug haze and a field full of cows, cutting off the dangling pink nipples of the bovines' udders with hedge clippers at Alain's insistence and then watching the animals thrash around and bleed. Then slowly die.

If Alain now planned to go beyond *that...*

Bruno already felt a coldness creeping up from the base of his spine.

The sights and sounds of those suffering animals had haunted Bruno since. Not to mention the chronic, bowel-twisting sensations he suffered from believing, thanks to a robust Catholic upbringing, he would eventually have to pay for taking part in such brutality.

The wrestling match with his humane substratum, though, had come *after* the fact, after the brutal act had long since been completed. During it, Bruno could only remember the purity of pleasure: the comfortable, drug-induced cloud he had floated on, the wonderful laughter he had shared with his best pal in the whole world, the powerful feeling of the hard wooden handles of the hedge clippers in his hands, the appealing *SHHHHWIT* sound of the clipper's two well-sharpened, metal blades coming together to form a single point, the curious, the sensual sensation of the rubbery udders first resisting the blades, then...

Then the horrible thoughts would always slide their way into the recalled scene like a pack of storm clouds on a sunny day: The slicing... soaking wet images of the slicing... first pleasant, now ugly. The udders splitting wide—spurting—then sometimes falling to the ground, sometimes left dangling underneath by a stubborn piece of skin... and then the bellowing and screaming—screaming cows... and kicking and twisting and thrashing and trembling and running cows—running left and right and in circles of confusion... bucking, bouncing... the gentle animals scrambling for escape and relief from the senseless pain just inflicted upon them by a pair of hooligans with hedge clippers.

SHHHHWIT...

No!

Oui to we. That's what it's all about—*oui* to we, Bruno thought, trying to change his mind. Me and my pal, Alain, forever together.

Bruno remembered one particularly beautiful bovine. Images were burned into his memory of how blood squirted out of her wet wounds more freely than the milk they were made to give. How the squirting continued for a minute, it seemed, then changed to a steady leak, then a drip, as old Betsy's heartbeat weakened. Then how the animal wheezed and snorted and staggered about looking dazed and sad—so sad, with those big, shiny, black eyes—and how she eventually collapsed to the ground, where she lay there with her body shivering, her nose oozing snot, her legs quivering and its teardrop-shaped, innocent eyes, blinking, looking up perplexedly as if she could see something coming down from the sky that no other living creature could.

Oui to we, *oui* to we, *oui* to we... .

And then her two killers stepped into the four-legged lady's line of sight, standing above her, smoking some joints, spitting on her, sharing a laugh at the surreal sight of her pathetic struggle as the bottomless black pools of the cow's pupils turned a bluish gray like the time-lapsed photography of a lake first freezing over in the winter.

Bruno couldn't be a part of such savagery again—no way. We or no we. Not this time.

Bruno knew he *had* to make his cold syrup-slow brain work faster. He *had* to stand up to Alain for once in his life and tell him he wasn't going to be a part of his going above and beyond—he wasn't going to, he wasn't going to, he just wasn't going to!

Innocent eyes, blinking, then turning bluish gray.

"Tell me, Alain, what you have planned because— "

"Because *what*?" Alain said, turning his face towards Bruno so fast, it looked like a spring had been sprung in his neck. He sounded annoyed that he'd been pulled out of his contemplative trance.

Bruno fought the urge to look away.

"Because what?" Alain's voice softened some, but not his demeanor. He stared at Bruno with the same searing intensity with which he'd been burning holes in the restaurant.

Bruno had to turn away. He gazed down at the pile of weapons on the seat, checking to see if they were all there, suddenly concerned that maybe Alain held something in his hand right now—

—like that scary knife—

—and was ready to plunge it—

What was he saying? They were best friends! Alain would never even *think* of doing something like that! Right?

Bruno peeked back up at Alain, feeling guilty for having thought the worst of his best friend. Alain had turned back to studying the restaurant. Bruno could see Alain's jaw muscles still tensing and relaxing.

Bruno prepared himself to go at it again, to make his stand, to tell Alain that beyond maybe an armed robbery, he didn't want any part of his plan.

Oui to—no! It was going to have to be *no* to we!

Bruno looked down at what lay on the seat between him and Alain. Was armed robbery all Alain had planned with two guns, a hatchet, a knife, some rope, some tape, and a video camera? Maybe. Maybe not. Bruno couldn't decide. It did seem like a lot of tools to carry for a quick couple of bucks. Or maybe it wasn't. Bruno wasn't sure. And his slow-as-sticky-shit brain wasn't helping any in sorting things out.

"I just want you to know that I don't... I don't want to... you know... with all these things here, I hope you weren't planning on, you know..."

The words for his defense slowly dripped out of his mouth. Bruno would never be a silver-tongued trial lawyer.

Alain turned and looked at Bruno—and Bruno had to look away again. He couldn't face the intense power that surged from his friend's pin-pricked pupils, burning away every paper-thin layer of self-protection Bruno had ever constructed, leaving him feeling naked and vulnerable. He had to look away to save at least *something* of himself, for himself. He was all for we, but he still had to protect his me.

Bruno swallowed hard and stared down at his feet. "Just... Just tell me what you want to do, that's all. Before we go," he said, his voice trailing off into the sounds of the struggling car engine, the heater, and the hiss of the sleet on the roof.

He could hear Alain take a deep breath and let it out in a more relaxed manner than before, as if he'd just surrendered to something inside himself. A white cloud of frozen vapor from his breath hung in the air like a morning fog.

"We take these things here," Alain said, sniffling and putting his hand on the pile on the seat, "and we get some satisfaction on this beautiful, opportunistic night, that's all."

"Opportun—" Bruno sounded out.

"Let me do the thinking, okay? We're out here for the fun of it," Alain said, leaning forward in his seat and looking out the windshield into the sky. "There may never be another night like this in our lifetime. It's a gift to us. *Carpe diem.* We gotta seize the moment before the moment seizes us, understand?"

We... Us...

They were such powerful words.

Bruno breathed a deep breath and tried to surrender to something inside, just like Alain had seemed to do.

"*Carpe diem,*" Alain repeated, his voice very low, barely audible above the other sounds around them. "It's as simple as that."

Bruno was silent for a moment as his sponge brain tried to squeeze some sense out of what Alain had said. The guy is so smart, Bruno said to himself. He knew what was best. Bruno couldn't make heads or tails of any of Alain's explanation—except the we and us.

"Simple, yeah," Bruno finally said. He felt a weight

slowly lifting off his chest, but he wasn't sure if he shouldn't just pull the weight back down on top of himself and try to scuttle under it like a ground beetle.

"Simple," Alain repeated.

And then silence again.

"Yeah, because..." Bruno started to say, his lingering nervousness provoking him to babble incoherently. "Because I didn't want... I... I know how you can get. I didn't..."

"Hey. Don't worry about it," Alain said, putting his hand on Bruno's shoulder and squeezing. He smiled at Bruno. "Trust me. Are we in this together? Do you trust me?"

"Y- Y- Yeah. Of... Of course. You know I do."

Alain's smile grew even wider as Bruno spoke that last sentence, the corners of his mouth curling up into razor-sharp points, giving Bruno a case of bone deep chills.

Somewhere inside of Bruno, he knew he shouldn't trust Alain. At the very center of his labyrinthine self, the heavy body of anxiety lumbered about and bellowed for attention like an angry Minotaur. It pounded on his inner walls, trying to shake him into making a stand before it was too late; to tell Alain he was staying in the car or going for a walk while Alain robbed, raped, and pillaged and went beyond himself. He just couldn't endure something worse than the screaming, bleeding cows.

But Bruno couldn't think of how to put the reverberations he felt coming from his center into something solid like words.

And, besides, could he *really* go against his friend. His bestest—and only—friend in the whole world? They always had the *greatest* times when they did things together. And the few times they'd fought in their life were some of the *worst* times for Bruno. The fallout period brought such intense feelings of dread and loneliness and...

He wanted to forget it, to shut it out of his mind, pretend it never happened, like a combat veteran's gory flashbacks. Nothing had been worse in his life than to be without Alain. Nothing.

Except maybe the screaming, bleeding cows.

And now Alain was getting ready to "go beyond himself" again. Beyond the cows—Bruno could feel their pain and suffering aching in his bones like stress fractures. The Minotaur pounded on his inner walls. He felt fear and doubt rattle and rise through his being, finally manifesting as a buzzing sound in his eardrums.

The ghostly screams of the suffering cows joined in, echoing from wall to wall in the back of his mind behind the reverberating buzz.

Oui to we...

To go beyond myself...

Us...

The screaming, bleeding cows...

Bang, bang, bang...

Oui to—

"I've got another surprise," Alain said. "Something I *know* you'll like, and I think this is the time to give it to you."

It felt like a hand had just been lowered to Bruno from a lifeboat as he'd been struggling to keep his head above the water of sanity.

Good old Alain, Bruno thought, grabbing onto the hand and allowing himself to be helped into the lifeboat. He's always there for me. He's my rock. *Oui* to we!

Alain reached over and unzipped one of the small pockets on the front of the backpack. He pulled out a palm-sized, plastic bag. He shook the wrinkles out of it and held it up to the streetlamp light coming through the windshield.

Bruno could see that the bag was half full with a fine, white powder. His tension began to melt away like a snowflake sliding down a warm windshield, leaving him with an awakened sense of clarity as to what had just been happening inside himself the last few minutes.

The Minotaur suddenly slipped into a pit, a deep, dark hole in the floor of its labyrinth that would hold it for hours, maybe even days, before it would be able to pull itself out and make itself known to Bruno's fragile conscience once again.

Bruno could now see how his thoughts had been a fantasy, a cruel joke played on himself *by himself.* A delusion of reality. But what he saw in front of his face—now *this* was the stuff of reality, and lovely Alain was its provider. He reached out and pinched the powder through the plastic at the bottom of the bag. It molded itself around his thumb and index finger.

Pure reality.

"Happy New Year," Alain said, smiling as he watched Bruno press and squeeze the plastic bag like a child playing with soft clay for the first time in his life.

Pure *moldable* reality.

Bruno smiled. For him, there was nothing finer in the world than cocaine.

Except for Alain's friendship and happiness.

"Let's get this party started," Alain said, opening the plastic bag and smelling its contents.

"All right!" Bruno yelled, changing the CD in backseat radio. He loved Christmas music because Alain loved it. He cranked up the volume—

> *Deck the halls with boughs of holly,*
> *Fa la la la la la la la la!*

> *'Tis the season to be jolly,*
> *Fa la la la la la la la la!*

—until the sound sent him tumbling off the molehill of his moral high ground, seared his eardrums, and blasted every last remnant of doubt and fear from his muddled mind.

The angry Minotaur inside could only howl in frustration and disappointment from the deep depths of its pit as Bruno chose to ignore the better person he *could have* been and the path of courage and commitment that he *would have* had to walk along alone to bring him there.

Instead, he chose to clutch self-surrender to his chest, affording him at least *one* positive in a sea of negatives. But a positive he too often felt he needed as much as blood, brain, or bones in order to live.

Belonging.

Chapter 7

On a normal dry evening, it took ten minutes at most to walk to the Royal Bank of Canada and back again. Tonight, Dean knew he and Peter would be lucky to make it in twenty.

The brothers moved cautiously along the thickening ice, each step bringing with it a risk of either bruises or broken bones. Every place they put a foot—on the road, the sidewalk, a patch of dead grass in someone's front yard—every place was seemingly trapped under semi-translucent, frosted glass. Everything they grabbed onto to help steady themselves—a railing, a fence, a parked car, a sign post, the drooping tree branches—everything was smothered in a blanket of heavy ice, a beautiful, milky plating, which burned to the bare skin's touch as if it were a rare jewel with its own built-in anti-theft device.

And still, the sleet generously fell from some bottomless bucket in the yawning black sky, strengthening its stranglehold on the city.

Dean and Peter slid their feet along the slick surface of

the sidewalk, moving like stiff, cramped-muscled monks, with their heads bent forward so their hoods helped shield their faces from the stinging, crystal needles dive-bombing them from above.

"This sucks donkey dick, boy," Peter said, most of his voice muffled by both the blood-red scarf and the coat collar he'd pulled over his mouth. "We *couldn't* have taken your car, huh?"

"Do you even *hear* what you're saying?" Dean said. His breath condensed on the scarf, making it soggy. It felt awful rubbing against his skin.

"What? So?"

"So-so. Funny, I always took you for the knitting type."

"Oh, boy, you are a regular *barrel* of laughs tonight! First, in front of Linda, and now..."

There was pain in Peter's voice, but Dean preferred to chase it away like a poisonous snake rather than let it get too close to him.

Smack him, boy. Give him one for me upside the head.

"Petey's got a girlfriend," Dean muttered.

"Yeah, well, at least my girlfriend can carry on a conversation. Can your right hand say anything beside, 'Beat it! Just beat it'?" Peter quoted Dean's right hand using both the words and melody to one of Michael Jackson's most famous songs.

"And *that's* what *you* call funny?"

"Funnier than anything you ever say, chump."

"I don't think so."

"Linda thinks so."

"*You'd* like to think so, wouldn't you?"

"No, I *know* so. And I know I'll be doing her in the broom closet sooner than you think."

Heh-heh! The kid's all right, eh, chickenshit?

"That's *real* classy, boy. I'm sure that'd melt her heart if you told her," Dean said, trying to ignore his father's voice in his head.

"And we're gonna be moaning and groaning and grinding in there while you're all alone up front serving a busload of Coke-bottle-glasses-wearing, buck-toothed Oriental dudes who can't read the menu or make up their minds and insist on taking your picture next to the shake machine. I can see you, getting all red in the face and panicky like you do when things are going to shit for you. 'Where's my coverage out front? Didn't anyone hear me say I need more coverage at the cash? And who's making the burgers? And who's doing the fries? Can I get someone to clean up the men's room? Chop-suey Charley, here, just overflowed it with one helluva egg roll. Joe, can you stop meditating on the meaning of life for just *one* second so you can make me a junior burger combo? And where's Peter and Linda? Are they in the broom closet banging *again*? Where's my coverage? I'm going to pieces here, people! I need my coverage! I need my coverage!' you'd be screaming while twirling around in circles like some short-circuiting robot. 'Danger! Danger! Danger! Where's my coverage! I need my coverage!' Now *that'd* be funny."

Dean didn't see anything at all funny about Peter's parody other than the fact his brother seemed to *believe* he was portraying the truth.

They were silent for a moment.

"I'm just kidding, boy," Peter finally said. "You can hit back, you know. I can take it."

He's a chickenshit pussy, that's why he doesn't hit back! Ain't that right, boy? You sure let that Horace Green scarecrow-of-a-safety push you around when it mattered most, didn't you?

Dean didn't respond to either prompt.

The cold, wet wind shoved at their bodies like a schoolyard bully unwilling to leave them alone until a score was settled.

Suddenly, something caught Dean's attention. He raised his head and squinted his eyes. The sleet shot under the hood of his coat and hit his cheek, abrading it the color and texture of pepperoni. As they approached the bank, he noticed it looked like a big, black gravestone.

For a moment, Dean thought there might be something wrong with his eyes. Then he realized the problem. Blackout.

"Holy shit, I just noticed the fucking lights are out!" Peter said.

"Do you *have* to swear so much?" Dean snapped at him, the mounting tension he felt inside causing a split in the surface of his normally cool demeanor.

"Yes! Yes I *fucking* do!" Peter snapped back, his mouth coming out from behind his scarf and coat collar and his voice booming and echoing off the wall of a nearby duplex.

"Why?"

"Because it's exactly the *opposite* of you! Fucking Golden Boy."

Peter sounded like he was expressing an honest-to-goodness emotion—but Dean could never be sure anymore. Both cynicism and sarcasm had been so securely sewn into fashionable teenage angst, it had become something of a second skin.

Golden Boy...

You don't know how wrong you are, Peter, Dean thought, the words *Golden Boy* moving about his mind, trying, like a sponge, to soak up and contain the entire history of his life.

Even if it could contain it all, boy, too bad that night *had to happen, huh? Wasn't much golden about it, was there?*

What you did to me?

The faint sound of Christmas music tickled Dean's ears, riding a gust of wind and a wave of needle sharp, frozen raindrops. Rather than ease his growing tensions, the familiar, jolly melody wrung his innards like a wet rag.

For some reason, Dean's thoughts drifted to Linda and Joseph. He hoped they'd be all right in the darkness that had, undoubtedly, swallowed them, too. Better yet, he hoped they had just upped and walked out of the restaurant and were now waiting in their warming cars for him and Peter to return.

Hurry, a voice said, suddenly zipping out of the blackness to sting Dean like a cold piece of sleet.

Or maybe it wasn't a voice. Maybe it was just a tree branch creaking from the weight of frozen water on its back.

Or maybe it was a single lyric picked out of the wind from the distant Christmas song.

Or maybe it was simply a sound bite from Dean's past.

Even though Dean had never believed he possessed psychic powers or even a butter knife-sharp intuition, he felt compelled to follow whatever- or-whoever-it-was's advice.

Hurry!

Maybe he wanted to move toward something; or maybe he wanted to get away—he didn't know which. He just knew he had to make this deposit and then get back and that he had to—

Hurry!

But the faster he moved his feet on the ice, the more they slid.

Chapter 8

"Shut the window—you crazy? It's freezing!" Alain said to Bruno while turning down the blaring music.

"I just wanted some fresh air—sorry," Bruno said, rolling up the window.

"You'll get plenty of fresh air—we're going. You ready for this?"

"Yeah. Sure," Bruno said, putting his hand on his right thigh to try and stop it from shaking up and down.

"Here, take the gun and stick it in your coat pocket—don't drop it, okay? I'll take the other gun and the knife here and you hold onto the hatchet and the rope and tape and the camera, okay? You're going to be filming me. You got that?"

"I'll try."

"Yeah, well, you do more than *try*, you hear me? You do it *right*. Or I'll be *very* unhappy."

Bruno nearly cut himself on the blade of the hatchet because it was so hard to see. The street lamps and all the lights in the buildings lining Cote-des-Neiges and Bedford had just gone out and the light inside the Buick was broken.

Snow and sleet swirled around the car, riding an explosive gust of wind. The car shook from side to side as the wind roared against the car's undercarriage. It sounded as if Alain had parked the car on top of a waking monster.

Warmth crept up from the Bruno's center and radiated out each of his limbs. It caused a spasmodic release in his muscles.

The cocaine.

As Bruno's muscles shook and trembled, he felt his head grow heavy and numb. Suddenly, a part of himself, a part that was neither liquid nor gas, but *felt* like both, wiggled free from his flesh and bones to float in the air.

Bruno wanted to scream for joy.

All fear was gone. All doubt was gone. Everything Bruno believed himself to be, gone. Everything he dreaded himself being or becoming, gone, gone, gone—left behind in the rotting sack of meat sitting on the car seat below.

Everything was perfect. Peaceful.

Bruno drifted above his body, enjoying the freedom, the bliss. His floating form slowly and rhythmically expanded and contracted as if it were breathing—although he had no lungs. He felt a pleasant tingling sensation emanating outward from the center of his new self. It felt so wonderful. Joyful. He knew he was smiling, although he didn't feel a mouth. He was deeply in love with this way of being. It was the only sane and fully satisfying way to be.

"We'll go through the front door, okay?" Alain said, his voice sounding muffled and distant, as if from deep inside a conch.

"Won't anybody see us?" Bruno said, feeling he spoke with his mind, telepathically. He didn't believe anyone could see him. Flesh was fantasy. Preserving his floating formless form was the only thing that mattered.

He wanted to laugh as he watched Alain look at his body. He wanted to yell that the real Bruno was hovering above it. He wanted his best friend to join him.

"Have you seen a single car going down this street in the last twenty minutes?" Alain said. "Nobody's gonna see us, don't worry. Besides, we'll have our fun in the back where no one can see us from the street."

"Our fun?" Bruno said, trying to follow along. Even though he felt like all that remained of him was his mind, it still wasn't a very quick one.

"Tying them up, putting a little scare into them. Having some fun, you know. I want you to get some good shots of me with the camera. I'm gonna be making a movie."

"Okay." Bruno said, already forgetting the first part of Alain's orders. He just liked to hear Alain talk because it made him tingle.

"And then you'll watch over them while I get the money and mess things up some—kids stuff."

"Yeah."

"And then we'll get out of there."

"Yeah."

"Hopefully they didn't do a deposit yet."

"Yeah."

"I didn't see anybody leave, so I don't think so. I'll be pissed if they did, though."

"Pissed, yeah. Kids stuff, right. Wait a minute, who's getting the money?"

"Just follow my lead," Alain said, sighing.

"Okay. You're the boss. Just give me a little puff. A little blow in the right direction."

"What? You *sure* you're ready?" Alain said, checking if he had all his weapons.

"I'm ready," Bruno said, his voice starting to tremble. His cocaine crash began—his body called his formless form back home.

But Bruno didn't want to go. He searched for something to cling to as he felt himself being sucked back into the sack of rotting meat on the seat.

Thhhhh...

No! No! Don't!

Thhhhh...

An earsplitting sound shook Bruno's head.

No!

Thhhhh...

The walls of his flesh and bone prison closed around him with a sloppy slurp.

Thhhhuup!

Bruno's awareness jolted back to reality. Electricity pulsed up and down his spine. His head spun and his eyes rolled back into his head. He released a raspy, guttural belch not unlike a death rattle.

"Let's go," Alain said, ignoring Bruno's return while opening his door and stepping outside.

Alain's voice didn't make Bruno tingle anymore. He felt himself thick and heavy. Dull and dead.

He wanted to tingle with life. He *needed* to.

Bruno bent far forward with his head near his lap and his hands pressed to the sides of his temples—damn his flesh and bone, he thought. He could feel his pulse throbbing— damn his blood and the heart that circulated it. He rocked back and forth in silence with tears in his eyes.

He tried to will himself outside his body again, but couldn't.

Trapped.

He let out a howl that rumbled up from the bottom of his

gut, then lifted the hatchet and smashed out the passenger's side window.

He desperately wanted his freedom back. He *had* to have it. He'd do *anything* to get it.

Even kill.

Alain stood outside and stared at Bruno through the windshield. He smiled, looking pleased with how the evening was progressing.

Chapter 9

Hurry!

"Goddammit! Get in there!" Dean yelled, hitting the key with his gloved hand to try and force it into the lock of the night deposit box installed into the exterior wall of the bank building. The frozen rain had ice-corked the keyhole.

Hurry!

"Just when you need something to work right..."

Dean suddenly felt he was back on a football field, where everything ran out of control, where everything and everyone schemed to bring him down or hurt him, and where few lucky breaks were won. Anxiety bubbled up from the depths of his soul and settled in his stomach, bringing with it nausea.

Forget the deposit, he told himself. Leave it for another day. Let the problem work itself out in its own time.

But he couldn't. He was *determined* to put that bank bag in that night deposit box. He made a decision and now he was going to make it work.

His entire world was suddenly focused on this key and

frozen lock. He wanted to believe that everything—the past, present, and future—would become safe, secure, satisfying, and serene if he *only* made that deposit. It wasn't unlike his borderline superstitious belief that the cleaner his restaurant was kept, the fewer problems he'd have running it—the *un*controllable controlled by the controllable.

"Come on! Work!"

"Tell it, boy! That's the way! Show that dirty lock bastard who's the boss!" Peter yelled. "This takes me back to those days when you used to whip M&M's at me so hard they left welts after I beat your ass at Sega basketball."

"Shut up! I don't need you to make everything worse."

Come on! Call him the *name! You know he loves it!*

"What bug crawled up your ass? Jesus! You should talk to Joseph. He'd help you with that anger. Did you ever hear his *I am now* bit?"

"Not now!"

"No, not *not now*—*I am now*. It's kinda cool when you get into it. It's supposed to help flush your mind clean of all the shit in it—and I know you got a lot of loaves clogging your pipes. Go ahead, try it." Peter closed his eyes and took several deep breaths. "He told me, don't just focus on the words. Focus on the meaning of it. 'Feel it purify your awareness,' is what Joe would say."

"Shut up, shut up!"

"Look at you, boy, you're going to break the fucking key. Let me try."

Peter tried to take step in front of Dean, grab the key, and take over.

"I can do it," Dean said, shouldering Peter away.

"Come on, let me try."

Say it! I know you want to.

"No, I got it!"

"You're gonna break it, boy!"

Come on, give it to him, boy! In memory of your pop!

"Shut up!"

"It's gonna break!"

Say it!

"What do *you* know! You're a fucking *loser!*" Dean snarled, his eyes looking like two burning embers at the bottom of a smoky campfire.

Them's me boys!

A wide-eyed Peter backed away from Dean. For once he seemed speechless.

Dean ignored the outcome of the nail bomb he'd just exploded on top of his brother and continued attacking the ice-covered lock with scary single-mindedness.

Hurry!

Something inside compelled him to work like a madman.

Hurry!

A voice—

Hurry!

—in his head. A voice that told him to—

Hurry!

—because something bad was going to happen if he didn't do what he was told.

Chapter 10

I am Gilles de Rais, Alain recited to himself. An insane sonofabitch if ever there was one.

While the cocaine released a whirlwind of repressed frustration and physical force in Bruno, it had a subtler, but nonetheless menacing effect on Alain. Taken in large enough quantities, the drug often made Alain believe he was someone different, typically someone more infamous, diabolical, and bloodthirsty than himself, like one of the serial killers or madmen whose biographies he loved to read. It was the perfect hallucinogenic marriage for someone so in love with lunacy.

The last biography he'd read was on Gilles de Rais— Bluebeard—the wealthy baron who was suspected of torturing and murdering hundreds of young children in 15th century France.

Alain felt an overpowering affinity for the maniac. He was the kind of guy Alain wouldn't have minded throwing back a few beers and doing a few broads with. And maybe they could have learned a thing or two about being bonkers from each other. One thing that Alain was sure of, though, was that Bluebeard would have made a much better buddy than bonehead Bruno.

As Alain and Bruno slid through the shadows, across the darkened street of Bedford towards the fast food restaurant, Alain tried to invoke the intervention of evil spirits—something Bluebeard had done many times in an attempt to alchemically produce gold out of base metals for his spendthrift self. Alain asked them to help in carrying out his own plan to completion.

To help him go beyond himself.

Alain heard the demons hissing in response.

The duo shuffled up to the restaurant. They crouched down behind one of four decorative Emerald Gaiety shrubs parallel to the restaurant's street-side window. The sorry-looking pyramid-shaped shrubs seemed encased in crystal, with each of their many branches sporting a shimmering pair of diamond earrings that wiggled in the wind.

Alain saw some stray beams of light cutting through the darkness in the restaurant's dining area. Generator light, he figured.

It was weak, but it was just enough light to get some striking, gritty, gray shots for his video.

He considered filming his fun in black and white since he'd always considered it spookier. Especially among the shadows. The problem, though, was the blood. In black and white, it only looked like pools of motor oil. Very industrial, far from the blossoming patchwork of reds and purples and browns and blacks in spilled visceral.

No, Alain preferred his gore in color.

Alain spotted some movement in the back of the restaurant. Shifting, brown shadows moving amid stable black. Curves melting into lines, lines expanding into curves.

Alain closed his eyes and breathed in deeply and called the evil spirits to him. He needed their help to pull this off. To go beyond himself.

Again, the spirits hissed all around him, chilling his head and heart with their voices.

He thought he heard them sound out a word, a phrase, a command—

Hiss...

Of course. No surprise. As they did with Bluebeard and his band of black magicians, they asked for appeasement with a human sacrifice.

SLIDE

67

Chapter 11

Dean sliced across the ice like a speed skater. It was difficult for Peter to keep up.

But it wasn't as if he wanted to.

Dean's nastiness had left Peter emotionally bruised. Peter knew he could be annoying, but he felt Dean's reaction had been way beyond normal impatience. He knew Dean held back from using the dreaded L-word only until his core reactor had overheated.

He wondered what could have caused his brother's explosion. A snotty little Frenchman? Lack of sex? A brain tumor? Constipation?

The longer Peter thought of reasons, the sillier they got. He couldn't stop himself. It helped him better recover from the stinging pain of being called a nasty name that reminded him of his darkest days with their father, when the despot used to whip little-boy Peter with that L-word until he was racked with stomach cramps from sobbing so hard.

If Mr. Golden Boy only knew what it was like to be

called that time and time again...

Try as he might to avoid it, Peter's mental search for a cause of Dean's insolence always fell upon himself. *He* was the reason why his brother was so miserable, why he was acting nothing like the fearless, faultless Golden Boy from the stories his mother used to entertain and inspire him with.

It's because Dean has to take care of such a... such a loser like me that he acts like such a boner.

It was plainly obvious.

The truth hurt as much coming from his own thoughts as it did from Dean's lips. He *was* a loser. He saw it all the time in the reflection of whatever mirror, window, or shiny appliance he happened to be looking in. The messy hair, the pimples, the fickle feelings, the big body housing what felt like a small and shallow mind.

Face the facts, boy. Why fight it? Just brand a capital L on my forehead—my own Scarlet Letter.

Dean pulled farther away from Peter.

"Slow down, boy," Peter yelled, breaking his promise to himself that he would never talk to his butt-head brother again. But he didn't want to be abandoned. His feet slipped out to the left and then to the right, nearly forcing him into a spread and twisted position fit only for a contortionist.

Dean didn't answer. He seemed even further away in mind than he was in body.

"You're acting like you left the goddamn bathtub running," Peter shouted, but received no response. "You got a hot date or something? Be sure to practice safe sex. Wouldn't want you to get any sores on your stubby."

His ribbing fell on deaf ears.

Screw him then. I'm never talking to the stubborn, insensitive sonofabitch again, Peter vowed to himself.

But all wasn't bad. The mention of a date brought the

soothing sight of Linda to mind. Provocative images of her fluttered across his mental movie screen. He felt warmth spread through his chilled body and a smile came to his face as he watched the syrupy, slow motion photography of him and Linda together. His beloved Linda. What he wouldn't do for her!

Suddenly, the Dean situation wasn't *that* bad.

The ferocious weather wasn't *that* bad.

Being an awkward, expatriate, loser teen with two dead parents wasn't *that* bad.

Not with Linda in his life.

He felt a surge of adrenaline wash over his muscles and nerves, stimulating to heavenly heights. He *had* to get back to the restaurant. He had to see Linda again before she left. The idea of saying goodnight to her filled Peter's head with so many passionate possibilities, so many seductive scenarios. He played each one over in his mind as he glided along, relishing the million and one ways he imagined Linda demonstrating her animal-like lust for him.

Oh, baby!

Peter burst forward, quickly closing the gap between himself and Dean until he was beside his brother, slipping and sliding down the street at a breakneck pace and with one word in mind.

Hurry!

Chapter 12

Alain knew the evil spirits would help him. After all, he had promised the hissing demons an attractive sacrifice. And if it had worked some two-hundred times for a raving lunatic like Bluebeard, why wouldn't it work for someone whose intentions were just as impure?

This is why he wasn't so surprised when he scurried up to the front door of the darkened restaurant with Bruno filming him from behind, grabbed the door's handle, gently pulled—

—and it opened.

Luck? Maybe. But he turned and gave a sinister smile for the camera as he listened to the gleeful hisses.

Alain and Bruno slipped into the warm and dry shadows of the restaurant.

Once inside, Alain closed his eyes and silently thanked the nasty netherworld beings, promising them extra bloodshed for their kindness—the way he imagined Bluebeard would have done.

Alain whispered to Bruno to get a shot of him crawling across the restaurant floor to a row of booths to the right of the entrance. Once there, Alain lay down flat with his ear pressed to the floor, looking as if he were listening for a stampede of buffalo. The sharp smell of lemon-scented ammonia assaulted Alain's nose, conceiving a monstrous sneeze in his sinus.

The evil spirits wouldn't let him birth it, he told himself. They couldn't.

And they didn't.

When he was positive nobody had either seen or heard him, Alain signaled Bruno to close the gap. Once he arrived, he whispered to Bruno to stay put and keep filming. He slithered into one of the booths' seats where he lay on his side in a half-fetal position. He could hear his heart pounding against the inner wall of his chest. He hummed a few bars of *Frosty the Snowman* to help himself calm down. Then he lifted his head until his eyes were level with a row of plastic ferns sitting on a divider beside his booth.

He heard people talking in the back of the kitchen. A man and a woman. They were speaking in English—something that soured Alain's stomach. Then, as Alain peeked between the ferns' plastic leaves, out of the shadows and into one of the stray beams of light stepped a dark-skinned man. Not a black man, but an Indian, it appeared. Seeing the man reminded Alain of something else he hated about his city—the immigrants who were spreading like weeds in a garden, choking out the *Quebecois* culture for which he was so proud to stand up, get drunk, and fall down in a pool of puke.

On the other side of the kitchen, in a separate beam of light, stood the woman. Alain could see she wasn't wearing the same brown and orange uniform as the Indian man.

Instead, she had on a sweater and a turtleneck, looking as out of place *behind* the counter as a fresh, green vegetable would have looked *on* the counter. By the relatively large size of her stomach compared to her thin legs and arms, she appeared very pregnant.

When he saw this, Alain turned to the camera and smiled. As Bluebeard knew, this was one of the *ultimate* sacrifices that could be made to the evil spirits.

Alain felt as if his heart was tapping into the power source that drove his lungs and was now overdosing on what it siphoned off. But this change in his physiology wasn't the result of nervousness. It was excitement at the idea of staring chaos in the face, walking into it, and coming through it still standing and in control.

This made him tingle like the days of old.

Alain leaned over and whispered his plan to Bruno. They would sneak up closer to the kitchen and take the two employees by surprise, quickly and quietly. No big-mouthed bravado and guns firing into the ceiling. Bluebeard was an urbane, calculating, demon-worshipping Baron, not a drunken, sloppy, rabble-rousing bandit. Sophistication should be an important part of bloodshed, Alain decided. Insanity wasn't just about smearing the devil's name in shit on a wall. That was an unfair stereotype. Insanity could be as much an art form as painting or ballet, every bit as subtle, complex, and beautiful.

And inspiring.

Alain could see Bruno's left eye, the eye not pressed to the digital camcorder's viewfinder, twitching while he gave instructions. He knew Bruno was going to soon burst from the cocaine-induced pressure building inside of him.

They crawled through the restaurant on the floor, Bruno hobbling along like a three-legged dog in order to get a good shot of Alain's ass as they moved along. Finally, they stopped in front of the counter and sat on the floor. While Alain fingered the trigger of his Glock for the camcorder's lens—figuring that would make for a powerful image in his video—he whispered to Bruno to get his hatchet ready with his free hand. Alain watched Bruno fumble with it, flicking his wrist, giving the hatchet a couple of chops in front of the lens—and almost hitting Alain's leg in the process. To Alain, Bruno looked like a young retarded boy with a twinkle in his eye, waving his brand new baseball bat in the air, eager to step into the batter's box and smack a game-winning dinger off the batting tee.

But Alain knew, from experience, that what was happening inside Bruno was as far from that innocuous impression as the planet Pluto was from the sun.

The plan was to be patient. To wait there in front of the counter until someone, either the man or the woman—it didn't matter who—came up front to the cash register or went to lock the door. Alain would then take the employee hostage while Bruno filmed everything, and then Alain would take the camera and film Bruno threatening to hack off his or her hands with his hatchet. Alain would then spring over the counter with camera and gun in hand—taping a nice Scorcese-esque hand-held dolly shot in the process—and take control of the other employee, who'd be too confused and shocked to resist.

What fantastic cinema! So powerful, so exciting! He already couldn't wait to edit it and include a fun Christmas song with the shocking images.

On the first day of Christmas,
My true love gave to me:
A partridge in a pear tree.

They waited for someone to come.

Alain punched Bruno in the arm when he started impatiently to tap the blade of the hatchet on the floor.

They continued waiting.

And waiting.

After five minutes, Alain figured something must be wrong. It was silent in the kitchen. Alain wondered if, while he was editing his video in his head, the man and woman had left the building without him realizing it.

And after he'd promised the evil spirits so much—this wasn't good.

Or even worse, the man and woman had heard him and Bruno sneak in and were now silently waiting just behind the counter, waiting to clobber him with a hammer or stick him with a knife when he raised his head to check things out.

Shit.

The thought of getting a knife stuck into his brain made Alain shudder. The thought of pain—his own pain—was *so* unpleasant: just to consider it was akin to experiencing it.

But others' pain... oh, now *that* was very different. That was sweet.

Alain promptly decided the two employees must be sitting silently in the kitchen, waiting for the lights in the rest of the place to come back on and business to continue.

But what business? There wasn't any business tonight. And what if the lights did come on with them waiting there?

Shit.

Alain prayed again to the evil spirits to help him out, to give him a sign as to what to do. He reminded the evil spirits about the young, pregnant mother-in-waiting with the fat, juicy belly just begging to be burst for their sake.

He thought he heard the spirits respond. A very soft hiss

off in the distance. He tried to interpret what they were telling him. They seemed to be instructing him to raise his head and peek over the counter—

—but he couldn't be sure.

Again, the thought of a knife or a hammer plunging into the top of his head in a silent, surprise attack made him shudder. His heart thumped. His lungs squeezed tight. A drop of sweat slid down his left temple and grazed the corner of his eye, making it sting.

He was happy Bruno wasn't capturing his anxiety on camera. But even if he was, Alain planned on editing it out.

He asked the spirits again what to do.

Hiss... .

They told him to stand.

Hiss... .

The spirits and Bluebeard were in this together.

Hiss...

To the end, my friends.

Hiss...

He had to follow their command.

He imagined blackness turning to blackness if the worst were to happen. If that was all death was, he'd be relieved. If he really would have to pay for all his prior sins, though...

Alain closed his eyes and slowly raised his head—

Expecting to be struck down to the ground—

Expecting blackness to turn to blackness—

Expecting the end to begin here and now with a violent meeting of metal and mind.

But he had to obey the hiss.

He had—

He heard the bang before he felt his heart stop cold and his knees buckle beneath him.

Chapter 13

"What took you guys so long?" Linda said, slamming the door closed behind her. She zipped up her coat and then slowly shuffled along the parking lot skating rink out to her car.

"Everything's all right here?" Dean said, out of breath from the rush back and sporting a limp thanks to a painful fall in the restaurant's driveway.

"See, didn't I tell you, Joseph, he'd be worrying about us?" Linda said. "Except for the power, sure. Joseph and I had a nice little talk in the dark, didn't we?"

Joseph nodded, but didn't say anything. He was taking time out from chipping away at his icy car to rub his bare hands together while blowing on them.

Peter felt the burning lava of jealousy fill the cavity of his chest and threaten to explode out of his mouth. If only his dumb-ass, demanding brother had made Joseph accompany him to the bank, he could have been the one alone with Linda in the dark where...

Anything could have happened.

Peter saw Linda struggling to clear the keyhole on her Honda Civic, and he acted quickly.

"Why don't you let me do that?" Peter said, slip-sliding over to Linda. "You go inside and keep warm—I'm already cold and wet."

Linda hesitated, and Peter thought she was getting ready to refuse his help as usual. But Peter sweetened the deal with a rare one-two knockout punch of chivalry and suavity.

"I wouldn't want you to slip and fall on this ice with— you know," he said, making eyes at Linda's belly.

Linda smiled, putting one hand to her belly and one on Peter's forearm, which was already stabbing away at the Civic. He stopped working and looked into her eyes, throwing all chivalry and suavity to the frozen winter wind by hoping she'd plant a warm wet one on his trembling kisser. Instead, she handed him the key to start the car once he'd broken through the frozen shell containing it.

So it'll take time to win her heart, Peter thought. I'm young and patient. I can wait.

Peter turned to Dean, who was working on his RAV-4, and blinked out a quick message.

M-I-N-E, his eyes said.

Dean smiled and shook his head. He had relaxed noticeably since arriving back at the restaurant.

Linda slid over to the back door of the restaurant and opened it. She turned around in its threshold and waved to Peter, who watched her while working, then flashed a knowing smile over at Dean and disappeared into the blackness spilling out of the restaurant inside.

Peter didn't like that smile she gave Dean. He wondered if his brother was taking strolls across her rolling hills and dewy pastures—lucky bastard. They were often together, stocking the condiments table side-by-side, wiping down the trays, refilling the soda machine. Peter stabbed the ice-covered Civic harder at the remote possibility of his brother's good fortune.

He wondered if he should follow Linda inside and take the opportunity to drink some hot chocolate with her and have an intimate chat—on any subject that *didn't* begin with a D, end with N, and have an E and an A crowding the middle. But then he figured she'd probably like him better for cleaning and warming her car than telling her about the latest Playstation game.

Playstation—

God, he really *was* a loser!

He had a hard time even *imagining* himself a better man!

Chapter 14

Alain and Bruno both heard the back door open and close. Someone entered, stamped their feet and shivered.

The person coughed. It was the woman.

She must have come back in after putting the trash out or starting her car.

Alain and Bruno had just made their way into the kitchen when the woman returned. They both scrambled to the darkest shadows like cockroaches, away from the weak beams of light crisscrossing the room.

The woman's winter coat made a swishing noise as she entered the kitchen area, making it easy to track her position. She opened one of the refrigerator doors, took something out and drank. She breathed heavily, which gave the shadows that surrounded Alain and Bruno a ghostly, sensual feel.

She moved close to Bruno—

Swish, swish...

—then Alain—

swish, swish...

—then Bruno again.

She heard something—a noisy pipe, a distant hiss, a man breathing—and turned quickly, hitting a metal cylindrical container on the side of the grill, which held a half-dozen spatulas. They rained down onto the greasy, brick floor and scattered in every direction.

She swore and then struggled to pick them up, her breath sticking in her throat each time she bent forward. She turned away as if she was going to leave them there for someone else to retrieve.

Alain thought she was going.

Swish—hiss...

She slowly made her way through the patchwork of light and shadows—seemingly more by memory than by sight.

Alain thought he'd lose his chance.

Swish—hiss...

She walked over to a closet whose door was half open—

Hissssssssssss...

—and reached her hand into the darkness to grab a broom and long-handled dust pan to pick up the spatulas.

Instead, she grabbed Bruno.

Chapter 15

Fifteen minutes later, Joseph was the first to unclog his car door's keyhole, rip open the stuck door and climb inside the freezerbox-like cabin. After he got his Ford Taurus started, rather than chip away at the one-inch-thick layer of ice on his car's windshield, he opted to turn the heater on full blast and wait for the warm air to do the work of birthing his metal baby from the its frozen womb.

"I'm going to wait inside with Linda," Joseph said, raising his hands up and wiggling his fingers so both Dean and Peter could see that he had no gloves. He was a minimalist by nature, but nobody could imagine the spiritual significance of, or reward earned, from practicing self-abnegation towards adequate winter wear. He must have simply forgotten them.

Joseph shuffled across the parking lot skating rink towards the back door. He curled both his hands together into a hollow ball, pressed his lips to the gap where both his thumbs met, and blew what could have been a beseeching note to the god of winter to stop this nonsense.

But the only sound heard was the hiss of the slamming sleet, adding layers to its sparkling empire of ice.

When Joseph arrived at the back door, he turned again, silently waved to Dean and Peter, and then disappeared through the doorway.

Old, rusted hinges screeched in apparent pain as they struggled against the door's weight.

Chapter 16

Bruno was finishing up when he heard the back door open and then slam shut.

He wondered what he should do—whether he should run to the closet again and hide or charge the door with his hatchet in the air like a savage and take his chances. But how could he tape everything if he did that?

Bruno dared himself to think that Alain sometimes expected too much from him.

Since they'd entered the restaurant, Bruno had been feeling stranger than he usually did when he went on his bumpy, cocaine-induced wild safaris of mind and body. What Alain had given him wasn't any ordinary powdered heaven. Now, as his high was winding down, he felt empty inside. But his powder-guided journey wasn't over yet. Filling this empty space were handfuls of grasshoppers climbing over each other, crawling and tumbling around, and popping up against the thin lining of his skin, panicking, desperate to escape their prison.

Pop, pop, pop.

Each time they popped, Bruno felt a part of himself twitch and itch. An arm—

Pop.

A leg—

Pop, pop.

His hands and face and tongue and hair and—

Pop, pop, pop.

They wouldn't stop jumping and crawling around inside. They were driving him insane, their oversized legs tickling, their hard heads slamming, their whirring wings buzzing against him, making him shudder and writhe and—

Pop, pop, pop.

Movement gave him his only relief.

Pop, pop, pop.

He could *not* stay still.

A grasshopper scrambled around inside his head, scurried over the backside of his eyeball.

Itch, itch, itch.

And now on the surface of his brain—

Itch, itch, itch.

He had to move towards the sound, towards the door that slammed—

He just *had* to move!

—towards the person who'd entered the kitchen.

He couldn't stay still in the shadows and wait. The grasshoppers would eat him alive if he didn't move.

Pop, pop, pop—chomp, chomp, chomp.

Eat him alive!

They were driving him crazy! Itching! Twitching! Tickling! Their legs pulling and poking at his guts—their toothless mouths gnawing the inside of his skin.

Chomp, chomp, chomp.

He itched like an angry rash. His muscles twitched uncontrollably.

He had to go after the guy who just came in. Surprise him—take care of him quick with the hatchet—try and end the grasshopper torture.

Pop, pop, pop.

Besides, it was only a matter of moments before the guy realized there was more than one other person inside the kitchen.

After he saw the girl.

It would have been impossible to miss her. In accordance with Alain's wishes, she had been splayed out on a food prep table in the center of the kitchen—unconscious, but not dead—ready to be hung upside down by her feet from a pipe discovered above the tiled ceiling.

Pop, pop, pop.

He couldn't take it one second more.

Pop, pop, pop.

They were driving him insane.

Pop, pop, pop.

Bruno plowed through the dark with both the camera and hatchet raised high.

Chapter 17

At times, it felt like they were picking apart the windshield itself, the ice was so hard and thick. The work left them with sore wrists and fingers and one broken scraper, which split into pieces after being used like a hammer. As fast as Dean and Peter finished one section of their windshields and moved on to the next, the preceding section coated over with a new frozen layer.

Chip on the left, chip on the right, scrape on the left, scrape on the right, chip on the back, chip on the front, scrape on the back, scrape on the front... and then all over again— the never ending carnival ride of clean-up.

When it was as close to being finished as it could be, when all their hard work had accomplished just as much as Joseph's heater, twenty-five minutes had passed with hardly a word spoken between them. It wasn't uncommon for Dean to go long periods of time without saying a anything, but for Peter it was rarer than a busload of horny nuns. Although he'd been trying Joseph's *I am now* awareness exercise to help calm his mind, his feelings still smarted as much as his frozen fingers.

"I'll go in and get the forsaken lovers," Peter said, wiping some sweat off his forehead with the back of his gloved hand.

"Hey, I'm sure Linda really appreciates your help, boy," Dean said.

Peter did a double take. His heart kicked against the walls of his chest like a bee-stung bull. He wanted to hear more, *needed it* to help heal the sore Dean had rubbed earlier. But, just the same, he knew better than to hold his breath.

"Yeah," was all Peter could bring himself to say as he hung his head and scratched his toe across the ice-covered ground, looking like a very young and timid boy.

The two brothers smiled awkwardly at each other. It was their version of a pat on the back or a hug. They both knew they had so much more to say to each other, and that it would have to be offered bit by uncomfortable bit soon enough, but now was neither the time nor place.

"Don't forget to lock the back door when you come out," Dean said, reclining back in the RAV-4's driver's seat, looking content to let Peter chase the other two out of the restaurant and into their cars, and handle the last few closing procedures on his own.

"Yes, master," Peter said, trying to keep the exchange going even if it meant starting a repartee of insults. He wasn't looking to quickly end this inexplicable, spontaneous renewal of their relationship.

"Did I ever tell you what a *putz* you are?" Peter said, again trying to get a rise out of Dean.

"About a hundred times every day," Dean said, his eyes closed, the RAV-4's radio tuned to some DJ's misguided, light rock ode to the weather.

"Fag music," Peter said, baiting Dean.

"Will you go?" Dean said, opening only one eye—the one closest to Peter—and glaring like a schoolmarm with it.

It worked, Peter thought, laughing to himself. I'm starting his engine.

"You know what? I'm gonna go inside and give Linda another baby right now," he said, figuring *that* one was sure to score.

"Go!" Dean said, opening both his eyes wide and sitting up in the seat, looking like he was going to lunge at Peter through the half-open window.

Bingo!

"Whatever you say, oh great one" Peter said as he carefully backed away from the idling truck, bowing like a geisha. When he reached the restaurant door and opened it, he turned and added, "Admit it, you'll miss me when I'm gone."

"Never happen," Dean said as he rolled up the window.

"What? Which? That I'm going somewhere or that you'll miss me?" Peter said, his body looking as if it was being swallowed by the kitchen shadows beyond the doorway.

"Never happen," Dean said again, his voice barely audible through the rolled-up window and the hissing sleet.

The door screeched and then banged shut like a heavy casket lid.

Part 11

Chapter 18

As he waited for Peter, Dean dozed off listening to the symphony of sounds surrounding him: the capricious ebb and flow of frozen rain and snow as it rode the wind's back, snapping and crackling against the truck, the constant, plunking rhythm of the wipers as they moved back and forth, laboring to keep the fogged-up windshield clean, the ceaseless, seamless breath of the bi-level heater blowing warm air, the idle of the engine gently percolating in the background, and the light rock melodies circulating inside the RAV-4, weaving themselves between and around the other sounds like a playful, swooping swallow with a blood red ribbon in its beak—

Dean jumped awake and into a world of flattened senses and cloudy thoughts.

Someone climbed into his truck.

He tried to wiggle his mind free from the remnants of his nap, but grogginess stubbornly clung to his consciousness like cobwebs to an attic corner. He'd never woken up well.

"Drive!" he thought he heard a voice say. "Drive! I... you... on!"

The voice became louder and clearer, but some words still escaped his awareness.

Dean thought he heard himself say, "What?"

"Wake up! Drive!"

He felt a hand grab the front of his coat and shake him. "We gotta fucking go—you gotta drive!"

Peter. His brother's face slowly emerged out of a vibrating sea of sleepy milk Dean's eyes had been swimming in, his features becoming more pronounced and colorful every moment.

"What? Where are we going? What's the hurry?" Dean babbled. His head felt thick and heavy.

He could see Peter's face clearly now. It was covered with droplets of water, which once had been sparkling pieces of ice. His eyes bugged out of his head. The skin on his face was tightly drawn and pale, as if he'd just been sick. His jaw trembled. And he seemed to be crying—although it was easy to confuse tears with melted sleet, sobs with shivers.

He gripped the front of Dean's coat. "You've gotta drive after them! They're all dead! We've gotta fucking catch them!"

Dean pulled away from Peter, thinking this was just another one of his brother's sick jokes. "Look, don't worry. We're gonna make it home in time to see *Cops*. And besides, if we don't, I set the—"

"Drive!" Peter raged, as he grabbed the steering wheel and pushed and pulled it. Bubbly, white foam collected at the corners of his mouth. The veins on his temples pulsated. "Fucking drive!"

When Dean didn't react to the command, Peter bent far forward and rested his forehead on his knees. He groaned and coughed and shook his head while saying, "No—it's my fault—no, no, no." As if those words were the trigger for an attempt at total purging of mind and body, Peter opened his door, stuck his head outside into the storm, and vomited.

At that moment, somnolent Dean made up his muddled mind what was wrong with Peter. It was obvious to him.

His brother was on drugs.

Where he'd got them or *when* he'd taken them or *why* he'd taken them were questions he didn't have the fully functioning faculties to answer. It didn't really matter, anyway, because Dean also made up his mind that he *hadn't* woken up and that this was all a crazy dream.

How their father would have reacted to Peter's panic sped across the dreamy landscape of Dean's mind, enticing him to hop in for a direct ride to irrational impatience. But he resisted.

"All right. Let's all relax. We're going, we're going," Dean mumbled, pulling the truck's shift stick into Reverse. He knew Linda had a spare key and would lock up when she left. He cautiously pulled the RAV-4 out of the parking lot, edging past Linda and Joseph's idling cars. "I'm not going to let you take control of my dream. I know *exactly* where to dump you."

"Here we are, driving. Driving, just like you want," Dean said, inching the truck down the parking lot's narrow driveway between the restaurant and an adjacent building. "You just calm down, close your eyes, and everything will be *all* right."

Dean had no idea where Peter wanted him to go. But it didn't matter. Regardless of what Peter *had* said or *would* say or how angry and crazed he *got* or *would* get, dreaming Dean knew where *he* was headed. He planned on doing a beeline straight to the hospital—probably the Jewish General about eight blocks north on Cote-des-Neiges—to dump his babbling, strung-out brother into the lap of a doctor.

Make a decision—take charge of the situation—*no problemo.*

That, or drive off the edge of the Earth and into Hell as he regularly dreamed of doing.

Whichever one came first.

Chapter 19

Alain and Bruno slipped and stumbled back to the Buick Regal. As far as Alain knew, nobody had seen them either going in or coming out of the restaurant—the streets and sidewalks were still empty. Because of this, he set a more leisurely pace than what might be expected from two murderers fleeing the scene of their crime.

Alain couldn't wait to watch the footage they'd shot. He hoped the scenes of the pregnant woman being gutted were sublime. If they were, he wanted to use it over and over throughout his gore-galore video—a visual motif symbolizing... symbolizing...

Symbolizing what?

He didn't care what it symbolized. He only thought it would look cool. And with something cute and funny, like *The Chipmunk Song*, playing in the background. (Especially the part where Dave is yelling at the chipmunks to "cut that out." He'd use that sound bite to death—to death, *funny*—to play over the images of that pretty bitch's bloated belly being sliced to ribbons.)

They found the body and windows of their car laminated in a series of progressively harder layers of semi-opaque, white rock. The windshield had to be cleaned off before they could drive. Alain wanted to hit himself for not leaving the car running with the heater blasting onto the windshield while they had been busy.

It was these relatively inconsequential, mental mistakes that provoked Alain to criticize himself harshly. This, as opposed to the physical mistakes, as when in the restaurant's kitchen he accidentally severed the tan man's right common carotid artery in his neck when he'd only intended to slit his external jugular. Although one could have argued that it had been a mental mistake due to a lack of concentration, Alain reasoned it was most probably a clumsy slip of his wrist. After all, both the hissing demons and a verse from *Do You Hear What I Hear?* delighted his inner ears as he sawed and hacked at the tan man's flesh.

His father and teachers had taught Alain that physical mistakes happened to the best and brightest of people and could be excused due to the human body's crude limitations. Mental mistakes, though, deserved punishment until old habits had dried and died and were replaced by more auspicious patterns of behaviour.

He made a mental note to let Bruno stand in for himself when it was time for the punishment to be meted out.

Alain used the Shark Bowie knife to chip at the ice covering the back window. Bruno used the hatchet to *carefully*—Alain couldn't stress that word enough to the high-strung klutz—work on the front.

As Alain slowly cleared the window, blood that had been smeared on the knife's blade wiped onto the ice's surface. It quickly sank into the ice and then spread in all directions as if it was alive and feeding and growing off the cold.

The sound of the evil spirits hissed in Alain's ears as he worked.

Do you hear what I hear?

They were still with him.

Alain could tell they were pleased, which was good. He delivered to them what he had promised.

On the other hand, though, he felt he had been shortchanged. Cheated, even. True, in some sense, he'd gone beyond himself with the demons' help—and for that he was grateful—and he'd gotten some great footage for his massacre movie, but he didn't feel the overwhelming sense of lasting satiety and satisfaction that he'd hoped for, that he'd expected, that he'd specifically asked the evil spirits to grant him. The tingle wasn't nearly as terrific as he'd wanted, needed.

But hadn't Bluebeard and his black magicians gone through the same sort of frustration with the demons of the dark every time they were supposed to help turn lead into gold? And after the baron had sacrificed to them small children by the bushels and in the most horrific ways imaginable?

Do you hear what I hear?

These evil spirits were a difficult, fickle bunch to please. Alain had tried his best for them. Especially with the pregnant woman. Her whimpering and begging—although brief and muffled because of her taped mouth—had been deliciously desperate. Especially when they'd strung her up while unconscious, revived her with some cold water to the face, then taunted her by scraping the knife over her smooth, swollen belly.

Do you hear what I hear?

To have this nagging displeasure and emptiness still

lingering inside after such a sacrifice...

It seemed unfair.

He didn't know what else he could have done to make things better, bloodier.

He was already thinking of a next time.

Alain couldn't believe how hard the ice was, how much difficulty the razor-sharp knife had in cutting through it. Nothing like the flesh of a young mother's belly, he thought, and then laughed because he could sense there was a joke in there somewhere—

—waiting to be born.

"Is my side good enough?" Bruno asked, showing off cantaloupe-sized holes in the ice on both the driver and passenger's side.

"Good enough," Alain said, walking to his door and opening it and throwing the knife in the back seat. "Let's get out of here. We've got work to do."

The stormy conditions were too opportune to head home and hide so early. The demons hissed to Alain that an end to his cravings, in the form of a true, tingling, unceasing satisfaction, awaited his discovery elsewhere in the slippery city.

Do you hear what I hear?

He'd come this far. He couldn't doubt the demons now.

It wasn't the insane thing to do.

Chapter 20

The RAV-4 skidded to a stop at the end of the driveway.

"Jesus, it's like an ice skating rink out here," Dean said, sounding more awake.

Peter leaned forward in his seat, trying to see through the new skin of ice spreading across the windshield, through the darkness stuffed into every nook and cranny of the city, and through the frozen precipitation that fell outside, blurring all fine details until the world looked like a stormy Impressionistic painting full of swirls and smears and speculations.

"When we get home, remind me to—"

"There! There they are!" Peter yelled, pointing at a pair of taillights a block away, heading north on Cote-des-Neiges.

"What? Who?"

"Them!" Peter said, the word spat from his tongue like a piece of bitter, rotten fruit.

Suddenly, Peter was back inside the restaurant, seeing the sadistic work of *them*. The blood. The gore. Joseph, still dressed in his winter coat and brown pants and black shoes, lying spread-eagle on his back on the food prep table beside the grill. Something slithery and slimy fell from his misshapen head through the thick shadows to the floor, where it splat. And the smell—the heavy stench of emptied bowels.

It was all bad, so bad. But that wasn't the worst.

Peter remembered how he had stood frozen in his spot, a moment slowing to a century as his eyes moved from Joseph up onto the food prep table, across to the grill, and then from the grill, up to the ceiling, where something hung, slowly rocking and twisting. Peter didn't want to see—

—the nakedness—

—the oozing blood—

—the cavernous, empty belly—

—the hands clutching at its ragged edges and entrails—

—the opened eyes, staring at him, lifeless, yet replete with shades of blame.

You! You did this to meeeeeeeeeee!

The images assaulted Peter as if they'd been sprayed across his brain by a machine gun, each surreal snapshot tearing into his soul with an unbearable caliber of horror.

He remembered suppressing a scream after he saw the carnage. But why?

He couldn't remem—

No, he *could*! It was because he heard a noise out in the front of the restaurant. He remembered ducking down and peeking through the gap in the soda machine. He saw two men scurrying out the restaurant's front door.

The front door.

The front door that was supposed to be locked during closing procedures—*oh, shit—oh, shit—oh, shit.*

The opened eyes, staring at him, lifeless, yet replete with shades of blame.

You!

Peter felt himself helplessly tossed about in a stormy sea of unspeakable horror and guilt.

He remembered running through the kitchen and out into the dining area, where he watched from the front window as the two men shuffled across the street towards a lone car sitting in the grocery store parking lot. Panic fell over him like a net, trapping him in a nightmare from which there was no escape.

His friend Joseph and beautiful, pregnant Linda—dead. Murdered by two psychos who came through... who came through—

The opened eyes...

You!

Who came through—

staring at him...

You!

He swallowed hard against the ascending gush of burning bile.

lifeless, yet replete with shades of—

You did this to meeeeeeeeee!

Who came through the door *he* forgot to lock.

The door *HE* forgot to lock!

The door *HE FORGOT TO LOCK*!

"We gotta go after them!" Peter shouted.

"Go after who? Look, you're starting to scare me, boy," Dean said, putting the truck into neutral and turning to face Peter—

—letting the taillights of the murderers dim into the wet darkness.

"You know, maybe I was right in thinking you're on drugs."

"Will you drop the fucking drugs bullshit!"

"Enough with the swearing. Are you trying to get back at me because of what I said to you before?"

"We gotta chase after that fucking car up there! We have no time for this shit! It's getting away!"

"I said enough with the swearing, Peter!"

"Fuck you! Look! There it goes!" Peter screamed, tears streaming down his face. The burning ball of rage in his stomach suddenly cooled and soured and made him want to gag. Horrific images of gore continued to flash in his mind as he sat and watched the killers pull further into the night.

He began to hyperventilate.

"Okay. Calm down. Relax. Okay," Dean said, looking uncomfortable with Peter's emotions. "If something bad *really* happened, like you say, I'm *more* than willing to give you the benefit of the doubt. We can go and call the police, okay?"

Dean sounded so insincere and patronizing. He obviously didn't believe Peter at all. Peter wanted to punch him out and take control of the wheel.

"They're fucking dead, okay? Joseph and Linda! They're fucking dead! Don't you get it?" Peter said in between gasps. "And those sonsofbitches driving away did it! If we don't go after them, nobody will. They'll fucking disappear. They'll get away with what they... what they did in there."

Something seemed to hit Dean *for* Peter. His eyes bulged as he listened to Peter talk. Then he stuttered and mumbled something incoherent. He took short, shallow breaths.

"Please. For fuck's sake, drive after them, Dean!" Peter glared at his brother. He felt the uncontrollable urge to bawl.

The corner of Dean's eye twitched. His leg bounced up and down at a jackhammer's pace.

"No," Dean finally said. "If what you're saying is true—

if what you're saying is true, we've got to go to the police."

"There's no time!"

"We'll call right away! Go! There's a phone right over there," Dean said, pointing to a phone booth on the sidewalk out in front of the restaurant. Peter could see his hand and arm shaking.

The murderers' brake lights continued fading.

"They're getting away! Look! Do you see? Fuck! You're ruining everything!"

Tears dripped from Peter's chin. Even though he was fighting with Dean on the surface, deep inside he'd already begun to mourn for his beloved Linda.

"The police will handle this. The police. The police are the ones... they'll do the job," Dean spluttered, sounding like he was trying to convince himself. He stared down at the steering wheel, looking as if he saw the control panel to a jumbo jet before him rather than the RAV-4's dashboard. "I don't think we should. It's not safe. If what you're saying is true, it's not right for us... I don't think..."

Peter couldn't believe how frightened his brother looked and sounded. He always thought Dean was the smart one. The strong one. The brave one. Dean was the one who would, without hesitation, lead him straight into battle like a fearless general. The one whom Peter ran to after finding Linda and Joseph murdered. He was the one who was supposed to know what to do, to help make everything all right, to lead the ride towards retribution. The one who—

"The police can handle it," Dean continued to babble. "If we go straight to the police right now and tell them, they'll hop on it. They're very good about that—I saw a report. They take these things seriously, Peter. The police can take care of everything and... and everything will be all right, you'll see."

Peter watched the Buick's brake lights completely dissolve into the stormy night. And with them went Peter's belief that the babbling Golden Boy brother sitting beside him was really made of gold through and through.

Chapter 21

Bruno shivered.

The window he'd broken wasn't helping any. The right side of his body was covered in tiny beads of ice that had shot through the open window as their car swerved from side to side, heading north along Cote-des-Neiges' cross streets.

The effects of the cocaine—the anxious feelings of both being bottled up inside his body and having hundreds of frantic grasshoppers filling him—had faded, the crashing, shore-shredding waves of high tide seamlessly slipping into the gentler, calmer flow of low tide. Low tide for Bruno, though, also brought low spirits. And a return of the ceaseless, sickening sensation that he'd just done something terribly wrong.

He couldn't remember quite what, though, but he knew it was bad. He knew two people had been hurt—badly.

But Alain had been so happy with his performance— he'd seen him smile—so it was good, right?

He couldn't be sure.

He strained his brain to try to remember the details. Smeared images came to him that he knew he shouldn't try to clear.

"Alain?" he said, intent on asking his best friend what had just happened and, more importantly, what role he'd played in it.

"What?"

Bruno didn't like the sound of that *what*. He knew he was bothering Alain.

"Alain, I... I... I'm cold," Bruno said, just to say something. He wasn't sure how to phrase the question he wanted to ask, the words dancing around him, taunting and teasing him just out of his reach like a pack of savage schoolchildren picking on the village idiot.

Which is just the way it was when Bruno had first met Alain back in grade school. Bruno was being teased during recess because all the kids knew he was a slow-thinking, easy target for verbal jabs and punches. They had danced around him, pointing at him, laughing at him, calling him such things as *Slow-Mo Bruno* and *Braindead Bruno*.

But then along came Alain. A boy who didn't have any friends—just like Bruno—but whom none of the other kids made fun of—unlike Bruno—because he scared them. Scared them not because he was large or had a big brother or anything typically intimidating like that. They were all scared of Alain because of the rumor. A rumor no one was ever really sure was true, but whose validity nobody wanted to challenge.

The rumor talked about what Alain, the surgeon's son, kept stored in the bottom of his school bag. A scalpel aptly called "Shiny Sharpy." The rumor talked about what Alain could—and would—do with Shiny Sharpy if provoked. The rumor gave all the kids nightmares. Nightmares which the kids would never speak about to their concerned parents. After all, the rumor explicitly stated that if they did leak a word to any adult, young Alain would catch them and cut out their tongues with ol' Shiny Sharpy and then eat the pink mouth meat raw so they could never squeal again.

That rumor.

As soon as Alain started talking to Bruno, having lunch with Bruno, inviting him over to play with his father's surgical tools and spy on his sister while she took a bath, the kids stopped teasing Bruno. And soon enough, even though he'd never hurt a fly in his life, Bruno suddenly found himself part of the Shiny Sharpy legends.

He was the one who would hold the little squealers down so Alain and ol' Shiny Sharpy could do their work.

The irony.

Bruno didn't know if he would have made it through school without hanging himself if it weren't for Alain. He owed his friend his life. And then some.

He shivered himself out of his reverie.

"I'm really getting cold here, Alain."

"Don't worry about it," Alain said, staring at something out his driver's side window. "Don't worry about it at all, my friend."

My friend. Those two words helped to chase away Bruno's chills and concerns about what had happened in the restaurant.

Oui to we...

"What do you see out there?"

"An answer to my prayers."

"And mine, too?"

No answer.

Bruno saw what Alain was looking at. It was a well-dressed, pretty, blonde woman standing in a parking lot, struggling to scrape the ice from the windshield of her black Dodge Durango.

Bruno shook and shivered hard enough to churn butter as he desperately tried to find the right words to his own prayers.

Chapter 22

*I shouldn't be doing this. I shouldn't be doing this. I
shouldn't be—*

"Can't you drive any faster?" Peter said. "We're never
gonna catch up to them unless you go faster!"

"I'm driving as fast as is safe in these conditions," Dean
said, slowing down to stop for a red light on a very steep
incline at the corner of Cote-des-Neiges and Cote Ste-
Catherine.

"What are you stopping for? Go!"

"The light's red."

"Who cares! There's nobody! We're gonna get stuck on
this hill, too! We're never gonna fucking catch them!"

"Calm down!"

"Do you want to catch these guys or not?" Peter said. "I
thought you were gonna go for it when we left the restaurant,
but the way you're going you couldn't catch a cold. Can't
you do any better?"

Can't you run any faster? Can't you do a cut-back any

quicker? Can't you push back that linebacker any more and get yourself a few more yards? Can't you do what I tell you? Can't you hurry, boy? Hurreeeee!

"I can't! I just can't!" Dean said, feeling himself being drawn into the hurricane of Peter's hysterics—and his own history.

When the light turned green Dean tried to accelerate. The tires spun on the ice's surface.

"Oh, great!"

"Don't worry about it. Relax. She's gonna go."

As Dean fiddled with the four-wheel drive switch, he and his brother fell silent. Under normal circumstances, silence would have been welcome. But Dean wasn't simply heading home to "enjoy" another half-heated Lean Cuisine, half-frozen Molson Dry, and the totally lame last half hour of Saturday Night Live—all the ingredients for a life half-lived. No, he was out chasing what Peter *claimed* were a pair of killers.

Claimed were a pair of killers...

It sounded surreal. This *had* to be the goings on of an elaborate practical joke, revenge for Dean having called Peter a *loser*.

He quickly ran over the facts that he knew—which weren't many—to try and see if he could see a seam in the joke's lining.

No, it *had* to be a joke. A sick, vengeful joke, for sure, but a joke nonetheless.

Then why did Dean feel so uncomfortable with that answer? Was it the look of absolute terror in Peter's eyes earlier? The kid was a born actor, but that performance was Oscar clip material.

He realized that as much as he *did* believe Peter's story, he *didn't* believe it either.

But that was nothing new. Often Dean realized that as much as he felt ashamed of his brother, he also felt proud of him. As much as he felt angered by him, he also felt delighted. As much as he cursed him, he also rejoiced in him. And as much as they argued together, they also laughed together.

But now, added to the clump of contradictions surrounding Dean's feelings towards Peter, were trust and distrust.

Dean pulled the truck to a sliding stop at another stoplight at the intersection of Cote-des-Neiges and Edouard-Montpetit.

"Not again!" Peter moaned. "There's *nobody*! Go!"

"What are you talking about? There's somebody right over there," Dean said, pointing left to a car at the intersection on Edouard-Montpetit. It looked like one of the windows was open. Or broken. Two dark shadows moved around inside.

"That's them!" Peter screamed, pointing with one hand and grabbing Dean's shoulder with the other. "That's the car I saw!"

Even though they had the green light, the car with the missing window wasn't moving.

Dean took a good look at the vehicle, squinting his eyes to see through everything—his foggy, icy windshield, the blurring sleet, the suffocating blackness of night. Something about the car's make and model looked familiar.

"We gotta go over there and kick their asses!" Peter said.

"Are you nuts?"

"Why are you still refusing to believe this is happening?"

"I'm not!"

You are!

"You are!"

"No, I'm just proceeding with caution, that's all."

It's so obvious you're grasping for an out from this, boy. It's goddamn pathetic if you ask me—and exactly what I'd expect from a pussy like you.

Their light turned green for the second time since they'd stopped. Dean started to move forward through the intersection and continue north on Cote-des-Neiges.

"What are you doing?"

"Joke's over, boy. We're going home. Can't you see how ridiculous all this is?"

"No! This isn't a joke! That was them!"

"Yeah. Okay. When we get home, the first thing I'm gonna do is call Linda. And the second thing, I'm gonna beat your ass black and blue for this."

"Fuck you!" Peter slapped the dashboard.

Pussy!

"Enough!"

Pussy!

"Fucking don't go!" Slap.

Pussy!

"Enough!"

"Don't! That's *them*, you asshole!" Slap, slap.

Tell the pussy—that's right!

"Peter!"

As Dean drove through the intersection, past the suspicious car still waiting on Edouard-Montpetit, Peter's arm snapped out like a whip. His hand grabbed the steering wheel and jerked it to the right. The RAV-4 swerved sharply.

"What the—"

Dean jammed his foot down on the brakes and pulled the wheel back towards the center. The truck's back-end swung around from the left, but then swooped back to the right as Dean regained control of the wheel. The sheet of ice covering the road had other plans for the truck, though. It flung the truck's body over to the curb, lifting it up onto the sidewalk, where it flattened a parking meter. It came to a stop a foot short of an ancient oak tree.

"You stupid bastard!" Dean yelled. "What was that?"

"You wouldn't listen to me! I had no fucking choice!"

"You could've just asked!"

They were silent for a moment. They both corraled their wild emotions, trying not to say anything they'd regret later once they'd returned to their tiny five-room apartment.

"Oh shit, this can't be good," Peter said, looking out the front windshield.

Dean followed his brother's eyes.

Heading up Cote-des-Neiges was a black Durango. About a half block behind followed a car with a missing passenger window.

Dean's jaw started trembling as he lost grip on his conviction that this was all a bad joke.

Or a bad dream.

No, this all seemed *too* real.

Chapter 23

This is...
This is what? What is it?
This is...
What? What!
This is...

Alain's cocaine high was all but gone. And with it, the voices of the demons faded into the incomprehensible crackle and hiss of the storm's fury, his sense of insanity dissolving along with it.

"Reach back there and start the CD and pass the backpack over here," Alain said, turning his head towards Bruno and taking one hand off the Buick's steering wheel. The car's tail end skidded out to the left in an exaggerated response to the turned steering wheel, nearly throwing the vehicle into a spin and Bruno out the missing passenger window. Alain quickly regained control.

"Where are we going? What are we going to do?" Bruno said, placing the backpack beside Alain and then turning to fiddle with the portable stereo in the backseat.

Alain could tell Bruno—the old Bruno—was back. The nervousness, the questions, the fidgeting. Bruno bit pieces off his fingernails, chewed them, then spat them out like sunflower seeds. But Alain had a way to make things right again. For himself, too.

"Just open the backpack, the small front pocket there, okay?" Alain said. "We're going to have some fun."

"But... didn't we just have enough?" Bruno shouted over the finale of *Angels We Have Heard on High. Blue Christmas* soon followed.

Bruno tried to steer the conversation, but Alain refused to relinquish the controls.

"Are you cold over there?" Alain said.

"Yeah."

"Then we'll fix that problem. Are you bored?"

"No, I—we—I—I don't—did we do something wr—"

"Yes, you *are* cold, I can see it. And your friend is going to fix that problem, too. Are you nervous?"

"Nervous?"

"I know you are. I can feel it. Don't worry, Alain is going to help you out. Have you opened the front pocket? Do I have to tell you to do everything twice? Open it. That's it. Okay, now take out what's inside."

Bruno reached inside and pulled out the clear plastic bag of cocaine.

"Nice, huh?"

"Yeah. I know this bag."

"You sure do. It's your friend—like me."

Bruno chewed his lower lip.

"What a great song, huh? Take a few snorts of your friend there and, next thing you know, you'll be high and dry and warm."

"I don't really feel like any of this right now," Bruno said, putting down the bag.

"What? Did you hear what I said? Take some."

"But it makes me all crazy and—and I think we did something real bad back there, but I don't remember it all—and I don't want to do that again—"

"Take some! I'm doing you a favor."

Here Comes Santa Claus played on the stereo.

Bruno didn't budge. He seemed to be planning what to do next. Finally, he said, "No, Alain. I'm sorry, but I don't want any. I'm sorry. And you can't make—"

"Bruno, you—you take some right now or so help me!" Alain's hand was balled into a fist, ready to strike.

"I'm tired of you telling me what to do all the time," Bruno said, the volume of his voice receding in contrast to the force of his words.

"Take some right now or I'll run this car off the road!" Alain shouted. The glorious music was making him bolder, crazier.

Cote-des-Neiges began to descend—a snaking descent down the west side of Mount Royal. Alain could very easily crash the Buick through one of the guardrails separating the road from a fifty-foot drop if he wasn't paying attention—or if someone distracted him.Or if he wanted to.

"Alain, please!"

"Take it now!"

"Why do you do this to me? No more."

"Bruno!"

"I don't want to hurt that lady! Please, tell me we—"

"I'll crash this car if you don't do what I told you to do! I'll crash it now!"

Alain let the Buick stray straight ahead when he should have been guiding it to the left. The guardrail became bigger and brighter as it slid into the path of the car's headlights. The tops of the trees waited just beyond, at the base of the drop-off, looking as if they'd catch the Buick with their tangled, icy arms.

Bruno's testicles were sucked up into his entrails. "All right! I'll take it!" he screamed, pulling his knees up towards his chest to prepare for the impact against the guardrail.

Alain jammed his foot onto the brake pedal and tugged the steering wheel to his left. The Buick's rear end swung out too far to the right and crunched into the guardrail. The guardrail threw the car back out into the center of the street, where it continued sliding down the steep incline like a bobsled with broken brakes.

And sliding.

Fifty feet—

—over a small ridge in the hill—

—down the other side, where the slope increased.

The car, picking up speed—

—sliding toward an intersection with Cedar Avenue, where a traffic light glowed red, where a black Durango waited.

Bruno screamed—

—as the gap between their car and the massive truck vanished. Alain wrenched the wheel to the right, trying to get the Buick to respond, to change directions enough to get by.

Both Alain and Bruno closed their eyes as the rear of the Durango loomed over them like a black gravestone. Metal screeched as it was ripped ragged—

Kshruuup...

—and it was over in an instant.

No direct impact.

Alain opened his eyes and saw a shimmering, snow

covered guardrail in front of him. The Buick had come to a stop in the middle of Cote-des-Neiges, turned counterclockwise a quarter turn. Alain looked out his driver's window and saw a small black object sitting in the road some five feet from their car. It was the Durango's passenger side mirror. The Buick had narrowly missed plowing into the back of the bulky truck, but had swept close enough to its side to tear off its mirror.

About ten feet behind the mirror sat the idling Durango, looking as if it were an angry black bull preparing to charge.

Alain wondered if the woman was going to get out and come talk to them—exchange insurance info, nervously reflect on how much worse it could have been, fuck them in her backseat—or whether he should go try and talk to her.

And take care of her then.

How insane would *that* be, taking care of the broad in the middle of such a normally busy road?

None of the Durango's doors opened. It looked as though he'd have to make the first move. Alain picked up one of the Glocks from the seat and put it in his coat pocket.

"I'm gonna go talk to her," he said to Bruno, whose jaw still hung to his chest from the close call. "You take care of yourself." He motioned down at the bag of cocaine on the seat. "And then grab the camera and film me, you got it. Watch for my signal, too. I may need your help if she tries to get away. Watch where she goes. She won't get far. Bring the camera if you have to follow, okay? It'll make for some great hunting footage. Don't let me down."

Bruno nodded and picked up the bag of cocaine. His hands shook.

Hark! The Herald Angels Sing! played.

Alain bent the rearview mirror and admired himself. He stroked the top of his eyebrow and wiped some white, crusted spittle from the corner of his mouth. He checked his clothes for blood from before. None.

He didn't think she'd be too scared once she saw him—looking so clean, so well-dressed, so respectable. A son of a revered surgeon. And, at the very least, not what she'd expect to be driving around in a piece-of-shit clunker car like the Buick Regal.

He decided he'd pick up the broken mirror and bring it back to her with wide eyes and outstretched hands—that would make him appear both helpful and innocent and allow him to get close. And he had to be sure to grin a lot—women trusted men who smiled. And look dumb and shake his head a lot in ah-shucks disbelief.

No, that's not it, he thought—look smart and confident and composed and witty, that's it—women liked wit and humor. Women wanted James Bond, not Forrest Gump.

"Is this supposed to bring us seven years bad luck," he'd say as he held out the broken mirror for her to take. And she'd relax and give a little laugh and maybe even silently thank God that it wasn't some sicko who had hit her, but a nice, attractive, even kind of sexy young man.

And then he'd reach for his gun as she took the mirror from him, as she breathed a sigh of relief.

Alain snatched the bag of cocaine from Bruno, opened the top, put his nose straight into the powder, and snorted the drug deep into his sinuses. When he lowered the bag, he had a white ring around his nose, which he wiped away with a wetted finger.

The drug immediately took affect.

This is the one, a voice said in his head, finishing the sentence he had stumbled over earlier. The song *See Amid the Winter's Snow* began playing.

This is the one—See amid the winters snow.

Alain opened the car door and stepped outside. The demons hissed around him once again.

This is the one—born for us on earth below.

And he smiled and waved as he started towards the truck trying to look as smooth and suave as one of his other favorite killers.

Yeah—forget that old fart, Bluebeard.

> *See the tender lamb appears,*
> *promised from eternal years.*

Hello, Ted Bundy.

Chapter 24

Blood everywhere in the kitchen.

Joseph spread out like a cadaver on an autopsy table.

Linda naked and hanging by her ankles.

Their eyes pop open and lock on Peter. Their mouths move to shape out a sound. Thick, bubbling, black blood spews out in vomitous cascades—followed by a throaty, ragged accusation:

Killerrrrrr!

Peter's eyes explode into round saucers.

"Can't you drive any faster?" he said, watching Dean gingerly balance the brake and gas pedal.

"You think I want to be out here? You're the one forcing me to go on this wild goose chase."

Forcing...

Peter couldn't remember ever having *forced* Dean to do anything—or at least Dean ever *admitting* to the fact that Peter had succeeded by such means. Although Peter was tormented by horrific images of gore, agonizing, guilt-crested swells of heartache, and a searing compulsion to exact merciless vengeance upon the murderers, Peter couldn't ignore the deeper, thunderous rumblings that stirred within. He couldn't put his finger on their exact cause, but he knew they had something to do with his older brother.

"This isn't bullshit, you'll see," Peter said.

"Sure it isn't."

"You gotta believe me."

"Of course I do."

"No, you don't. It's fucking obvious you don't."

"But I do. I *really* do."

"Yeah, right. They're all dead and you're not even upset."

"But you're wrong. I am. I *really* am. I'm crying on the inside."

"Fucking patronizing jerk."

"Doesn't say much for you then, huh, worshipping a jerk like me as if your life depended on it?"

"You know, I hate you sometimes."

"The feeling is mutual, my friend. Except with me, it's *all* the time."

Tears welled in Peter's eyes. He fought off a whimper. "Asshole. I really do fucking hate you," Peter said, wanting to open his door and jump out and instantly end the torment and helplessness soaking him to the bone.

"Yeah, until you need your next ride, lunch, or piece of advice to keep you from being such a loser."

Why was life being so unfair? He was just a kid. What had he done so wrong to deserve all this? He needed to sob out all the poison that had been accumulating in his body since as far back as he could remember.

But he couldn't.

Because what he saw happening in the road up ahead sucked the sadness right out of him.

Chapter 25

It seemed to Bruno that Alain appeared inside the Buick like a phantom. Bruno had taken the cocaine as he'd been told to do, and now he floated free of his physical form in a silky stratum of satisfaction.

"Did you see? Did you record it?" Bruno thought Alain said, as he toyed with the steering wheel and automatic transmission stick.

"Did I—huh?" Bruno asked, his voice rising and falling like a raft on a rolling sea.

"Did you see what the bitch did? Were you paying attention and filming? She must have gotten scared—probably saw you or something—and just took off! Without her mirror!"

"Mirror?"

"Fuck!" Alain said in English. And then in French, "She took a right down Cedar. We're gonna lose her."

"Where are we going now, Alain?"

"We're going to have some fun if it *kills* us," Alain said, turning the Buick around so he could head back up Cote-des-Neiges to the intersection at Cedar Avenue where he'd hit the Durango.

The Buick's wheels stripped away layers of ice as they tried to pull the car's weight up the hill from a standstill.

"She's going to get away," Bruno said in a sing-song voice. "She's going to get away. She's going—"

"Shut up! Come on car!" Alain shouted, gunning the engine. The rear tires whined and smoked on the road's slick surface.

"There goes the fun—she's getting away," Bruno sang again. "She's getting away."

"Shut up!"

Weeeeeeeennn . . .

The tires sounded as though they were a screeching, starving, abominable beast.

"She's getting away. Guess it's just you, me, and the ice now—she's getting away."

At that moment, a pair of headlights pierced the heavy sleet and darkness from the top of the hill, on the road Alain and Bruno had just slid down.

"Now see what you—" Alain started to say. He jammed his foot down on the gas pedal.

"Oh wow, lucky us!" Bruno said. "I sure hope they see us, because if they don't, we're as good as dead. Are your lights on? Make sure your lights are on," Bruno said, reaching over and flicking down one of the levers coming out of the steering column, causing the windshield wipers to stop.

"Don't touch that!"

"But I want to make sure our lights are on."

"They're on!"

"Well, you didn't answer me!"

"They're on—shut up!"

The oncoming headlights grew bigger and brighter. Alain rocked back and forth in his seat as he pressed the gas pedal.

"Come on!"

Bruno copied him, but ended up rocking back and forth in the exact *opposite* rhythm.

"They're coming."

Weeeeeeeeeeennn . . .

"They're coming to get us."

Weeeeeeeeeeennn . . .

"They're almost here."

Weeeeeeeeeeennn . . .

"Fun time is over!"

Just then the Buick's tires pealed away the last layer of the road's icy crust, finally finding something they could bite down on. The car hurtled forward and up the hill, throwing its two occupants against their seats like test dummies.

Alain cut the steering wheel sharply to the left, pulling the car onto Cedar Avenue before the oncoming vehicle crumpled them.

"Ha!" Alain shouted, hitting the steering wheel. "What was that you were saying, dipshit? We're back in business!"

Conversely, the sudden blastoff start hastened Bruno's crash landing from his cocaine high. In an instant, he was a trapped man again, ready to rage for release.

He thought of slitting open this lady's belly like he had the other one—or maybe it was Alain who did that while he recorded the festivities, he couldn't remember.

He hoped no squirming surprises would fall out this time.

The last woman ended up resembling a Russian doll. Upon opening her gut, rather than seeing her spirit fly free, he found another flesh and bone prison waiting inside. And when he slit that writhing, purple sack of screams and juice open from end to end, he thought he'd found another—but he couldn't remember.

For all he knew, it had been a bad dream. A dream he'd soon be waking up from, in his big warm bed, with a fresh day of fun-seeking ahead.

And with his best friend, Alain, to share it all.

Chapter 26

Dean saw the headlights shining at them from a car facing the wrong direction, but he resisted the urge to slam on his brakes. He'd been driving around in Montreal winters long enough to know that brakes weren't always one's best friend. Instead, he took his foot off the RAV-4's gas pedal and coasted.

"That's them!" Peter shouted, as if Dean were on the other side of a large room. "Ram 'em!"

But Dean was a long ways away from being able to ram them. Instead, seeing that same Buick again rammed something into Dean.

He felt as if he'd just been hit in the solar plexus by a linebacker and had his wind knocked out of him. The perpetrator of this unpleasant sensation wasn't a linebacker, though, but the equally merciless, frightening face of reality.

Peter is right! Linda and Joseph are dead! You are chasing a pair of killers!

"Maybe they just spun out on the ice—regular people, you know. Maybe they need our help," Dean said, as one last, desperate attempt to spin this sinister reality facing him into something as savage as a kitten.

But even Dean didn't believe his own words.

He had the RAV-4 slowed down to walking speed as it came within fifty feet of the other car. He could see its wheels spinning and smoking as it fought for traction on the ice. Its frantic attempts to break free of the ice's slick grip made Dean queasy. He hated to see or be around things that struggled—like the time when he was nine and he watched his dog, Pickle, get hit by a car, slide down the ragged, ripping road on his back, and then crawl into the woods, bloody and with a broken skull and a missing eye, where he died an hour later after Dean tried to do everything he could to save the animal. He'd pushed the broken skull back together, chased the ants and flies away from the soggy, slimy eye socket, and whispered in Pickle's ear that everything was going to be all right while the dog's helpless, high-pitched whine slashed pieces from his heart.

Sounds familiar, don't it, boy?

He did everything he could. Everything except call his father, who he knew would have put a bullet in the dog's head without a second thought. Pickle might have suffered more, but at least he died knowing that somebody loved him.

Just like me, boy. I know you loved me with all your pussy heart.

Dean could see the passenger window missing in the Buick, and inside it a person's face reflecting the RAV-4's headlights.

A person who had killed two of his friends.

Dean felt the tears well up in his eyes. His stomach clenched, trying to hold back a sob.

Suddenly, the Buick took off like a missile. It shot pieces of sand and rock and broken bits of ice out from its back tires and came, first, straight at Dean and Peter, but then turned sharply to the right, fishtailing back and forth, and disappearing into the darkness down Cedar Avenue.

"Go! Go after them!" Peter shouted, grabbing for the steering wheel.

Dean didn't think. He put his blinker on and turned to the right down Cedar Avenue. He didn't drive fast, but he *did* follow.

He didn't want to be a coward any more—he was content with being a coward. He didn't want his brother to think of him as a coward—he couldn't care less *what* his brother thought of him. He believed what was happening—he didn't believe what was happening. He wanted to face the challenge, to feel his heart pumping, his blood racing, his sweat dripping—he wanted to go home and submerge himself in soothing beer-soaked-sleep. Dean could see the Buick turn to the left far ahead.

Somewhere, somehow, the coin was tossed inside him, the decision made.

He sped up, plunging straight into the swirling, swarming storm of frozen stingers slapping against his truck. He chased after the Buick with a momentary blossoming of confidence, courage, and decisiveness he'd rarely experienced since the Sugar Bowl.

But he knew his heroic behavior was on borrowed time.

And as the RAV-4 suddenly slid out of control and spun 180 degrees in the middle of the street, with Peter cussing in his ear like a trucker with Tourette Syndrome, and with a bladder full of urine, delivered straight from the fear factory, waiting to let loose, Dean had to wonder if his time had *already* expired.

Chapter 27

"Get *down*," Alain whispered.

A vehicle's headlights reflected off the faces of several large, gray stone, Second Empire style houses lining the south side of Ramezay Avenue. At the corner where Ramezay Avenue twisted sharply to the south, changing into Ramezay Road, both Alain and Bruno scurried behind some burlap-covered, shoulder-high Boxwood hedges lining the border of an exquisitely landscaped front yard.

Alain lunged and slid out of control, banging his knee on one of a series of large icy lumps spread out under the snow in the shape of a semi-circle—some decorative stones serving as a border to a flower garden. He cursed in French—*rich fucks*—while rubbing his knee and scowling at the mansion.

He untied a bit of the burlap covering on one of the hedges for spite's sake. Just enough to let the sleet work its magic on some branches.

Bruno tapped Alain's shoulder. "Down there," Bruno

whispered, stabbing his finger towards a house on Ramezay Road. "The woman. Her truck."

Alain smiled, happy to hear Bruno so involved. He reached into his left coat pocket and fingered a CD he'd brought from the Buick. He intended on playing it in the pretty blonde's house—for inspirational purposes.

They took baby steps across the glazed ground, moving through the mansion's modest-sized yard, toward the huge house at which Bruno had pointed. Before stepping out from behind the hedge wall, Alain peeked to see what was doing with the oncoming vehicle.

It was closer than he'd hoped.

Alain put his arm across Bruno's chest, keeping him from sliding too far forward, where he might be seen. The approaching vehicle inched along Ramezay Avenue, its engine hardly audible above the many sounds in nature's stormy symphony. Alain could tell it was a Toyota RAV-4. It slid to a stop only thirty yards from Alain and Bruno, at the junction of Ramsey Avenue and Ramsey Road.

Alain's heart pumped a tsunami of blood through his arteries. His mind raced around like Jacques Villeneuve on a Formula-1 track.

Hadn't they seen a RAV-4 recently? Did the driver know who Alain and Bruno were or was it just a coincidence that he was creeping around the same neighborhood? Would he recognize the car Alain and Bruno had parked around the corner? And if he did, would he continue to pursue Alain and Bruno on foot?

That thought *really* unsettled Alain. Too much chaos for his taste. Try as he might to embrace a more "carefree insanity," Alain felt most comfortable with his plans, ideas, and fantasies being played out on a stage after they had been well-choreographed and well-rehearsed. Not that he didn't appreciate his own sort of "neurotic insanity" and its attention to details and control, but like many people, Alain secretly pined to succeed at those things that he most often failed.

Alain felt his stomach climb down from his chest when the RAV-4 started moving again along Ramezay Avenue. At least he wasn't turning down Ramezay Road, where he and Bruno were heading.

Alain asked the demons to help prevent the truck's occupant from interfering. They responded immediately with a fierce hiss.

Translation—

Even if whoever was in the RAV-4 *did* see their Buick, he and Bruno weren't in it. It was empty. And even if whoever was in the RAV-4 searched around, he would never find Alain and Bruno because they would be down the street in the blonde's house.

Translation—

They'd better get their asses moving.

Alain tapped the back of Bruno's shoulder and motioned towards the house with the black Durango out front. It was a whopper of a home—which was saying something, since everyone who was someone with money in Canada seemed to have a whopper in Westmount.

Alain and Bruno moved as quickly as they could out from behind the hedge wall, onto the slick sidewalk, and then down Ramezay Road.

The blonde's house occupied the rounded corner where the steep, snaking, southbound Ramezay Road ended, intersecting St. Sulpice Street. The majestic home climbed three stories into the sky, its busy, multi-leveled roof a series of triangles stacked on top of triangles growing out of triangles, broken up only by the two square chimneys located on the right and left sides of the main gable roof, and the single prominent turret that stood in the center "elbow" of the house's V-shaped ground plan. Cut into the turret at its base was the front door and, above that, a story-high Rococo window, through which a winding staircase could be seen stretching up to a tent-like skylight above.

Alain didn't know who owned it. A fat bank president, a Gucci-suited CEO, a famous athlete, a corrupt politician—they all had homes up on "the hill". And they all seemed to have sexy, blonde, buxom babes to keep their beds warm at night.

Alain told Bruno to check out the Durango and see what sort of alarm system it had—if any—in case they needed to hot wire it for a quick getaway. Alain knew from experience that a lot of these fat cats didn't bother with alarm systems because, to them, money flowed freely like water from faucets. To have their car stolen was certainly an inconvenience. But what it *really* meant was they would then have an excuse to enjoy the drug-like consumer high of picking out a spanking new BMW, Saab, Lexus, Volvo, or Porsche, and showing it off to their friends.

Last filthy rich sonofabitch to have a new car is a rotten egg!

At least that's the way Alain had always seen it played out. He smoldered in anger to think that an insane monster as himself came from such a dirty, green bloodline.

He considered bringing the loaded Glock over to show his parents.

While Bruno inspected the Durango, Alain slid over to one of the large picture windows, which revealed a wide, spacious living room. He ducked down between the face of the house and one of a line of hip-high bushes in front and peeked inside. He could see, among other things, a grand piano, a fireplace, and a couple of Chinese-red walls hung with hand-painted plates and Impressionistic landscape paintings.

He pressed his face against the frosty window and peered deeper into the house. He saw through the living room and its two opened, arched entranceways and into other rooms—rooms with lights on.

The blonde cut back and forth across a distant opening. She stopped for a moment where Alain could inspect her surgically enhanced features. She leaned against something—a counter, most likely—while eating a carrot stick and talking on the phone. She was probably chatting with a friend or her husband about the accident.

Alain guessed she was alone, although he knew from experience that in these castles, two people could easily live under the same roof and neither see nor talk to each other for hours on end. He had to be careful.

The blonde disappeared into another part of the house with the cordless phone still pressed to her ear.

Alain reached into his pocket and stroked the Glock. He closed his eyes and listened to the hissing sound around him, hugging him, containing him in its *sssssssibilant* womb.

Bruno touched his shoulder, making him jump.

"It's alarmed," Bruno said. "A good one, too. We won't do much without the keys."

"Then let's see what we can do about that," Alain said, enjoying a tingling rush of adrenaline as he visualized his plan.

He had a hunch about this blonde. The demons had hissed ideas into his ears.

He told Bruno to stick close with the camera and film his every move, and then he looked inside the house for any sign of the woman passing by distant doorways.

When he was sure she'd disappeared into a faraway room,

Alain slipped and scurried up to the front door. He gave a nervous little laugh at the brass, lion-head door knocker staring him in the face like a ferocious protector, and pointed it out for Bruno to film a close-up. He directed Bruno to get a tight shot of his hand as it grabbed the matching brass door handle.

Alain thought of his good fortune with the restaurant door.

He tried to turn the handle.

Someone down there likes me, he thought, as a rumbling gust of wind whipped a stinging tail of ice needles across his face and the evil spirits hissed in delight.

He would have winced if he weren't so busy smiling for the camera.

Chapter 28

"Pull over here, that's their car," Peter said. "And this time try not to crash the fucking thing."

Dean did what he was told.

"I saw somebody moving around down that side street—I think it's them," Peter said, hopping out of the RAV-4. His open coat flapped wildly in the gusts of wind, which rumbled down the slick and slanted streets of the affluent mountainside neighborhood.

Dean fixed his scarf, zipped his coat up to his chin, put on his gloves, and then did what he was told.

Part of Peter was shocked at the ease with which Dean followed him—especially after their most recent squabble.

But most of Peter concentrated on shoveling the cold black coals of revenge into the furnace of anger blazing inside him in order to continue fueling the instinct that had brought them this far. The sick bastards who had slaughtered Joseph and Linda so savagely would soon be getting a taste of justice—dealt by Peter's own hands, in Peter's own merciless court of law.

They gingerly shuffled along Montrose Avenue to the corner where Ramezay Avenue took a sharp turn south, pouring itself into Ramezay Street. Peter didn't know if his eyes, doped up on the potent drugs of revenge and wishful thinking, had hallucinated the two dark shadows he'd seen at the end of a hedge wall. He was operating mostly on hunches.

"I think they went down there," Peter said, pointing down Ramezay Street.

"How do you know?"

"I just *know*!" Peter said, not wanting to let Dean in on the fact that he *did* have *some* doubt. Like their father, Dean was always on the attack when Peter expressed doubt, becoming hungry and vicious like a shark smelling blood in the water.

"Isn't that the truck we saw?" Dean said, pointing to the black Durango parked on the side of the street.

"Holy shit," was all Peter could say, realizing he wasn't *entirely* happy to have been right about his hunch.

But then he thought of Linda.

As they arrived at the Durango, Peter glanced inside the truck and then up at the house in front of which it was parked.

"They might be inside there attacking her already," Peter said, pointing at the house while shuffling towards it.

"What are you going to do? Just walk in?"

"I'm not gonna fucking call ahead, am I?"

"What if it isn't the house?"

"It's the house."

"How do you know?"

"Boy... Trust me for once, will you? I just know."

Peter crept up to the front door and put his ear to it. He turned to Dean and whispered, "I think I hear something inside."

"You *think*?"

Peter frowned at Dean and said, "On three, we go in and take them by surprise."

"What? Peter, wait! This is crazy," Dean said, his eyes bulging, his jaw trembling from the cold—or fear. "What if they have guns?"

"Don't worry about it. We're not going in there yelling and screaming," Peter said, finding it hard to keep calm. "Keep it quiet. Stay low. Move quickly. You've seen the way the pros do it a million times. You take the bigger guy. *Especially* if he's got a gun. Ready?"

Dean's silence said it all.

"You ready?"

"No. Don't."

Peter could hear Dean's teeth chattering.

"Let's do this," Peter said with false confidence, suddenly imagining himself on the big screen as the lead actor—an action hero—in a Hollywood movie. It helped take his mind away from the cold and crazy reality of his intentions.

Peter, the big action star... The hoards of women that'll be pulling off their panties for me.

Linda.

Deep breath. "One."

The piles of money I'll be sleeping on.

Joseph.

"Two."

Dildo Dean worshipping at my feet.

Linda, Joseph, Linda, Joseph, Linda, Linda, Linda...

"Three."

Peter pushed his shoulder against the front door, prepared to dive and roll through the foyer and then outrun a spray of bullets nipping at his heels, exploding the wood and walls

into a heavy shower of debris.
    Just like in the movies.

Chapter 29

Alain and Bruno glided silently from the foyer into a wide hallway, and then over to check the living room followed by the library. Each time they approached a room, they stood on either side of the its entranceway, Alain with his Glock drawn and pulled to his chest, the barrel pointed straight up at the ceiling like he'd seen in all those cop shows, and Bruno recording his every move.

On Alain's nod of three, he would bring the gun down to a pointed, ready-to-shoot position with Bruno standing behind him, filming over his shoulder. They'd both step through the entranceway, Alain searching to the left side of the room, then the right. Bruno made sure the camera saw what Alain saw.

Each room was empty.

They moved quickly down the hallway, pulling the same search-and-destroy dance at the dining room, kitchen, and den entrances. They soon cleared the first floor of the house, paying little attention to the luxury surrounding them: the grand piano, the crystal chandelier, the leather sofas and chairs, the damask-covered Victorian settee, the red oak floors covered by genuine, two-inch-thick Oriental rugs, the collection of oil and Tiffany lamps carefully placed for maximum exposure to party guests' eyes, the 12-foot vaulted ceilings...

Everything stank like home to Alain and Bruno, boring them to tears.

But not the hunt for the blonde. That wasn't boring. The hunt was fun. Suspenseful. A real salivator. A tried-and-true tingler.

But where was their prey? Their search of the expansive first floor turned up nothing, meaning their sweet, succulent mark must have gone upstairs. Maybe to take a shower, just like the soon-to-be-dead-buxom-babe did in all those slasher movies they rented and watched after the cop shows.

Alain and Bruno found their way to a staircase, a fifteen-step walled-in area, which had, sitting at its top, a circular mirror framed in sculpted brass hanging above an ornately designed hall table. A small, dark gray sculpture of Mercury, the winged messenger god of the Greeks, stood on the table, looking as if it were about to make a mad dash to the left, down the hallway—maybe to the master bedroom to warn the woman. Alain pointed his gun at the god as he took a couple of steps up the stairs, trying not to cause any creaking in the carpet-covered step beneath his foot.

He stopped at the third stair and listened and watched Mercury, the Glock held out in front of him and swaying back and forth because of his tiring, aching shoulder. His finger stroked and picked at the side of the trigger as if it were a giant hangnail.

Bruno knelt prayer-like on the bottom step and studied Alain through the camera lens. From that position, he saw he had a clear shot of Mercury. Between Alain's legs was a triangular space, and at the center of that space and just above the edge of the top stair sat the god's wing-hatted head. A perfectly framed head on a carpeted platter—an ideal gift to Alain, if he could just—

—capture it.

Bruno laid down the camera and took out his Glock from a waterlogged pocket of his winter coat. Even though Bruno had never fired a gun in his life, his cocaine buzz rid him of his usual inhibitions, allowing him to confidently raise the firearm and point it up the stairs at Mercury's head between Alain's legs. The gun swayed left and right and up and down as he tried to line up its sights with the target.

Bruno's bloodshot eyes watered, blurring his vision. He blinked often until they cleared—

—only to see double—two spaces, two heads, two—

The two Mercury heads circled around each other like a pair of UFOs in a dogfight.

Which one to aim at?

Bruno chose the target on top and pressed his finger to the Glock's trigger. But that target suddenly disappeared, and Bruno saw that his gun was instead aimed square at Alain's ass.

He tried again, quickly aiming the gun while there was only one daemonistic target.

Then another appeared.

Then another.

He blinked hard—and again—and again, trying to focus. Wanting to hunt down this god's head so he could offer it to his own god, Alain.

Bruno kept the sight of his gun aimed at what he thought was the real Mercury head and followed it as it circled around and around. It was hypnotizing. Bruno swayed left and right, the gun's site moving with him. His eyelids grew heavy.

When the Mercury head's circling slowed, Bruno aimed the Glock, again, at the one he believed was real, put his finger on the trigger and started to squeeze.

Just then, the sound of a door closing upstairs caused Alain to spin around and come quickly tiptoeing back down with the grace of a ballerina, nearly ramming his crotch into Bruno's gun.

Alain gave Bruno a harsh look and then pushed him back out of the stairwell and around the left corner. Alain then hopped over to the right side. He gave Bruno another look, one even more severe than before, which carried every bad word and insult known to mankind in its wrinkled eyebrows, pulled back lips, and bared, gritted teeth.

The clack of another closing door pulled Alain's eyes away from Bruno. Bruno breathed a sigh of relief, as if a red-hot branding iron had been removed from his skin.

Alain peeked around the corner and surveyed the staircase. He immediately pulled his head back, straightened his body and leaned flush against the wall on his left. Bruno did the same. Alain positioned the Glock close to his chest, the barrel pointed up at the ceiling. Bruno did the same.

Alain poked his head around the corner again, but this time he jerked it back as if he'd just been hit in the face with a rock.

"She's coming," he mouthed over to Bruno, who stood on the other side of the stairway. "Get the camera ready."

The approaching footsteps kept an uncanny rhythm with their thumping hearts.

Until the blaring music smacked slivers of sound into their ears.

Chapter 30

Peter had tried to break into the wrong house.

Dean wanted to give the kid *such* a punch in the arm for making a mistake like that, for nearly busting into the home of an innocent family. But he didn't feel he needed to *add* to Peter's pain after he had hurt his shoulder ramming it against the locked door.

Like dear old Dad would've done, right, boy? That time he kicked you on your twisted knee while you were still rolling around on the ground in agony during practice and then, in front of all your teammates, calling you an embarrassment to fathers everywhere, you remember that? You played a helluva game that weekend, though—one of your best—so what's the problem?

What *was* the problem? Success born out of sadistic means. Action fueled by a complex mixture of two parts fear, four parts loathing, and six parts masochistic need for both love and acceptance from the very person who refused to give it. Had there ever been a more potent cocktail for pro-activity than that?

Dean had never experienced one.

But that didn't stop him from at least sensing that *something* was wrong with that method, and choosing to try and steer clear of its practice. But he often felt the deepest currents in himself pulled to it like metal to a magnet.

Because you've got my blood in you, boy, that's why. You can never get away from your blood. You carry it with you everywhere. *It feeds you. It gives you life. It* rules *your life. It is your destiny.*

That voice. That damn, deriding voice.

Sometimes he felt so hopelessly entangled in a world of ambiguity, a world of interpretation, a world that could as easily paralyze as inspire.

The world of memories.

Dean's attention returned to the matter at hand, to where Peter was leading him. For the last couple of minutes, Dean had been silently following him around. Now he found himself standing in the yard of the house next door.

Peter looked through one of the front windows.

"What the hell are you doing?"

Peter pointed at something inside the house. "They're in there—that's them."

"Oh, *now* that's them, huh?" Dean said, rolling his eyes under his winter coat's hood. "The people next door only *looked* like them, right?"

Peter ignored Dean's sarcasm as he backed away from the window, gingerly stepping on the ice and snow as if they were hot coals.

"What are you doing *now*?" Dean said.

No answer.

Dean heard the sagging branches of a large oak in a

neighbor's yard across the street squeak and creak as they strained under the weight of the building ice and the force of the bullying wind gusts. As if Dean's awareness carried its own weight, one of the oak tree's thickest branches suddenly tore itself away from the trunk and crashed to the ground.

"Did you *see* that?" Dean said, watching the large tree branch land on the neighbor's sloped front lawn and then start sliding down hill until it got snagged in some bushes. He turned to see if Peter was paying attention, only to find his brother with his ear to the front door and his hand on its knob.

"Peter, don't! Please!" Dean said, forgetting about the ice and taking a quick step in his brother's direction. His foot found no traction. It slid forward, threatening to wrench Dean into the splits.

He recovered, but not before his kneecap twisted and popped in and out of place. A blade of pain scraped up and down the inside of his leg.

As Dean rubbed and pressed his throbbing kneecap, he watched Peter turn the door handle, praying that it would stop rotating.

It didn't.

Peter turned and smiled.

"Don't do it," Dean said. "Please."

"And pretend like these fuckers didn't do anything wrong?" Peter whispered. "No way."

Peter's skin was pulled tight across his face. It seemed to glow. He moved confidently and quickly.

Now there's *a man with the decisiveness and courage of a true leader! And to think, I wasted so much time on you!*

Dean wondered if Peter had found his courage in the self-help section of one of the water-stained, dog-eared *Men's Fitness* magazines that always sat beside the toilet at home.

"Peter, please. I don't want to see you get hurt."

Peter ignored Dean as he cracked open the door and slipped inside.

Goddamn stubborn, careless punk.

Wish you had half his cajones, don't you, boy?

For a moment, Dean thought about returning to the RAV-4 and the security and familiarity that he craved as acutely as he did an end to the throbbing knee pain. But he couldn't leave Peter.

Dean shuffled slowly, stiffly, toward the house. He pushed open the heavy door and slipped into the darkness inside, half expecting to find Peter impatiently waiting there.

He wasn't.

Instead, there was music. Loud music—a Maria Callas aria was being pumped into the many halls and rooms, thanks to well-positioned, powerful speakers.

Dean stood in the dark, frozen in place in the foyer. As much as Peter was a pain in the ass, he gave Dean something positive. He didn't know what it was called, but he could feel it missing from himself like an amputated limb now that his brother was out of sight. Dean wasn't sure where to go next. To move through the shadows of the house on his own accord violated everything he believed about his nature.

Pussy nature.

Dean gripped the door knob—the dial of freedom that he only had to turn and pull on to let himself back outside—and tried to recover his breath, which he just noticed had stumbled down into the depths of his chest like a blind coal miner.

It felt as if a hand swooped through the darkness and landed on his shoulder. Dean flinched. That wet and wheezing voice sounded in his head.

Don't be afraid. There's no monsters in the dark, boy.

Only me.

Rage bubbled up inside of Dean. He wanted to find the voice in the dark and attack it—just like he'd felt *that night*—after the same wet and wheezing voice commanded him to do what, in his gut, he wanted so *desperately* to do.

Do it, boy! Do it!

A surge of emotional electricity coursed through his body—not unlike the tingling current he'd felt *that night.*

When we were so close, you could smell my dying breath.

When he held his father's broken body in his arms.

When I called in my latest and greatest play.

When Dean felt both the power to giveth and the power to taketh away amplifying his senses.

Dean let go of the doorknob and rode the surge, turning and walking confidently through the darkness of the foyer. He moved to his left and walked down the hallway, stopping at the entrance of each room for a second or two to check for Peter.

Nothing.

As each step brought him deeper into the stranger's house, the bolstering surge disappeared as steadily as the setting sun against a Pacific horizon. He felt he was descending into the belly of the bitter beast—

One of my favorite expressions before every game, remember—the belly of the beast.

—where his self-worth would soon be seared away in a wave of digestive juices, with anything of remaining value being shit out as the waste it was.

I knew you'd come running back.

He could feel his knee starting to ache again.

Just can't let go, can you, boy?

Where was everyone?

Boo!

Each step made the uncharacteristic nature of his actions throb like an exposed nerve.

Goddamn punk, Peter! What did you get me into?

In the room up ahead—the kitchen, by the looks of the white tiled floor—a light glowed. Its rounded, luminous edges spilled out onto the carpeted floor and walls of the hallway like a pool of sweet, golden honey. Dean was drawn to the warmth and security it symbolized. But he was also well aware that there he could come upon the surprised and undoubtedly surly owner making a late night snack—or, worse, sitting with a shotgun, waiting for an intruder to poke his head around the corner.

Dean stood in the hallway just outside the kitchen and listened. He heard noises—indefinable rumbles and grumbles—mixed in with, but clearly separate from the music. They seemed to originate from another part of the house. Or from his own twisted, protesting organs—he couldn't be sure.

Dean weighed and measured each one of his actions like a paranoid carpenter. He stood in the hallway pondering if he should peek around the kitchen corner—which would make him a harder target—or if he should just walk into the kitchen with his hands up in the air as a sign of surrender.

He finally chose the latter. Without taking too much time to think about it—and, thereby, calling to mind the thousand-and-one better reasons he'd come up with to turn and run—Dean took a deep breath, put his hands in the air above his head, suppressed his fear as best he could, and stepped into the light.

He closed his eyes as he entered, the child in him still believing that if he didn't see the danger it wouldn't harm him.

Maria Callas hit—and held—a note that seemed humanly

impossible.

But no blast of buckshot accompanied it.

He opened his eyes and found a kitchen before him as big as his apartment bedroom and living room put together— made all the larger by the lack of a justifiably vigilant resident.

As if his eyes and neck muscles were being steered by a driver in his brain, Dean spotted a white cordless phone on the wall opposite the kitchen entrance. The impulse to leap for it and call the police jolted him, making his pained knees buckle.

But then he realized he was looking at only the phone's base. And then the worst—that the handset lay on the windowsill just to the right and below the base, the battery cover on its back torn off, a square black hole where the NiCad battery pack should have been gaping at Dean like a toothless, old coot.

Hee, hee, hee, hee, hee, hee, heeeeeeeee...

Someone had planned ahead.

Dean's pulse pounded in his temples. He stepped farther into the kitchen; just long enough to notice the bowl of fresh fruit and a gold foil-wrapped gift sitting atop the island counter to his far left before—

—a pair of hands snapped around his head, one plastering itself against his mouth like a piece of tape, the other against his forehead.

The hands pulled Dean's head backwards. His arms flew out to his left and right, his hands grabbing for the wall on each side of the kitchen entrance. His legs twisted underneath him as if conspiring to place him in the most vulnerable position possible.

Adrenaline surged through his body causing him to bounce back on his feet. Dean ripped his head free of the hands and whirled around, fists clenched and teeth bared.

His brother's face gawked back at him.

"Bang, you're dead," Peter whispered.

"You sonofa—" Dean started to say, but Peter put his pointer finger to his lips to signal to him to be quiet. He then pointed to his eyes, which started blinking out in code.

H-E-R-E, he blinked. 2—he motioned with his fingers, B-Y S-T-A-I-R-S.

Dean started to blink out a return message, telling Peter that they should just call the cops and let them handle it, but Peter had already turned and crept away down the hall.

Peter motioned for Dean to follow, and then put his finger to his lips to remind him to be quiet. Even though they would have had to speak in a loud voice to be heard over the music, Dean felt their breathing was well miked and would be broadcast over the speakers just as stentoriously as Callas.

As he followed behind, Dean silently cursed Peter—yet again—for getting him involved in this mess and for not letting it end right here, right now. But at the same time, he felt so relieved that he'd found his brother safe, and that he didn't have to be in this house alone any more.

Peter turned into the darkened room just beyond the kitchen. Dean couldn't tell what the room was at first, but when he nearly bumped into an eight-foot high bookshelf, he assumed it was the study. Peter glided through the room, proving to Dean that either his youth blessed him with better eyesight or that he'd already been through the place—or both.

They exited that room by the back and walked into a spacious area that Dean guessed was the family room, from such things as the large-screen projection television and a table in the corner with a pewter piece chessboard lying on top.

Peter stopped in front of a folding door that seemed to open into a closet. He waited for Dean to catch up. When he did, Peter very slowly opened the folding door to reveal another small room—a laundry room.

He could tell they had finally arrived at their destination by the way Peter slunk into the laundry room in slow motion and ducked behind a dryer, careful not to let the sleeves of his winter coat make a *whooooshing* noise as he moved. Dean reluctantly followed Peter and ducked down behind a washer. He looked over at Peter who motioned with his head toward another door at the far end of the laundry room.

Dean peeked around the edge of the washer, his eyes straining to see through the thick, liquid-like blackness to the open door and beyond. His vision was immediately drawn to a walled-in, carpeted stairway that glowed faintly from a second-floor light. Dean couldn't help but think that the stairway resembled a giant esophagus, with the light above coming from the outside world, faintly illuminating the belly of the bitter beast in which he and his brother roamed.

Suddenly, the gray-black shadows framing the stairway entrance rippled, as if an invisible stone had been cast into it.

Motion.

And voices.

The voices were so soft compared to the music and melted so naturally into the orchestral accompaniment of Callas's song, they could have been mistaken for sleet spraying against the windows outside.

Dean squinted till his eyes ached. He saw two black shadows skulking in the gray murk on either side of the stairway.

Dean's mind started playing tricks on him. He wondered—wished, really—that he and Peter had stumbled upon a late night, kinky sex game, and he stifled a laugh—a very nervous laugh.

But his eyes wouldn't be deceived as easily as his brain. He saw one of the shadows holding a gun.

Dean's heart climbed up his chest with spiked shoes and a pickaxe. He felt each breath had to force its way through a windpipe lined with flypaper. He suddenly understood why all those bears he saw in the zoo paced back and forth. The sensation of being trapped caused it. It wasn't just boredom, as his uncle Bobby had tried to tell him. It was something more sinister.

More scary.

Dean's leg bounced up and down. It was the next best thing to pacing back and forth that his brain and body could devise.

He felt like he'd just been given the play: A Fullback Trap on fourth and goal on the five. Two minutes, eighteen seconds remaining. The ball was coming to—

You, pussy! What are you gonna do with it this *time? Drop it?*

Dean looked over at Peter, who watched the same thing going on by the stairwell. He tried to get Peter's attention by waving his hand, but Peter didn't look. Dean tapped the carpeted floor, but Peter still didn't look. Instead, his brother stared at the shadows by the stairwell, looking as if he were a cat digging in its back legs, getting ready to pounce.

Dean's leg wouldn't stop shaking.

He *had* to get Peter's attention. He didn't know if Peter had seen the gun, too. He *knew* what Peter wanted to do, though—he could sense it. He had to stop him.

Now.

Maria Callas's voice soared among the clouds.

Dean took a chance, leaning out from behind the washer

into the middle of the room, waving his hand at Peter.

No response.

He found a stray sock behind the washer. He balled it up and threw it at his brother. It hit him on the side of his head and bounced dangerously into the center of the room, threatening to draw attention.

No response.

Peter's leg twitched.

Dean's trembled.

Another moment in the music swelled.

Dean waggled both his hands and mouthed Peter's name as his brother arched himself into a sprinter's starter position.

No!

Dean reached across the shadowed gap towards Peter— to stop him—to keep him from—

Peter, no!

Callas exploded in a fit of emotion so stunning, it could have moved mountains to tears.

Peter burst towards the stairs—

No!

—with Dean stumbling behind, determined to see to it that his baby brother didn't leave him alone again in this dark and dangerous world, this belly of the bitter beast.

Chapter 31

As unfathomably powerful as the army of magicians making up the human mind is, one of its strongest, most revered generals of wizardry, a leader who can elevate the troops from the deepest swamps of despair to the highest peaks of achievement with one uplifting image, can also be its most crippling enemy.

Alain heard the footsteps coming fast, but he wanted to *believe* they came from around the corner and up the stairs. A force hit him from behind and seemed to blast loose the few things Alain felt were solid about himself—his teeth, his eyes, his limbs, the gun in his hand.

He slammed into the wall, which knocked the wind from him and exploded red and yellow stars behind his shut eyelids. He fell to the floor like a sack of dirt.

His breath caught in his throat. In place of the missing oxygen, panic nourished his blood and brain. He pulled his knees to his chest as he rolled from side to side on the floor—trying to groan, but finding no air to make a sound. Alain's whole body throbbed. His eyes watered—his penis wanted to.

Even though a thick coat of pain was sloppily painted across the surface of Alain's mind, he had the urge to stand up quickly and return to his hiding spot at the foot of the stairs before the blonde saw him.

His mind was a jumbled jigsaw puzzle of thoughts trying to be put back together to form an acceptable reality.

Maybe the blonde hit you. But we checked the whole lower floor of the house. Maybe she came down the other stairs and sneaked up on you. But how could such a small woman hit so hard?

Wait a minute, where am I?

He realized his hearing had been affected. It was as if his ears were submerged under the same salty seas as his eyes, his heartbeat playing the part of the rhythmic clunk of a faraway ship's engine, his rushing circulation playing the ebb and flow of the waves overhead.

No more of that annoying opera shit—thank God!

Alain forced his eyes open to a slit, forced them to strain to see through the murky pool of salt water collected on top of them. The blurred shadows hung heavily from the walls and ceiling above him like a jury of dark, menacing jungle apes. Even though they weren't moving, Alain believed they'd come crashing down on his head at any moment.

Then one of the shadows did move.

It radiated a boundless, seething energy. Through Alain's smeared sight, it seemed as though the shadow first looked down at him and then looked away and pointed and said something—something muffled, nearly muted to Alain's ears. But he detected pitch—a low pitch. A man's voice.

Where had he come from all of a sudden?

Where is my gun?

Where am I?
How could I screw up so badly?
What will the demons think? Say? Do?
Stupid! Stupid! Stupid! Sssssssssstupid!

His hearing began to return.

The shadow man turned his attention back to Alain as if he had been thinking out loud on the floor.

The shadow man suddenly doubled—tripled in size, as he landed on top of Alain with the weight of a falling tree. Alain felt the drops of precious air he'd finally eased back into his lungs explode up his windpipe and out from his lips. A new wave of pain crashed on top of him, burying all his senses with a blackness thicker than mud, soaking him straight through to the marrow in his bones.

Alain wondered if this was death.

And if he'd soon be tried and convicted in a demonic court for his careless crimes against insanity.

Chapter 32

It had been over six years since Dean had hit another human body. But unlike riding a bicycle or using a typewriter, where learned movements are stored in the muscles' memory for a lifetime, knocking someone off his feet was a technique whose potency was a strict function of practice.

Keep your head up and just drive your shoulder into the son of a bitch's solar plexus, boy, and push, push, push the pussy to the ground! It's simple!

But Dean never found it so simple. Nearly every time, no matter how much he promised himself he'd do it differently, at the moment of contact Dean would revert back to the matador's *olé* technique.

Rather than launching himself like a missile at the far shadow beside the stairwell and taking it out with a direct blow, as Peter had done, Dean ran up to the other shadow, grabbed it by its shoulders, and simultaneously spun himself counter-clockwise while flinging the shadow away—and hoping with all his heart it went tumbling to the ground.

But it didn't. It stumbled a few feet into the hallway, regained its balance, and then stood motionless for a moment, as if surveying the situation.

Even though Dean couldn't make out the shadow's face, he could sense by the way it stood there that it was confused. Dean's brain tripped over itself as it tried to decide how to rush the shadow again without hurting himself.

How many times did I tell you not to think!

Plenty of time for the shadow to raise its right arm and point something at Dean.

"*N'approchez pas!*" the shadow said, in a quivering voice.

"He's got a gun!" Peter shouted.

Dean's reaction was instinctive. He closed the gap between himself and the shadow with a single lunge, bringing his right arm above his shoulder as he moved and then chopping across his body at the shadow's right arm. Even though both Dean and the shadow wore heavy winter coats, it felt to Dean as though their forearm bones had cracked together.

Dean winced. The shadow yelped. Something flew out of the shadow's hand and landed with a heavy *clunk* on the carpeted floor. Neither Dean nor the shadow, which was stumbling around on its heels, went after it. Instead, Dean grabbed the shadow around the shoulders by the coat and pulled it towards the floor as he backed away. The shadow stumbled forward in the same direction as Dean and then finally gave way to the top-heavy force, crashing face first into the carpet with a grunt and moan.

Dean leapt over to the black lump that the shadow had been holding. He picked it up. As he'd suspected, it was a gun. He pointed it at the shadow, which was slowly pushing itself up onto its hands and knees.

"Don't move," Dean said, pointing the gun.

"All right! You got the asshole!" Peter said, standing over the other shadow with a gun pointed at it.

"Get up," Dean said to the shadow.

"What? Don't make him get up," Peter said. "You gotta keep the motherfucker down on the ground where he's submissive and vulnerable."

With that last word, Peter let a kick fly into the side of the body lying at his feet.

"Don't do that!" Dean snapped.

"What? They're fucking killers!"

"We don't... we don't know that... for sure," Dean gasped, suddenly realizing how winded he was. Apparently, working out in the gym didn't entirely prepare one for the physical demands of subduing killers.

Dean's shadow spoke to Peter's shadow. "*Alain, es-tu correct? Qu'est-ce que tu veux faire*—"

"What the fuck is he saying?" Peter said.

"I... I think he's just asking if your guy there's all right."

"Well, tell him to shut up!" Peter said. "Stick the gun in his face! Kick him in the fucking head!"

Peter unleashed another kick into his prisoner. The guy let out an agonized moan.

"Peter—come on!"

Pussy!

"You wouldn't be saying that if you'd seen—"

Kick.

"fucking—"

Kick

"Linda cut up!"

Kick.

Dean pushed his detainee onto his stomach. He held the gun to the back of his head. Unlike some accounts Dean had heard of people feeling an intense rush of power when they held a gun in their hand, Dean felt more enervated than invigorated. Although, as a young man, he'd many times fantasized about shooting his own father to death with everything from poisoned darts to bazookas, now that he held a real gun in his hand for the first time in his life, he felt as clumsy and awkward with the hardware as a virgin on her wedding night.

"All right, one of us has got to go call the cops and find whoever lives here and tell them what happened," Dean said, his breath sawing his throat raw.

"You go," Peter said without hesitation.

Dean recognized the tone in Peter's voice. It said to Dean that if he left him alone with these two, he might soon have a murderer as well as a punk for a younger brother.

"I think you should go," Dean said.

"I'm fine here—you go."

"Listen, I think it'd be better if *you* go—now!"

Peter's prisoner mumbled something to Dean's, who then mumbled something back.

"Shut up!" Peter said, drawing back his foot and preparing to kick the man on the ground again.

"Peter, no!" Dean said.

Peter stopped his kick in mid-swing, and Dean breathed a sigh of relief. But then Peter got down on his knees, grabbed his captive by the hair and stuck the Glock in the guy's mouth.

"You sick son of a bitch! You *like* cutting up pregnant women, you sick fucker! You got a taste for blood? *I'll* give you a fucking taste of blood, motherfucker!"

Peter jammed the barrel of the gun so far into his captive's mouth that he gagged.

"You like that? Does it make you horny, bitch? You want more? You want more, you sick fucker?"

"Peter, calm down!" Dean called. He could see Peter's

finger on the Glock's trigger—one mistake away from becoming a murderer.

"I'll give you more! I'll make it *real* sweet and slow!"

"Peter, relax!"

"I'll give you something to fucking remember!" Peter screamed into his prisoner's face, spraying spit and tears like a sputtering showerhead. "I'll give it to you! I'm your man! I'll give it to you like the dirty bitch you are!"

"Peter—stop it, *now*!"

Dean leaped away from his prisoner and grabbed his brother's shoulder.

"Stop it, Peter," he said again, this time talking right into his ear while shaking and squeezing his shoulder. "Please. If you don't do it for my sake, do it for Linda's. She wouldn't have hurt a fly—you know that. She wouldn't want you to either. Even for her sake."

Just then the other man started to get up, looking like he was going to bolt past everyone and down the hallway.

"No!" Dean shouted, spinning and pointing the Glock at him. The man froze in place and stretched his arms high in the air.

Dean found himself caught in the middle, his head turning left and right between his brother and his captive as if he were watching a tennis match, wondering which problem to take care of first in order to regain some control of the situation.

Uh-oh, stand back! Decision time!

Dean decided to take care of his captive first. He made him lie face down beside the other man and put his hands behind his back. Peter calmed down and made his captive do the same.

Dean felt he'd dodged more than one type of bullet there with Peter. The kid had guts, sure, but his lack of self-control almost got the better of him. For the first time that night, Dean saw how his careful nature had been useful. Up to that point, it had been Peter's gung-ho, take-no-prisoners attitude that had gotten them to where they were—catching a pair of killers, perhaps, and saving a woman from becoming their next victim.

Which reminded Dean: Why hadn't the woman these two sickos were stalking made her presence known? She *must* have heard the commotion. She *must* know that the "good guys" had won.

Dean asked Peter again if he'd go and try to find the woman and a phone, warning him about the one in the kitchen being broken. This time his brother agreed, putting the gun in his coat pocket and striding confidently up the stairs and into the warm, inviting light.

Soon this would all be over, Dean told himself as the surrounding darkness squeezed tight against his body and his shortened breath sawed at his throat once again.

The shadows hissed and howled.

And whispered.

Chapter 33

"What are we going to do?" Bruno whispered to Alain in French under the blaring music.

"How do I know? I didn't expect this," Alain said, his voice sounding as deflated as his punished body felt. "All I know is this guy watching us is an amateur."

"Maybe if we both jump at him, we can take him."

"Spoken like a true savage—I'm proud of you."

"You are?"

"I don't think he could shoot that gun even if he wanted to."

"So we're jumping him?"

"Be quiet, you two," the man with the gun said.

"*J'comprends pas*," Alain said to the man.

"No, I know you understand some. *Every*body understands *some* English," the man insisted.

"*J'comprends rien, monsieur*," Alain said. And then talking to Bruno in French he said, "What a stupid anglophone asshole. He must be an American. I can tell by his accent."

"So what do we do?" Bruno asked, sounding more than willing, if commanded, to risk his life rushing at an armed man.

Alain knew he must still be high from the coke. The down and dependent Bruno wasn't nearly as daring.

"We wait for the right moment. If he comes around in front of us and we have a good shot at him, we try it. If not, we wait for another opportunity."

"But the other one's calling the police right now."

"I thought I told you two to be quiet," the man with the gun said, his words carrying as much force as an anorexic trying to lift an automobile.

"The police—spare me," Alain said, ignoring their captor. He listened carefully for the evil spirits' voices. They were hard to hear. "Besides, I have a feeling something is going to happen to help us get free before any police arrive."

As if on cue, the Marie Callas music disappeared into the darkness. The fresh silence seemed to amplify all ambient noises.

The man stopped pacing around Alain and Bruno and crouched down in front of them. He held the Glock out of reach, but in plain view. His frightened eyes roved over their facial features as though they were metal detectors searching a sandy beach for sharp objects.

"You know, you two really don't look like the killers they show on all those cop shows."

Alain thought the guy looked like a big, dumb, former football player from the States who probably couldn't let go of his glory days.

"Maybe that help will come sooner rather than later," Alain said to Bruno in French and smiled. Then he looked up at the man with the gun. "*J'comprends pas,*" he said as he calculated how much closer the guy had to come before commanding Bruno to strike.

Chapter 34

A hand grabbed Dean.

He shouted, leaped up onto his feet and whirled around. It was Peter.

"Goddamit! Stop sneaking up on me like that!"

"Sorry. I came down the other stairs," Peter said, motioning to another part of the house. "I didn't find anyone."

"What?"

"Yeah, I was calling and shit and looking in all the rooms, but there was no one."

"What about a phone? Did you find another phone?"

"Yeah and no. I found the base to one upstairs, but the phone wasn't there."

"Jesus Christ, I can't believe you couldn't find a—this house is the size of a goddamn football field and there are only *two* phones. Run next door and call from there."

"What? Since when did *you* become boss of this operation?"

"Now's not the time, Peter. Just go next door and call, all right?"

"Fuck you, *Dean*! I just did your dirty work for you checking the house—*you* go next door if you want the phone so bad."

The two prisoners on the floor watched and listened.

Peter paced back and forth only inches away from Alain and Bruno's heads, muttering to himself.

"Fucking pushy sonofabitch... What are these two cock suckers' names?"

"I don't know. I didn't ask."

"What are your names, you sick fucks?" Peter said, crouching down in front of the prisoners and putting his face close to theirs.

"*J'comprends pas.*"

"They keep saying that—claiming they don't understand."

"Yeah, I got *that. Quelle est...* No, *que... C'est quoi... Como se—*"

"*Quelle est votre nom*?" Dean said over Peter's shoulder.

Peter turned and glared at Dean. "Oh, listen to Shakespeare here."

The two men looked at each other for a moment. Peter swore he saw one of them smirk. Finally, one of them said, "*J'suis Guido et lui est... Guissepi.*"

"Guido and Guiseppi—good," Dean said.

"Guido and Guiseppi—they ain't named Guido and Guissepi, boy! They're fucking with you," Peter said, standing up and nudging Dean out of the way. He raised his foot, preparing to smash it square into Alain's face. "What's your real fucking names, assholes?"

"Peter, don't!"

Peter saw the guy whom he wanted to kick flinch. It felt

good. So rather than ease up, Peter cocked his foot several inches further back, looking like he was going to place kick Alain's head right off of his neck, taking great pleasure in watching the guy's face try and fold in on itself for protection.

"Alain *et* Bruno! Alain *et* Bruno!" Alain said. "*Moi, c'est Alain et lui, c'est Bruno.*"

"Oh, would you listen to that," Peter said, putting his foot down and feeling all puffed up. "At least those *sound* right."

Dean said, "Okay, Alain and Bruno. I'm Dean and this is Peter. Listen, we're here to—"

"What the hell are you doing? What the—*Boy*, don't tell them *our* names!" Peter said to Dean, trying to push him away. "You gotta be tough with them." The tone of Peter's voice sharpened. "Okay, Alain, listen up, douche bag. *Pour quoi* did you kill *les deux personnes dans... dans* the motherfucking restaurant, motherfucker?" Peter's hand sprung out from his body like a switchblade and grabbed Alain's hair. He bashed his head into the floor. "Tell me, motherfucker! *Pour quoi, pour quoi!* Tell me in English! *Pour quoi!*"

Dean yanked his brother's arm away from Alain's head.

"What! What? Why did you stop me? Why do you always—why, huh? That there's a piece of shit!"

Peter stormed off, kicking at something invisible on the floor in front of him. He found it *so* hard to control himself, especially when the images of Linda and Joseph's bloodied, butchered bodies strobed in his mind.

"Fuck!" he yelled again, and hit the wall with his fist. "What the fuck are we gonna do now with them? Ask them their favorite team, beer, and titty movie and then blow them?"

"If you'd just listen to me and go next door and use their

phone, maybe—"

"Yeah, everything'd be just fine then—I *love* how the solution to every problem is always so clean and easy in your mind," Peter said as he paced toward the laundry room.

"If you'd just calm down, maybe things wouldn't seem so complicated."

But Peter didn't act like he'd heard. Instead, he thought of Linda as he traced his finger along an interesting pattern in the waist-high mahogany wood divider which separated the light peach wall above from the pleasantly contrasting flowered wallpaper below.

"You realize, don't you, that if I'd listened to you back at the restaurant," Peter said, "there'd be another dead woman in this—"

It was as if those words—*dead woman*—were the pop of the starter's pistol. Out of the same pitch black shadows of the laundry room that Peter and Dean had earlier sprung from came a blood-chilling shriek, followed by an extended arm with a small black container in the hand of a short, petite, blonde-headed body. The woman stood sideways as she scampered forward clothed only in a white cotton terry robe.

"Get out of my house!"

The small black container that she held out in front of her squirted a thin line of liquid at Peter's face. Pepper spray. He turned away quickly enough to keep it from hitting him directly in his eyes, but the spray still had a debilitating effect. Feeling as if his lungs and throat were collapsing in on themselves, Peter grunted, doubled over, then fell to the floor, gasping and coughing and pressing his hands to his face.

Dean put his hands straight out in front of him, the gun still stuck in his hand, his finger resting softly on its trigger. He tried talking to the woman.

"Please, lady, we're here to help. We're not the—"

But before he could finish the sentence the woman screamed an obscenity as she quickly shuffled sideways across the floor towards Dean like a boxer in a ring. She pressed a button on the top of the pepper spray container. It responded with a powerful stream squirted straight into the center of Dean's outstretched hands. Several tiny drops splashed off his fingers and into his eyes. Dean sounded like his breath had just been ripped from his lungs. He fell to the floor, groaning and covering his face.

The woman screamed as she ran down the hallway and out the front door of the house, having exercised enough personal justice for the night. Her foot hit the ice-covered step outside and kept going, flipping her body backwards. She landed on her rear-end, got up as if she hadn't felt the blow, hastily took another step, and fell down again. She started to crawl on her hands and knees across the ice toward her neighbor's house. She was in hysterics, tears of pain and panic streaming down her cheeks as her real emotions let loose, her bare knees bruising, her hands rubbing themselves raw on the frozen ground.

The world hissed dispassionately around her, absorbing her cries for help.

Halfway to her neighbors, she fell face down onto her stomach in exhaustion. Something inside the front pocket of her bathrobe pushed itself into her abdomen like a small fist. She rolled onto her back, her eyes squeezed shut to prevent them from being pierced by the stinging sleet shooting down at her, and put one of her red and throbbing hands inside her robe pocket. In it she found a cordless phone.

She took it out and dialed.

Back in the house, more sounds of suffering.

Unlike the woman's, though, the suffering coming from Dean and Peter was heard loud and clear by Alain and Bruno.

But they weren't about to do anything to help stop it.

In fact, coughing and puffy-eyed, but otherwise fine, they were getting ready to make things much worse.

Chapter 35

Alain was going to kill those English-speaking sonsofbitches for hurting and humiliating him.

With every part of his body still screaming in agony from the pain of Peter's beating and his eyes, nose, and mouth leaking like squeezed oranges due to the lingering mist of pepper spray, Alain stumbled over to the dropped gun nearest him. Bruno, who hadn't been roughed up as severely as Alain, retrieved the other Glock with more spring in his step but less slosh slobbering down his face. Together, they stood above the squirming and groaning and coughing brothers, looking like slaves who'd finally swiped the whips from their masters.

Shooting them would be so easy, Alain thought. Insane, sure. But a hackneyed type of insanity. No originality and effort put into it at all.

The serial killers he'd read about took killing to new levels. They raised murdering to the realms of art—as he, in turn, wished to do. He understood how many of the maniacs had a tumor full of mysterious and dark urges aching in the depths of their being, ready to split and spill at any moment. He appreciated how that growing pressure, in turn, often drained itself, without obliterating its host, in intricate and symbolic forms, or personal signatures, upon a canvas of flesh. He knew what the subsequent sense of satisfaction and relief—and sometimes hope—felt like. But also, how that satisfaction and relief inevitably faded away, only to have the same tumor of fiery tumult in the soul's center once again over-inflate with perverse poisons.

These were some of the same profound and powerful forces that Alain saw inspiring not only killers, but the likes of Picasso and Michelangelo and Dostoyevsky to do what they did, to continuously attempt to go beyond themselves in order to finally extract from their being the toxic tumor which always threatened to fully expand and choke to death any lingering sense of their humanity.

These were the same forces Alain liked to believe he felt moving around inside his mind and body—the anxious forces of a misunderstood genius.

Being his own harshest critic, though, Alain felt he lacked the personal signature that the greatest creators and destroyers possessed. Or, at best, he couldn't recognize its pattern yet, the preferred mode of dress of his internal urges.

No, shooting was too easy. Hardly a personal signature—or at least one worthy of his talent. Shooting would be like the Harlequin novel of literature, the trailer home of architecture, a mostly lazy, convenient, half-assed investment of himself in the arts of insanity and murder. He needed to add some poetry to the mix. Something personal and perspicacious. Something straight from the heart.

"I want you to run to the kitchen and get me something," Alain said to Bruno, catching sight of an enticing image in his mind and deciding to follow its beckoning to see if it took him someplace special.

Alain told Bruno what he wanted from the kitchen and why he wanted it, and Bruno laughed, still obviously experiencing some sort of residual high from the cocaine he'd snorted earlier.

This was good. Alain needed his full cooperation.

Bruno scampered down the hallway to the kitchen making mooing sounds. Alain heard him pulling out drawers and letting them crash to the floor, sending their contents shimmying loudly across the terra cotta tiles.

A minute later, Bruno returned carefully carrying what Alain wanted as if were a highly volatile piece of plutonium.

"These are fine," Alain said, taking them from Bruno and testing them in the air. They weren't good ol' Shiny Sharpy, but they'd do.

"What are you going to do with them?" Bruno asked, beaming from the compliment.

"You mean, what are *you* going to do with them?"

"Me?"

"Yeah, you. You did such a great job in the restaurant earlier—"

"I did?"

"Why not try your skills on these two?"

"Skills? What skills? I don't have any—"

"Oh, but you do. I've seen them. Start on the young one here. Hold his arms down with your knees. I'll film."

"But I—"

"Just do it!" Alain shouted, not wanting to waste a moment.

With a paradoxical gentleness, Bruno uncurled Peter from the fetal position, turned him groaning and coughing onto his back, and lay his arms out perpendicular to his sides, as if getting ready to nail Peter to a crucifix. He stepped over Peter so he straddled his body. He crouched until his knees came down on top of each of Peter's arms at mid-bicep; his rear-end crushed down on Peter's heaving chest.

Manson had his family do most of the dirty work for him. I have Bruno.

Bruno looked up at Alain with wide eyes.

The damn cocaine was wearing off!

"Now get a hold of his hair—come on, hurry up, Bruno," Alain said, keeping one eye on what Bruno was doing through the camera's viewfinder, and one on Dean, who was recovering faster than Alain had hoped.

Bruno gave Alain a pleading look again.

"Bruno!"

Bruno reached down and grabbed a clump of Peter's sweat soaked hair.

"Let's go—now take these," Alain said. He let out a mooing sound like the one Bruno had made moments earlier.

The left corner of Bruno's mouth twitched as he took Alain's offering.

The corners of Alain's mouth curled into a satisfying smile as he caught sight of his own personal signature as if it were the last word in a word search puzzle he'd been studying for hours.

It was so obvious. It had been there all along.

It was a signature that wasn't so much identifiable by *whom* he killed or *what* he used to kill or *where* he killed or *when* he killed or even *why* he killed, but rather how *he* didn't kill at all—how he had someone *else* kill for him.

Genius—of the maddest sort.

He felt himself rising above both the demon-worshipping, cold-blooded killer in the restaurant and the suave, smooth-talking maniac out on the open road, as he approached the much-revered level of the *great* artist—the type that books and films showcased. The cosmic creator of destruction. The director of death.

He tingled with joy as if he'd just received an acceptance letter to an elite club.

"Let's start with the ears—*a la* Van Gogh," Alain said, framing his shot in the camera's viewfinder as he imagined Scorcese would. "Try and make him smile for the camera, too. Aaaaaand action."

Chapter 36

As if his swollen eyes, which felt like two sizzling fried eggs, and his itching and aching lungs, which tried to suck in air through a cotton-clogged throat, weren't enough, Peter thought a three-wheeler ATV was parked on his arms and legs, threatening to crush them into the slimy substance of road kill.

His hair was being pulled, its roots threatening to let go after a valiant but painful protest.

Peter opened his eyes to see what was on top of him. It felt like a draft of cold air raced across the hallway from some crack in a faraway floorboard and ripped across his greasy corneas like a circular saw. He struggled to try and focus his vision, but he might as well have been looking at the world through a beer bottle—everything took on a dark, distorted, muddy appearance.

He could tell, though, that it was a man pinning him to the floor.

Peter's head jerked forward. A hand, he thought, lowered

towards his face. It held something. That something swooped across his line of vision like a razor-beaked buzzard, dove directly at his right eye then veered off to the side of his head. Its cold metallic body pressed against his ear. Peter wanted to believe it was an ambulance technician performing a pain reduction procedure—

—but he wasn't reducing the pain at all. Without a doubt, his discomfort was increasing—

—exponentially.

Peter struggled against the man's weight, but he couldn't get enough leverage or momentum to throw him off. He tried to move his head, to get away from the cold, metallic sharpness—

He felt sharpness!

—touching his ear—encircling his ear where it connected to his head. It slid back and forth, the chill coming off its two metal sides entering Peter's body and snaking down his spine.

Peter let out a scream.

But nobody came to help.

He yelled his brother's name.

Nothing.

The sharp pieces of metal suddenly slid away from his ear. But only for a moment. Before Peter could even *consider* if his yelling had literally saved his skin, the pieces of metal returned—this time pinching Peter's earlobe between their dagger teeth.

Pinching hard.

No!

Pinching *very* hard.

No!

As a last resort, Peter's body shook and thrashed like an epileptic.

A sound that wriggled down Peter's ear canal; an altogether pleasant and appealing sound—

SHHHHWIT...

—if flesh hadn't been the cause of it.

The cold, sharp pieces of metal came together like two long lost lovers, slicing through Peter's earlobe on their way to meet each other, their *rendezvous* eliciting an erotic-like eruption of warm, bubbling fluid.

Scissors! They were scissors! And they'd cut off part of my ear!

Peter screamed, as much from the sheer *idea* of having a piece of himself severed as from the pain.

The chunk of earlobe brushed against the side of his neck as it dropped inside an opening in his coat and shirt. It came to rest wedged between the bare skin above the lump of his clavicle bone and some bunched -up shirt fabric. Peter believed he could feel the piece of ear pulsating like a slug against his flesh—and he bellowed.

"*Arrete de pleurnicher comme un bébé,*" Peter heard a voice say. It sounded like the guy named Alain. "*Veux-tu vraiment savoir c'est quoi souffrir? Je vais te le montrer. Bruno—vas-y! La langue,*" Alain said.

Peter couldn't understand more than a couple of words.

Alain and Bruno started having an animated conversation. Peter couldn't follow along, but he could tell they were talking about him and that it had something to do with Bruno not wanting to follow Alain's orders.

Even though Bruno had just taken off his earlobe with a pair of scissors, Peter had no choice but to cheer the slow-sounding sonofabitch in his mind. Whatever order Alain had given him, Peter knew it couldn't be good.

But Bruno folded to Alain's demands after only a baby's breath worth of resistance. He pulled Peter's head up off the floor once again by the hair.

Here it is!

Dean!

Come on down!

Dean!

You're the next contestant on Your Death Tonight!

Dean, help!

Peter tried to shake free again, but Bruno wouldn't budge. Through his blurred vision, he could see the scissors coming straight at him from above. He expected them to veer to the left and take off his other earlobe. But, instead, it moved front and center. Two sharp points poked Peter on the bottom lip. Then they pinned his lip against his teeth—

Ahhhh!

—then pressed harder.

They bullied their way through the lip's soft skin until they hit the waiting wall behind—Peter's teeth.

Peter wanted to scream, but he knew if he did, it would be like opening the door and inviting the bloodstained blades inside the warm, wet cave of soft, mushy mouthparts. Some of the blood found its way past his teeth and to his tongue.

"*Ouvre la bouche,*" he heard Bruno say.

The scissors' blades sliding up and down on the front surface of Peter's teeth, scraping and scratching at their enamel—

Krrrrr-krrrrr-krrrrr...

—looking for a space to squeeze through. They pressed hard; they felt like they'd push right *through* a tooth if all else failed.

They suddenly slipped across his teeth and bit into his upper gums. Fresh blood flowed like gravy from a punctured Zip-lock bag. It quickly filled the space between Peter's bottom lip and gums and then spilled down his chin.

"*Ouvre la bouche! Aide-moi donc,*" Bruno said.

Peter shook his head left and right. Bruno let go of Peter's hair. His head bounced against the floor. Bruno slid forward on Peter's chest. His free hand came down hard on Peter's face, pushing it into the floor, while the fingers pried open his lips. Bruno stabbed the blades against Peter's teeth, using them as a battering ram. If he couldn't push through, he was going to *break* through.

Alain cheered Bruno on.

The pointed tip of the closed blades zipped down from six inches above Peter's head. It hit hard and with surprising accuracy. Just an inch or two in any direction and it would have punctured through Peter's face.

Dean!

It hit a second time—

A third—

Dean!

Peter didn't know if he should struggle or what. If he moved, he was sure Bruno would miss his teeth and hit him somewhere less resistant.

A fourth time—

—and Peter felt one of his incisors buckle under the force and move.

Move! Like in my nightmares!

The scissors jabbed again. This time the pointed tip wedged itself in a space between Peter's upper and lower incisors. The space wasn't big, but it allowed Bruno to then use the scissors as a crowbar instead of a battering ram.

Bruno pulled down on the scissors' handles.

Alain cackled.

Either because of the force from the leverage they had or because Peter's jaw was getting extremely tired, the blades opened a tiny space for themselves—

—and slipped inside.

They quickly slid deep inside Peter's mouth, missing his tongue and rocketing right to the back of his throat, where they grabbed at the uvula dangling from the ceiling of his palate like a boxer's speed bag.

Bruno squeezed.

Peter gagged, the force of which jolted the scissors' blades away from his uvula. But the gag also opened Peter's mouth, giving Bruno the opportunity to move the scissors about unhindered.

Bruno withdrew the scissors from the back of Peter's throat and fished around in the front for a big, red, throbbing piece of mouth meat—the trophy for his efforts.

The scissors stabbed beneath Peter's tongue and gripped it at its base. They squeezed, threatening to tear through the flesh.

Peter screeched. He waited for the intense pain to come...

But it didn't—for a second—

Two—

Three—

It seemed Bruno—*God bless his tender heart*—was having a hard time getting up the guts to complete the job.

Alain jumped up and down, first cheering him on, then yelling commands, followed by words that sounded like threats. Then he stuck the camera beside Bruno's face, aiming it down at Peter.

Peter felt a surge of strength welling in Bruno. His hand shoved Peter's head down into the floor harder than ever. The starving scissors opened wider, taking more tongue meat between its two long, sharp teeth. Peter could feel Bruno's body stiffen, building his strength for the big snip—

When Alain yelled for him to stop.

Peter's ever-clearing eyes saw Bruno turn his head

towards Alain with a twisted look of confusion painted across his face. He obviously didn't understand what he was doing wrong.

A thick silence filled the house like a toxic gas, crowding out the oxygen, making it difficult for Peter to breathe. The scissors still pinching the bottom of his tongue didn't help either.

Alain said something to Bruno in *sotto voce* and Bruno whispered something back.

And then silence as they both listened.

Peter could hear a gust of wind rattling windows somewhere in the house. But that was all. Whether it was on purpose or because his mind was distracted, Bruno squeezed the scissors harder against Peter's tongue. The blades started to slice. Peter whimpered and his whole body quivered. When Bruno's attention moved to Peter he recoiled. He loosened his grip on the scissors, then slid them out of Peter's mouth.

Blood leaked down the back and sides of Peter's tongue and down his burning throat. He swallowed it fast and often until he gagged. He turned his head to the side and spit. His tongue felt as though it were swollen to the size of an elephant's testicle.

Suddenly a mix of laughter and coughing came tumbling across the floor from behind Peter. A familiar laugh and cough—Dean's.

"Ha-ha, you stupid sonsofbitches! They've got you now!"

"*Ferme-là!*" Alain said.

"What is it?" Peter said, his voice butchering all vowels and consonants to match his tongue.

"Finally this is over!" Dean said again, still laughing and coughing.

"*Ferme-là!*"

"What is it?"

"Don't you hear it?"

"*Fermez-là! Vous deux! Fermez-là!*"

"The police! The police are coming! I heard their sirens! So did these sonsofbitches—that's why they look so scared! Finally, this is over!" Dean said, and then he let out a triumphant shout of jubilation as if he'd just scored the winning touchdown on a fourth down play with time running out.

PART III

Chapter 37

It felt as though freshman safety Horace Green, the Missouri Tiger football player who'd haunted Dean's memories for years, launched his body at Dean all over again, hitting him with the force of a sledgehammer, stopping him short of the goal line.

How effortlessly that single play's emotional significance had expanded as a function of time. Coupled with the memory of *that night*, those two events had effortlessly become the roots of all the weeds of defeat in Dean's life. As if being stuck in the situation he was in—poked in the back with the same gun he held in *his* hands only several minutes prior, held hostage by the same hooligans who were just *his* hostages, and having wasted time and energy celebrating the belief that he was going to soon be rescued and returned to his comfortable life in the somber sea of *status quo*— could be traced back to, above all, one missed touchdown and one particular night spent with his dying father.

Why not?

It seemed so obvious to Dean, he couldn't possibly imagine someone else missing the connection. Sure, there were a plethora of other lesser moments contributing to his dire perspective, but it proved much easier to draw his self-effacing impulses from two mountainous events rather than a multitude of molehills. He was a man who'd proved to himself with the regularity of sunrises that he didn't have what it took to... to... to what?

He never knew how to finish that thought.

But it was only the first part that really mattered—an *incomplete* thought used to define himself *completely*.

The four of them moved quickly through the hallway, the armed Alain and Bruno shadowing Dean and Peter. Even though Dean had occasionally joked to some of his employees that his bulky winter coat felt thick enough to stop bullets, he wasn't about to test that declaration.

The front door was still open from when the frightened woman had exited in hysterics. She was nowhere to be seen outside. There were no policemen crouched behind their cruisers with their pistols fixed on the darkened foyer either, waiting and wondering if they'd be forced to take a life tonight.

There was only ice and fallen branches. And nature's frozen, stinging tears falling from the sky.

"Where are the fucking cops?" Peter said.

The sirens remained far off in the distance. There was little doubt they were responding to another call for help.

Dean wondered if his brother, who was obviously in pain by the way he held his hand to his cut ear, and undoubtedly burning with rage because of it, was about to try something stupid; to slip and stumble into Bruno on purpose so he could start a scuffle and try to get the gun. It wouldn't have been out of character for the kid who had once been kicked out of Cub Scouts for putting poison ivy leaves in the scoutmaster's salad.

The thought of it—of his and Peter's life possibly ending in mere seconds if they couldn't quickly get those guns away from Alain and Bruno—made Dean's legs wobble like Jello pillars. But, just the same, the thought of going along passively with these monsters' demands and being taken far away and beaten and tortured to death made him want to vomit on his boots in self-disgust.

Why, isn't 'pussy' your middle name, boy? I always thought it was.

Enough!

What's so bad about dying? Shit, you've thought a lot about what dying is since that night, haven't you? Didn't you once even think about taking your own—

Shut up!

If his life was going to end in the next few minutes, he didn't want the lights to go out with that voice scraping around inside his skull like a spoon cleaning out the pumpkin pulp for Halloween.

Peter made no heroic move to snatch the gun, and Dean wasn't sure what he should have felt.

That means both my boys are gonna go die like a pair of squealing pigs in the woods—I'm so proud!

They all stepped outside and onto the ice, moving in a single line down the walkway with the same lack of speed and duck-waddling awkwardness as a chain gang with ankles shackled together.

The storm had intensified since they'd been in the house. Everywhere around them, the world crackled and popped and rumbled.

Out of one beast's belly and into another.

Dean figured they were turning left at the end of the walkway, heading up the sidewalk and back to either his RAV-4 or their Buick. But instead, they stopped at the black Durango everybody had been following earlier that night, albeit for very different reasons.

Like a sleight-of-hand magic trick, the truck's keys appeared in Bruno's hand. He turned off the truck alarm, which automatically unlocked all the doors, and brought the puffy-eyed Peter around to the driver's side.

It was then that something happened which would have made Dean chuckle if he'd seen it in a movie. In real life, with real guns being pointed, though, it wasn't so funny. Bruno and Peter had come around the front of the truck and approached the driver's door. When Bruno took his left arm off Peter's back and reached over his gun to open the Durango's door, Peter slid backwards along the glare ice, away from Bruno and down Ramezay.

Dean wondered if this was it, if Peter was taking a major risk to try and help them escape. But then he noticed the look of honest-to-goodness helplessness stretched across his brother's bloodstained face as he struggled not to lose his balance.

Bruno yelled at Peter to stop. He pointed his gun at him. But his threats didn't work. Peter looked as if he were being pulled into an invisible vortex while riding a surfboard. His arms were fully extended and waving up and down and side-to-side, searching the frigid air for stability. He started off in a full-standing position, but the further he slid the more he crouched.

Alain yelled for him to stop, too, and pointed his gun. At that moment, Dean thought about chopping Alain's arm. But he couldn't get his own arm to move. What if he didn't knock the gun loose? What if it was the wrong choice and he ended up getting both himself and his brother killed for it? What if...

Peter waved his arms in front of himself and shouted "no" toward a flustered, threatening Bruno and then fell forward, ending up on his hands and feet. As lubberly as it looked, now that he had four body parts digging for traction instead of two, he was able to stop sliding. While remaining in this position, he slowly walked himself back up the hill to the Durango in a manner that harkened to pre-caveman times.

Dean wanted to lunge for the nearest tree when he saw Bruno hand a squinting, watery-eyed Peter the keys. He felt his own eyes still itching, burning, and leaking from the pepper spray—and he knew he'd barely been hit. He feared Peter, if tested, would qualify as legally blind.

Dean climbed stiffly into the front passenger seat of the Durango, his knee clenched and cramped from twisting it earlier. Alain climbed in behind him, all the time keeping the Glock pointed at the back of his head as if on this ice and with his gimpy knees Dean could, at any moment, scamper into the woods like a frightened gazelle.

"Okay, go," Alain said to Peter, once everyone was inside.

"Go where?" Peter said, his voice sounding slurred, his breathing heavy. "He wants me to drive in this shit? Didn't he see me sliding around out there?" He turned to Dean for some answers.

Dean had none. He was concerned that Peter's awareness was just as impaired as his mouth, lungs and vision. He found it hard not to stare at the dried blood caked on the side of his head, below his missing ear lobe.

"*Joue cette CD,*" Alain said. Dean looked at the compact disc, then at Alain's gun. He took the CD, turned and pressed it into the Durango's stereo CD player slot. It wouldn't go in all the way, though, because the truck wasn't running.

"Go!" Alain said again, this time jabbing his gun into the back of Dean's head.

"Ouch!" Dean said, reaching back to grab his smarting skull "I guess, just drive. We'll figure out where he wants to go after."

"Does he know I don't have a license?"

"*Câlisse! T'es fatiguant! Maudit innocent, condui le camion!*" Alain said, pulling the gun away from Dean's head just long enough to thrust its barrel into the side of Peter's skull, near his right ear. Peter's hand flicked up and grabbed the side of his head as he leaned forward in his seat and groaned.

"Are you all right?" Dean asked.

"It's got Excedrin written all over it, I can tell you that," Peter said, still grimacing from the pain. "I thought *your* noogies were nasty—shit."

"*Ferme ta gueule!*" Alain shouted. "*J'veux rien entendre!*"

"What did he say?" Peter asked, rubbing one of his half-open eyes.

"I don't know. I think he wants us to shut up."

"*Eh, ferme-la! Tout'suite!* Go—come on!" Alain said, raising his gun between the two brothers' heads, threatening to bash—or shoot—either one of them with it if they dared challenge his authority.

Peter turned the key in the truck's ignition. With the same precise timing as a car bomb, the moment the Durango's engine roared to life, the moment the radio's speakers exploded with a chorus of a hundred voices—

> *Dashing through the snow,*
> *in a one horse open sleigh.*

—the world outside erupted with red, white, and blue lights, which ricocheted wildly off the ice like a laser show in a hall of mirrors, and sirenic sounds, which brought some of the overloaded branches on nearby trees crashing to the ground.

> *Through the fields we go,*
> *laughing all the way.*

"Go! *Condui!*" Alain barked, looking back at the two police cars that had just turned onto Ramezay about seventy-yards away. He poked his gun onto the side of Peter's head again, using the international language of violence to insure his command was well understood.

> *Bells on bobtails ring,*
> *making spirits bright.*

Peter reacted by jamming the truck's automatic transmission into drive and stamping his foot on the gas pedal. All four of the Durango's tires screamed in pain as they smoked and spun on the ice. The truck turned a quarter-turn clockwise, then a quarter-turn counter-clockwise, then back again, as it slowly moved forward searching for traction.

> *What fun it is to ride and sing,*
> *a sleighing song tonight.*

The two cruisers were no more than ten car-lengths behind them. They'd have the Durango surrounded in a moment.

> *Oh...*

"Go! Go! Go!" Alain kept yelling, while looking out the back window. He thrust his body back and forth in the seat to try give the Durango the added momentum it needed.

Ohhh...

Peter suddenly picked his foot up off the gas pedal.
"*Qu'est-ce-que tu fais là? Vas-y! Vas-y!*" Alain screamed, his eyes bulging to the breaking point.

Ohhhhhh...

Dean felt the Durango drop back into one of the burned-out grooves. Peter didn't wait around for it to come to rest, though—no time; the cruisers, which weren't breaking any land speed records thanks to the conditions, closed within a couple car lengths.

Ohhhhhhhhhhh...

Peter stomped his foot onto the gas pedal again. This time, the tires found something to grip. The sudden acceleration threw everyone back against his seat as the Durango squirted out in front of the two approaching police cars, fishtailing its way down Ramezay toward St.-Sulpice.

Jingle bells, jingle bells,
jingle all the way,

"Here we fucking go!" Peter shouted. "Driving for the visually impaired!"
Dean wanted to puke as he gripped the door's armrest, suddenly more afraid of the man behind the wheel then the

one holding a gun to his head.

> *Oh what fun it is to ride,*
> *in a one-horse open sleigh.*

Chapter 38

Peter had demanded so much explosive acceleration from the Durango to free it from its ice trap that, once moving, it simply had too much speed to cleanly handle the fast approaching turn onto St.-Sulpice.

He wrenched the steering wheel to the right. The truck hardly responded. It squirted through the intersection and straight towards a modest-sized stone house on the south side of St.-Sulpice.

The Durango crashed through the waist-high wall of bushes lining the street side of the house's property. The bushes slowed the truck somewhat, but it continued planing across the front yard toward the stone house.

Peter pulled the steering wheel as far as he could to the right and stepped on the accelerator. The Durango's tires smoked and screamed again, but this time they quickly broke through the ice layer on the front lawn and found ground.

The Durango's engine whined ferociously. The truck

curled away from the house as its wheels dug into the cold, hard earth, violently tearing up and spitting half-frozen clumps of grass and dirt behind itself, some of them hitting the side of the house, one of them breaking through a picture window. The Durango swung around in a small arc and accelerated, crashing through a line of shrubs that separated the front yard it had just ravaged from the neighbor's property. It cut down a three-foot-high baby hemlock, rolled over a child's blue plastic sled in the driveway, crunching it flat and shooting it skyward from under the wheel. It demolished a plastic Santa's sleigh, sending the reindeer's broken body parts spraying in every direction, before crashing through another set of bushes and pulling back onto St.-Sulpice with the two police cars bringing up the rear.

Peter gained more control over the roaring black beast. The police were so close behind, Dean was sure that the first chance they got, the officers were going to ram the truck into one of passing trees posing as an ice sculpture.

Peter took the first right and headed north up the steep, slippery slope of Mount Pleasant Avenue. The Durango's tires spun wildly as its progress slowed and its body swerved left and right like a slalom skier.

The pursuing police cruisers had no better luck. Looking like two boxers bobbing and weaving beside each other in the ring, both police cars quickly fell a half block behind the determined Durango. A few moments later they gave up the chase.

Alain watched the cop cars abandon their hunt through the camera's viewfinder. He let out a shout of joy, followed by a high-pitched, fluttering laugh.

Dean didn't have the nerve to turn his head all the way around to see if Alain truly was in a good mood—a mood buoyant enough to be willing to reason and negotiate their release. But when he turned his head only slightly, he saw Bruno out of the corner of his eye. The bull-necked sidekick wasn't looking out the back window at the police. He was looking at Alain, a watered-down smile tremulously stretched across his lips.

Before Dean could blink, Alain's celebratory mood spun on a dime and he began snapping commands at Bruno. Something about the camera. Dean saw Bruno take the video camera from Alain and put it up to his own face. He was filming Alain.

Look at him, boy. He's like a fricking dog—does everything he's told to do. Doesn't it make you sick! Doesn't it make you want him to do something radically stupid like... like take the ball around the outside on your own, when it matters most—

"I can't concentrate with this fucking Christmas music playing!" Peter shouted, slapping Dean out his reverie.

The infectious melody of *Jingle Bells* was a jarring, surreal soundtrack to the unfolding events. Dean knew he'd never be able to listen to that particular song again without reflexively grabbing something for support.

"Oh, shit!" Peter suddenly exclaimed in his new injured tongue accent. "Buckle your seatbelts! Here we go again!"

There was no way of telling whether they were the same two police cruisers that had just given up or a fresh pair of back-ups responding, but twin cop cars raced west down Montrose Avenue, heading straight for a collision with the Durango at the intersection of Montrose and Mount Pleasant. Dean could tell they were approaching too fast to stop on the slick surface. Both the cruisers simultaneously went into a slide, breaking apart from their single lane, single line formation—one shooting to the left, one to the right. It was as if they'd finished the stem of the Y and were now moving on to the double-lined head, leaving their skid marks spread across the ice's surface like smoke trails from a pair of sky writers.

"They're gonna hit us!" Dean yelled.

Since they both had a clear view of the impending impact, Dean and Alain reflexively threw themselves as far as they could to the other side of the truck.

Dean's face fell against Peter's arm. He pressed it into his brother's sleeve, closed his eyes and grit his teeth.

"Dear God," he said, "just make it quick."

Chapter 39

Space and time were reduced to the size and speed of snail spit. Everything contained within was thrust together—held there for a moment's moment, where smothering silence tried to extinguish the awaiting cacophony—and then pulled apart with the audacious, roaring intensity of a gorilla being held down and having his balls beaten with a hammer.

In the midst of the millisecond of chaos, Dean's life flashed before his eyes. But the review contained little he hadn't already seen and used to rebuke himself with.

"Ha! Did you see that? They missed us!" Peter shouted. "The sonsofbitches slid right around us—one in front and one behind! You stupid sonsobitches—ha!"

The stupid sonsofbitches...

Dean lifted his head from his brother's sleeve and peered through the frosted window outside. The Durango was somehow north of the intersection, past the point where the impact was supposed to have happened, where death had been waiting. Dean turned his head all the way around to look out the back window, ignoring the stunned-looking Alain and Bruno and their guns and threats, and saw the two cruisers. They were struggling to turn themselves in order to again give chase.

A dumbfounded Dean turned his wide eyes from the windshield to the back window to the windshield again. "How the hell did we..." Dean started to say, feeling as though he'd just taken part in either a miracle or the greatest magical illusion ever performed.

"I don't know," Peter said, his voice trembling with excitement. "I just took my foot off the gas and the truck slowed and... and... one just went like two inches in front of the truck and the other like a half inch behind us. I swear I could fucking count the nose hairs on the dude that passed us in the front, he was so close!"

Dean wanted to hug his brother. He didn't know how the kid had done it, but somehow he'd kept his composure—

Made the right choice.

Somehow he'd had the courage to face the situation—

Instead of running away like a weeping pussy.

—and do what he had to do. To take the truck straight up and through the danger.

It didn't take long for the two police cars to get back into the slow, slippery chase. The reflections from their flashing blue and red lights skipped and danced off the ice-sculptured world, swirling around the Durango like taunting phantoms.

"*Tourne à droite,*" Alain said to Peter, putting his gun up to Dean's head as if there were any doubt who was still boss.

"Left, right? That's what he said?" Peter asked Dean.

"No, right," Dean said.

"Fucking useless French classes."

Peter carefully turned off Mount Pleasant and onto The

Boulevard, which was much flatter and stretched four lanes wide. In between the one-way streets branching in and out of The Boulevard, every square inch was stuffed with two, three, or four-story stone or brick mansions with beautifully landscaped front yards, the likes of which would have taken Dean a hundred years of scrimping and saving and selling burger-and-fry combo meals to afford.

The police cars remained about two blocks behind the Durango down the remaining length of The Boulevard. At the end of road, Alain told Peter to turn left onto Cote-des-Neiges. They were soon heading north, back in the direction of Dean's restaurant.

Peter coasted through two stoplights under the command of Alain, with the help of his big gun barrel whispering sweet nothings into Peter's ragged ear.

The sense of wonder and gratitude—and even envy—that Dean had felt toward Peter after he'd seen them safely through the near-collision soon dissipated into a gnawing, nauseating sense of dread.

The stupid sonsofbitches...

Peter seemed to be enjoying his role as getaway guy too much.

Alain shouted at Peter to turn right onto Remembrance Street—

He-he-he, how appropriate, huh, boy?

—towards Mount Royal, but the street was blocked by two sawhorse roadblocks with a yellow and black striped reflector running horizontally across their centers. A sign hung off one of the sawhorses. It said the street was closed because of the severe conditions. Obviously only a fool on a suicide mission would have had reason to try and drive up and down a mountain.

Apparently, though, Alain *was* that foolish—betting either

that the police wouldn't be so brave as to follow or that, if they did, the four-wheel drive Durango would outperform them both.

Peter eased the truck to a skidding halt just before the roadblocks. Mount Royal Park looked so peaceful, so surrealistically beautiful, as the variety of trees bowed under the weight of the white snow and glistening ice in subservience to nature's power.

"He wants me to go through these things?" Peter asked, pointing to the shiny sawhorses.

Alain leaned forward in his seat, put his gun up to Dean's head, and said, "*Passe les barricades. Et sans que la police nous suive, sinon tu peux dire bonjour à sa peau. Compris? Maintenant!*"

"What did he say?"

Dean had understood perfectly, but didn't want to say it. He didn't *need* to say what he and Peter already feared.

"What's going on?" Peter asked.

Dean wanted this nightmare to be over... but some unwakeable beast in which they all were trapped kept on dreaming the unimaginable in ever-swelling waves of horror.

"Just drive," Dean said with the plaintive voice of a coroner giving autopsy results at a trial. "And... Good luck."

Chapter 40

"Go!" Alain screamed.

Peter's foot stomped the accelerator. The Durango's tires scratched, screeched and spun—

—and gripped the ground. The truck crushed the two roadblocks.

The police cars followed.

Alain cursed venomously.

The police sirens sounded pissed and impatient.

Notre-Dame-des-Neiges and Mont Royal Cemeteries abutted each other, together filling nearly the entire north side of Mont Royal Park, from its surface to some six-feet under, with sentimental concrete slabs, wood coffins, and moldy bones.

Dean glanced at one of the cemeteries to his left and wondered if he'd be its next resident.

Are you kidding me, boy? You're gonna be laid to rest next to me—on the eastbound side of the Mass Pike!

SLIDE

Dean didn't want to breathe in deeply. He didn't want to smell the rotting bodies in the ground. He discovered a few years ago that he was unconsciously holding his breath whenever he drove past small cemeteries. When he had attended his mother's recent funeral, the intense emotions surrounding the burial made his own existence next to unbearable. He nearly passed out from it all—from choking back the tears as well as the imaginary stench of the slush pile of putrified organs and black, blistery, mother's flesh being burped out of the ground among the army of tombstones.

And the sweet stink of soiled pants—don't forget that smell, huh, boy? Remember—here on Remembrance Street—that smell in the car that night as my skin everywhere sagged and turned grayish white, except for those pepperoni stains where my blood was pooling. Remember—here on Remembrance Street—how my body stiffened as the rigor mortis started to set in, and my glassy eyes, with the dime-sized dilated pupils, bulged as if they were about to burst—remember that here on Remembrance Street?

Remember?

Of course you do—you're on Remembrance Street! You've always been! You can't get off it!

Remember, you thought I was coming back alive? And you know... in a way I was. Because surely it was the images of me in my eleventh hour that have haunted you in your dreams and jumpstarted the flow of memories more than any other, hasn't it, boy? How will you ever be able to forget? It sometimes feels like they're stamped on the back of your eyelids, doesn't it? In a way, I bought another lifetime for myself in that moment. A lifetime in your memory. There's not a life support system in any hospital in the world that could've kept me more alive and energetic and powerful and influential than you continue to do in that pea brain of yours. In exchange for the sperm, headaches, frustration, disappointment, money, and sweat from the strappings I invested of myself in trying to raise you right, you've, in turn, helped me to transcend death, boy. To come as close to touching immortality as one possibly can in this day and age.

All I can say is, keep up the good work! For once you're doing something right!

"Shit! They look like they're gonna try to push us off the fucking road!" Peter shouted.

Through a fingernail-width scratch across the crusted surface of the passenger side mirror, Dean saw the bright headlights of the cruiser bearing down on them.

"*Plus vite! Envoye plus vite! Comment peuvent-ils être juste derrière, envoye, pèse sur le gaz!*" Alain shouted, his voice cracking in mid-sentence.

The cruiser gained ground.

Bruno put aside the camera, raised his gun and aimed it out the back window. But Alain grabbed his arm and rebuked him. He then turned to attack Peter. "*Toé! Tu ralentis!*"

"Whoa! He's not!"

"What did he say?" Peter asked. He was sweating as if it were a hot summer day, and some of the dried blood on the side of his head near his cut ear mixed with the sweat and trickled down where it dripped from his chin.

"He said you're slowing down."

"I'm not! I don't know what's happening!"

"*Je vais te tuer, s'ils nous attrapent, tu comprends?*" Alain said, turning his attention to Peter. He pointed his gun at the back of Peter's head.

"Come on, give him a break!" Dean said.

"What did he say?"

"He's doing the best he can!"

"*Ferme-là! Envoye! Conduit!*"

The cruiser's headlights closed in. The whooping, flashing MUCP monster was about to climb onto the Durango's back—

"*Conduit!*"

Closer—

"*Conduit!*"

Closer—

And then it hit.

Chapter 41

The force of the impact threw everybody forward in their seats. The Durango slid clockwise like a second hand—but Peter regained control, pulling it back straight.

The cruiser hit again—*Bam!*

"Go! Go!" Alain screamed.

Bam! A hard jab right to the bumper, but no knockout punch.

The police were trying to force the Durango off the road and into one of the many parking lots, which passed in and out of view through the smeared darkness and strobing lights.

The Durango suddenly gained some ground on its pulsating pursuers.

"*Bon!* Let's go! Go! Go! Come on!" Alain yelled over both the sirens and the song, *Children, Go Where I Send Thee,* blasting on the stereo, the extent of his displayed English vocabulary stretching to only that which was shouted at hockey games.

Dean peered ahead through the windshield and up the mountain. Just ahead, two dark orange metal, skeleton-like towers—the French and English Radio Canada antennas— stretched up so high into the night sky, they might have been solely responsible for the ice storm hanging overhead, having snagged it in its cloudy center as it passed by.

They arrived at a traffic circle, which completely circled a parking lot. This was the area where, in warmer weather, people parked their car and then went to picnic on the rolling grassy hills of the park, or to jog along the many small trails stretching through the woods, or to take a leisurely stroll further up the mountain to Le Chalet. There, the observation point offered a unique and breathtaking panoramic view of the entire southern part of the city of Montreal as it stretched from the peaceful, pastoral heights of the modest Mont Royal to the winding Saint Laurent river below like a carpet cluttered with a child's building blocks.

The mountain, blanketed on one side with the deep sleep of death, on the other, with the buzz and chatter of life. So much life and death united on one modest mountain in the center of this metropolis; artists couldn't have conceived a more fitting monument to a city's soul.

It was here Dean had first come, upon returning to Montreal after *that night* on the Massachusetts Turnpike. The city's expansive soul had helped to air out his own. He spent much of his time walking a trail that leads from the two orange Radio Canada towers to the giant steel cross— the Cross—that stands upon Mount Royal's highest point. Whereas de Maisonneuve had planted the original wooden version of the Cross *after the fact*, to thank God for stopping the floods from washing away his settlement, Dean looked to the Cross that summer to help rescue him from the flood of memories and tears he was drowning in.

He was still waiting to be saved.

The Durango sped counter-clockwise around the loop, moving with the grace of a one-legged skater. Its back-end fishtailed to the outside of the traffic circle, where it banged against the steep surrounding snow bank. It ricocheted back onto the road, in line behind the front end, and crawled forward another few feet before trying to make another break for the distant woods.

There, progressed slowed—

—and slowed and—

—then, at the twelve o'clock hour on the traffic circle, at the steepest slope so far encountered on the climb up the mountainside, the Durango came to a sliding halt.

Alain panicked and screamed threats and waved his gun around.

The Durango slid backwards towards the cruisers as if the truck had decided to give itself up, whether its occupants liked it or not.

"Go! Go!"

Peter pumped the gas pedal up and down against the floor, but it didn't help. He stabbed his foot on the brake to try and stop their regress, but nothing happened. The Durango glided back down the sloped traffic circle, as frictionless in its motion as a space capsule slicing through the deepest, darkest parts of the universe.

It picked up speed as it descended.

"Go! Go! Come on!" Alain shouted, his head flipping back and forth between the back window and Peter.

The lights and sirens intensified. They migh as well have been powerful tractor beams, the way they drew the Durango towards them. The sirens let out an unusual sounding whoop, as if they were beginning to celebrate their capture—

—or plead for the approaching wall of black metal to

have mercy on them.

The Durango thumped into the first cruiser at the loop's two o'clock hour, back and front bumpers clanging together.

During this night, while many apparent laws, both natural and man-made had been flouted, Newton's third law of motion alone remained unsullied. The cruiser reacted to the hit by bouncing backwards and into the one following. All three automobiles then slid for several feet, bumper to bumper, looking like a short train, until the train's caboose slapped into a concrete-hard snow bank. The line of vehicles came to a jolting stop. A shock wave shivered through all bodies, both metal and flesh, like a nervous chill.

For a moment, all movement ceased except for pounding hearts and pumping blood.

Chapter 42

Peter gunned the Durango's engine, but the truck didn't move.

"Go! Go! Come on! Go!" Alain screamed for the umpteenth time. It did nothing to help unstick the vehicle. The ice, which had helped them avoid being caught up to now, had finally delivered them into the hands of the law.

"*Il faut qu'on sacre notre camps d'ici,*" Alain said, while fumbling in the dark for the handle to his door and searching for the woods in the distance.

The vehicles suddenly shifted. The Durango and middle cruiser slid to their left, looking like the top part of a tree starting the arc of its descent to the ground. Outside Peter's window, the dark shadow of the snow bank on the south side of the traffic circle stretched to the sky. Five feet from hitting it, Peter stomped on the Durango's gas pedal again. This time, the truck responded. It lurched forward, fishtailed left, then right, then lurched forward again. It rocketed around the bottom half of the loop in the opposite direction, traveling faster than it did on its approach. It would have slid off the left side of the road—and probably not have stopped until crashing through a fence and mowing over a few gravestones in Notre-Dame-des-Neiges Cemetery—had it not been for an unusually high curb, which literally kept the Durango on track. The curb helped "sling" the truck around the remainder of the traffic loop and toward the top of the mountain.

The cruiser that had been the meat filling in the three-car sandwich followed the Durango down the wrong side of the road, leaving the second cruiser's tail-end hopelessly stuck in the snow bank's grasp, its siren screaming into the night to be set free, like a baby doe caught in a bear trap.

The Durango left the traffic circle behind and reached the highest point of the mountain road at walking speed— the easy part completed.

Now, all they had to do was descend.

The Christmas Waltz played on the stereo, its cheery lyrics laboring hard to stomp out the raging fires of dread within the Durango, but having little success.

Nobody said a word. It was as if they all knew they might have only a few minutes more to live.

Peter navigated the first part of the descent with godly grace. He simply took his foot off the gas pedal and let the Durango coast down the ski slope-like mountainside, flanked by a slanted wall of stone stretching high into the night on the left side of the road, and a sudden, severe drop-off on the left.

The driver of the patrol car, obviously caught up in the excitement of the chase, wasn't so careful. He accelerated as much as he could into the descent, caught up with the Durango, and then, in a bit of weirdness that Dean thought he only ever would see in a cartoon, slid *past* the Durango.

Coasting speed brought the Durango's speedometer up to 60 kilometers per hour. The truck stayed in the middle of the road for the first several hundred yards, nearly kissing the bumper of their police pursuer-come-escort the whole way.

The world seemed to close in around the Durango and cruiser as they passed between sheer, gray rock walls.

The road curled sharply to the left. Peter threw the steering wheel in that direction, but got only a hint of a response. The Durango rotated counterclockwise a quarter turn—a turn that would have ordinarily been enough to make the curve—but its body continued in a straight line, following the police cruiser into the chain link fence lining the roadside. They both bounced back out into the center of the road and continued down the hill.

"Holy shit! I can't believe we didn't go crashing through that thing!" Peter shouted.

The Durango and police car shot down a short straightaway, passing another popular observation point just off the road to Dean's right. He could see the entire northeastern part of the city stretched out before him. It looked like a patchwork quilt of light and dark spots. Over half the city was dealing with a blackout—freezing cold and too lost in its own problems to care what was taking place half a small mountain away.

The truck's weight advantage over the car began manifesting itself in greater slide speed. Like two horses racing down the final straightaway to a photo finish, the Durango looked to glissade down the right lane and past the cop car. Below them the road twisted severely to the right.

Through no fault of either of the drivers, the Durango and cruiser pressed together, touching sides in the center of the road, and then drifted apart—

—and then pressed together again.

"*Rentes-y dedans!*" Alain suddenly shouted at Peter from the back seat while tapping the side of Peter's head with the gun.

"Shit! I'm trying to drive here! What did he say?"

"I... I don't know," Dean said.

"*Rentes-y dedans!*" Alain shouted, this time pointing his gun at Peter's head.

"I don't understand."

"*Fonce, maintenant!*"

"I don't understand! What the fuck is he—"

A gunshot exploded in the truck's cabin.

Chapter 43

The sound wave *punched* Dean in the temple as a bullet tore past Peter's face and obliterated the driver's side window. The glass splintered and then exploded outward. Cold, sleet-spiked air gushed into the cabin.

The bullet streaked across the narrow gap separating the two sliding autos and ripped into the cruiser's roof.

The cop inside panicked, probably having imagined that he and the Durango's occupants had called a temporary truce in order to concentrate on making it down the mountain alive. His car swerved to the left toward the edge of the road, and then reflexes brought him back hard to the right. It would have gone into a spin if the Durango weren't there to block its turn. The cruiser hit the truck just behind its front left wheel.

Peter responded by trying to swerve the truck to the right, away from the police car.

Too much.

He pulled the steering wheel in the other direction.

Good enough. But the two vehicles streaked toward a sharp turn flanked by a massive rock wall.

The cruiser suddenly rammed into the side of the Durango. Dean screamed as the jagged rocks blurred just beyond the frosted window beside him.

They were going to barrel into the turn too quickly. The wall there waited, looking hungry for metal and mayhem.

Peter responded to the cruiser's assault by throwing the Durango to the left. The cruiser pushed back, but was overpowered.

The painful sound of scraping metal and roaring wind gushed through the broken window.

The cruiser fought for control—and self-protection. In the process, the cruiser's back end swung sharply to its right and smacked the Durango near its left rear tire—the equivalent of a swooping, unseen uppercut landing beneath a jaw.

The Durango spun.

Its left front end swooped hard to the left and crunched the cruiser near its front right tire, forcing the cruiser's front end to the left, until, like two twirling figure skaters, the vehicles were performing a perfectly synchronous spin as they slid toward the waiting rock wall.

They turned a full 180 degrees, until they were both facing up the hill they'd just journeyed down.

Dean grit his teeth—

—this was it—

—a second stretched to a century—

—Dean reached out for Peter—

His hand never made it across the cabin. The truck and cruiser hit the waiting wall of rock backside first in an explosion of red and orange signal lights and crushed license plates and the ominous, thunderous crunch of bending bumpers.

Dean thought he heard Hell's Gates swinging open.

Chapter 44

Rather than let them crumple against the wall like paper cups, the laws of physics had other plans for the vehicles. The rate they were spinning and the angle of the rock wall helped to ricochet them both back out into the middle of the road, still rotating.

The Durango came to a rest with its front end facing down the road, but cocked to the side. The cruiser didn't have as clean a finish. It continued straight across the road, caught in a tighter twirl than the Durango. Its front end shimmied up a slick snow bank. The cruiser flipped onto its roof like a turtle, its flashing lights darkening with the same abruptness as a snuffed candle.

For a moment, the only things that could be heard was the truck's idling engine, squeaking wipers, and the eerie hiss of the sleet spraying its roof.

The Durango's headlights lit up some of the cruiser's interior, and Dean could see the policeman hanging limply upside down in his seat, his safety belt keeping him from falling onto the underside of the roof. He didn't appear to be moving.

Dean prayed for him to wake up. His awareness then shifted to the backseat of the Durango, where Alain was barking at Bruno. Bruno seemed reluctant to carry out one of Alain's demands. Dean tried to understand what was being said, but the power of his mind to focus was patchy.

Something about the cop...

Alain raised his voice with Bruno. If Dean didn't know better, he'd have thought Alain was scolding a dog that had just pissed on the back seat.

"What the hell am I supposed to do now? Go?" Peter asked Dean.

"*Toé, je t'ai déjà dit de la fermer!*" Alain shouted, and he slammed the butt of his gun against Peter's bloodied ear.

Peter yelped and cupped his hand over his ear.

Alain yelled something at Bruno, cursed, then opened his door and climbed out of the truck, mumbling the whole way. He reached back and grabbed the camera from Bruno and took it with him in one hand as he shuffled toward the cruiser. He held a gun in his other hand.

Peter cut the Christmas music to silence with a spin of the volume knob.

Dean turned to look in the back seat. Bruno's gun met his eyes like a shaking, nervous cobra. Dean turned back and watched Alain approach the overturned cruiser.

"Is he going to shoot that cop?" Dean asked Bruno. Bruno responded by adjusting his gun's aim in between Dean's eyes.

Dean squinted through the windshield and crowded darkness to see into the cruiser. The cop was still hanging upside down, motionless.

Alain was nearly half way to his destination.

"He *can't* do that!" Dean said. He turned back to Bruno. "Bruno, you've got to listen to me. You can't let Alain kill that cop. I heard you. You didn't want to do it, right? So you don't want him to do it, either. Listen to me! You've got to stop this from happening!"

"*J'comprends pas,*" Bruno said, his voice quivering.

Dean turned and saw that Alain shuffle past the halfway point, and still the cop wasn't moving.

"Bruno, please! Put down the gun. Let us go." Dean tried to stay calm. "We can save him. We can save *you.* Please!"

Bruno's arm shook. Dean watched his eyes look past the gun, past Dean's head, out the front windshield, and at how close the predator was to his trapped, helpless prey.

"Please!" Dean said. "I *know* you're not like him—please!"

"*Je... Je... J'comprend pas,*" Bruno said, sounding like he didn't believe his own words.

"Bruno! This is your chance! We can get away! We can save that cop! Let us help, goddammit!"

Dean took a deep breath to calm himself. He slowly put his hand up and reached back towards the gun.

"Careful. The guy's a nutbar," Peter said, watching what was happening.

"*Non!*" Bruno said. "*Je... J'comprends pas! J'comprend pas!*"

Dean moved his hand closer to Bruno's gun, as if he were reaching out to pet a mad dog.

"Please. I know you understand. Please, Bruno. We can help."

"He's almost there, boy," Peter said, referring to Alain. "The sick fucker's filming his approach! Look at him!"

"It's now or never, Bruno," Dean said. He could tell Bruno was close to surrendering, close to abandoning his belief in Alain for a brighter, saner bunch. "Please."

Dean's hand was only six inches from the front of the gun's barrel.

"Hurry up, boy," Peter said. "Hurry."

Bruno seemed to be lost in confusion. His eyes kept darting left and right, unable to meet Dean's for more than a moment. Maybe even too confused to react if Dean quickly grabbed for the—

"Hurry, boy," Peter said.

"Bruno."

"Wake up, cop! Wake up!" Peter screamed at the windshield.

"Bruno!"

Bruno's arm shook.

"Bruno! Give that gun to me now, you hear me!" Dean shouted.

Bruno's eyes darted to Dean. Dean knew he'd gotten through to him that time, that he was the kind of person who was born to follow.

Dean swore he saw Bruno lean forward to hand him the gun.

The sounds of two shots being fired overpowered the hissing sleet, idling engine, squeaking wipers—

—the desperate men—

Dean's arm flicked forward.

Chapter 45

Bruno pulled the gun away with a surprising quickness.

"Oh, no! Oh my fucking God, no!" Peter shouted. "That sick fucking bastard!"

Bruno's eyes bulged. He pointed the Glock at Dean's head again with a new look of conviction.

"He's coming back," Peter said.

Dean's ambition flew out the broken window and away in the swirling wind. Both he and his brother sat slumped in their seats, exhausted.

"*J'ai bien fait ça, comme tu me là demandé,*" Bruno said to Alain once he'd climbed back into the truck.

He did good. He did just what he had been told to do, Dean understood.

Alain grunted, shook the glistening sleet from the front of his hair, then pointed his gun at Peter.

"*Fonce.*"

As Peter drove the Durango past the overturned cruiser, Dean told himself not to look inside.

But he couldn't resist. He grit his teeth and choked back the urge to whimper as he assaulted his eyes with the brutal image of the officer's opened skull. And to think that that violent act had been recorded—on purpose—to be watched over and over again. He wondered if Linda and Joseph's murder had been recorded, too—and if Peter wondered the same.

Dean dropped his head back against the seat's headrest. His hands squeezed and twisted his coat like sponges. He couldn't catch his breath. His jaw muscles pulled tight and trembled, threatening to snap. His teeth chattered. Sweat condensed on his forehead and dripped into his eyes, making them burn like bee stings.

Peter brought the Durango down the remainder of the mountain with the innate skill of a Tibetan Sherpa. Everyone sat silent, nervously watching the hard-fought but wavering results of the teenager's slippery battle against nature's finest drops.

Once the truck spun ninety degrees to the left. Another time, ninety degrees to the right. Another time, it slid around a curve in the road, pressed to the icy fence along the outside the whole way, threatening to break through it and tumble end over end, bouncing off each of the boulders and trees below like a pinball.

But still, the young man fought on—as if a higher power were at work in him, giving him more courage and concentration than usual.

The air in the truck's cabin was as thick as porridge with suspense—either the Durango would slide *down the road* to the bottom of the mountain still in one piece, or it would slide *over the edge* and to the bottom of the mountain, ending its journey as a blood and gasoline-soaked avalanche of bolts and broken body parts.

"We got this thing. This baby's ours," Peter mumbled down at the steering wheel. "I am not my fear. I am not my pain. *I am now.*"

Dean recognized those words.

Joseph.

Peter brought the truck around the last sharp bend in the road. He moved the Durango far to the right of the road, preparing to enter the curve on its inside edge, and giving himself as much space as possible for the inevitable slide to the road's left outside edge.

"This baby's ours," Peter said again, his voice slow and scratchy and sounding aged beyond its years. "*I am now. I am now.* You're ours, baby. Just help get me through this one here, *D*, and we can go home and party."

D. Dean knew Peter wasn't talking about him. He was referring to the Durango, speaking of it as the *only* other member of his team.

Dean remembered how Peter nicknamed him *D* about three years earlier. It had been a short-lived nickname—lasting barely a year—but it was a relentless break from the usual *boy* tag. The words of camaraderie that Peter used when speaking to the truck—we, us, ours—was something different. The message that Dean got from their meaning and tone was that the truck and Peter were close. That they shared a special bond. That they'd survived a lot together in a short period of time—and now had to survive just one more challenge, relying on their trust and confidence in each other to see them through.

It made Dean ache with envy.

But that's been our life together, boy! Hasn't it? You have your own special D. D—for daddy.

Dean shivered as a few pellets of sleet streaked through the broken window, across the Durango's cabin, and somehow found their way past his scarf and down his shirt.

To Dean, Peter's affection for the truck distinctly *excluded* him from playing a part in getting the brothers through this. It seemed as if the magical myths of Golden Boy had finally been penetrated, understood, and discarded as stories for starry-eyed suckers.

Think about it! Think about how pathetic *that sounds, boy! And especially now, when your life is only a slip, bump, and a thump away from becoming a warm meal for the squirrels and raccoons! I went to all that trouble to raise you well and here you are, jealous of the way your brother is talking to a truck! Oh, if I only had hands, I'd slap you silly! I guess I gotta be content with badgering you from the great beyond, though, until you either shape up or they ship you out in a straight jacket to the local loony bin—ha ha!*

The Durango hit the turn at 50 kilometers per hour. It continued in a straight line, crossing the entire width of the road, which curled to the truck's right. Peter's crash course in handling ice had obviously taught him to work *with* what he was given rather than against.

Joseph would have been proud.

Peter was able to turn the front end of the truck against the slide, bringing it around clockwise so it faced in the direction the road continued. In so doing, he had the treads of the truck's tires pointing nearly at right angles to the slope and slide, which helped give at least a semblance of traction and to slow the truck before impact.

The two doors on the driver's side came up hard against the snow bank. The bulky truck took the hit well, though, bouncing directly off the bank and back into the center of the road, where it started to glissade once again in the right direction.

"You're getting good at this," Dean said.

"Yeah. Should hire myself out as a getaway driver for bank robberies and drive-bys when this is all done," Peter said, grinning.

Even though he grinned, Dean felt a sense of sadness behind Peter's words that hung heavy between the brothers like a line of wet wool blankets. The thought that *if* Peter got out of this grave situation alive, the *best* he could hope to aspire to be in life was a common criminal. Dean wondered if Peter really thought that or if it was just his habitual off-color humor back on display.

Or, if it was his brother's off-color humor *further* colored by the truth that Peter had lost one of the greatest motivating forces in his life: Linda.

Dean knew that if they made it through all this, the real work would only just begin—for both of them.

The Durango slid past the last grouping of trees and rock. To its left appeared a clutter of apartment buildings, to its right, the wide open remainder of Mont-Royal Park, which gently sloped several hundred yards down from the steep, tree-lined mountain to the north/south running Park Avenue.

It was a beautiful area. On a different night and with different conditions, it would have been the point in the journey when one sighed deeply at the sublime juxtaposition of pure serenity positioned in a sleepless city's center.

But not this night.

And not when, five hundred feet in front, six police cars sat in a row, blocking the only way off the mountain.

Chapter 46

"Oh, shit! Don't these guys know when to quit?" Peter shouted, slamming the steering wheel with the palms of both his hands.

"I think *those* guys are our friends, remember?"

Alain leaned forward, pressed his gun to the side of Peter's head, and said, "*Tu te souviens-tu de ma promesse?*"

"*Je ne comprend pas,*" Peter said to Alain, his teeth chattering from the cold air gushing through his broken window. "Shit! There's no way around them!"

"*Trouves un moyen,*" Alain said, knocking the barrel of his gun against Peter's ear again.

Dean looked at Alain suspiciously out of the corner of his eye. The guy seemed to understand more English than he kept claiming. That meant he and Peter had to be careful when talking to each other.

The Durango approached the roadblock fast. Too fast— and with no way to stop. Peter touched the brakes, but the truck only became *impossible* to control then. It was best to let it roll in order to gain some semblance of traction. But that didn't help them any when the road ended in one hundred feet—

Seventy-five—

"*Trouves un moyen.*"

Fifty—

Thirty-five—

"Shit!"

"*Trouves un moyen!*"

Dean gripped the sides of his seat, preparing for the impact. Preparing to ram right through the police car barricade. He was surprised bullets hadn't been tearing holes through them when the cops saw that they weren't about to stop.

Peter slammed his foot on the gas pedal. The wheels spun frantically, mostly ineffectually, but the Durango picked up some speed.

Twenty feet away—

"*Trouves—*"

Fifteen—

"*—un—*"

Ten—

"*—moyen!*"

It looked as though Peter were going for the car on the farthest right of the roadblock—to blow through it for the touchdown like a running back carrying straight up the middle.

"*I am now!*" Peter shouted as he threw the wheel hard to the right while stomping the gas pedal onto the floor. The Durango canted, but then righted itself as it exploded through a foot-high snow bank on the side of the road, missing a cruiser by inches, and jumping up and onto the open field of

Mont-Royal Park. The ice was so thick on top of the tightly packed snow, it held the Durango up enough for the truck to slide roughly over it. The truck bounced up and down and left and right, threatening to flip like a hockey puck squirting across a gouged-up ice rink.

Peter looked as if he were trying to gain control of a jackhammer gone mad.

The Durango demolished the remnants of a snow fort as it off-roaded across the field, racing towards the far corner and Parc Avenue. The police cars left behind each hurried to move out of their formation and pursue the runaway Durango.

One of the cruisers quickly backed up onto a crystallized snow bank, jamming a camel hump of ice up underneath its body, which lifted the back tires off the ground. It teetered back and forth helplessly as its engine roared with displeasure.

Another cruiser started off on the chase with the other three, but at the corner of Mont Royal and Park, it lost traction and slid sideways down Mont Royal and off the road.

The Durango rocketed past a monument to Sir George Etienne-Cartier, leaving a hanging cloud of crystalline water in its wake. Its wheels dropped in and out of the plethora of hardened boot prints dimpling the park's surface around the statue. They frantically thumped up and down against the wheel well, sounding like a popcorn maker-gone-mad.

The Durango went airborne for a moment as it launched itself over a snow bank. The truck cleared the sidewalk and landed on Park Avenue in one piece, finishing its jump with a nifty 390-degree spin in the icy center of Park, which left it pointing due south.

The three remaining cruisers closed in fast.

Peter coaxed the Durango up to a respectable speed.

The road conditions on Park were no better than on the mountain, except Peter now had four lanes to work with.

And he used them all.

The Durango's back end swung left and right like a compass needle as it crawled forward up a long, but mildly-sloped hill. Dean felt nauseous. He put his head back against the seat headrest, raising his eyes up to the roof of the truck's cabin.

When was this going to be over? I'm going to die from the anxiety of waiting *to die!*

Something bright on the mountain caught his half-opened right eye through the side window. A series of lights. He turned and peered through the prism of ice on the upper third of the window, which distorted their rays, spreading each one of their concentrated points of purity out across the glazed glass surface like flowers of light in bloom. A crack in the crust of ice gave him a clear view to the mountain. The lights were coming from the top. From a structure. A symbol. A sign, perhaps.

A cross.

The Cross shone down at Dean—a sort of radiant reminder to carry with him into the darkest, coldest regions of the blackened city. As it slowly disappeared behind a line of trees, its glowing image remained imprinted on the backs of Dean's eyelids.

Memories... to stimulate... or enervate...

The Durango struggled to the top of the hill on Park and then came down the other side, nearly tripling its speed. Peter kept the truck near the center of the road most of the time, only once scraping the passenger's side against a concrete barrier, creating sparks which shot out behind the truck like the flaming propellant in a Space Shuttle booster rocket.

Alain told Peter to turn off Park and onto the one-way

Pine Avenue, heading west along the south side of Mont-Royal. The road was full of steep hills and hard curves and tree branches—piles of arboreal arms, large and small, that had been torn from their body by the weight of the ice—all of which challenged Peter and the Durango to keep from sliding into any one of the many brick-faced, blacked-out apartment buildings or McGill University halls lining the road. There were no large snow banks or fences or sturdy walls of rock to absorb the blow of a blunder. A slip-up here could bring an unwelcome, oversized tin can with four occupants crashing into the livingroom of any one of the passing homes.

An uncharacteristically concentrated Peter orchestrated the road perfectly, climbing and descending the hills at just the right speed, handling the corners well enough—which was all that mattered. Most of the tree branches that he ran over crunched under the weight of the truck's tires. Several, though, banged the truck's underside with frightening force.

The police fell behind on an especially steep hill in front of Royal Victoria hospital. Alain shouted a joyous profanity at the sight of the fading cruisers. He'd had Peter drive the Durango through some of the most winding and steep streets in Montreal, under the worst road conditions, with the police in pursuit.

And he was prevailing.

"*I am now*," Peter whispered—

—but only for a moment.

But then a deeply understood awareness of *I am now* made it obvious that life was a fluid, dispassionate continuum of nothing but—

—moments—

—to slide through.

Chapter 47

The three cruisers somehow caught up—maybe using tree branches for traction, maybe raw will power. Alain swore again, but joy had been bled from the words, leaving them to stink up the truck's interior with the foreboding stench of doom. He shouted for Peter to pull off Pine, handle a hairpin turn to his left, and then head down a very steep and short McGregor Avenue.

All the cruisers followed.

The second cruiser, though, didn't make the turn completely and slid up onto the sidewalk, clipping the corner of a wood fence, propelling splinters of its brown frosty lumber across the ice-covered lawn like arrow-shaped toboggans. It wasn't enough to end the cruiser's night, though, as it spun and squealed its way around and back into the pursuit.

The Durango scooted through a red traffic light at an intersection, and knocked over a bus stop sign as it took as quick a left as possible onto the eastbound, relatively flat Doctor Penfield Avenue.

Dean felt safer on this level surface... but Alain had something else in mind. Two blocks down Docteur Penfield, he made Peter turn right onto Musée Avenue.

Musée dropped straight down like a displaced frozen chute from a luge course. It abruptly ended at the intersection with Sherbrooke, across from the Museum of Fine Arts, whose post-modern structure made it look more like a majestic monument to a future dimension rather than a depository for yesteryears' treasures.

Musée was lined on both sides with cars parked in front of expensive, stylishly canted apartments and houses. The Durango had no more than three feet of empty space on either side before it would be rubbing metal skins with another vehicle. Peter paused the truck at the top of the hill—just enough time repeat his mantra—before taking his foot off all the truck's pedals and letting it go free.

The pause had given the three cruisers time to close the gap. The lead cruiser fought to control itself and make the turn onto Musée as the Durango descended.

The truck picked up speed fast. Dean's stomach lurched up his esophagus. Peter's hands shook as they fought the steering wheel for control.

No more than fifty feet down the hill, the Durango lost its composure, Peter's *I am now* quickly superseded by *I am now in trouble.*

It began as a little swivel in its back end—no more than a couple of feet in each direction—but then quickly grew in size as Peter overcompensated with the steering, reflexively trying to jerk the truck in the opposite direction. The Durango's left end gouged the side of a BMW first. It then arced across the avenue and slammed into the door of a Land

Rover, tearing its side mirror off. Back it went to the other side, hitting hard into an Audi, before rebounding to the other side and putting a nasty dent in the side of a Lexus.

The three cruisers followed suit, swinging wildly from side to side like wrecking balls as they slid uncontrollably down the steep avenue, the cars and trucks they smashed sacrificing themselves to keep the cruisers on the avenue, out of their owners' living rooms, and still in the chase.

The Durango exploded out of the bottom of Musée like a launched rocket, its backside dented and torn and smeared with the colors of a dozen battered victims. It nearly tipped over as it shot across Sherbrooke, rotating counter-clockwise 45 degrees to try to avoid hitting head on with the Desmarais Pavilion. Its wheels squealed and burned through the ice, fighting desperately for traction. The truck jumped the sidewalk, slapped a mailbox to the moon, and slammed its back end into the corner of the pavilion, sending pieces of concrete scattering.

Peter's stomped his foot onto the gas pedal, pulling the Durango out of its skid and east down Sherbrooke Avenue.

The first police car in pursuit performed almost the identical move as the Durango, zooming out from Musée, sliding across Sherbrooke while spinning, and slamming, tail end first, into the same crumbled corner of the pavilion before continuing onward.

The second police car came off Musée and made the turn, avoiding contact with the damaged pavilion corner and everything else as it passed the other cruiser.

The third police car slid off Musée much faster than the others, spinning like a helicopter rotor blade as it streaked straight toward the center of the museum. It jumped the sidewalk and hit the ice-covered front steps of the pavilion at a tremendous speed. The steps acted more as a ramp than a barrier. The car launched into the air straight at the pavilion while still rotating, swooshing through the sleet-filled air. Its lights flashed, its siren pulsed as it cleared the pavilion's front doors and burst through the museum's pane glass roof, which stretched at a severe slant from just above the line of front doors up several stories to the building's peak.

The police cruiser disappeared inside as if it had just been swallowed by a monstrous beast, its headlights beaming out of the freshly opened hole in the roof as though a spotlight inside was signaling the museum's latest, greatest exposition.

The Durango was finally, once again, on flat ground. It picked up speed, racing through the red traffic lights without hesitation.

Dean couldn't help but flinch each time they approached an intersection showing a red light. Even though he'd seen less than a half dozen cars driving around all night, he couldn't let go of the notion that maybe, just maybe, a car would come out of one of the side streets at the exact same moment they were passing through, causing a tragic—albeit welcome—end to it all.

The two remaining cruisers followed no more than a half a block behind the Durango as it skimmed east across the ice through one red light, past McGill University; through another red light, past Park Avenue again, past St. Urbain, St. Laurent, St. Denis...

Dean's jaw hurt from gritting his teeth too hard.

The pursuing cruisers stayed close.

Dean felt they were driving too fast across the crusty white streets. Far too fast to stop if they needed.

Past gas stations, past banks, past depanneurs, past video stores and clothing shops and duplexes and condos and high-rises and hospitals—it was all a blur of buildings.

Yes, far too fast—even for a dry, summer night.

Suddenly, the traffic lights weren't functioning any more—they were in a blacked-out region again as they raced past St. Hubert, past Lafontaine and Lafontaine Park.

The cops closed in.

Dean was reminded of his recurring dream: He felt they were in a race to the end of the world. He feared that the darkened shapes all around them would suddenly give way to nothingness—complete blackness as the truck plummeted off the cliff at the world's edge and into oblivion...

"*Gauche ici!*" Alain shouted. "*No, droite! No, gauche, gauche!*"

"What? Which? What!" Peter shouted back.

"*Droite!*" Alain screamed.

Peter ripped the wheel to the right to try and turn onto a small street called Champlain. The Durango kicked into a sliding spin as it glided past Champlain and continued along Sherbrooke. It continued for a full block before slowing and stopping in the center of Papineau, facing north.

"*Tournes! Reviens sur tes pas! Tout de suite!*" Alain screamed, waving his gun all around.

"What? What does he want?" Peter shouted to Dean.

The cruisers approached fast. They seemed to have increased their speed.

"Turn around!" Dean shouted, translating Alain's command to Peter.

Peter forced the wheel as far to the right as he could and pressed the gas. The tires spun helplessly on the ice.

"*Tourne! Envoye! Go!*" Alain screamed, watching the approaching cop cars' headlights getting bigger and brighter.

"I'm trying, goddammit!" Peter shouted.

The Durango pulled itself forward and turned in the center of Papineau so it faced south.

The cop cars were nearly at the corner of Sherbrooke

and Papineau. Dean thought he could feel the heat of their flashing lights on his face.

The Durango's wheels spun again, this time beginning a slow crawl forward and along Papineau.

The cop cars shimmied and shot out onto Papineau. They both went into synchronous spins as they tried to take the corner with too much speed behind their bodies. They slid across the four-lane street and toward an Esso station on the corner. The first car scored a direct hit on the gas pumps, mowing two of them down with one chop from its swinging body. A geyser of fuel erupted underneath. A spark was born somewhere in the twist and tear of metal against metal and the entire entanglement was instantly engulfed in a roaring rage of showering flames.

The second cruiser glided by the burning cruiser, but not before lightly brushing its rear, pushing the crackling coffin further into the flames.

Dean could hear Alain shouting at Bruno to get some footage of the spectacular crash that had taken place behind them as they pulled away.

The remaining cruiser acted quickly after it slid to a halt. It struggled back onto Papineau and began pursuing the Durango again, its flashing lights and wailing siren giving no emotional sign of grief over a friend lost.

"*Ils sont toujours derrière nous,*" Alain said, looking out the back window. And then to Peter: "*Prend le pont Jacques Cartier.*"

"Is he talking to me?" Peter said to Dean.

"*Oui, c'est à toi que je parle!*"

"He's telling you to go over the Jacques Cartier Bridge."

"Where's that?"

"*Hey, le cave, tourne à gauche,*" Alain said, leaning forward and pointing.

For a moment, Dean entertained the idea of grabbing Alain's arm and breaking it in two. But the killer's arm was in the back seat again before he could consider acting further.

"Shit! They've got a road block up!" Peter shouted.

Up ahead, the half-loop entrance ramp up onto the Jacques Cartier Bridge was closed off by the same striped and flashing sawhorses they'd rolled over earlier in order to climb Mount Royal.

"*Rentes dedans!*" Alain said. "*Et après tu continues!*"

"He wants me to smash through them, huh?" Peter asked Dean.

"Why am I not surprised?" Dean said, grabbing the side of his door.

"I wonder why it's closed," Peter said.

"You're joking, right?" Dean said.

"*Ferme-la! Je ne veux plus rien entendre!Toé, conduis!*"

The Durango shattered the backs of two of the wooden sawhorses as it barreled through them. Dean prayed for one of them to splinter just right and puncture a tire or two, laming the truck.

But no one answered his call.

He and his brother were all alone on this one.

Chapter 48

The Jacques Cartier Bridge is one of five major bridges spanning the St. Laurent River on the south side of Montreal. The lights, which normally line the many girders of the bridge's imposing body, were off. So were the lights that hung above the roadway. The bridge, whose gray outline could still be seen against the black, spitting sky, had the look and feel of a brontosaurus carcass stuck in the river, only the bones remaining of what was once a majestic and meaty beast. The Durango would drive up onto its head and climb the sloping road of its neck and spine. It would continue along the back bone and pass through the center of the dinosaur, through its rib cage which towered above everything, and then come out the back end, still on the spine, and travel the remainder along the long tail, above Notre Dame Island, and to the other side.

So simple.

The Durango moved surprisingly well on a surface that

had been deemed too dangerous to drive on.

Something didn't feel right to Dean, though. But then had *anything* felt right tonight?

The Durango built up speed, gaining distance on the lone chasing cruiser.

Alain screamed out for Peter to go faster.

The bony belly of the bridge beast lay ahead.

The faster the truck went, the more Dean felt they were sliding along not a three-lane bridge, but a tightrope. One from which they'd be thrown into the river below at any second, where even if they survived a more than hundred-foot fall onto the ice-jammed surface, they'd quickly find themselves struggling for air beneath the freezing black water.

"*Plus vite! Come on!*"

The Durango slipped to the right, slamming into the side of the bridge. Dean saw only darkness in the side window. He felt as if he were hanging out in space, just waiting to feel the gut-lurching sensation of falling.

Peter pulled the truck back toward the center of the road. The bridge's green, rib-like girders closed around them like a giant steel cage. For some reason, Dean felt safer there.

Boom!

Something slammed hard against the windshield; white frost exploded across it in a star-point pattern. In the center of the star was a crack.

"Holy shit! Did you see that?" Peter said. "Is the cop shooting at—"

He didn't finish before another one hit the windshield—*boom!*—this time right in front of Dean's face. It completely blocked his view. He put his face up close to it to inspect it. It was a mix of ice and snow falling from the bridge's girders.

Boom! Boom!

Two hit the top of the truck's roof.

Boom! Boom! Boom! Boom!

It started coming down hard, continuously pummeling the Durango from above.

Boom! Boom!

The dormant beast had been awakened. The frozen bombs cracked and covered the hood and windshield with white stars. Peter struggled to see through them. The ice and snow was so dense and hit so hard, the wipers couldn't push aside what had accumulated.

Boom! Boom! Boom!

Dean couldn't see out his side of the window. It felt they were heading straight for the edge of the bridge.

Boom! Boom! Boom!

The Durango swerved.

"I can't see shit!" Peter yelled.

Boom!

The Durango drifted to the left lane, then the right lane—

—too close to the edge—

—and then it started to tip, came back hard onto all four wheels.

Boom! Boom!

Dean thought he heard Peter scream—then he realized it came from his own throat.

Dean felt the Durango spin and slide—slide forever.   It hit something, went airborne—

—a liquid burned the back of Dean's throat—

—and slammed down.

Dean couldn't swallow the sting away.

This is it! The express elevator to a wet and icy hell!

Alain screamed. Bruno screamed for Alain.

The Durango hit something—Dean couldn't see what; his eyes were squeezed shut. There was a whooshing sound and then a deafening crunch of folding metal and then—

—an explosion of white and then—

—in an instant, the truck came to an abrupt halt. The momentum whipped Dean's body forward until his seatbelt snapped taut, his face slapping against the inflated air bag. The ice continued pummeling the truck, as if trying to teach it a lesson to never trespass again.

Peter immediately threw open his door and jumped out, trying to take advantage of the chaos to escape. Without looking back at Alain or Bruno, Dean followed. He immediately fell several feet to the ground, twisting his sore knee to what felt like its breaking point.

Somehow, the front end of the truck had risen up on the railings as if contemplating suicide, its back wheels on the bridge surface, its hood poking through a hole in the criss-crossing girders large enough to make the leap if it so chose.

Dean tried to stand, but he immediately slipped to the ground, partly because of his knee, partly because of the slick surface. He covered his head with his arms as heavy, large chunks of ice and snow fell from the girders and exploded all around him.

Boom! Boom! Boom!

He had to get away. He knew that the next *boom* he heard could be a gunshot. He tried to stand up, but slipped down again.

Just then, something drew his attention away from the fear of being shot or hit from above. He looked up and saw a pair of headlights coming at him fast—accompanied by the same familiar whooshing noise. It was the police cruiser. It swerved left and right as the falling frozen bombs—playing no favorites—battered it unmercifully.

Dean had to move—quickly. He put one foot in front of the other to run, but fell again.

Whoooooooosh...

He could almost taste the chrome on the cruiser's bumper.

He tried to throw himself forward, as if he were diving headfirst back to first base on a pick off attempt. It worked better. He slid several feet and immediately tried it again. Several more feet this time and one lane away. But he couldn't make it far enough, fast enough. If the police car swerved toward the inside he was as good as a new hood ornament.

Fortunately for him the cruiser slipped to the outside.

Dean dove again just as the cruiser brushed by. It smashed into the back end of the Durango, lifting the truck up into the air and through the opening in the girders.

For a moment, it fell—

—but the truck's bumper, already twisted and dented into the shape of a postmodern sculpture, snagged itself on the bridge's structure. The Durango's underside slammed against the side of the Jacques Cartier, its attempted plunge to the river momentarily foiled.

The cruiser bounced around, sounding like a concerto of hammered trash cans. When it finally came to rest, its front left side was completely obliterated, crushed and crumpled like a stubbed-out cigarette.

There was no movement inside the cruiser.

Or the dangling Durango.

Chapter 49

Dean's sleet-assaulted-eyes squinted and scanned from the accident scene to the road, searching for Peter. At first he couldn't see him. A bubble of panic expanded and rose inside his belly at the thought that his brother had been swept over the edge of the bridge during the accident. Then he caught sight of the faint outline of a figure in the darkness some twenty feet away, waving his arm over his head. It took Dean a moment before Peter's voice registered in his mind above the howling, gusting wind and crackling sleet, as he was still deafened from the explosive sound of the impact.

He moved toward his brother as though he were a thirsty man rushing to a lake mirage in the desert, all the while protecting his head with one arm to avoid having it being crunched flat from falling ice and snow. Dean took baby steps, sliding his feet along the slippery surface the entire way. Even so, each bit of effort sent a ragged sword of pain stabbing through his knee, which felt swollen to the size of a cantaloupe.

When he arrived at his brother's side, he wanted to tell him what a great job he had done, how inspiring his driving performance had been, how, given Peter's less-than-auspicious history of bad behavior, Dean *never* would have imagined the kid could find the necessary resources inside himself to do so well under such adverse conditions.

But he couldn't bring himself to say any of it. He didn't know why. Maybe because Peter's recently revealed ability to dig down deep and be more than the sum of his past was exactly what Dean waited desperately to discover in his *own* being.

So instead, Dean simply hugged his brother. It just happened. In a way, the hug was trying to speak for him. It was the first time he'd hugged Peter in years.

Peter's eyebrows knit. He looked confused. And embarrassed. But he didn't pull away. His lips parted as if he were about to speak—maybe to try and reciprocate— when the pop of a gunshot ripped through the chaotic rumbling, hissing, crackling sounds around them. Dean and Peter quickly turned towards the Durango just in time to see its back window bulge upward from the force of a second shot, and then collapse down into the truck in a thousand-piece jigsaw puzzle.

"Where the hell are the other cops?" Peter said, responding to the lack of approaching sirens and flashing blue lights. "Isn't anyone gonna come help us out?"

"I don't know. Let's hope. Maybe your driving scared them all away. We're on our own for now, though, I guess."

Dean pulled his hood over his head to give himself extra protection against the falling ice. He pulled Pete's hood over his head as well, then grabbed Peter by the coat and tugged him in the same direction he'd spontaneously decided to head—across the bridge, *away* from Montreal, toward St. Helen's Island.

"What are you doing? Where are we going?"

"Trust me. I have a hunch."

Oh, help me Lord! We all know how successful those fricking hunches can be!

"A hunch? You're lucky I'm too beat to kick your ass, boy, and take charge."

Peter *did* look like he'd been through the wringer; his otherwise youthful face was pale and haggard, with crusted smears of blood spread across his cheek and chin as well as filling and highlighting the spaces between his teeth.

"But what about this cop?" Peter said, pulling in the other direction. "He might need our help."

"Hey, as far as he's concerned, we're the bad guys—come on," Dean said, tugging Peter's arm. "You're starting to sound like me, all soft and sentimental—let's go."

"Shit, I can say the same thing about you, boy. Leaving the cop behind is so cold it makes this fricking ice feel like burning lead."

"Question is, is it good or bad?"

"Question is, will it get us out of this shit alive?"

"Question is... what's the question?"

"I don't know, but the answer is yes and no."

They had to share a needed chortle as the dark, merciless world seemed to collapse on top them. Even though the humor was brief, it served as an effective aperitif in whetting Dean's appetite. He hungered to share more—more of *everything*—with his brother.

But now was not the time.

Their long overdue, brotherly bonding had waited this long; it could wait a little longer, Dean told himself. They were both young. They had an entire lifetime left to take care of unfinished business.

Besides, inspired by Peter's uncharactericstically calm and focused performance under pressure, Dean had to concentrate on encouraging this change he felt taking place inside himself—from the cowardly hunter to the brave-hearted hunted, from the frightened, dependent child to the courageous, independent man.

He'd felt it happen a couple of times that night—only to be buried and re-buried by familiar avalanches of indecisiveness and frozen fear. But this time he felt he was psyched enough to *finally* dig himself out from that suffocating mess.

What proof he had of this internal shift, he didn't know. But this time he believed he'd found within himself that which was needed to stand courageously and victoriously atop everything that he'd perceived holding him down since he could remember.

"R-I-P Horace Greene," Dean said to himself. "I'm carrying this thing operation straight to the promised land. And there's not a *damn* thing you and your kind can do *this* time to stop me."

Another gunshot sounded.

Dean felt his own words catch in his throat, making him cough, gag—

—choke.

Part IV

Chapter 50

Bruno stretched his arm through the crushed trunk and towards the busted-out back window as if he were trying to touch the face of God. The muscles, tendons, and ligaments of his shoulder sizzled with pain, feeling as if they were about to snap, rendering his arm as limp and useless as a sock full of hamburger.

The Durango dangled from the edge of the bridge like a freshly-slaughtered pig in a Chinese market. The truck's ragged bumper, which had wedged itself between a girder and the railing, creaked and stretched and strained to hold the Durango in place.

Inside, Bruno and Alain stood on the back of each of the front seat headrests. The seats had collapsed forward during the collision, and rested on the half-deflated airbags.

Bruno felt his body being pulled towards the windshield below his feet as if it were an immense magnet attracting not metal but human flesh. He made the mistake of looking down and out the cracked windshield.

But only once.

Through the infinite splits in the glass, he followed the path the Durango's headlights slicing through the space between itself and the ice-clogged river more than a hundred feet below—a path he could go down if he simply surrendered to the magnetic pull, if he just let himself be sucked through the split glass and over the truck's crumpled hood, and then down, down, down, flailing helplessly against the sleet and wind like a rag doll—

It took his breath away, the thought of falling so far, of leaving Alain behind.

He turned his head and eyes up, turned away from the illuminated path to his demise.

Alain, who was crouching on the back of the front passenger's seat, reached down between the airbags to the dashboard, seemingly unfazed by what lay beyond the windshield, and turned the radio's volume up. *Grandma Got Run Over By a Reindeer* threatened to pulverize all glass in the vicinity to glistening crumbs.

Bruno's head throbbed. The music made it difficult for him to concentrate on the task at hand. Alain bobbed his head and smiled.

Alain gave Bruno a boost up towards the Durango's trunk. Bruno stretched his arm as far as it would go, but his fingers were still a good two feet away from the opening.

"You there?" Alain shouted.

"No. I still can't reach it," Bruno said, squinting his eyes against the frozen rain that zipped through the shot-out window.

"Stretch, dammit!" Alain shouted. "We don't have time for your bullshit, Bruno!"

As if Alain's words were its cue, the truck groaned and

sank an inch towards the river.

"Stretch!"

Bruno heard the flesh-magnet windshield salivating for a taste of his flesh as he passed through it on his way down.

Thank God, Alain is there for me.

"Come on!"

After another unsuccessful try, Alain lowered Bruno to the driver's seat.

"Did you hear the truck?" Alain shouted above the music. "It's going to take a dive any second. You want to go with it? Then stop standing there gaping at me like a fucking idiot!"

Although Alain's words were firm and angry, Bruno couldn't help but sense he was stifling a laugh.

"This time just try and climb up onto the back of the backseat. It's simple."

Alain gave Bruno a boost from his rear end, raising him up so his head and shoulders hovered above both headrests. Bruno tried to pull himself up onto the back of one of the seats, but his hands kept slipping on the ice-glazed leather.

He tried again—

Slip.

"Dammit, Bruno!"

And again—*slip.*

"You fat ass!"

The music blared louder in the trunk area, the volume making the surface of Bruno's eyes vibrate.

If Alain would only turn it—

Slip.

The truck groaned and shook with another failed attempt.

"Hurry up! My back's breaking here, you cow!"

"I'm trying my best. The music doesn't—"

"What *about* the music?"

Bruno could feel Alain's pull his hands away—the flesh-magnet windshield pulled, sucked, yanked—

Bruno's bowels started to let loose as he felt himself fall. He landed on the back of the front seat and quickly grabbed at whatever solid and secure his hands hit first. Something hot and sour splashed against the back of his throat as he gagged.

Alain's mouth twisted into a half-grin, half-sneer as he watched Bruno.

Bruno hung his head in shame.

"All right, think, Alain. You're obviously working with a complete moron; think." Alain's leg bounced up and down as he thought. The truck soon responded, bouncing and shaking. Rattling. Groaning.

"Uh, Alain? Your leg."

"Shut up! Think, Alain, think. How can I get out of here? Think, think..."

"Alain! Your leg! The truck!"

"That's it! I've got it!" Alain's leg stopped bouncing.

Bruno sighed in relief.

"It's so obvious. The door."

"The door?"

"That's right, the door."

"Oh. Of course. The door."

Chapter 51

"We can open your door there—since mine's all crushed and stuck, see," Alain said, while Bruno's eyes followed along. "We can climb out onto yours and then smash out the side window in the back there and then climb up onto the truck and up onto the bridge."

We. *Oui* to we.

Bruno shivered and swallowed a lump. "I don't know."

"Do you have a better idea?"

Silence.

"I can film you. I'll even put on one of your favorite songs. You know, the one about Grinch?"

"But I thought that was *your* fav—"

"What do you think about *that*?"

"But if you're filming..." Bruno's eyes felt they were being pulled toward his feet, toward the cracked windshield on the other side of the seat, toward the light path leading straight down to the river. He stiffened his neck and raised his chin. He wasn't going to look; he couldn't look. He'd surely fall if he looked. "What if... What if I need you... your help?"

"Open your door. Hurry," Alain said, as he prepared the camera.

"But—"

"Do you hear yourself coming up with a better idea?"

"Well, if you give me a ch—"

"Just shut up and *do* it! Let's go! And remember to smile for the camera," Alain said, as he raised it to his eye. Bruno saw the red light go on.

There was nothing he could do now; the camera was recording.

Bruno gave the door a slow, soft push. Very gently, very carefuly, very—

The door ripped out of his hand, shaking the entire truck as it swung wide open, nearly tearing itself off its hinges. The bumper groaned. The wind roared into the truck's cabin, icy pins and needles riding the rushing air and smashing Bruno's face.

"Okay, go," Alain shouted to Bruno over the howling wind and music. "Wave to the camera before you go. Wave bye-bye."

"What? I... I can't climb out there," Bruno said, waving as he was told to do and then looking at the open door, which resembled a miniature plank laid out aboard a pirate ship.

"Do it! Now! We don't have all day, Bruno!"

"But—"

"Are you quitting on me? Are you? After all I've done for you, this is how you thank me! By quitting?"

Bruno flushed. Alain laughed.

Bruno didn't.

He swallowed hard and looked out at the door. It seemed so tiny. Like he would barely be able to fit his big toe on it.

The howling, growling wind made the door shake up and down. The sleet crackled against it, slicking up its surface and filling the recessed area of the window.

The truck shifted. The sound of metal grinding and tearing accompanied Bruno's stomping heart.

"Do it! Go! Now!" Alain screamed, his face growing so red it was almost purple. "I don't know how much battery juice I've got left on this thing!"

A snicker was crouched just beneath Alain's voice, chilling Bruno's bones.

Bruno, whose concentration was blistered by the blaring music, pulled his hood over his head, stooped forward, and slowly slid the top half of his body out onto the door. A gust of wind swooped underneath him, nearly lifting him into the air. The door shimmied. Bruno's eyes peered straight through the door window, catching sight of the headlight path to the river. Bruno turned his head to the side, slamming his eyes shut. He flattened himself, pressing the side of his face to the door, then reached his hands out and grabbed the door's edges, squeezing them until his fingers ached. His throat burned again with that same sour stomach acid. He gasped for air. The wind roared, forcing itself down his throat, freezing the burn.

He didn't want to go any further. This was too much. He could not do it. He just could n—

"Get going! Now! Go!" Alain screamed.

Bruno could feel something hard pushing against the back of his left leg. It was Alain's gun. He was using it to poke Bruno, to provoke him to continue on and...

And what?

He wasn't so sure anymore.

Bruno opened his eyes. The side of the bridge was just three feet or so to his left. But there was nothing to grab onto—only flat, green, ice-coated steel, with extra large, round bolt heads sticking above its surface. He could see that the Durango's back tire was flat and that among the many dents in the side of the truck, there was a long and deep gouge down its side. It was suddenly very important to Bruno to know how far that gouge continued toward the truck's front—his brain's way of avoiding dealing with the terror of the task at hand.

"Move!" Alain shouted, poking him in the leg again and snapping him out of his self-protective contemplation. And then, "Oh, I *love* this song! That Grinch is one mean sonofabitch, isn't he? Isn't he!"

With his arms still hugging the door, Bruno inched himself forward while pulling the lower half of his body from inside the truck out onto the door, carefully keeping as much of it as possible away from the window.

A gust of wind kicked against his stomach, rippling his coat. His fingers burned as he squeezed onto the edge of the shaking door, which shook all the harder from Bruno's trembling body. He heard soft, low-pitched whimpering. It was coming from his own mouth.

"Now stand up!" Alain shouted.

Bruno didn't want to let go of anything.

"I... I can't!"

"Come on! Just stand up! Nothing's gonna happen! It'll give me a great shot of you. Very flattering."

The truck's bumper groaned and creaked and then stretched, causing the Durango to drop another inch. The door jolted. Bruno squeezed his eyes shut and gagged.

"See, the more time you waste... Stand! Go!"

Bruno slowly brought his knees up closer to his chest and arched his back as high as it would go.

"Good. Good."

The door bucked.

Bruno shifted his body backwards, first onto his toes and then onto the bottom of his feet, and slowly raised himself up until his legs were about two-thirds of the way straight—but with his hands still gripping the edge of the door.

The wind pushed on his right side, trying to tumble him over.

He didn't think he'd ever be able to let go of the door. It was then that he realized the mistake he'd made climbing out there. He should have climbed out backwards because now, in order to stand up and still have a firm grip on something, he had to let go of the window, turn around, and then grab for the door frame.

"Did it all wrong, huh?" Alain shouted, reading Bruno's mind and body language. "I saw that when you went out, but I didn't want to tell you. Now you have to turn around so you can climb up the truck."

Bruno swore he could hear Alain chuckle. Why? What was so funny? Their *lives* were literally hanging in the balance!

Bruno let go of the sides of the door first before moving. Slowly, he stood up straighter, his arms extended out to the side.

"Wow! Look at that! He's a daredevil!"

He carefully turned his feet and body counterclockwise. The bullying wind went from punching him in his right arm to pummeling his back. His right foot started to slide backwards along the thin layer of ice covering the interior of the door. It was dropping into the mini skating rink forming on the door's window. Bruno picked that foot up—and for a brief moment, he balanced on one leg.

"Good. That's good. Now dance to the music!" Alain shouted.

Bruno rushed to put his foot back down on the door, to feel anything but air beneath his boot. His foot immediately slid backwards. Bruno reacted by leaning forward. His foot kept slipping toward the window behind him. He tried to pick it up again, but the wind hit him hard, making him teeter. He fought back with flailing arms.

"That's it! Good! Good! Man versus that bitch Nature."

His eyes looked down for a moment's breath, only to have that same breath sucked from him by what they saw. His body was leaning out over the edge of the door farther than he had thought. He panicked and started to fall forward. He threw his head and shoulders backwards and clawed at the passing sleet.

It worked.

But then a well-performed act quickly turned ugly again, and Bruno fought against momentum to keep from pitching over the door's edge. The wind barreled into his body. The door shook. Bruno stepped backwards, to try and once again find balance. His foot thudded hard against the window— the same window that it had been trying to avoid.

It broke through.

"Oh, baby!" Alain shouted.

Bruno was falling.

Chapter 52

Bruno's right leg disappeared through the hole like a piece of spaghetti sucked into a hungry mouth. His body collapsed on top of the window, shattering it, sending its pieces into the howling darkness. His right arm sprang out from his side, grabbing for anything, for life.

It overshot everything.

But the window's glass-less frame jammed itself under Bruno's right armpit, preventing his entire body from falling through.

The Durango creaked and groaned.

"Alain! I need you!"

"You don't need me! You need to be put out of your misery! Shot dead like a broken-down race horse!" Alain said, raising his gun beside the camera, which was already pointed at Bruno.

"No! Alain! What are you doing? Alain!"

"Dead man falling through!"

"Alain, no!"

"Or better yet, I should just wound you so you'll feel yourself falling and hear yourself screaming every inch of the way!"

"You're crazy!"

"Sweet words from such a stupid man."

"Alain! No!"

"Should I wound you in the hand or in the arm or maybe in the leg," Alain said, moving the gun from body part to body part.

"No!" Bruno struggled to climb out of the broken window. He moved with a speed and grace that was normally foreign to him, spryly pulling himself up onto the door like an adolescent gymnast, ignoring the wind, the sleet, the height, the slick surface, death. Suddenly he was standing back on top of the door facing the Durango, with his hands clutching the inside of the doorframe. His explosive movement had stolen his breath from him and he gasped for air.

He expected his shins to be blown apart by a gun blast at any moment.

Instead, he heard laughter coming from inside the truck.

"Did I tell you how much I love this song?" Alain said, starting *The Grinch's Song* over again. "I guess I know how to get your ass moving, huh? Now hurry up! Climb up the side of the truck so I can get out of here!"

"Climb up? Where? Where do you want me to go?" Bruno wasn't in the mood to argue with Alain about what he'd just done. He could feel the panicky courage he'd just benefitted from leaking out of him, leaving behind the cold, cramping ache of hopelessness.

"Climb onto the window frame there in the trunk."

"Frame? But... I can't. The window's still there."

"Well break it out, moron!"

Bruno released his gloved right hand from the doorframe, clenched it into a fist, and then slammed it against the ice-crusted window. It harmlessly bounced off, barely cracking the frozen surface—never mind the glass. Electrical shocks of pain streaked from Bruno's hand up his forearm.

"I can't break it, Alain!" Bruno shouted, while shaking his hand and grimacing.

"Well, try again! Swing harder!"

Bruno did what he was told, but nothing broke. Each time he hit it, too, the door he stood on protested.

"Can you shoot it out for me?"

"No! Just ran out of bullets!" Alain shouted. The same hideous laughing as before shadowed his words.

The truck creaked and swayed from side to side.

"Alain! I can't break it with my fist! Please, shoot it out!"

"I told you, I have no bullets!"

"Alain!"

"Hit it hard, you pussy!"

Bruno did, but nothing broke. He wanted to cry. He nearly slipped back through the hole in the door's window. His hand throbbed.

"Alain! Why? Why, Alain?"

"I can't hear you! The music is too loud!"

"Please!"

"I don't want to hear whining! I want to hear breaking glass!"

Bruno took a moment to think what to do. His sense of loneliness standing out there was as crippling as his fear of falling.

An idea suddenly streaked across his mind like a hawk, and he grabbed at its tail feathers before it flew away.

"Those two Americans are getting away!"

Alain's laughter and baiting stopped. Bruno cocked his

head to the side to try and figure out what was happening inside the Durango.

The window that his sore right hand had just been pummeling suddenly exploded in front of his face.

Chapter 53

"Now no more excuses! Get up there!"

Bruno could see Alain now through the windowless frame. His face was dimly underlit by the Durango's green glowing dashboard, making him appear more reptilian than human.

Bruno put his right foot at the center of the inside edge of the window frame. Because the truck was suspended off the bridge at an angle, as soon as Bruno put some weight on his foot it slid to the right corner of the window. Nothing life-threatening, but nothing like adding more to worry about to his already long lists of nausea-inducing concerns. He grabbed the window frame and pulled himself up, his left leg following behind once his body was as stable as it could be. His left foot abruptly slid to the right corner of the window frame to join the other foot. Standing up straight now, he was able to reach as high as the railing from which the Durango hung.

But not far forward enough.

There was a nearly two-foot gap separating the bridge from Bruno's outstretched arm. He stood on his toes on the edge of the window frame and reached his right arm up and forward until he felt his shoulder blade was going to slide around front and become a breastplate. He could only close the space to about a foot. There was no way possible to reach it from the position he was standing. And there was nothing higher to climb onto.

"Hurry up!"

Unless...

"What's taking you so long!"

He reached up and out again, stretching for the round, metal, icy railing with every bit of his physical being. He closed the gap to within ten inches. He stooped onto the window frame's edge on his tiptoes and closed the gap to nine inches. With his left arm, he pulled his body up towards the railing with every last ounce of his strength and the gap became eight—

The truck creaked and shivered and then sank away from the bridge, increasing the gap to nine inches. Bruno's heart sank along with the truck.

"Come on! Stretch, dammit!"

In all this effort, Bruno did see how he could get to the railing easily enough. But it would take a risk he wasn't sure he could force himself to take. He saw that because he could reach his arm high enough, but not far enough forward at the same time, if he lifted his arm as high as he could and then let himself go, let himself fall forward into empty space, gravity would be a friend and help connect his arm to the railing—

—while at the same time acting as a mortal enemy as it tried to pull his floundering body away from the railing and send it hurtling to the river below.

Did he have any other choice, though?

"Come on! I'm gonna give you ten seconds to get moving and then I'm coming up whether you're still there or not!" Alain yelled. "And if you're still there, you won't be much longer!"

How could his best friend be so cruel? Didn't Alain like him anymore?

But now was not the time to answer a questions like that. Now was the time to move.

"One, two, three..." Alain started to count.

Bruno got up onto his tiptoes and reached as high as he could.

"Four, five, six..."

He made the mistake of looking down to gauge the gap separating himself from the railing. A sour sting, compliments of the stomach, assaulted his throat again.

"Seven, eight, nine, and..."

He had to go. He knew Alain was serious. He pulled his eyes away from the howling hole between him and the bridge and looked up at the railing. Only a few inches, he told himself.

"Ten! Here I come!"

This was it.

Chapter 54

Bruno let go of the window frame with his left hand so he'd have two hands to grab for the icy railing.

It was all or nothing.

He pushed off with both his feet as best he could. Rather than give him a boost toward the sky as he'd hoped, the swirling, sadistic wind yanked him down into the blackness. The side of the bridge grew to insurmountable heights before his eyes.

Somehow the railing fell square into the palm of his right hand, and he squeezed with all his might. But he misfired with his left hand, hitting the railing with his wrist. As he tried to compensate, his left hand slipped away and circled like a spoon trying to stir the soupy, stormy space surrounding him. His body slammed hard against the side of the bridge, nearly knocking his breath from him.

He held the railing as tightly as he could with his right hand. His body twisted and turned in the raging wind, threatening to unscrew itself from his shoulder joint.

He knew he wasn't going to make it. His felt his fingers slipping on the icy railing.

This was it. The end of Bruno. The end of his friendship with Alain.

The beginning of the punishment for all his wrongdoing.

He looked up at the sky rather than down at the river waiting to swallow him. He knew there was nothing but suffering waiting for him down there. But maybe up in the sky... maybe there was some sort of salvation. Did good intentions count for anything?

He squeezed his eyes shut as his fingers slipped away from the railing. He waited for his body to pick up speed as it sliced through space towards the ground. He expected to feel his stomach lurch into his throat as if he were about to puke up a cantaloupe. He expected the shit and piss to flow freely into his underpants. He listened for the sound of his own scream to replace Alain's music as the soundtrack to his death.

But instead, he felt he was floating in the darkness behind his eyelids. No speed. No sickness. No sound.

Dying wasn't so bad after all—at least until the judgment began.

A voice—perhaps his own, perhaps an angel's, he didn't know—spoke to him. "Hold on!" it said.

Did it mean hold on, death would soon stamp out all his fears like a foot to a glowing ember?

"Hold on!"

There it was again. How long did it take to reach the river? It was far, but it wasn't *that* far.

"Hold on! I've got you!"

Who had him? The voice came from above. Was an angel carrying him down to the river to dunk him and do him in and then whisk him away to heaven?

Heaven... How's *that* for a joke! Heaven! Someone like him!

Dying was making him giddy.

"Hold on!"

"I'm holding!" Bruno yelled back. "Hurry up! The suspense is killing me!"

He didn't know he could be so ironic. So funny. It saddened him to realize this so late in his life. The next life around he'd be a stand-up comedian.

"Grab the railing!"

What railing? He was falling!

"Grab the railing!"

Bruno felt light-headed. Dizzy. Confused.

"Open your damn eyes and grab the railing now!"

That was a different voice. It came from behind him. A recognizable voice. Alain's. What was *he* doing falling down to the river, too?

Oh, no! Alain isn't... The truck didn't...

Bruno pealed open his eyes like he was told. The side of the bridge loomed in front of his face, the flattened back tire of the Durango just to his left. His right shoulder screamed agony, the muscles, ligaments, and tendons straining not to allow the ball and socket joint to dislocate. His body twisted left and right like a heavy sack of potatoes. For the first time he realized that something both squeezed and pulled on his hand and wrist. He looked up and saw a pair of black-gloved hands gripping his hand from over the railing. No angel. But a welcome sight just the same.

Who was it? One of the Americans? He hoped it was that guy named Dean. Bruno knew that he could be trusted, counted on. It showed in his eyes.

"Grab the railing!"

But the American didn't speak French, did he?

Bruno grabbed onto the railing with his free hand.

"Now the other hand! Come on!"

Bruno grabbed onto the railing with his other hand. The helping hands attached themselves to each of his forearms.

"Now, let go of the railing! Trust me!"

What choice did he have? He let go. Rather than fall, Bruno felt himself being pulled up towards the top of the bridge.

What would he say to the American guy when he got up there?

"Kick your feet up to the edge!"

How could he thank him after he and Bruno had tried to kill him and his brother?

Bruno was able to swing his right leg up to the topside of the bridge and use it to help pull himself up.

"Almost there!"

His head rose up above the side of the bridge to the height of the base of the railing. He could see his savior's black boots. He wasn't sure what color or kind of footwear the American guy had been wearing, but he told himself they were black boots. Using the helping hands, Bruno was able to pull himself up onto his right knee. From there, he pulled his left leg up to the three-inch wide edge so he was now on both knees with his arms up over his head, above the railing. If he was let go, he would have surely fallen backward and over the edge. But he knew he wouldn't be let go. He just knew it.

"Okay, now slowly and carefully stand up."

Bruno did as he was told. His legs were shaking from fatigue as he straightened them. His knees were throbbing. The helping hands kept Bruno's arms taut so he wouldn't and couldn't lean backwards into empty space.

Bruno kept his eyes down, turned away from the stinging sleet swirling around the edge of the bridge like shards of glass in a whirlpool, and fixed on the boots. He saw them slipping and sliding backwards and forwards and left and right on the ice, fighting for traction.

"Almost there," the voice said, encouraging Bruno on. "Now lean forward over the railing and I'll pull you up here."

Bruno did so. He felt himself sliding over the top of the railing and gently to the ground, the helping hands guiding him there the whole way.

Once Bruno was on top of the bridge, safe and secure, the hands suddenly became cold and forceful with him, changing as quickly in character as a nebbish Dr. Jekyll morphing into a nightmarish Mr. Hyde. They wrenched Bruno's arms behind his back. They seemed to want to tie them into knots. Two cold metal rings slapped against his wrists, binding them together. A knee pushed into Bruno's back, holding him face down and flat on the icy surface of the bridge while squeezing the air out of him like toothpaste from a tube.

"You're under arrest," the voice said, its tone changing from encouraging to accusatory.

Bruno turned his head toward the Durango. "Alain," is all he could think to say, but it wasn't nearly loud enough to warn his friend. And even if it were, what good would it do? Alain had to get out of the Durango sometime soon if he wanted to live.

And Bruno decided he wanted him to live.

"Alain," Bruno gasped again with the little air he had available under the crushing weight.

"Don't worry, my friend," the cop said into Bruno's ear. "Your matching dirty sock will be by your side soon enough."

Bruno wondered if the cop, too, had ever entertained the

idea of being a stand-up comedian or sitcom writer in a future life. He watched him move over to the railing and reach his hand down and towards the side of the Durango.

"Don't worry, I'll catch you!" Bruno heard him yell to Alain. "Trust me! If you make it this far, I'll make *sure* you get somewhere safe and secure and warm and dry, I promise!"

Bruno couldn't help but close his eyes and think how good that promise sounded. How good it sounded that this would all be over soon and both he and Alain would still be alive. And could get back to being best of friends.

"Get ready, I'm coming!" Bruno heard Alain shout. "I'm coming, Bruno—don't worry! I'm coming, buddy!"

Chapter 55

Peter followed Dean south across the Jacques Cartier, out from under the ribcage of icicle-bombing girders and onto an open stretch of the bridge. Each ten feet seemed to take ten minutes to cover.

Several pops from a gun were heard above the hissing sleet and howling wind. Neither one of the brothers turned to look.

Peter flinched with each pop, his body reacting as though a bullet was about to tear flesh from it. He felt he was living one of his childhood nightmares. The one that, regardless of the differing circumstances that precipitated, always ended the same, with him frantically trying to get away from the snarling, unseen monster he could sense lurking under the stairs or behind a tree or in the closet. Those nightmares where his feet kept slipping on a slick surface or sinking into knee-deep sand, or felt like two heavy concrete blocks which he struggled to lift in order to escape as the monster came closer and closer—

—and closer, its long, black nails scraping against the back of his heels...

I should have pushed those bastards over the side while I had the chance.

Peter felt a strangely disproportionate mix of anxiety and comfort at his brother's newfound desire to lead their get-away. He would follow his brother, though, because like most people, his desire to have faith in a power greater than himself was overwhelmingly strong. But he would follow with a watchful eye.

Two more popping gunshots slapped Peter in the back. He ducked. Those seemed louder. Maybe because the two freaks were closing in on them from the shadows—although Peter didn't want to turn to find out. Or maybe because the wind was gusting hard into his back, carrying these sound waves to Peter's ears faster than previously.

"Are they right behind us or what?" Peter said.

"I don't know. I don't even want to look," Dean said, hardly sounding confident as he spoke through chattering teeth. "We're toast, though, if we stay on this bridge."

"More like popsicles."

In Peter's view, Dean's decision to head out of the city rather than toward it was dumb—d-u-m-capital-B*oy, is that idea dumb!* Yet, in a strange twist of irony, the plan only further accented Peter's profound, even irrational *need* to believe his brother knew best.

They walked for what seemed like an hour, but was, in fact, only fifteen minutes.

As an aching coldness seeped into Peter's bones making them feel as brittle as chilled pretzels, panic scurried about his skin. With each slippery step, he repeatedly asked himself how he could have *ever* let Dean convince him to go this direction. The other way, toward the city, the way that *he* had wanted to go, at least made *some* sense. The Jacques Cartier stretched out in front of them into the pitch-black smear of the South Shore for what seemed an eternity.

Two more pops.

"Shit, we're fucking dead!"

"No, we're not—shut up! I hear you still breathing. The island. The entrance to it is right up there," Dean said, pointing to two gray stone pillars marking the driveway entrance to the park island below. "We go down there and..."

"And what? Get shot?"

"Hide. There's plenty of brush—"

"—to get shot in—"

"—and trees we can use for cover."

"Yeah, *falling* trees."

"Look, what do you want? Stay out here in the open and just let those psychos take target practice on us?"

"No, but if we'd gone the other—" Peter started to say, before stopping himself. "I just don't think you've thought all this through."

Dean threw his hands up into the air. "I can't *believe* who's saying that!"

"Hey, it's been my thinking and doing that's gotten us this far—alive! You haven't done—"

The wind shifted, bringing with it a face-assaulting sting of sleet that cut Peter off mid-sentence. Once the discomfort passed, though, Peter didn't bother to finish his sentence. They'd have plenty of time soon enough, he told himself. They'd have plenty of time.

When they reached the exit ramp, Dean promptly sat down on its icy surface, took a deep breath, whispered something that sounded like *I am now* and disappeared into the shadows engulfing the island below.

Peter couldn't believe his eyes—or ears.

"Hey, asshole, come back!" Peter shouted. "That's *my* phrase." He threw himself down the ramp headfirst. As he slid, he yelled "Geronimo, jerk-off!" motivated less by a need to escape the armed whackos than by the desire to stay close to his brother, just in case his newfound courage was the real deal.

Just in case the Dean of legend and lore had finally shown up to play the game.

Chapter 56

Alain ignored the chunks of ice falling off the girders, knowing they would never *dare* hit him. He smelled the wind, imagining himself to be an animal. He smelled nothing. He tried his eyes, first looking along the bridge towards the city, but saw nothing silhouetted against the faint glow of the few remaining city lights. He also saw nothing the other direction, towards the South Shore.

Where had they gone?

"Alain?"

They could only have gone either right or left, and with conditions being as bad as they were, they couldn't have gotten far.

"Alain?"

He tried to tap into his other animal instincts to see if they would give him a clue.

He sensed something...

To the right, toward the South Shore, away from the city—that's the way. But what if they went toward the city and were crouching down in the shadows near the sides of the bridge, below the faintly glowing horizon?

It *was* possible.

He needed more convincing evidence than some tingling spidey-senses. A noise.

"Alain?"

A smell.

"Alain?"

A—

"What do you *want*?" Alain said, looking down on the ground where Bruno lay on his stomach, his hands cuffed behind his back. The policeman was lying stiffly across Bruno's hips and legs, like a fallen tree. He had dropped there after Alain had pumped two shots into his face... after the considerate cop had taken such care of Alain's camera before helping him climb from the Durango back up onto the bridge.

"I can't get up, and I'm afraid some ice is gonna fall on me. Can you take these cuffs off me? Please?"

"Actually, I was thinking of leaving you here. I'd love to hear you try and stutter your way out of *that* one."

"No! Alain! Please! Don't leave me! Please!" Bruno begged, as he rocked his body from side to side, trying to shake off the dead weight. Alain thought he looked like a seal with its tail trapped under a stone. He laughed and filmed Bruno.

"All right, you big baby. Just calm down." After finding the cuff's keys in one of the cop's pockets, Alain freed Bruno, who wiggled and squirmed his way out from underneath the body.

Alain searched again for a reliable sign of the Americans' whereabouts. He smelled the air again—nothing.

He looked—nothing.

He listened...

"Alain?"

"Shhhhhhh!"

He listened...

The wind howled. Distant sirens whooped, but for some reason he knew they weren't coming for him—or the dead cop. The sleet hissed and crackled against the frozen surface of the bridge and the two vehicles. Nothing—

"Alain?"

–human.

"Alain?"

"I said shut up!"

And there it was. Off to the right—toward the South Shore. A sound. A human voice riding atop the swirling wind. The word *Geronimo*, and then something else—the voice's volume starting out strong, but then fading, as if the person was moving quickly away.

"Alain?"

"What! What do you want?"

"I have to go to the bathroom," Bruno said, squeezing the front of his pants like a three-year old.

"Go on him," Alain said, pointing down at the dead cop.

Bruno looked down at the dead man. His mouth contorted in repulsion.

"That's all right," Bruno said. "It stopped. I don't have to go anymore."

Alain knew that wasn't true, and it concerned him. Bruno was disobeying his orders. If he got too defiant, he'd have to be dealt with—sooner than expected.

All the sick ones were paranoid, Alain told himself. It's what kept them on top for so long. They trusted no one. They believed that everyone was out to get them—

An ice bomb dropped from a girder, exploding on the

ground just inches to Alain's right.

—as well as every*thing*. The only choice, the *safest* choice then, was to *get* before being *gotten*.

Alain stepped calmly through the falling chunks of ice. Bruno, on the other hand, raced as quickly as he could out from under the bridge's girders, darting left and right and starting and stopping and slipping and falling the entire way. Alain stopped and filmed Bruno, knowing the footage would help compose a sentimental, slow-motion montage leading up to the bozo's bloody end in his movie *magnifique*.

Alain took his time, confident that he'd still catch up to those two American fools no matter *how* fast or far they went.

After all, it was always that way in the movies.

The movie killers *always* operated as if guided by powerful, invisible forces—

—hissing...

and hissing...

and—

Chapter 57

Dean wobbled up onto his feet at the bottom of the ramp, just in time for Peter to crash into his legs, cutting them out from underneath him and exploding tiny neutron bombs of pain in his knees. Dean tumbled on top of his brother and the two of them slid several feet face-to-face. In a romantic comedy, this sort of meeting might have been the deciding moment when a kiss was stolen. But in this situation, personal boundary violation alarms shrieked.

Dean quickly flopped off Peter and onto the ice. He quickly scanned the terrain around them. Even though his eyes could pull in only enough reflected light to make out the muted outlines of objects no more than ten feet in front, Dean had visited the small island enough on brighter, warmer days to be somewhat familiar with its layout.

East of the Jacques Cartier bridge was the amusement park. West of the bridge, where Dean and Peter were, was a beautiful park with small, rolling hills, a conveniently-spaced mix of deciduous and evergreens, and an eclectic scattering of tourist attractions. Winding its way partly around the island was Tour de l'Isle road—where Peter and Dean sat.

Dean remembered that to their right were Saint Helen's Island Fort and its accompanying museum, a parking lot or two, a rather steep hill that dropped down to another parking lot for the amusement park, and then the Saint Laurent river. Through the sagging, creaking limbs of some nearby trees, Dean could see the faint bar-graph contours of the city along with a few patches of twinkling neighborhoods lining the distant shore of the river. To their left was the Lévis Tower, about two stone throws' distance. But in that direction were mostly rolling hills, with occasional heavily-wooded spots surrounded by picnic areas, and a couple of large open fields used for playing football or frisbee or sunbathing in the summer.

"So what now, boy?" Peter said, after he'd tried to stand, only to fall back down. The ice was especially thick and smooth and slippery in this area due to the accumulated runoff from the exit ramp.

Dean didn't know what to answer, but he knew if he wanted to impress upon Peter that he was still willing and able to lead them out of this mess, he had to respond with conviction. He looked around the park as if he were waiting for it to give him a clue. It hissed and crackled one singularly icy note, which was often interrupted by the crunching sound of a falling tree branch.

"Well, boy? Commercial's over—I gotta have your answer."

This was it. He *had* to decide—and decide *well*. Their lives depended on it.

Dean's whole body trembled. His teeth chattered. His knees throbbed. His breath stuck in his throat like hair in a clogged drain. The memories of both the Sugar Bowl fiasco and *that night* rubbed their cold and slimy bodies against his brain.

"I think we should get the hell out of here and hide—hide in the woods or something," Peter said. "They'll never find us in the dark."

A violent, cracking sound wave ripped across the island and through Dean's gut on its way to the bridge.

Peter was giving him the benefit of the doubt.

He's giving you the ball, boy!

He *had* to decide—and decide *well.*

Their lives depended on it.

"I've got a better idea," Dean said, swallowing the cold, phlegmy mass of cowardice that had collected in the back of his throat. "You may fall down again, though, when you hear *this* one."

Chapter 58

The ice and wind made progress across the bridge tedious. The fact that Bruno wouldn't shut up made it near unbearable.

When he was nervous, Bruno talked incessantly and asked questions about the stupidest things. "When did they build this bridge? Do you think this bridge would ever fall? Is it bigger than the Champlain bridge? They always seem bigger when you walk over them as opposed to when you drive over them, huh?"

Shut up! *Shut* up! Shut *up!*

Alain wished he had that big bag of cocaine on him right now, but it had been left back in the Buick. Bruno was much quieter, easier to control, and more evil when he was high. But even if he wasn't, even if the cocaine was ineffectual on him for some strange reason, the powder-filled bag could have *at least* been used to plug up that chattering hole in his head!

"Alain, what if..."

"Alain, I was just thinking..."

"Alain... Alain... Alain..."

Shuuuuuut uuuuuuuuuuuuup!

Alain wondered if he should shoot Bruno *tout de suite* and be done with him, get him out of his hair, be free of his cloying anxiety. But then he wouldn't have anyone to kill for him any more. That was no good. Having a slave killer was supposed to be his signature. As nettlesome as Bruno was, Alain couldn't get rid of the dope yet for that reason alone.

After talking himself out of the need to lay Bruno down for a dirt nap, Alain was feeling pretty self-righteous about his flexibility as a fruit loop. Most serial killers seemed to be stuck on a broken record of compulsivity, but Alain saw himself able to weather the ever-changing winds of insanity's storm better than most.

He liked that about himself. He liked to imagine his future biographer would too.

Up ahead were the mini-white towers marking the descending entrance to St. Helen's Island. Alain had been to the park many times. His parents used to take him to the amusement park when he was a young boy. Upon arriving, they'd drop him off at the entrance with a hundred dollars in his pocket and a promise that they'd be back to pick him up at sundown. They never wanted to go in themselves. Couldn't be seen in such a low-class gathering spot. Fine with Alain. He didn't want to be around them and their kind anyway. He liked being alone—or so he believed. The truth of the matter was he hated it. But within the context of his present *modus operandi*, he convinced himself that liking solitude—even seeking it out and wallowing in it—was what all proud, mentally disturbed people were *supposed* to do.

Alain called upon his senses again to deliver him to his

prey. He looked, but saw nothing. Listened—nothing. H e smelled the air—

Something.

Something faint, but nonetheless there. The smell of cooking oil. It rode the wind coming in from the west. It was the same smell he remembered coming from the two Americans. The sour stink of their restaurant. It came from down the ramp. That would explain the shout he'd heard earlier. The two were probably trying to find a hiding place in the shadows.

Wrong move.

Not only did Alain know the amusement park like the back of his hand, but he knew the rest of the island—the woods and hills and tourist attraction parts of the island—even better. He should have. He often left the amusement park after only an hour or two of roller coaster rides and bumper cars to go explore the park by himself or walk along the Saint Laurent river and gaze over the river at the cityscape seemingly just a well-spit phlegm ball away, or trap some of the friendly, trusting squirrels who'd practically climb into his lap for caramel-coated popcorn—where he'd then catch them by the tail as they tried to get away and swing their bodies against a rock or tree until they split apart, spilling their innards everywhere.

He had loved the sensory overload their deaths gave him: the feel of them trying to pull away—sometimes digging their back claws into his hand to gain some leverage, sometimes even twisting and bending and trying and bite his hand—their pathetic squeaks for mercy during the first few wacks, the heavy smell of their urine and feces thickening the air like the scent of a mid-summer thunderstorm rain, the wet, popping noise they made as their gray bodies blossomed, bursting out with red, glistening petals of flesh...

The classic beginnings of a lunatic.

Yes, he *was* insane. For real. He always wanted to be and now he felt he'd finally arrived. It had taken quite a few years to find the right time and place to move from animals to humans, but this night he'd finally done it. He couldn't help but feel proud of himself. He smiled at the idea of his overachieving, hypocritical parents joyfully beaming at their boy's accomplishments.

He itched, though, to add two more people to his list of trophies.

Trophies... Yes, that's what he'd forgotten to get from the others. Most crazed serial murders took something from their victims to serve as symbolic representations of their accomplishment. Other people—like his totally fake father— got gold watches and fancy pens and vacations and whatnot from their employers as a way to honor their years of service, but since serial killers were their own employers, they had to reward themselves with a putrid piece of each of their creations, isn't that right, Alain? Isn't that right? Alain? Isn't it?

"Alain? Isn't that right?" Bruno was saying.

"Yeah, yeah, whatever. Sure," Alain said, having no idea what he was responding too.

He told himself not to forget to get something from the two Americans. Something fitting. Maybe he'd finish what he'd started back in Westmount and get the younger one's tongue, because he talked so much and so fast in that awful English language. And from the older one, he'd slice off one his bulging biceps—flesh and all—stuff it between two fresh slices of mustard-slathered pumpernickel and enjoy.

Perfect.

"Alain?"

And maybe he'd throw in the brain of someone else he

knew. He always figured Bruno's brain was as filled with holes as a chunk of Swiss cheese. It would make quite an addition to his collection, especially considering their history together. Many serial killers always seemed to have at least one victim who was close to them, who trusted them, who sometimes even helped them. Since Alain's deranged parents or slut-bag sister weren't available this night, Bruno would have to do.

"Alain?"

And he'd do just fine. The more he talked, the more perfect he became.

"What now? What! If you have to take another piss, just do it over there! I won't look."

"No. It's not that. I just wanted to tell you that I think those two guys went down there," Bruno said, pointing at the exit ramp to the island below.

"Yeah, I know."

"And that I think we should get going after them before they get too far away."

"Right. Brilliant plan."

No, he'd let Bruno hang around a little longer. Sometimes his Swiss cheese brain seemed to work well enough. Without the cocaine, though, Alain didn't know how useful Bruno would be when it *really* counted. When flesh had to be damaged, pain inflicted. He'd have to keep a close watch and not hesitate to lay his longtime lackey down for that dirt nap.

Alain surveyed the ramp and decided that the easiest way to descend would be to slide straight down its middle into the darkness below—quietly. He told Bruno what they were going to do—stressing the quiet part—and Bruno treated the news with a childish glee. Alain reminded himself to be patient and that soon enough he'd be free of this mush-brained burden he had to bear.

Bruno begged to go first. Seeing it as an expression of his power—like a king having one of his servants taste-test all the food for poison—Alain obliged.

Alain felt anxious when he observed the way the road abruptly disappeared into the soupy darkness below. It was as if he'd be sliding into a void—where either eternal emptiness or eternal damnation awaited.

Neither of which soothed his unstable soul.

Did the insane feel fear? Probably. How many times had he seen them in movies or documentaries screaming and thrashing about in apparent terror of the demonic voices in their head or the drooling, decaying visions of death haunting them, bursting out from underneath the bed sheets or peeking at them from around every corner, grinning and growling, promising to skin their crazed asses alive as soon as they fell asleep?

Alain shivered.

Sure, the insane felt fear. Alain was as normally abnormal as all of them.

Bruno threw himself onto his stomach on the icy off-ramp in an attempt to slide down it face forward. Unfortunately for him, he had started his slide a couple feet above the point where the road began descending from the bridge. As a result, he lost most of the momentum he had gained on the near friction-less surface, and his slide came to a halt only three feet down the ramp.

"Ooops, I've got it. I know what I did wrong. Just wait. I'll do it again," Bruno said, as he struggled to stand.

Alain's blood bubbled. He wondered if a bullet pumped into Bruno's chest would give the lug enough momentum.

Bruno got up into a half crouch and threw himself forward again. This time he disappeared into the blackness below as though he were a load of dirty clothes sliding down an unlit laundry chute.

Alain quickly followed, throwing himself forward and down—with camera and gun in hand—onto his stomach. He almost made the same mistake as Bruno had by starting the dive into his slide too soon.

The wall of absolute darkness below came at him fast and furious, and he flinched as if he were about to slam his face into something solid. But he streaked through it, gliding like an Arctic seal across an ice flow. His eyes strained to see.

Some blacks lightened into grays as shapes seemed to rise up out of the inkwell world, soft and hazy, gradually hardening as their images dried on the surface of his retinas.

A human figure lay straight ahead. Alain could immediately recognize it was Bruno.

Damn that clod to hell!

Alain pushed hard against the surface of the ice with his boot tips. He pressed as hard as he could, straining to steer his body. It wasn't until he jammed the gun's grip into the ice's surface, though, that he began to turn. His body rotated to the left quite sharply.

Alain turned his head to watch Bruno as he slid by him, feeling quite pleased at his ingenuity in avoiding a collision—

—only to catch sight of another figure lurking straight ahead.

Before he could blink, one of the figure's legs swung forward, striking Alain's right forearm, sending the Glock flying out of his hand.

Chapter 59

Dean saw an opportunity, made a split decision, and acted.

The Glock sat in one of the killers' hands, pointing straight ahead, just asking to be kicked away like a teed-up football. As the killer slid face first across the ice towards him, Dean swung his leg at the gun. He missed the gun, but instead felt his foot connect with the killer's forearm. He watched the killer's arm jerk to the right, He heard the weapon hit the ice, sounding more like a child's castaway toy than something deadly. The Glock came to rest only a few feet from the other killer.

The eagerness with which Dean had kicked rewarded him with both good and bad results: the killer lost his gun, but Dean lost his grip on the ground. At the peak of his foot's follow-through, his left leg flew out from underneath him. He crashed to the ice. Pain exploded in his lower back and then radiated out to every limb. Dean bellowed as tears squeezed themselves out of his pinched-shut eyes, pooled in the corners, and then spilled over onto his red and raw cheeks. He opened his eyes just in time to see one of the killers plunge on top of him.

A pair of hands closed around Dean's throat as Alain's growling face materialized out of the darkness. It appeared to be twisting itself in several different directions simultaneously, as if a demon were trying to claw its way out from beneath the skin. Alain's eyes were so dark they seemed to be sucking the very blackness out of the night. As he squeezed, Alain hissed something in French through gritted teeth.

The bottom of Dean's breath dropped away. Lost. Inaccessible. Unreachable no matter how hard he tried to gag it back out of his innards and through the hand-made blockage. He tore at Alain's forearms, but it was a tough angle from which to generate an explosive, wrenching force. Alain's arms felt like two thin steel pipes beneath his coat.

Dean's head throbbed as his brain screamed for precious, oxygen-rich blood. He dug his feet into the ground, searching for the traction needed to buck off Alain, who was straddling his body and sitting on his diaphragm. Dean's feet slid backwards and forwards on the ice, finding nothing stable to push against to help himself.

The world smeared again. This time, though, an army of globular, purple phantoms swirled around and around on the surface of each of his eyes.

Escorts to the nether world, maybe.

His strength faded as fast as his consciousness. He tried with every last bit of effort to pull Alain's arms away, but his own arms were overcooked noodles. He tried to punch at Alain's face, to gouge at his eyes, to grab at his lips and teeth and tongue, but his hands limply fell away.

Death by strangulation. How fitting, eh, boy?

A familiar apathy suddenly fell over Dean. He tried to relax, to just let it happen. Better to get it over with quickly than to drag out the inevitable.

The inevitable. What was he saying? But it was the truth, wasn't it? He should have known all along that he wasn't cut out to be the—

Alain shouted out in pain as his hands sprang from Dean's neck and grabbed at his own head. At the same moment, a chunk of ice the size of a baseball dropped down onto Dean's chest. Without thinking, Dean seized the opportunity. He grabbed Alain by the front of his coat and pushed him away. He wanted to jump on the sonofabitch and pound him like a veal cutlet, but the fact that he'd just been nearly strangled to death demanded respect. He coughed and gagged and gasped for precious air.

But each cough and gasp gave Alain more time to recover.

Although only seconds passed until Dean felt strong enough to continue fighting, in his mind it seemed there had been enough time for Alain to both plan and prepare his bruising response. But when the last of the purple phantoms that had been staining each of Dean's eyes melted away, clearing his vision, Alain was several feet away, still struggling to pick himself up off of the icy ground.

It became a race to see who could get to his feet first— and to the gun.

Alain had the head start, but Dean had in his favor a familiarity with the extraordinary capabilities of the body and mind in the crunch of competition.

Extraordinary depths of chickenshitheadedness too, huh, boy?

Dean rolled onto his stomach, which was no easy task on a near frictionless surface. From there, both he and Alain struggled to a standing position with the grace and speed of two crotchety centenarians. Their efforts to stand mirrored each other, giving the impression of a well-choreographed stage performance with an underlying, eclectic message.

They both uncurled to an erect position simultaneously, facing each other. In perfect synchronicity, they turned their heads to the gun lying on the ground.

"Get the gun!" Dean heard Peter shout. He couldn't really make out where his brother was positioned in the dark, but he could tell Peter was close.

Alain seemed to hear Peter's voice for the first time, too. When he froze in place, surprised by Peter's proximity, Dean took the opportunity to answer back.

"Are you all right?"

"I've got the other dude under knife point!"

"Knife?"

"Well, icicle. You got my special delivery?"

"Huh?" Dean said. He was so happy to hear his brother's lively voice.

"The ice ball. I nailed that other fucker right in the side of the head when he was on top of you!"

Alain squinted into the darkness.

"Yeah, you, you baby-killing fucker!" Peter shouted. He must have had superhuman vision to see Alain's reaction, because Dean sure couldn't make out many details on the killer's face.

Just as well.

Alain lunged forward. He stepped quickly with his right and put it down too hard. His legs slid apart until he nearly did the splits. His arms waved wildly in the air as he fought to maintain his balance.

"The gun, boy! Get it!"

Learning something from Alain's mistake, Dean shuffled his feet on the surface of the ice without picking them up. It worked well, but it was slow.

"Go, boy! Go!"

Dean picked up the pace, sliding each alternate boot forward further. But then he noticed he was being pulled to the left by an invisible force—due to gravity and a sloping terrain. He tried to adjust, but started to lose his balance. His stomach twisted at the thought that he was going to end up back on the ground.

"What are you doing? Get the gun—come on!"

Come on, boy!

Dean waved his arms in the air as he fought for his balance. Both he and Alain looked as if they were conducting invisible, inaudible orchestras.

"Come on! You've got him!"

Hurry, boy!

The gun was within diving distance.

"Dive for it!"

Dean's foot slipped.

Hurry!

I can't.

"Get the gun! Go!"

Sliding... Sliding... away.

Hurry!

I'm doing all I can!

Peter's cheerleading wasn't helping Dean. How quickly his brother's voice went from being among the sweetest sounds on the planet to the sourest.

Alain regained most of his balance and, stealing a clue from Dean's more effective approach, shuffled rather than stepped forward. He closed the distance between himself and the gun fast.

"Come on, boy!"

Dean quickly compared their respective distances to the gun. Dread rippled through his body, shattering what remained of his already waning courage.

"You got the bastard! Come on!"

Why bother? He was barely moving. Alain was. He had *so* far to go. Alain could already reach down and pick up the gun... and point it at him... and put him out of his—

"Boy!"

It was the Sugar Bowl all over again—

Boy! What are doing! I thought I told you to—

He didn't want to score that touchdown. He had let himself get smacked out of bounds by that scarecrow of a safety, Horace Green, on purpose.

Ha! Ha! Ha! Ha! Ha! Ha! Ha!

He was born to lose.

"Boy!"

Too late. Alain fell to his knees, picked up the Glock and aimed it at Dean. Dean had no time to worry about falling. He pivoted and, with a surprising amount of grace and explosiveness, bolted away from Alain and towards the nearest hole in the bushes, paying no attention to the slippery surface as he scampered.

Look at him go! Boy's talented at running away!

"Boy, no!"

He heard a pop behind the voice, and simultaneously a bullet screamed by his head and cracked into the center of a nearby tree trunk. Dean lowered his head and hunched his shoulders long after the bullet had passed him—but he was at least ready for the second one.

But the second one didn't come his way. Or the third. Or the fourth. Even as Dean crashed through the hole in what ended up being only one row of bushes, and landed face down in another clearing, he could tell by the difference in the pitch of the gun's discharge that Alain was shooting in a different direction.

Peter.

Dean jumped to his feet with cat-like quickness. Although ice covered the ground he stood upon, it wasn't the same flawlessly smooth surface as near the ramp. Here it was rougher, more lumpy and bumpy, and it possessed a grain of sorts—something to push off against.

Dean moved up to the row of bushes and peeked through, squinting until his eyes were just slits.

Everyone was gone.

Dean whispered Peter's name, but his voice was dissolved by the sizzling sound of the sleet. Dean knew something was wrong.

"Peter?"

Nothing.

What should he do next? Go after them with no weapon?

The hissing sleet's intensity increased.

Dean felt so alone. Both of his knees throbbed mercilessly. He felt cold and wet for the first time since... all night. His teeth chattered. A sob welled up in his chest.

Peter.

He didn't know where to go, what to do. There was only blackness around him. And vague forms—some living, some not—any one of which might turn hostile without a moment's notice and fall on him or jump on him or put a bullet into him or...

The world was such a vile, hostile place.

Peter.

He wanted to crawl under a bush and not come out until it was all over.

Until all the people in the stands went home, right?

Until bravery could go back to being the stuff of movie heroes; the stuff of which dreams were made.

And he, the child dreamer.

Chapter 60

The pine tree stood out in a sparsely wooded area of the island. Its normally open, inviting arms, which typically created a swaying, seductive, triangular form, pulled themselves close to its trunk this stormy night as if the tree was frightened and freezing. It whimpered like a lost and lonely child, giving off a symphony of sorrowful creaks with each wind gust.

Peter lay on his stomach behind the protesting pine—or what he thought was behind it in relation to where he had last seen Alain and Bruno.

And Dean.

In the thick darkness, he checked himself as best he could for any bleeding bullet holes. His breath caught in his throat like a cork as he fingered a tear on the backside of his coat. But after several times of sticking his finger in the hole, checking it for blood, and finding nothing darker than the night smeared on it, he was convinced the rip came from something more benign than a bullet.

He thought he heard voices nearby, but it was so hard to tell with the sound of sleet ceaselessly hissing and crackling both around and on him. He was pretty sure that if they were voices, they came from somewhere on the other side of the pine. His sense of direction had gotten scrambled during his frantic flight.

Why did Alain shoot? Bruno had been positioned between Peter and Alain with a makeshift icicle knife pressed against the side of his Adam's apple—the perfect bargaining position if things got ugly, right?

Wrong.

Bargaining apparently wasn't part of Alain's vocabulary. The maniac had shot in the direction of his partner without hesitation. As soon as Peter had seen the Glock flash, he pushed Bruno toward Alain and then dove for the nearest cover. The knee-high row of bushes had offered him a blessing he only now could fully appreciate. They were unable to stop his barreling body, trapping him between themselves and the gunman. Instead they allowed Peter to crash through their frail branches, where he spun and slid some twenty feet down a short hill into a relatively flat and open area—perhaps a parking lot. It was at that point that he'd made out the solid black presence of the pine off to his right. He'd half-crawled, half-slithered across the surface of the ice, frantic to get as far away from where he guessed Alain and Bruno stood. He had moved toward the tree as if it were a parent offering protection from the neighborhood bully. The *gun*-toting neighborhood bully. Now that he was there, all he could think of doing was to wait.

Wait for what, though?

He heart pounded against his chest and the hard glazed snow. He thought about Dean. He wondered whether that first bullet Alain shot had found its mark. As he quickly replayed the scene in his mind of Dean and Alain racing for the gun, he didn't know if he could believe what he had seen. It seemed as if Dean had given up right at the moment when he most needed to push himself to the limit. But why?

Apparently gone was the tough talking, courageous fighter who'd come up with the idea to ambush Alain and Bruno when they slid down the park's entrance ramp.

The thought made Peter feel hollow inside. And desperate.

But Peter couldn't be absolutely *sure* of what he'd seen. It *was* very dark. The ice *was* nearly impossible to move on. Maybe what he'd seen had nothing to do with giving up. He wanted to give his brother the benefit of the doubt. But too much had happened that night for Peter to go on believing that some... no, a lot... hell, *everything* that he'd ever heard from their father—more than their mother—about Dean's legendary courage, his coolness under pressure, his ability to lead and conquer, was true. Their father seemed to worship everything about Dean, from the ground he walked on to the stink of his shit. Only in the last hour or so, though, had Dean suddenly shown even a *spark* of courage and leadership—and it was plain to see he handled it like a flaming charcoal briquette.

The hollow space inside Peter began filling with sadness. A thick, heavy sadness that expanded as it siphoned off his energy.

The sound of voices slapped Peter back to the present moment.

This time he was *sure* of what he heard, even with the white noise of sleet smothering everything. It was Alain and Bruno, and they were close. He still wasn't sure of the direction from which the voices came. It sounded as if they were somewhere on the far side of the tree, but he checked behind himself just to be sure. He could see barely ten feet into the darkness, the icy rain slamming into his peering eyes making even the attempt torture.

They could have been eleven feet away, preparing to pounce, and he wouldn't have known.

The voices spoke again, and Peter shivered.

Fear took the place of sadness, filling the hollowness in a flash flood.

He didn't feel safe or secure anymore next to the tree. He had to move. But where? The voices seemed to double in numbers while, at the same time, circle around him, surrounding him like a pack of wolves.

Was he hallucinating?

No. Even though his mind told him one of the pairs of voices was just an echo, that he wasn't *really* being surrounded, he still felt trapped.

He wasn't sure which set of voices was real, though—the ones to the left, to the right, behind, in front—they kept shifting direction.

And closing in on him.

Or pulling away?

Left, right, in front, back—

Where to go to get away? Or should he stay? In which direction did safety lie? Or was it right where he was?

I am now, I am now, I am now, he said to himself, trying once again to benefit from the clarity, calmness, courage and concentration those words had given him in the truck. But instead, his mind released a swarming army of distracting thoughts.

He tried to hide himself within the swarm. It didn't work. His fear expanded inside him like a mushroom cloud. Rather than he containing the fear, the fear quickly contained him. His teeth chattered. His body shivered and sweated—his fear,

SLIDE 309

an impenetrable, enveloping sack of suffering.

Dean. Where was he? He needed him bad—Mr. Golden Boy—just in case.

Just—

Right.

Mr.—

Left.

—in—

Golden—

Right.

—case.

Boy.

Peter dove into his thoughts again, pretending not to hear the voices, and suddenly...

Suddenly, something with the form of a thought, but packing the power of God's grace, exploded in Peter's head. He wasn't trying to think of his father and all the years of heartache the old man had caused him, but...

there he was...

in his mind. And, as the voices closed in around him, Peter inexplicably and instantaneously understood everything: why the abuse, why the favoritism, why the tyrant continued to live even though he lay six feet under in the cold, cold ground. He looked upon it the way someone dispassionately observes a complex tapestry of interwoven images hanging on a wall. He didn't know why, but he understood.

He understood!

—behind, in front, left—

It was so obvious!

Right, left, behind, in front—

He knew he'd have a hard time putting it into words, but he couldn't wait to at least *try* to share the details of his discovery with Dean—it was so damn—

—in front, behind, right—

—obvious! He couldn't wait to see his brother's face when Peter told him—

—right, left—

—that now he understood—

—behind, in front, left—

—everything!

—left, right, behind—

The hollowness inside him emptied of fear and filled, instead, with a pure and peaceful light of awareness and wisdom.

—behind, behind—

It was *so* obvious. The stains of jealousy and anger began fading from his soul. Why didn't this happen to him before? Why had this enlightenment come to him in the midst of chaos?

—behind, behind, behind—

He was bursting with excitement.

So much so that he whirled around and, while still trapped in the self-perceived safety of his own buzzing mind, nearly blurted out "Cool!"

But the blinding pain of a severe blow caused a train wreck of syntax in the back of his throat.

Chapter 61

Dean huddled behind a row of bushes with his knees pulled to his chest. His body rocked back and forth. His teeth clicked together. His eyes fixed on the sizzling cold ground, but they were really searching inside for answers.

What had gone wrong?

I'll tell you what went wrong! You fucked up again, boy! You got your brother killed because you couldn't come through when you had to—what a surprise!

Shut up, Dean muttered at the familiar voice in his head.

You're really all alone now, boy! And you've got no one to blame but yourself!

Shut up!

No! Stand up! Take charge, goddammit! Don't make me look like an asshole! What do you think I was preparing you for all those years?

To drive me insane!

No! To drive you to stand up for yourself! To take charge

of your life! To get you to give up your dependence on me!

That's ridiculous!

Is it? Well, you may be able to criticize my techniques, but you won't be able to find fault with my intentions. I tried to free you right up to the end. Remember how? Remember that night?

No! I don't want to.

Remember it!

No!

But the voice wouldn't stop.

Remember racing along the Mass Pike to get back to your mother's place in time to see Peter, me in the passenger's seat beside you, ready to cough up a lung— remember that?

I don't want to! Leave me alone!

Tears streaked down Dean's cheeks as the memory of *that night* bullied its way past the traumatic circumstances at hand and through the front door of his awareness.

That coughing got to you, didn't it? And when I touched you... Your stomach is probably still tied up in knots from it, huh? Remember how I kept telling you what a worthless piece of shit you were? Remember that? Remember how mad you were getting? How much you hated me at that moment? How much you hated life and what it all seemed to be about—always feeling fearful and anxious, always following orders, always being yelled at, always being criticized for never being good enough, and forever being physically and emotionally ground down—from diamond to dust. And then sitting there and having to watch—what am I saying? choosing to watch—as the author of your miserable existence blackened and leaked and split at the seams like a rotting banana as death leached the life from him. How did it feel to watch that? Were you happy? Of course not! You weren't happy I was leaving you. I created you, every thought and feeling and fear inside of you came from me. To lose me was to lose yourself, right? Quite the paradox, huh, depending so much on someone you so despise? But not if I could help it. I wanted to leave you with something you could count on to get you through life. I wanted to leave you with a pair of balls as big as watermelons and filled with the courage of kings!

Shut up!

That's right, I wanted to grind your ass into the dirt! I wanted to see you as good and dead as me! If I was going down, you were going down with me!

No!

That's right, I did what I did to you because I loved you, son. It's true I made mistakes. But when you have a son someday, you'll see that sometimes your best intentions become your child's worst nightmare. I'm sorry for—

Through his sobs of anguish, Dean saw his mind skipping like a record. Except, each time it skipped it played a different song.

That's right, I'm actually not dead at all, boy! I've shrunk down to the size of a peanut and I'm living in your ear right now!

What was going on here? Was he finally going mad?

No, he was pretty sure his sanity was still intact.

Dean was suddenly acutely aware of the malleability of his thoughts and memories. Under more normal circumstances, he would have been panic-stricken by this realization, as his well-structured, well-compartmentalized sense of self slid away from his controlling grasp. After all, the entire present and future of his life has always been cut from the cloth of the past, regardless of its pattern. But now, for the first time, he was truly seeing both how much that pattern shaped his decisions and how his decisions shaped the pattern.

But why now, of all times?

For some reason, that realization brought a greater calmness. He took a deep breath and listened some more, motivated as much by curiosity as by an inability to find the courage to face his present problems.

I was so glad you came down to be with me during those last days. See, it gave me a chance to finish what I had started the day you first showed signs of being clingy and dependent. A Mama's boy, a model of insecurity. A model of faggotness. I couldn't accept that, no way! I knew the world would eat you alive. So I decided to launch a campaign to toughen you up—even if it meant sacrificing your feelings towards me. To have you there when I died was a way to try and put the final touches on a job not yet quite finished. That was why the abuse never ended, why there was never any sickly sweet dialogue between us full of tears and apologies or long musings on the meaning of life from a dying man's perspective.

Was that true? Was that what he really wanted? Dean couldn't be sure anymore.

As long as I could flap my jaw, I was gonna try and finish the job I'd started as best I could. I was going to show you that life was about the fight, the endless fight to survive and conquer. You needed a killer's instinct, boy, that's what. Something I saw you severely lacked. You needed the constant presence of anger and hatred burning inside, powering your person like the plutonium rods in a nuclear reactor, to get you through life. To be your constant companion. Something to call on. Something to trust.

That night, *it all came to a head. Things got pretty wild during that ride home, didn't they? Remember when I puked on your shoes? How close to the edge did that push you? Nobody wants his shoes puked on. It's tough to get the smell completely out, and then you're left carrying it around with you everywhere as a constant reminder. Which reminds me, have you thrown away those shoes yet or are they still sitting in the back of your closet, adding a lightly sour stink to the already stale air back there?*

Did he? No, of course not. He never did. He didn't even remember his father puking on them. Where was this coming from? Had these recountings of past events been *that* factually wrong all along?

What was real? What could be trusted?

Strange, though, how you were able to endure such a horrible thing with almost no emotion. Yeah, you hated it, hated me, hated life and God for even having such a horrid thing as puke, but you dealt with it calmly—I was watching closely. On the other hand, though, the constant badgering and name calling and criticism—how about that? That's the stuff that got to you, huh?

That's true. He remembered it as clear as day.

Like Chinese water torture. Ceaselessly drip, drip, dripping on your head—each drop insignificant in and of itself, but taken as a whole... That's what really *got to you, huh, boy? That's what made you drive so goddamn recklessly* that night.

No, no! It was because he was *telling* me to hurry, Dean said to himself.

You ain't no race car driver, that's for sure. You must have been doing ninety when that deer came out from the right.

Or was it a skunk? Or a fox?

Made you flinch—I saw. You jammed the foot on the brake, and the car skidded, fishtailing left and right. The smell of burning rubber filled the cabin, remember that? Remember screaming, too, as the car started to spin? Shit, the sonofabitching thing slid over and hit something on the side of the road, and the next thing you know we were tumbling end-over-end.

Side-over-side.

Ten times, at least.

Two times, at most.

But it was enough to throw your sonofabitching old man right out the busted out window, wasn't it?

Because you didn't put your seatbelt on, like I kept *telling* you!

So there we were. Damn near the middle of the night, hardly another car on the road, remember? You picked up my broken body in your arms, held my head on your lap, real Hollywood-like, and you started laughing.

Crying.

Sobbing like a baby. Your old man had just about had enough, right? But he ain't dead yet. He's got one trick left up his sleeve, don't he? Remember what it was? How could you forget it, right? He asks you—

—tells me—

—to put him out of his misery. To kill the sonofabitch. To wrap your hands around my neck or press me to your chest or bash my skull in with a rock—bottom line, to put me out of my goddamn misery. You were bawling like a baby then.

I was scared.

You were scared—boo-hoo. Well, how do you think I felt? I was dying! I could hear the devil feeding his fires in preparation for my arrival as we spoke!

I wish you'd told me how scared you were—for once.

Yeah, right. Don't try to infect me with your pussyness! Don't try to infect me! Anyway, so I gave you your orders—

just like in the Sugar Bowl— and you remember what you did?

I cried.

And?

I held you close.

How close?

I squeezed you hard. Real hard.

And I was wheezing and coughing and spitting up blood and begging for you to squeeze harder, to squeeze the life out of me, to be a fucking man for once! And you remember what you did?

I think so.

Probably the most cowardly act, as far as I'm concerned. What?

Probably the most heroic act, as far as I'm concerned.

I kissed you on the forehead and then I...

Yeah?

I told you that I was sorry, but that I was going against your call, taking the ball around the outside one more time...

You didn't say that!

No, that's right. I said... I... I said...

Dean couldn't remember what he'd said. He'd always told himself that he'd told his father he was taking the ball around the outside one more time, but now he knew it wasn't true.

You let me suffer there on your lap, choking on my own blood, until I died.

I tried to make you comfortable.

Well, you goddamn failed at that! I was in agony!

This was the point in Dean's recollection when he usually lashed himself with a whip of guilt for all the choices he'd made which brought him to that moment.

Why did I even keep in contact with him all these years?

Why did I come down to be with him when he was sick?
Why did I put up with his abuse even then, when *he* needed
me most? Why did I agree to drive him home to see Peter
before dying? Why did I let him get to me with his usual
bitching? Why did I drive too fast? Why did I crash? Why
did I run to see if he was hurt instead of just walking away?
Why did I hold him in my arms? Why, when he looked up
into my eyes, his own eyes big, blue, and beseeching, his
jaw trembling, his broken teeth, bloody and jagged, his nose
twisted, blackened with mud, and leaky, did I not do him
that one favor he asked of me?

I can't. I can't.
That's what you said!
I can't.
Your goddamn motto for life!
I can't.

And he didn't. He didn't kill his father when his father
wanted it most. Here was a man who was responsible for so
much suffering in Dean's life, here he was in his most
vulnerable moment, begging to be put out of his misery, and
all Dean could do was hold him in his arms and weep for
him as he slowly expired.

Why couldn't he kill him?

Dean once thought it might have been a passive-
aggressive sort of revenge inflicted on his father, but no
matter how deeply he delved into his memories, he couldn't
recall feeling vindictive towards the old man as he lay in his
lap dying.

Dean didn't know why he'd done it. But the bottom line,
what he had come to know for years, was that his decision
had been somehow flawed.

It had to be. It always was before—his father made him
feel it was so—and it would always be.

But Dean could now see more clearly than ever how much he was a product of his father's conditioning. And how the voice in his head and most of the memories he maintained had all been shaped by his mind to coincide with that conditioning.

But how much of it was actually true?

Dean felt something inside himself suddenly crack. A warmth seemed to ooze out of this crack and spread through his body. It wasn't unpleasant, but it wasn't familiar. It made Dean squirm out of his crouched position and stand. His mind felt fresh and fearless, clear and light. Although he sensed it was only temporary, Dean knew this was a direct result of his epiphany. A part of him wanted to continue searching for more definitive evidence of the unreliable nature of his memories, knowing that he'd only had a taste of what was possible and that his transformation was far from complete, but he knew he had a more important search to conduct.

For Peter.

Dean shielded his eyes against the sleet and looked around. The blackness pressed against his eyeballs like contact lenses. He had no idea how much time had passed. He hoped it was no more than a few minutes.

He searched for the Jacques Cartier bridge, but couldn't see it. He was surrounded by creaking and crackling trees whose sagging branches looked near the breaking point. He squinted his eyes and slowly turned himself around three-hundred-sixty degrees. The slope of the ground near him gently sank to his right. He was sure he'd come uphill when he'd rushed to get away from Alain. But had he wandered downhill without even realizing it? He couldn't remember. He might even be farther west on the island than where he had started since he couldn't see the bridge any more.

He decided he'd walk downhill.

Dean slowly slid one foot in front of the other, keeping his eyes focused on the ground at his feet since they did little to help him see much of anything in front. His heart jumped in his chest each time a branch broke off a nearby tree and crashed to the ground.

But he felt no fear. Instead, he felt strangely detached from the sensation of his jumping heart. Each thump arose out of emptiness and returned to emptiness—exactly where Dean felt his awareness comfortably and naturally resting.

After walking for what felt like a quarter-mile—but in reality was only twenty feet—he had not yet come back to the area they had all started from. He didn't recognize where in the park he stood. All the trees looked the same. Dean felt panic rising inside himself at the idea that he was lost, but he watched it crest and fall like an ocean wave, and then disappear. Following close behind were all sensations, all emotions, all thoughts. None of those things existed independently unless...

Unless he held onto them.

Like the memories of *that night*. How hard had he worked to hold on those? And for what? Over time, those memories had yellowed and warped to the point where they could hardly be considered accurate snapshots of the past.

It was time to define himself differently.

Bullshit! I made you! You need me to survive!

It's just in your head—keep going. Old habits die hard. The voice isn't real—don't stop.

You're trying to tell me all those slaps upside your head weren't real!

Get control of yourself, Barret. Don't let yourself slide too far from the task at hand.

Pussy! Psycho-babbling pussy! You ain't nothing! You're

worthless! You're meaningless! You can't do a single goddamn thing right! You—

Focus on the tangibles, he thought. One foot carefully in front of the other. Sweeping the eyes left and right. Watching for falling branches. Looking for a missing brother...

Feeling my stomach squeeze tight... Feeling my stomach... squeeze... tight... Feeling...

That's as far as reality goes right now. Tangible-type stuff. That's all that really matters.

I am now.

The words bubbled up from the depths of his subconscious. As before, he felt he was watching everything spontaneously occurring within and without from an untouchable position simultaneously both familiar and foreign.

I am now.

The dispassionate awareness those words brought to him further reinforced his revelation—

I am now.

—about how much his own mind had played a part in both imprisoning and torturing himself throughout the years.

I am now.

An aching sensation rose within himself—an aching to be close to his baby brother once again.

I am now.

An aching to begin trying to heal a host of injuries inflicted upon the siblings in the name of the malleable memories of their father.

I am now.

So much suffering for the sake of sand castles.

Chapter 62

"Bring him over here," Alain said in French to Bruno.

Bruno pressed the gun into Peter's back. He noticed how Peter limped from the injury he had gotten when the tree branch fell on him. It was because of that falling tree branch, and Peter's subsequent shout, that Alain and Bruno were able to pinpoint exactly where the kid had been hiding.

Fate. Its game could be so cruel sometimes, made worse by the fact that one couldn't call a time out or substitute in another player.

Bruno nudged Peter along, not wanting to cause him any more discomfort than necessary.

"Over here," Alain said, pointing to a spot on the ground. The spot was next to a colosseum of stone seats and stairs set into the side of a small but steep hill.

Bruno remembered coming there with Alain several summers earlier and sitting under one of the trees and smoking joints while watching bikini-clad girls playing

Frisbee. Girls, who Alain endlessly vilified for their "obvious sexual promiscuity" and their "pathetic attempts" to stay attached to someone—especially the slobby, abusive cretins they called their "boyfriend"—at all costs to their self-respect. They were all useless sluts in Alain's eyes.

"We're going to play a little game with him, have some fun," Alain said.

Bruno enjoyed games. Especially ones like tag and hide-and-seek. But he didn't think either of those games was on Alain's agenda.

"Place the prisoner here, at this spot," Alain said. After Bruno did so, Alain approached a trembling Peter and tore the wet, ice-crusted gloves off his hands. "Take these and put them on top of the hill up there." Bruno took the gloves and started to move toward the stairs some ten feet to the right, but Alain stopped him. "No, not that way. Take them *straight* up."

So Bruno tried to take them straight up as he was told. He made it less than three feet up the hill before sliding back down. Alain laughed and slapped Peter on the back. Peter didn't respond.

It upset Bruno that Alain laughed at him as if he were an idiot after he had tried so hard to please. But even more so, it upset him to see Alain sharing his joke with someone else—even if Peter seemed like a nice enough kid.

Bruno tried to climb up the hill again, this time taking extra care to dig the toes of his boots into the icy surface as best he could and to grab with his hands lumps of ice and protruding rocks or sticks. Again, he made it only a few feet before sliding back down. Alain laughed and attempted to get Peter to join in with pats and nudges.

A sharp pain jolted Bruno's gut. Although Alain's actions were the cause of it, Bruno instead blamed it on Peter. He was the *real* reason.

Bruno suddenly wanted the kid dead.

These feelings surprised his sober mind. As far as he could remember, he had never *wanted* anyone dead. He may have played *some* role in *some* people dying—sure—but he had never *wanted* them dead. Alain did. It was *his* fault.

No, no, not *his* fault.

Never.

He didn't know *whose* fault it was—and it didn't matter. But now... now if anything bad happened, Bruno knew it would be his *own* fault—a mere extension of his murderous desire to make Alain *his* and his alone.

"Come on, man, get those gloves up there!"

"I'm sorry, Alain, but it's too slippery."

"It's too slippery, he says," Alain said to Peter in French. But Peter only looked blankly at him. "What a pussy, huh?" Alain said, poking Peter in the chest with the gun while motioning over at Bruno. "I can't get him to do anything right."

Bruno boiled. "That's not true!"

"Look, he's having one of his temper tantrums."

"No, I'm not! Stop talking to him!" Bruno shouted, stamping his foot—and nearly losing his balance.

"I'm waiting," Alain said, tapping his foot on the ground in a feigned display of impatience. And then he turned to Peter and said in a softer voice—but still loud enough for Bruno to hear—"Watch how quick he jumps when I tell him to. Bruno! Bruno, I'm waiting! Now!"

Even though Bruno heard what Alain had said to Peter, he found it impossible to defy Alain's impatient command.

"You see. Look at him. He's my slave," Bruno heard Alain say, as he turned and tried to climb the mountain—only to slide down yet again.

"It's impossible!"

This time when Alain again tried to share a laugh with Peter at Bruno's expense, Bruno took the gloves and, in exasperation, threw them up towards the top of the hill. One of the gloves landed a couple of feet short of the goal and then slid back down to Bruno's feet. The other made it to its target on top and remained there.

"Not exactly what I asked for, but lucky for you, we don't have time for me to punish you for your sloppy work." Alain stepped away from Peter and focused on directing Bruno. "Make yourself useful. Grab the camera and film this. We're gonna capture a classic here. Let me show you—come here."

Alain showed Bruno where to stand and how to frame the shot for maximum dramatic effect. Bruno liked it when Alain grabbed his shoulder or elbow to pull him where he wanted, or when he slapped *him* on the back and encouraged him to "do it right." It felt so good. So right. It was the way it should be—was always going to be.

Bruno couldn't stop thinking about what had just happened.

Alain came back to me for a reason. He needs me. He wants us to be friends. He tried to be friends with Peter, but it didn't work. He saw how much better I am for him than... anyone else.

Oui to we.

Bruno's hateful feelings toward Peter abated—and then might as well never have existed a moment later. He was swept away by delight. The bond between him and Alain was strong. The evidence was indisputable. He couldn't think of anything that could break it.

"Are you ready over there?"

"You bet, buddy," Bruno responded, his mind romping in anticipation of hearing the ground rules to Alain's game, capturing the whole event on tape, then sharing his efforts with his best bud back at home over some nachos and beer.

Maybe Alain would let Bruno invite Peter along.

******

Dean leaped to the side as the ice-encased top of a bent-over maple tree suddenly tore free from its trunk with an ear-splitting crack and crashed to the icy ground several feet to his right. Much of the treetop's frozen sheath smashed like glass upon impact, its countless fragments scattering in every direction, making a tinkling sound the entire way.

I am now, he said to himself, trying to avoid thinking what would have happened if he'd been standing under the tree. If anything, that mantra pulled his mind and senses out of the storm of thoughts, memories, and emotions battering his inner being and placed them square in the center of the here-and-now storm around him. His awareness had a clarity, sensitivity, and strength of focus he'd previously known only in the midst of a football game, when he was sometimes able to intuit what was about to happen around him: holes opening up in the warring offensive line, thick, muscular arms springing out of the chaos to grab at him, the fakes the growling linebackers would fall for. It was a powerful ability, but one that defied logic. It often required an inordinate amount of faith to follow the direction of signals so subtle.

Dean had to be careful where he moved. The broken ice bits had spread out all around him like ball bearings, making each slippery step even more treacherous.

He heard another crack, and part of another tree crashed

to the ground, followed by the familiar tinkle of shimmering, frozen shards. The world seemed to be collapsing around him, finally succumbing to both the weight of nature's wrath and the interminable pull of gravity. He looked down at his arms and noticed that a thick shiny layer of ice had built up on his coat.

It was only a matter of time before his top, like the tops of the trees, gave into gravity's demands, broke off, hit the ground, and shattered into a million fragments.

He had to get out of this place.

He had to get to some shelter before he froze to death.

But first he had to find Peter.

Dean had no idea where to go. Between the cracking trees and the hissing sleet and the roaring gusts of wind, little could be heard. There were absolutely no clues as to which direction to head.

The only choice Dean had was to follow his newly awakened intuition. It said to go to his left, like it had many times on the football field when, if given the chance to think it over, he would have picked right.

So he went to his left.

And as he stepped in that direction, a large tree branch swung down from above him to his right, and slammed onto the spot where he had just been standing.

✳✳✳✳✳✳

Speaking in French and in a voice that fit comfortably between that of a circus ringmaster and *The Price Is Right*'s Rod Roddy describing a fabulous showcase, Alain announced, "The game's rules are simple, ladies and gentleman. The prisoner—er, contestant—you see standing before you has just lost his gloves."

Bruno laughed at that part, amused by the Alain's twist of the truth.

"The contestant has recovered one of his gloves, but the other one has found its way up to the top of yonder mountain peak," Alain said, pointing to the top of the hill.

Again, Bruno laughed when Alain called the twelve-foot hill a *mountain*.

"Very simply, ladies and gentleman, the contestant needs his other glove so the first one isn't lonely, right? He must recover the other glove so one of his hands doesn't freeze, correct? So, ladies and gentleman, in order to avoid such a tragedy, the contestant you see standing before you must now climb a very icy, very treacherous mountain, rivaling that of Everest, K2, and... and... and some other big-ass pile of dirt that I can't think of right now—"

Bruno laughed so hard, Alain had to stop and wait.

This was *so* exciting. Bruno could barely contain himself as he watched Alain through the camera's viewfinder.

Alain continued: "The contestant sees his glove up on top of the mountain and will soon move to retrieve it. But since he is a rather *stupid* contestant, rather than take the icy but *far* more accommodating stairs just to our right—Vanna, kindly show the viewers the stairs if you would," Alain said, cueing Bruno to get a shot of the stairs.

"That's it, Vanna. Thank you."

"You're welcome," Bruno said, in his best Vanna voice.

"Ladies and gentleman, the contestant will not be climbing those stairs, but instead will be attempting—and I cannot express the word *attempting* enough—to climb right up the icy mountain side here before us! Isn't that right, contestant?"

Peter looked blankly at Alain.

"See! Stupid as Vanna over here."

"Hey!" Bruno said in his Vanna voice, mocking insult, but instead loving every precious second of attention Alain paid him.

"Vanna, why don't you show everyone just how slippery this mountainside before us really is. Please, demonstrate for the people at home."

Bruno put the camera down and gladly attacked the hill, making it a foot further than the other times before his feet slipped out from underneath him. He slid down to the hill on his stomach.

"Thank you, Vanna. Can we have a nice round of applause for Vanna, ladies and gentleman?" Bruno stood up and did a bow—then remembering that he was supposed to be a woman, did a curtsy and stepped aside to pick up the camera. "So, if everyone is ready, let the game begin. Contestant, ready and... go!" Alain shouted, pointing up the hill at the glove. But Peter just stood in place, looking confused and nervous.

"Contestant, go! Go!" Alain shouted.

Peter shrugged his shoulders and looked first at Alain and then at Bruno.

"He really doesn't understand French," Bruno said.

"Piece of shit," Alain muttered. "Vanna, will you *please* explain to the contestant what he has to do while we take a commercial break. Quickly, quickly."

Bruno walked over to the shivering, confused Peter and looked into his eyes through the camera. Big mistake. The frightened, helpless boy he saw pulled on his heart, ruining his fun. He reminded Bruno of a little puppy he'd had when he was a young teenager. The one that used to go into the laundry room and squeeze itself into a foot-wide space between the washing machine and dryer, with its head lowered, its ears pulled back until they seemed to disappear, its tail between its legs, its flesh quivering. Bruno could never begin to put two and two together to comprehend why the dog acted that way whenever Alain was around. He had never seen Alain do anything to the dog, so he had just figured the lovable mutt to be crazy.

Bruno lowered the camera and his eyes and began explaining in his best broken English—his *fran'glish*—just like Alain had drilled into his head to do whenever he was called upon to speak the "devil's tongue."

"Alain says to go and get *la gant* over there-la, *comprend-tu?*" Bruno said to Peter pointing up to the top of the hill.

"You gotta help me get out of here, man," Peter said to Bruno in a breathy, desperate whisper.

"*J'comprends pas,*" Bruno said, looking away from those eyes and down at the camera. Peter's eyes looked so much like his scared puppy's. He couldn't let them penetrate his skin—and soul. He couldn't—for Alain's sake.

"Bruno. Please. The two of us. We can make it out of here."

Bruno looked over his shoulder at Alain, who gave Bruno a wide-eyed look that he understood to mean "hurry up," and then turned back to Peter, leaned close to his ear and said, "Sorry." He then raised the camera and stuck its lens inches from Peter's face. He peeked into the viewfinder to make sure he had a good shot—and then he closed his eyes so he couldn't see Peter's gloomy face.

"Has the contestant been instructed what to do, Vanna?" Alain asked.

"Yes," Bruno said in French to Alain over his shoulder, and then he turned to Peter and, from behind the camera, pointed up at the glove on the hill and said, "*Le gant.* Let's go! Come on!"

"But that's fucking impossible!" Peter said. "You slipped down it three times yourself, you *know* that!"

Bruno just shrugged his shoulders and looked to Alain, then back into the viewfinder. He bit his lower lip and said, "*J'comprends pas.*"

"And if I don't get it?" Peter asked, looking first at Bruno and then at Alain for an answer, his eyes about to drop out of their over-stretched sockets.

Bruno asked Alain what would happen to Peter if he didn't make it, being curious himself. What Alain told the camera with obvious relish made Bruno's stomach slam against his other organs in a fit of frenzy.

"What did he say? What's going to happen?"

Bruno kept the camera between his head and Peter's as if it were a shield. He looked down at his shoes, absolutely unable to meet Peter's pleading, puppy-dog eyes with his own as he backed away.

"Wait a minute! What's going to happen to me?" Peter shouted, looking frantic.

"Let's go!" Alain shouted, clapping one of his hands on the side of his leg while raising the gun at Peter.

"I—I—I can't make it up there!"

"Come on, let's go!"

"You can't do this to me!"

This was too much, Bruno thought. He wondered if Peter felt the same way he had felt when he was trapped out on the truck door. He really didn't want to see Peter get killed. All that jealous rage he'd felt earlier was gone. The truth was he kind of liked the guy. He didn't know why—he hardly knew him—but he seemed nice. He seemed like the type of guy Bruno could really get along with if he didn't already belong to Alain.

"Please! I'm not gonna fucking make it!"

Bruno squeezed his eyes shut behind the camera each time Peter turned his way and pleaded.

The thought of trying to put a stop to this streaked through Bruno's mind as suddenly as a lightning bolt. And stayed just as long. Aside from running away with Peter, he couldn't get his brain to even *imagine* how to escape this mess. And running along this ice was impossible. Besides, his and Alain's friendship had been through too much this night.

When he weighed the consequences of helping Peter against the pay-off for following Alain's orders, the scale tipped heavily in one direction.

Bruno chewed his lower lip as he watched Peter, through the camera's viewfinder, slowly approach the hill, nearly slipping to the ground before he even got there. He prayed silently to himself that the kid would make it.

"Let's go," Alain said. He raised the Glock waist high, pointed it at Peter, and started to once again give his play-by-play. "The contestant approaches the hill. He's looking anxious. His hands are probably already freezing, and he hasn't even touched them to the icy mountain yet. Just wait until he feels what's waiting for him. He looks up at the glove—at the jackpot, let's say—at the top of the mountain. It's maybe twelve, fifteen feet away, but it might as well be a mile for this young warrior."

Bruno wasn't feeling as excited or amused about the commencement of the game as he had earlier. He trembled. Nausea swirled around in the pit of his stomach as though an oily eel were chasing its own tail. The camera shook. He knew Alain would be very angry with him for that.

Why, why, why did Alain have to take everything too far! Everything was going great! Everybody was about to have some fun!

"This is very exciting, ladies and gentleman. The contestant falls forward onto his hands and feet—no knees—he's decided to do the knee climb. No, I'm sorry, he's going back up onto his feet—this is understandably a very tense moment for him. It does appear, though, that he's taking the slow approach. No trying to run up the hill like our resident idiot in a dress, Vanna, tried to do earlier. Oh, he's made his first move. He's put his right hand forward and is searching for something secure to grab onto. But we all know that there's absolutely nothing secure on that hill; that's what makes this so damn exciting, huh? Huh, Vanna?"

Bruno nodded. Blood was seeping from his lip, he'd been biting it so hard. He didn't want Peter to die. If he confronted Alain about it... maybe even used his gun to get Alain to listen...

No, that's crazy! Alain and I are best—

"The contestant's right leg is coming up, his foot is trying to find someplace to dig into. He's seemed... Yes, he's seemed to have found it, ladies and gentleman, because he's just brought his left foot up and is digging it in. And there's his left arm—so that's four limbs moved, about one foot of ground covered. He only has to do that same thing maybe ten or eleven more times—how exciting!"

Bruno kept looking back and forth from the ground to the viewfinder. He didn't want to see what was happening, but he had to make sure he had a good shot for Alain.

"And there's his right arm going up. His right leg. His left leg—

"—oh, his left leg just slipped out from underneath—

"—this is so exciting. But he's recovered, folks! He's actually regained control! That shows you what a *fine* competitor we have for you today. And there goes his left hand. And his right hand. And his right leg."

Bruno prayed as intensely as a monk.

"Left arm."

Come on, Peter!

"Left leg. Right arm."

Bruno wanted to shout some encouragement, but he was afraid of the consequences.

"Right leg—I know, this is getting a bit tiresome, isn't it, ladies and gentleman?" Alain said. "So let's add some fun."

Bruno eyes were fixed on Peter as the crack of the gunshot blindsided him, slamming into the side of his head like an invisible snowball, causing a full-body flinch. He looked into the viewfinder for Peter just in time to see pieces of ice spraying out from a spot a foot above Peter's head. He saw Peter's hands let go of the ice to protect his face.

The kid disappeared out of the viewfinder as he slid towards the bottom of the hill.

✳ ✳ ✳ ✳ ✳ ✳

Left, right, left—

—straight—

No—which way? Which way!

The park started to spin around him. Each tree, each bush, each rock, each hill looked the same.

Dean felt his intuition fading in direct proportion to his rising frustration. He tried to force his mind to tell him where to go, but the clanking wheels and pistons of processed thought drowned out intuition's whispers.

Which way! Which way!

I am now—I am now, dammit!

The mantra did its job of helping to bring him into the present moment where intuition resided, but waiting there this time was the caped, cackling, long-fingered fool of panic. It screeched as it trapped Dean in its bony arms.

Dean's restored intuition wasn't completely muted, though. One thing he sensed for sure—he knew that something bad was about to happen. He knew if he didn't get to Peter soon, he'd never see him alive again.

Hurry, a familiar voice said inside his head.

A familiar voice that, for once, sounded less like his father's and more like his own.

******

Peter's hands sprang off of his head and slapped onto the icy hill, effortlessly changing from one attempt at self-preservation to another. They first slapped and pressed against the hill, along with his feet, trying to use friction to slow his descent, but when that didn't work, the fingernails tried to dig into the ice.

Bruno could hear a low-pitched, plaintive whine coming from deep within his own throat.

This game isn't fun at all!

Alain raised his gun and shouted triumphantly as Peter's body slithered to the bottom of the hill.

"Looks like we have a loser! You know what that means, everybody!"

Bruno couldn't contain himself. "No!" he yelled as he lunged forward, trying to grab at Alain's arm.

******

Dean thought he'd heard a gunshot to his right and behind, nearly in the *opposite* direction from the one reason had him recently heading—but in the *same* direction as intuition had previously pointed. His heart felt as though it were a fish flopping around in a wet paper bag.

Going against every well-trained fiber in his body that attempted to pull him away from the sound, Dean rushed toward the gunshot, hoping it wasn't too late.

His mind bucked like a bronco. The more he squeezed his spurs into its sides to try and gain some control, the more it thrashed about.

What if Peter is injured? Will I know what to do? What if Peter is dead? Will I freak out? Am I going to live? What will I do without him? What if I'm shot and not killed? What if I can't walk again? What if no one comes to find me? Is it so bad to freeze to death? Where are the police? Why am I here? Where did this all go wrong? Why can't I feel braver? Why am I—

Focus!

I am now.

Dean passed through a hilly, thick settling of trees where he had to dodge two large, falling limbs with his name on them, and into a more open area.

He wasn't so sure he was still heading in the right direction any more. His restless, self-immolating mind had done little to help and a lot to quiet his intuition's softly spoken suggestions.

The park began to spin around him again in an indistinguishable blur. His throbbing, loose knee caps wanted to drop into his socks.

I am now.

He thought another sound would aid in putting him back on the right trail. A laugh, a sneeze, a voice, a fart...

Anything but another gun shot.

****

Peter lay on the ground curled in fetal position with his arms covering his head. He waited for the explosive force of a bullet to explode into his skull, delivering blackness and eternal sleep.

But it didn't come.

Instead he heard Alain and Bruno yelling at each other. It sounded like Bruno was making a stand—of sorts. As soon as Alain raised his voice several decibel levels, though, Bruno backed down.

Although Peter couldn't comprehend many of the words of their heated argument, and although, in the end, Alain obviously retained his title as lord and overseer of Bruno's life, Alain's victory hadn't been complete: Peter was still alive. He had understood enough—at least in tone—to know that it was Alain's idea that he should die and that Bruno had a problem with it. Although Peter despised them both, he found himself in the odd position of silently cheering for Bruno.

Bruno, it seemed, stood for life.

Bruno, quite possibly, was his only chance. Unless Dean came around sometime soon. But what were the chances of *that* happening? Hadn't he heard them arguing?

Peter climbed up off the ice as Bruno made his way over to him, looking as if he had something to say. Peter swore he smiled as he approached.

"You go again."

"I get another chance?"

"Second chance, yes. *C'est ca.*"

"But I still won't—," Peter started to say as he looked up at his glove. This was it. What good would pleading do him? He saw what these guys did to a pregnant woman. "Fine— assholes. Get that fucking camera out of my face!"

"Never mind that. Just go," Bruno said, glancing at Alain behind him while gently pushing Peter towards the hill.

"Just fucking try to stop me," Peter said, taking deep breaths, trying to psyche himself up.

I am now, I am now, I am—

"Just remember, I did all I could," Bruno said as he stepped away.

Peter flinched when he heard the comment. It seemed so strange, so out of context. But he yanked his mind away from contemplation of Bruno role in this night's insanity and to the task at hand.

I am now.

Peter faced the hill again. He didn't want to admit to himself that his mantra was failing to conjure up the same clarity of being as in the Durango. Peter looked up the slippery slope. The glove might as well have been sitting on the top of Mount Everest, it looked so far away. But he thought he was going to make it last time—was *sure* of it, in fact, after he got the "feel" of the ice—and then Alain had to shoot at him and ruin it all. A shudder of hopelessness rumbled through him at the thought that he'd never make it up there for the simple reason that Alain would never *let* him. But he tried to chase it away into the darkness around him and replace it with another thought to help him focus.

I am now.

"You're mine, motherfucker."

He attacked the hill the same measured intensity he did the first time; slowly, steadily, moving no more than one limb at a time as he'd seen mountain climbers on television scaling walls twice as steep and a hundred times as high.

But they didn't have a crazed gunman waiting at the bottom doing a stress-inducing play-by-play of every move and slip-up, who was ready to shoot at them whenever the impulse struck.

As he laid himself face down onto the ice at the base of the hill, his many thoughts quieted, clearing the way for the sense of *I am now.*

The ice seemed to be burning the skin off his hands. The fingers on his right hand, already abraded and bloodied and numb from the first attempt, scraped along the slippery hill high above his head searching for a frozen lump or indentation to grab. He found a lump—perhaps the same one he had used during his first climb—and tightened his throbbing fingers around it.

He heard Alain chattering away. By the tone of his voice, he sounded as if he were calling a ballgame. It annoyed Peter, distracting him from his task.

With his right foot, he found a familiar ridge in the ice.

This was going to go better than he first thought. If he had made it more than half way up before, there was no reason why he couldn't make it all the way up—sans bullets raining around his head. And if he made it to the top, he knew exactly what he'd do. He'd save himself, that's what. Screw Bruno. Screw Dean. Screw *I am now*. He didn't need any help. He'd do it all himself. If—*when*—he made it to the top, he'd take off! That's it! They'd *never* be able to catch up to him, ha ha.

That psycho-idiot, Alain, hadn't thought of that when he came up with his little death game.

Energized by his fantasy, Peter climbed with a new confidence. Left hand, left foot, right hand, right foot, left hand, left foot—it was almost *too* easy. The glove grew larger as he drew closer to it. Five feet to go. Maybe four. Right foot, left hand, left foot, right hand. Four feet—tops. He slowed up once he passed the point he'd reached last time, expecting a bullet to explode the ice around his face any second. But none came.

Right hand, right foot, left hand, left foot... the bumps and indentations seemed to have been laid out for him by some mythical forest fairy. He told himself when he got back home, he'd have to embellish the story when he told Dean how difficult a climb he'd had. Add extra blood on his hands, extra bullets in the air, maybe even a few falling branches and tumbling boulders that he'd had to avoid , while retaining his balance, as they came crashing down from above.

The glove was three feet away—closer to two, even.

This is almost too easy!

And then...

As Peter confidently jammed the tip of his right foot between the surface of the ice and a tree branch captured within—perhaps the easiest step Peter had had on his climb to the top—his foot slipped, causing his body to lurch to the right. His fingertips dug into the ice's surface, searching for something to grab onto.

Nothing.

Falling.

Sliding, down.

Down—bullet waiting at the bottom.

Left hand shooting out—searching—grabbing for the branch he just slipped off. His ring finger hooked it and then bent back, nearly breaking. Peter shouted. His descent slowed. His right hand pressed against the ice, trying to find friction. His legs swung sharply to the left, spinning his body sideways. His sore ring finger unhooked from the branch—

—sliding down. Down. Face first. Kicking toes into the ice. Pushing hands, applying the brakes.

Sliding down.

Down. Down.

He came to rest at the bottom of the hill, at the feet of Bruno and Alain.

He saw Alain carve a sinister smile, then hand the gun to Bruno. Alain said something to Bruno, but Peter didn't understand.

By the terrified look in Bruno's eyes, though, Peter could tell it wasn't good.

******

Hurry!

Find Peter!

Dean slipped and slid through a clearing, then came to a hill that stood between him and where he wanted to go. It proved to be difficult for him to climb so he decided to go around it, trying to maintain his sense of the direction from which the gunshot had earlier sounded.

Hurry!

Time running out... Find Peter...

Dean discovered a way past the hill, only to meet up with a pile of boulders and fallen tree branches. Rather than try to climb straight through them, he took the time he needed to go around them, falling to the ground once as he did so.

Time—

He had no idea if he was on the right track any more.

—running—

Each time he'd change his course to pass around something, he'd have to pause a moment and think—guess, really—where to go next.

—out—

A line of trees with bushes between them stood in his way, but these didn't challenge him enough to have to avoid. Dean pushed his way right through them, snapping off a bunch of tiny, frozen branches from several of the bushes.

Hurry!

Where is he? Got to find him!

Across another short clearing, down a hill, up a small hill, past a children's playground... Dean felt exasperated. He'd been rushing about for what seemed like an eternity now without any luck. He needed a sign that he was doing the right thing, that he was headed in the right direction, that he was making the right—

Where? Where!

Hurry!

His need for a sign was fulfilled almost as suddenly as it arose.

The sound of loud voices rode the crest of a gust of wind

above the hissing sleet.

He was close. Real close.

$$* * * * * *$$

Bruno glanced at the gun, cold and lifeless in his hand, then at Alain, whose eyes reflected a searing inferno of anger and hatred and bloodthirstiness.

Shoot Peter? He couldn't do that!

Bruno looked at Peter, who had crawled across the ice whimpering at the sight of the gun. He sat crouched in the corner where the concrete seats/stairs abutted the hillside. He had his right arm pulled over his head, covering as much of it as possible. His right leg was pulled up against himself as if he felt it would shield him from any bullet, from death. He peeked over the top of his arm and looked at Bruno with pleading eyes.

He could *never* shoot him. What was Alain talking about? He wasn't a killer.

"I can't," Bruno said, looking away from Peter and trying to hand the Glock back to Alain.

"Shoot him! Now!" Alain said, refusing to grab the gun and instead pointing fiercely at Peter. He picked up the camera and began filming.

"But... But..." Bruno stammered, unable to think quickly.

"No buts! He lost the game! You saw! Don't be a sore sport, Bruno! Do it!"

Alain pointed the camera at Bruno.

Bruno felt his hand holding the gun rise—reflexively—at the tone of Alain's demands. But then something else inside stopped it. His hand shook as if it would be torn apart any moment by the two opposing forces.

"Do it!" Alain shouted, as he lunged at Bruno from behind the camera and slapped him in the face.

Bruno felt a sadness and humiliation welling up inside. His lower lip quivered and his eyes grew wet.

"Do it!" Alain shouted again, slapping the weeping Bruno, causing tears to fly from his face.

"Don't do it!" another voice shouted. It was Peter's.

"Shut up!" Alain screamed at Peter in French, and then turning back on Bruno, "Do it! Shoot him!"

The tension inside Bruno made his face ripple and shake.

And then a thought as blasphemous as that of a dog biting his master streaked through his mind. What if he raised the gun at Alain? Not to shoot him, of course, but just to make him—*help* him—to see his side of the situation.

But what if Alain misunderstood and leapt at him and the gun fired and...

He chased the thought away like a raccoon from the garbage.

But it came back as soon as another humiliating slap stung his face.

"Don't," Bruno said, starting to blubber. "Please don't hit me."

Again a slap.

"Don't, Alain. Please."

"Then do it! Shoot him!"

Bruno looked at Peter and, once again, saw his puppy dog from long ago hiding from Alain in the space between the washer and dryer.

"No... I can't..."

Slap.

"Don't!"

"You will!"

"No!"

Slap.

"Don't do it!" Peter shouted.

"Shut up! Do it!"

"I... I can't!" Tears everywhere. Bruno just wanted to be at home in his big warm bed with his blanket wrapped around him.

Slap. Slap.

Bruno brought the gun up at arms length. He looked at Peter, then Alain.

"Do it! Pull the trigger or I'll beat you like the dog you are!"

"Don't, Bruno! Please!"

How could he shoot his own puppy?

"Please!"

Slap.

"Do it!"

"No, Bruno!"

A rage pushed its way past the shame, the humiliation, the sadness. The gun swung from the left to the right—Alain, Peter, Alain...

"Shoot *him*!" Peter shouted.

"What are you doing?" Alain shouted. "Don't point that thing at me! Shoot *him*!" Alain screamed, slapping Bruno again and then retreating behind the camera lens. "*Him*!"

Bruno couldn't take the pressure and humiliation one moment longer.

He pulled the trigger, then ran.

Chapter 63

A gunshot.

From just beyond a clump of trees and shrubs at the top of the hill to Dean's left.

Even though the sound was a blessing in helping Dean to adjust the direction of his pursuit, he couldn't convince himself that the explosive, cracking sound meant anything but...

But what?

He didn't want to think about it.

Dean struggled halfway up a slippery slope before falling on his face and sliding back down to the bottom. Without thinking, he attacked it again. There was no time to find his way around it. He couldn't lose his place again in the dark and indistinguishable chaos of the island. He was too close.

His second attempt would have proved nearly as ineffectual, if it hadn't been for a well-placed tree branch dangling in front of his face near the top of the slope. He grabbed it and pulled himself up.

Even though he couldn't see much further than ten feet in front, he could sense that he was standing before a large, open field. He wondered if it was the same field he had played a game of touch football one afternoon on with several teenage employees of his. If it was, he remembered that there was a set of stone bleachers built into the side of one of the hills running the length of the field. He slowly stepped into the open area. It seemed slicker here, the ice feeling like the greased surface of a mirror. He groped about in the dark for...

For what?

He didn't want to think about it.

A few steps further and he knew for sure it was the same field he'd played football on. The stone bleachers appeared out of the blackness before him, plated with ice.

Unless the echoes had played games with him, he believed the gunshot had come from around this area. He wanted to call out Peter's name.

He crept slowly along the ice to his right, squinting against the wind and sleet.

A sound caught his attention up ahead, making his stomach twist and the hair on his neck bristle.

Without thinking, he ducked down into a crouch. He didn't know if what he'd heard was made by a human, an animal, or...

Or what?

He didn't want to think about it.

He stood up from his crouch and proceeded—hesitantly. The sound had spooked him, pulling his mind back away from its concerns with the present task at hand and into the whirlpool of *what ifs* that it ordinarily steeped itself in.

Dean checked the stone bleachers and reassured himself

that they were placed into the hill like steps; there was nothing there to hide behind.

Another sound, this time behind him.

It sounded human.

A human suffering.

He inched forward in its direction, cocking his head to one side to better hear through the cacophony of crashes and hisses.

There it was again...

It was between a groan and a howl. And overflowing with sadness. It wasn't loud, but it was continuous. As if the sound possessed a rope that it threw out to all passers-by, Dean pulled himself across the ice toward it. Its volume increased somewhat; he could tell he was getting closer.

His heart drummed. The pounding pain in his knees had ceased. His palms moistened inside his gloves. He slid his tongue across his teeth. They felt as if they had a thin, blemished skin coating them.

Where was the sound coming from? It seemed he was standing right on top of it. Or... Or maybe... Maybe he was imagining the entire thing. Maybe the sound of sadness was coming from inside himself.

No, that was ridiculous. It was obviously coming from somewhere very, very close. Dean scanned the area again.

Focus.

All the time, something scratched his insides raw in protest, not wanting to find what he suspected—what he knew—what he *feared* most would be there in the dark.

His ears scanned the howling wind, then told his eyes to stop at a large tree branch. He stepped forward.

The sound. It was coming from there.

Without thinking, Dean moved to the dark shape on the ground. It was a body. A male body—could be any male body.

The man lay face down, his head turned to the side. Dean's heart slogged away in his throat. He moved the branch, then grabbed the man's far shoulder and gently pulled it towards himself, turning the body over.

He recoiled, wide-eyed. Blood covered the man's face like a mask.

But because it was like a mask, that meant it could be anybody, right? Dean reasoned with himself, his hands shaking as they pulled the injured man—the man who could be *any* man—closer.

That same sorrowful sound rose out of the red mask. It gurgled and then climbed into a soft wail for a second or two, only to fall weakly back into a sloppy gurgle.

Dean gently pulled the injured man—the man who could be *any* man—into his lap. The man protested the move with an agonizing cry. Dean wrapped his arms around the injured man's shoulders, lowered his head down near the injured man's chest—*any* injured man's chest, *any* other injured man's beside *Peter's* chest!—and gently rocked back and forth, saying "shhhhhh" and "it's all right" over and over.

He could feel the man trembling in his arms.

"Shhhhh..."

He felt himself trembling, too. And weeping.

"It's all right... It's all right..."

Dean raised his face to the sky as he continued to rock the whimpering man. He let the viscous sleet tear into his cheeks and mix with the tears that flowed, fast eroding the wall of denial that he'd hastily thrown up when he first saw the body. He had had only time to construct a wall big enough to block out one thing: a name for the person on the ground. And now the tears washed away the wall and let the name come forth in a whisper that belied the vastness of the horror and pain he felt.

"Peter—no," Dean said, nearly choking on the words as his voice cracked and splintered into shards of various emotions and feelings. Hurt, anger, hate, sadness, frustration, panic, out of control, lost and lonely...

Great heaving sobs ripped through Dean's body, nearly cracking him in two. He looked down at Peter's face, whose familiar contours and shapes and creases still showed through the thick mask of blood.

He noticed the blood continuously dripping out the side of Peter mouth.

Dean had been avoiding looking into his brother's eyes... until now. They were less than a third of the way open and showing only the bottom whites.

A sudden surge of electricity seemed to shoot through Peter, forcing his chest to buck. His mouth quickly filled with blood; he gurgled, gagged, then coughed, spurting red droplets into Dean's agonized face.

Dean turned Peter's head to the side to let the blood drain from his mouth. He curled himself forward so he could see Peter's face. His brother's eyes sprang open, fully, and locked with Dean's.

"Peter? Are you all right?" Dean said, at the same time feeling the question was both ridiculous and necessary.

Peter didn't answer. He continued to stare wide-eyed at Dean as though his big brother were a demon.

A wet, ragged sounded from around Peter's head as he tried to move his lips, to speak. That was when Dean saw the dark and gaping hole in Peter' throat.

Dean looked away so as not to scare Peter by his terrified expression.

"What is it, Pete?" Dean said, keeping his eyes averted from his brother's throat. It had been so long since he'd called him anything besides "boy" or "jerk" or "little shit" or "idiot".

Peter tried to say something, but nothing resembling a human speaking voice came out of his mouth.

"I can't understand. I'm sorry," Dean said, feeling the sobs heaving up the front of his body from his stomach.

Peter tried to speak again, but it only made him cough and spit. Dean felt his brother's frustration. Peter closed his eyes tight and started to tremble as though he had a monstrous chill. Dean pulled him close, trying to keep him warm.

Dean found it easier to deal with the situation by concerning himself with his brother's position on his lap, whether his head was properly supported, whether his ungloved hands were covered, warm...

A part of Dean knew that to try and stop the bleeding in the type of wound Peter had on his throat would be...

What?

He didn't want to think about it.

"There. There you go. How's that?" Dean said, trying to keep his voice upbeat and his mind away from confronting the consequences.

Peter's eyes had closed.

"Peter?" Dean said as he tried to literally shake the life back into him. "Peter? Wake up! Peter! Pete! Wake up! Pete! Please!"

Peter's eyes snapped wide open and blinked. Dean put his face close to Peter's both so he could see his brother's eyes well, and so his head would shield his brother's face from the sleet. Dean followed what they signaled with mixed emotions. He already pined for their playful banter.

Quick blink, long blink, long blink...

Dean held every blinked letter in his mind until the next one and the next one was signaled, until he could string them together and form a word. It was as if Peter had the most important things in the world to say to him and he didn't want to waste a single second.

Quick blink, quick blink, long blink...

H-E-

His eyes looked as though they were fluttering, they were blinking so fast.

H-E-A-R-D-A...

Dean tried to sound it out in his head as Peter signaled, but it wasn't until his brother had finished with the last word that Dean could make sense of it. Then it all came together in an instant.

H-E-A-R-D A S-C-O-P-E, Peter had blinked, raising his eyebrows as best he could at the end to show it was question. And then managing to crack a shaky, half-smile, his teeth glowing white next to the crust of dark blood slicking his face.

Heard of Scope?

A sob quaked through Dean's body again.

Never had his baby brother's teasing sounded so good.

Chapter 64

What did I do? What did I do? What did I do? What...

Bruno couldn't get the image of Peter's terrified face out of his mind. How could he have shot him? He had looked just like his puppy with those eyes pleading for forgiveness, for mercy, for one more chance. But there couldn't be one more chance. Alain had wanted the job done right then and there. So... he'd done it. But why? Why? Why! Why did Alain make him do such bad things!

He hoped Peter was all right. Even though Bruno had turned and run as he was squeezing the trigger, he knew he'd hit the kid. A bit of bad luck had been the real perpetrator, because Bruno wasn't trying to inflict a mortal wound—and he was even hoping to have missed Peter all together. But he didn't miss—damn intrusive bad luck. If he had been really trying to hit him, he would have missed for sure. But because he wasn't aiming, wasn't even *wanting* to hit Peter, he ended up striking the poor guy in a place that would have scored *beaucoup* points in a Nintendo game. Stomach shots, heart shots, throat shots, head shots... these were what gave the most points and brought the enemy down the fastest.

Poor Peter, poor guy.

When a jocund Alain finally caught up to Bruno after he had shot and run, for an instant Bruno had had the same desire as earlier to turn the gun on his friend.

Poor Peter, poor guy.

But when Alain told Bruno that what he'd done was good, really good, Bruno's perilous plan was immediately discarded.

Poor, poor—

Good Bruno.

"Where are we going now?" Bruno asked Alain, whom he went from fleeing to following.

"Down by the river."

"What are we going to do down there?"

"Wouldn't you like to know."

"Look for the other guy?"

"We *could* do that. Or..."

"Or what?"

"Or I could kill you."

Bruno laughed at Alain's joke.

"I'm serious."

"Come on, Alain. Stop that."

"Well, you're going to kill your*self*, I should say. Like the good doggy you are."

"That isn't funny. You're scaring me. Stop it."

"All right. I'll stop. For now. But soon enough the subject will come up again."

That Alain! What a kidder! He's always teasing. How could he possibly kill me after what I just did for him? I'm good Bruno. Alain told me what I did was good. I'm not a good doggy—I'm good Bruno. I do everything I'm told. And as long as I do, Alain would never want me gone. Besides, he says I'm going to kill myself. That's... That's just silly! A real silly joke—ha ha. Kill myself? That's a laugh out loud joke—ha ha ha! How could I possibly kill myself? I don't want to die. I have Alain's friendship to live for.

Bruno laughed out loud as he thought of Alain's joke. His friend sure knew how to make him feel better. He'd almost forgotten about Peter. Killing himself was the craziest thing he'd ever heard. The idea that someone could be *that* obedient, that spineless!

If they weren't moving so fast through the park, he would have doubled over in laughter.

But instead he found himself furtively wiping half-frozen tears from his cheeks with a trembling hand, as though he were a junkie who'd just come to the realization that the drug he'd relied on for so long to give him temporary tastes of living was now one hit away from giving him eternal death.

Chapter 65

Alain couldn't bring himself to be too pleased with everything. Bruno had given him a lot of trouble when it came time to shoot Peter. And Alain swore he saw a Bruno considering whether or not to shoot him, his maniacal master.

That was the final straw. Now it was time to get rid of the ass. He was dead weight. *Dangerous*, dead weight.

Alain thought it would be a fabulous and fitting ending to Bruno's life, as well as to his epic Christmas music-filled movie if he could force Bruno—no, make Bruno—no, *command* Bruno to commit suicide in front of the camera. Bruno had taken other people's lives on Alain's command, so why not his own?

Alain could barely contain himself at the thought of the power surge he'd receive when he pulled Bruno's strings like a marionette one last and insurmountably great time. All that would be missing was the appropriate music to go along with the moment. He'd have to dub it in during postproduction. Perhaps *I'm Getting Nuttin' for Christmas*, with the stupid scrotum sac gasping his last breath in the middle of the song's chorus.

"What are we going to do down by the river?" Bruno asked again. He obviously didn't believe Alain's deadly intentions. Alain knew he wouldn't—that's why he'd said it. It was fun to toy with the oaf and watch him sweat and move his lips while he silently talked to himself.

It excited Alain to think that he was both insane enough to want to kill his friend and powerful enough to get his friend to do himself in. How many serial killers could put *that* on their resume?

"Are we going to do something fun down there?" Bruno persisted.

"Yeah, something fun," Alain said, annoyed by Bruno's questions, but at the same time trying desperately not to upset the shithead by snapping at him. He was going to need Bruno—the cocaine-less Bruno—to be more comfortable and trusting of him than ever before.

That's why he was letting Bruno continue to hold both of the guns, even after that dangerous look he'd had in his eye earlier. How could anything bad happen if Bruno was the one with the guns, right?

Alain decided to try a joke out on Bruno. Laughter always seemed to calm the ol' raw rectum down.

"Hey, Bruno, did you hear about the whore who had her appendix taken out and then after started making a lot of money on the side?"

Bruno gave a little laugh, but nothing like Alain was hoping for.

"How about the whore that takes this guy up to her room only to find out that her period has just started. She's embarrassed and feels bad for the guy, so she asks him if he wants a drink. 'Who the hell you think I am, whore, Dracula?'"

Again, Bruno laughed softly—and even more insincerely than the first time.

"What the hell is your problem?" Alain shouted, finding it hard to control himself.

"What?"

"Why are so serious all of a sudden?"

"I'm sorry. I... I'm just a little scared. I don't know whether you're serious about killing me, Alain."

"Of *course* I'm serious! I *told* you I was serious, didn't I?" Alain was risking a lot by refusing to backpedal. But only to gain so much.

Bruno seemed to weigh each word of Alain's response on his rusted scales of discrimination, trying to detect if and to what degree each of the words was loaded with double meaning.

Alain held his breath, wondering if he'd gone too far.

"Oh, I get it," Bruno finally said. "This is like you always do—you try and scare me so I don't want to go, and then you get mad at me and call me names, and then I force myself to go because I don't want you to be mad at me anymore— but I still don't really want to go because I'm still scared— and then you make fun of me and how scared I am the whole time and... and..."

Oh, he is so stupid!

"Yeah, I don't know how you saw through to my real intentions, but you did," Alain said, trying his best to sound impressed. "Let's go."

They moved across what was a parking lot on a summer day. As they stepped out of the lot and carefully inched their way down a steep hill, Alain squinted his eyes against the sleet to see through some of the spaces between the crystal chandelier-like tree branches. He couldn't see the Saint

Laurent, but he could see bits of the city lit up here and there, across the river. He wondered what all the people with lights on were doing? Watching TV? Fucking? Thanking God that He chose their family to have electricity instead of their neighbors?

The thought of God brought Alain's eyes up to search for a familiar landmark: the Cross. Between a dangerously heavy oak branch above and a leaning pine below, Alain saw the Cross. It glowed. It still had power, of course. The people down below without electricity might freeze to death, but as long as they could look to the top of the mountain and find their comforting symbol of eternity, hypothermia was a non-issue.

Fools.

Alain often told himself there was no God. He did so because he believed that if there were a God, and if He *were* so great, why would he have created someone as incredibly evil and insane as Alain? Alain could never see past that point—mainly because he couldn't see past the idea that there was anything, divine or not, greater than his insanity.

The two killers made it down to the bottom of one hill, only to find themselves atop another. The last before reaching the amusement park's parking lot beside the river.

Alain could now see the Saint Laurent—or at least the space where he knew it lay—below him. It looked like a great, bottomless, snaking, pitch-black pit had been torn into the earth. As his eyes traveled along its length, he saw a spot in the river that was illuminated. Alain's eyes followed the light up away from the ice, fearing for a moment—but only a moment—that it was the great God that he'd always refused to believe in beginning His descent from the heavens to pay retribution. The light seemed to be made of a vibrating substance, caused by the billions of droplets of half-frozen water passing through its rays. Alain's eyes arrived at the source of the light: the Durango. It still dangled from the Jacques Cartier bridge, its dark body easily mistakable for a worker's platform.

"Okay, we're here. So what did you want to bring me all the way down here for?" Bruno said.

"We're not there, yet."

"You have a surprise for me all the way down *there*?" Bruno said, pointing towards the shore.

"It's no surprise. I told you what I have in store for you."

"Stop teasing, Alain. Stop it."

The stupid oaf-assed bastard is getting way too pushy!

"Let's go down to the river."

"Well... All right. But I'm going only because I don't really believe you. I mean, I may believe you just a little bit—and that's what's making me a little scared right now—but I really do trust you, Alain."

"As well you should."

"I know you would *never* hurt me."

He wasn't sure why, but Alain suddenly didn't want to wait until they got down by the shore. He wanted Bruno and all his nonsense gone from his life *immediately*. No waiting. Hell, he'd even take care of it himself and *not* film it, that's how desperate he was.

But that would be compromising, wouldn't it? And he really didn't want to settle. This was going to be his greatest accomplishment ever. He might never have another opportunity like this again. He couldn't settle.

Life was far too precious to settle.

Chapter 66

M-U-C-H 2 S-A-Y.

Peter's shorthand blinking was difficult to decipher. Dean had to repeat what he thought was being said—sometimes several times—to be sure he understood.

"You have a lot to tell me? Is that what you're saying?" Dean said, sniffling often to try and hide the sobs wanting to explode from him.

Peter nodded.

Dean didn't know what to say. He had a lot he wanted to talk to Peter about as well. But their time was fast running out.

"I had a lot to tell you," Dean said. "But where to begin?"

I-M-P-O-R-T, Peter blinked, and then raised his eyebrows signaling it was a question.

"What's important?" Dean translated.

Nod.

"What do I have to tell you that's important?"

The circumstances invested that question with a stirring significance it never would have had if asked in the midst of daily routine. Looking down at his dying brother, Dean realized that very little of what he'd thought important earlier seemed worth wasting precious time on now. The present moment was made all the more agonizing for Dean, though, by the fact that so many wasted moments between him and Peter had preceded it.

Why couldn't I have been a bigger man back then? What was I so goddamn scared of? Back then I was scared to bridge the gap between us and now I'm scared that I'll never have the chance to do what I was always scared to do! It's insane—

—how easily fear fits into the various clothes of circumstance. Only to ruin them, one and all.

J-U-S T-L-K

"Just talk?"

Nod.

"Problem is, so much of what I wanted to say before, now seems..." Dean's voice drifted off.

I N-O

"You know."

T-L-K H-A-R-T

"Talk ha— Oh, talk from the heart, right?"

Nod.

Dean had to double-check that it was Peter—the punk—who'd just said that.

"Okay... You know... When I look there..." Dean started to choke up, knowing what he felt was a dam of emotion ready to burst. "When I look there, all I see is... love."

M-E 2

The tears flowed in full force. Dean lowered his head next to Peter's. "I love you, Peter," he whispered in his ear.

It was the first time he'd ever said that to him.

Peter coughed hard. Blood sputtered from his lips, some of it hitting Dean in the face. Dean gagged, but not from the blood hitting him. He gagged because of his inability to help his brother. There was no way to relieve Peter's suffering— or his own.

Except...

I am now.

Dean said those words to himself several times as he tried to comfort Peter. He suddenly felt the most amazing thing. He felt his awareness expanding to a point where it didn't feel boxed in, cornered even, by the onslaught of painful emotions. He felt as if he were witnessing the goings on both inside and outside himself from the deepest, most essential part of his being. A part of his being that lovingly embraced all, yet remained powerfully unaffected by all.

It was with this level of awareness that Dean found the quiet strength to express some much needed humor as he stared at death in the bloodied face of his brother.

I L-O-V-E U 2, Peter blinked up at Dean.

"Sure, their early stuff is great, but they've gone progressively down hill since *Joshua Tree*," Dean said, referring to the rock group U2.

Peter's body shook, and Dean though he was having a seizure. But in soon became apparent that it was a laugh.

N-E-E-D T-H-A-T, Peter blinked, his eyes glistening with tears. L-I-K-E T-H-I-S

"You like this?"

Nod.

"Me, too."

W-I-S-H M-O-R-E

Dean's stomach twisted as the thought of all those wasted moments throughout the years fought its way into his mind.

"Don't say we won't have more moments like this."

N-O

"Please. Don't say that," Dean said, his expanded awareness fast collapsing in on itself and focusing squarely on the growing sense of panic. "I can get you out of here and to a hospital."

N-O

Dean started to lift Peter off of his lap with the intention of picking him up and carrying him. Peter gurgled and groaned so intensely, Dean stopped.

N-O, Peter blinked, looking as if it took every drop of energy he possessed to open his eyes wide for emphasis.

"Oh, God, no. Oh, God. Don't leave me. I love you so much," Dean cried, his head falling forward onto Peter's chest. "Why did I wait so fucking long?" He clutched Peter to himself and sobbed uncontrollably. "What was I protecting?"

Dean felt that life up to that moment had been some type of game of which he'd never possessed the directions, rules, and helpful hints. Instead, he'd just kept fumbling and bumbling, trying to figure out what to do with all the pieces on the board before him.

If fate would only give him and his brother a second chance.

Pleeeeeeeeeze... For God's sake, pleeeeeeeeeeeeeeeze!

I am now, I am now, I am now, Dean said to himself, desperately trying to use the mantra to medicate his mental anguish. But this time they were only words.

His intensifying desire for deliverance stood in the way.

Chapter 67

A-F-R-A-I-D, Peter signaled to Dean, as he shivered.

"I'm here for you, buddy," Dean said, pulling Peter close to him. "I'll protect you."

Peter appreciated his brother's efforts, but it wasn't helping much. What Peter was afraid of, Dean couldn't make disappear, no matter how much he hugged and squeezed and claimed he could beat up the bad guys.

Peter didn't know how it was possible, but the world around seemed to grow darker.

"I wish we could start all over again."

Peter nodded as best he could. He felt so weak. Insubstantial. He felt as if he were a piece of sleet melting and mixing into the surrounding swirling world of disparate elements.

The endless creaking of the weighted trees and the hissing sound of the sleet were suddenly so loud, he could barely hear Dean. The wound didn't hurt any more. He was surprised Bruno had shot him. He'd thought for sure the guy was going to turn the gun on Alain. When the bullet hit, though, he knew he'd been hurt bad. In the throat—how *couldn't* he have been hurt bad? But did that mean he was going to die?

What did that mean, "die"? He was too young to have ever given the concept any serious thought. Sure, he'd seen it happen a million times on television and even a few times that night, but those had been *other* people. Their deaths hadn't given him a clue as to what it was like or what it meant, or even an acceptance that it would happen to him someday, too.

But was he dying? It seemed to be happening so easily— too easily—for such a troubling concept.

D-I-E, he signaled to Dean, raising his eyebrows as high as possible in order to show it was a question and not a command.

Dean's eyes leaked again. That was the only answer Peter needed. Dean spoke, but most of what he said was drowned out by the loudening world around Peter.

The features on Dean's face grew darker by the second. Reading his lips became next to impossible. His eyes, though, seemed to shine brighter than the rest of him.

B-L-I-N-K, Peter signaled to Dean.

"What? Why?"

Instead of signaling the word "blink" out again, Peter rapidly opened and closed his eyes, hoping Dean got the point.

He did. D-O-N—, Dean started to signal.

C-L-O-S-E-R, Peter interrupted, wanting Dean to put his face closer so he could see his eyes. They were fading so fast. Everything, fading—

—so fast. So much sooner than expected. Dean put his

face so close to Peter, their noses were nearly touching.

D-O-N-T G-O, Dean signaled. Several tears rolled out of his eyes, slid down to the tip of his nose, then seemed to reach out into empty space, closing the gap between the brothers until they finally connected. The tears gently dripped off both sides of Dean's nose and onto Peter's, where they descended to the corners of each of the young man's eyes.

As everything grew darker around Peter, he felt very light-headed. His entire body tingled and vibrated. It wasn't an entirely unpleasant sensation, but it was frightening because he knew in his ever-slowing heart that these sensations were a sign—*the* sign—that he was about to embark on a profound, uncharted journey. A one-way journey, perhaps, that might absorb him into permanent nothingness like a sponge soaking up a drop of water or zap him through a wormhole to a different universe. Or perhaps it was simply the next stage of a long running cycle right here on Earth. A cycle Joseph had often talked about in great detail, much to Peter's delight and dismay. Joseph's descriptions were of realms where ego's shields and weapons such as greed and pride and fear and hatred would fast become the very incarnate substances of hell.

Still, it was something that only supposed to happen to others. Never himself.

Until...

"You'll want to merge with God," Joseph had said, "but it will require you to let go of every concept you have of yourself and die completely. That's what the *I am now* practice is supposed to begin to help you do, to see through the ego, to *die* to the ego. In a way, it takes a lifetime of practice to prepare for a good death. Most don't realize, though, that every moment we die and are reborn. Every moment we have a chance to let go and finally recognize, finally become that which we've *always* been looking for. What have you done in your life to prepare your spirit for your death, Peter?"

Or maybe Jesus was going to meet Peter, his grizzled beard blowing in the wind like a kite tail as he rode a flaming chariot pulled by seven snow-white stallions down from the heavens... with a glowing yellow taxi sign hovering above the Divine One's head in place of a halo...

All of these thoughts and memories—some sublime, some ridiculous—raced through Peter's mind like a film set on high speed, but none filled him with the sense of comfort he craved. Instead, as his thoughts began to fail him, he suddenly understood how little comfort they were *ever* able to offer him. How thoughts were as strong and substantial as an actual strip of film; resistant to the occasional tug and twist against its integrity, but otherwise flimsy and weak and often useless when attempting to support the weight of an individual's most profound and important problems—like an impending death.

"Don't go. Don't leave me. I'll be a better brother—I promise," a voice said, somehow finding its way through the static and hum.

"Let go and let things be," another voice suddenly said, this one clearer and louder than the first. And female. And familiar. Maybe Linda's. Maybe his mother's.

"Peter! Peter!" Peter recognized this voice as Dean's. It was sounding fainter than before, but it had no direction external to himself. Instead, it seemed to have risen from the center of his ever-expanding being.

But what was happening to him suddenly felt so right, he couldn't bear the thought of even *trying* to go back. Not even to try and say a better goodbye to Dean. None of that seemed to matter anymore. For some reason he knew Dean would be all right, no matter what happened to him. And for some reason he knew that his mother was all right and his father was all right and Linda and Joseph were all right and that he would be all right if he just let go and—

—dissolved.

And then for the briefest instant, he could see again. Except, this time, it was a type and quality of vision lying somewhere between a lucid dream and wakefulness. He could see that he was slowly rising above himself—or the now lifeless body that once housed his spirit—which Dean cradled in his arms, apparently oblivious to the fact that it now belonged more to the Earth's bacteria than to his baby brother. Peter felt neither the sleet falling nor the wind gusting, even though he could see they were as strong as ever. Instead what he felt was himself expanding as he rose like helium mixing with the sky. He briefly wished he could lower himself and touch Dean's shoulder to let him know that he was fine, but found himself instead rising up and away from the scene faster and faster and towards a bright, vibrating light above.

Dean, and Peter's former body, were soon half their original size, then the size of dogs, then the size of ants, then the size of grains of sand...

Peter tried to yell goodbye to Dean, but by that time everything he had been and known had vanished, leaving him to be more than he ever could have known was possible, dissolved into a ever-present light that was at once everything and nothing.

Chapter 68

Gone.

Even though the tears flowed freely from his eyes, Dean felt an unusual—even unsettling—calm in his chest as he watched his brother take his last breath.

Gone forever.

But the calm didn't last for long. As he felt it burn off like morning fog on a lake, he scratched and clawed to keep it from completely disappearing. But the harder he tried, the more easily it slipped through his fingers—and the more intense its replacement, rage, grew.

Rage at the losers that had done this to Peter, rage at himself for not being there in time—along with everything that he'd done or not done that he had gotten them into this deadly situation in the first place—rage at God for having created death, even rage at death for not being more discriminating in choosing the latest occupant of its distant domain.

Around and around his head this rage buzzed, harassing

him like a horsefly, trying desperately to get him to commit to it, to chase it, to obsess over it, to try and grab hold of it and never let go. But Dean fought the urge. And as a consequence, the urge intensified; rage buzzed louder, demanding more of his attention.

Dean gently laid Peter's body down on the ice. Although most of his face was swallowed in darkness, Dean could make out a look of peace—a soft smile—stretched across the young man's lips. Rather than comfort Dean, though, it made the rage's harassing buzz deafening. Dean felt a deep, aching longing to see that dead smile on his brother's face bend and stretch into a grin of joy, followed by a belly-busting fit of laughter.

But it would never happen.

Gone.

And buzz of rage would soon shred his eardrums.

Dean stumbled away from Peter's body, walking like a stiff-legged zombie, due both to his frozen, weak, cramped knees and to the fury that numbed his mind. He headed only where the lay of the land and his feet and the elements took him, leaving behind the body, but carrying close to his heart an album of snapshots of his beloved brother; most of which would have caused him to smile, to giggle, to howl with laughter any other day.

Peter's face and body spotted red with chicken pox...

Peter talking tough about his ability to ride the Rotor at Riverside Park and not feel a thing... and then vomiting in the trash for an hour afterward... .

Peter trying to tackle Dean by his ankles in a one-on-one game of football, only to be dragged across the lawn for twenty yards until he was covered with dirt and grass stains and tears of laughter... .

Buzz... Buzz...

Peter and Dean blinking to each other across the dinner table, calling their father every name in the book, trying to make the other laugh so he'd have some explaining to do to daddy dork...

Buzz... Buzz...

Each snapshot seemed to multiply exponentially the number of harassing horseflies of rage buzzing in his mind. Dean fought them, swatted at them to get away, to leave him alone with his fond memories, but it only intensified their attack. He stumbled through a spinney of oaks and birches in a daze, grabbing a loose, frozen, three-foot length of fallen branch as he passed through and swinging it above his head like a staff, as if trying to defend himself from some invisible, harassing phantom. He cracked the branch hard against the nearest tree, once—

—twice—

—a third time, growling like a savage bear, not caring if anyone heard him, as the stick exploded into several jagged, frozen fragments. The three-foot branch was suddenly reduced to a mere foot in length, but it didn't stop Dean from attacking the innocent tree.

Buzzzzzzzzzzz...

He took a step closer and began battering the tree trunk on its right side with a barrage of forehands, followed by a series of swift backhands to its left side. Each blow, a blow against fate. He tried to punish fate as it had just punished him, trying to *at least* get it to apologize for the mistake it had just made.

But no apology came. Only the grunts and growls of his anguished soul could be heard above the storm.

Soon the remaining section of the branch disintegrated in Dean's bloodied hands. But not his rage. He continued to act—react—without thought; his expression was as pure as it had ever been. He backed away from the tree, turned, and part-ran, part-stumbled, part-slid down the hill he'd been standing on, screaming his lungs raw. Unable to stop or turn, he crashed into the trunk of a birch as though it were a linebacker blocking his path, bounced off, then continued barreling straight down the hill, paying no attention to the shrubs and thickets he burst through as he built speed.

Amazingly, Dean kept his balance most of the way down the glare ice hill. But it only postponed the inevitable. A fallen tree branch caught Dean by both of his ankles like a safety making a superb open field tackle, sending him flying face forward and onto his stomach. He crashed through several fallen branches, which shattered on impact, the pieces following his descent.

One protruding stick imbedded deeply in ice refused to break,though, when Dean plowed over it. It scratched across his face, very nearly gouging his eye as it traced a path from the inside edge of his right eyebrow, along the side of his nose and over his lips. He tasted blood, but didn't know if it came from a tear in his lip or a front tooth ripped from its foundation—or both.

The physical pain he felt in his face helped diminish his emotional torment. Perhaps because physical pain was something he was more familiar with, more drawn to if given a choice between dealing with that or dealing with a troubled soul. Or perhaps it was because the physical pain tore him out of his soul's domain, where the future is often woven out of the threads of the past, and placed him squarely in the here and now, where there were no killers, no storm, no dead brother or co-workers—only agonizing flesh.

When Dean's sliding descent finally stopped, he slowly turned over onto his back, opened his eyes, and squinted against the sleet up into the sky at what the few remaining lights from the nearby city illuminated. He saw a dark gray, thick covering of low-altitude clouds. They seemed to swirl and bubble as they passed by, like a river covered in glutinous, boiling oil. His eyes swept across the sky, searching for Peter's spirit, which he imagined was stuck somewhere above, looking for an escape hole in the clouds.

Blood collected in the back of Dean's throat.

He rolled to his side and spit. No teeth came out. He took off his glove and put his hand to his mouth, first checking his front teeth—which were still all there—followed by his lip. Stars shot across his mind's eye as he touched what was a cut running vertically from just above his upper lip, through his bottom lip to the top of his chin bone. Even though he didn't have a mirror, Dean could tell the cut was deep, slicing through his entire lower lip. He tried to spit the accumulating blood out of his mouth again, but the intense pain made it impossible.

He pulled himself onto his feet—no easy task since both his knees felt like pummeled veal chops—and squinted to see if he could recognize where he was. It took all of a second. His location was unmistakable. Around him was a large parking lot—the amusement park's main lot. Behind him was the hill he'd just come down. To his left stretched the parking lot, disappearing into the darkness several yards away. To the right, the same, except for the haunting, majestic form of the two-humped Jacques Cartier bridge. Straight ahead lay several yards of the parking lot, beyond which flowed the Saint Laurent river.

Dean couldn't believe how far he'd traveled in his rage. He felt physically spent, resulting in a contradicting combination of physical feelings. His head itself felt it was going to fly away like a helium balloon, but according to his rubbery neck, it seemed full of rocks rather than gas. His torn lip felt closed tight due to the swelling, but the blood that continued to drip from his chin demonstrated otherwise. And his limbs felt an odd mix of limpness and rigidity, as if he'd just played a three-overtime playoff game and had carried the ball over a hundred times...

Around the outside or up the middle?

The question came out of nowhere and was spoken not so much in his father's voice as his own voice representing his father's—as it had always been. It made him shiver. His eyes drifted towards the Saint Laurent and across it, and rose above the cityscape along the river to the pitch-black shadow of the mountain framing it from behind. Atop the mountain, Dean could see the orange Radio Canada tower, its lights powered by a generator, still shining a warning to air travelers. And just to the left of that, the Cross, the lights nailed along the edge of its body, illuminating its shape for everyone in the city below to take solace in.

Rain or shine, God didn't take any breaks.

Dean shuffled stiffly towards what looked like a miniature lighthouse sitting on the raised and rocky shore above the Saint Laurent. He'd seen it several times before when he'd come to the island—even walked up and examined it, and concluded it must have once been some sort of a signal tower for the boats coming up the river, to warn them where the island's coast lay. He remembered there being a small room in the center of the fifteen-foot high structure. The room had been spray-painted with all sorts of political graffiti and was missing a wall, exposing it to the elements, but he hoped it would offer him at least some shelter from the bad weather— and a hiding place from Alain and Bruno—until morning.

As Dean approached the structure from the west side, he heard voices. He could tell they were close, but the ceaselessly stormy elements made it hard to pinpoint where they were coming from. He felt exposed standing out in the open in the parking lot, so he scurried as quickly as he could toward the lighthouse. The voices seemed to be coming from all sides—he couldn't be sure he was moving away or towards them. He pressed his body against the lighthouse's six-foot-high stone foundation.

The voices were closer than ever.

Assuming they were coming from somewhere in the shadows of the parking lot, Dean started to shuffle around the lighthouse's foundation, away from the parking lot and towards the river.

The voices grew louder, not necessarily because of proximity but because the tone of the conversation changed, becoming more argumentative. Even combative.

Dean continued to slowly move around the base of the lighthouse.

Louder.

One voice was pleading. Another was shouting orders.

A swirl of wind suddenly carried the voices away so they seemed to be on the other side of the island. Dean relaxed, only to have the wind change, bringing the voices close again. He tensed.

Another sliding step. Then another.

The voices flew far away on the wind. Then near. Then far. Then near.

Step.

Then nearer.

Step.

Then very near.

Then so near, Dean could have reached out and touched the tongues from which the voices had been born. Literally.

Alain and Bruno stood behind the little lighthouse, on the shore of the Saint Laurent.

Chapter 69

Alain had had enough of Bruno, enough of the stupid questions, the constant companionship, the dog-like obedience. And besides, taking care of Bruno interfered with his insanity. An insane person was supposed to act impulsively and irrationally. Alain believed Bruno's presence kept him from flying, from truly going beyond himself. He was frustrated at being the idiot's babysitter. Sure, he'd be losing a pair of helping hands and what began as a promising killer's signature, but Alain believed he'd be gaining so much more if he were a single slayer.

And gaining more badness was never bad. It was basic math.

The decision had been made... The time had come...

Alain snatched both guns out of Bruno's coat pockets. He threw one away into the distant darkness and pointed the other at his lumbering lackey. Alain told Bruno to drown himself in the river. He hummed *Silent Night* as he watched Bruno's face alternately expand and constrict in reaction to his insane order.

Alain believed that if he could get Bruno to kill himself, it would be the perfect conclusion to their twisted relationship—as well as his monstrous murder movie.

"W-W-What are you talking about?" Bruno said, backing away from Alain and toward the river behind him. He stopped at its shoreline. "D-D-Drown myself? I-I-I'm not going to do *that*?"

"Oh, yes you are."

"Are you crazy? Why would I do that?" Bruno said, snickering nervously.

"Drown yourself in the river *now*, Bruno," Alain said, pointing the Glock at his head to make sure he knew it was no joke.

"Alain! Alain... B-B-But I thought we were friends!"

"Friends! We *are* friends! Think of this as a *favor* I'm doing for you."

"A favor?"

"Yeah. Like putting down a dog when it's sick."

"Sick? But I'm not—"

"Oh, but you *are*," Alain said, feeling himself so unchallenged by Bruno's slow-mo thought processing. "We *all* are sick to some degree. The only thing that separates those who succumb to their sickness from those that find a way to live with it is adaptation."

"Adap-what?" Bruno said, his wide-eyed face blank with incomprehension.

"I embrace my sickness. And, to be fair, to a lesser degree, I think you embrace your own, as well. But, see, your sickness is stupidity. Mine is boredom. I don't think you can ever let go of your stupidity and change and move where my need for excitement takes me."

"Change? I-I-I can *try* and change, Alain. I can change.

I'm always willing to change. For you. I'd do *anything* for you, Alain!"

"Bah! I don't need someone to kiss my ass and cut up my victims anymore. I'm through with that useless child's play."

"I-I-I can hotwire you cars and drive you around. You-Y-Y-You're always gonna need *that*."

"Pathetic, Bruno. Really pathetic. You see what different levels we're on. That may be enough for you, but I need much *more* than that. I used to think you helped define me—and you did, for awhile—but that's old news now. "

"What's old news?"

"See! Stupidity! Go drown yourself, slave! I *command* you! Sacrifice yourself for your master—and make sure you splash around a lot so it looks good for the camera."

"No! I won't! I want to understand, Alain! I want to be your friend! Forever! Like we always talked about!"
Bruno began to cry.

Alain took a step closer to Bruno and the barrel of the gun to his forehead.

Bruno closed his eyes and raised his arms above his head as if he were surrendering to the police. "Please. Please don't," he said. "I love you, Alain. Please don't make me."

"You're sounding like a fag. In the river. Walk until you fall in. It'll be funny. I'll get a good laugh. You know how you like to make me laugh, right? Right!"

"Right. I like to make you laugh."

"You might even make it onto one of those funny video shows. Don't you want to be a celebrity?"

"I want to be with *you*!"

"No! I want you to want to be a celebrity!" Alain shouted as he pushed the Glock's barrel into Bruno's forehead.

Alain could hear the rusty wheels in Bruno's brain trying

to grind out a reason why this wasn't a good idea. But the dope couldn't generate anything other than a couple of false starts at a response, followed by a seemingly resigned sigh and then a torrent of tears and snot and blubbering.

"In the river," Alain said, unmoved by the show of emotion. "Turn and walk."

"But Alain... I don't want to go!"

"In the river!"

"Alain!"

"Shut up! The more you think about it, the more painful it will be. Don't think, do."

"Alain!"

"River, Bruno! Or else I'll shoot you right here on its banks. And that won't make me laugh like watching you drown will. You like to make me laugh, don't you? You want me to have a nice video, huh? Turn and walk into the river—now!"

Bruno turned away from Alain and faced the Saint Laurent. He started to move towards the ice flows packed against its banks, and Alain did what he could to contain his surprise and excitement at how easy this was going to be.

"That's it. That's a good boy. Now you're being smart. Turn around and wave to the camera once. Good! That's it. See, you're making me happy. That's what you want, right?"

Silence.

At the edge of the river, Bruno gingerly put one foot out onto the ice, which was relatively flat, unbroken, and unscarred by the river's current.

"That's it. Keep going. Find any place you want to drown yourself in," Alain said. And then added more to himself than to Bruno: "Fucking idiot."

Bruno didn't take another step. Instead he took his foot off the surface of the frozen river and turned to face Alain.

A fierceness filled Bruno's eyes, a fierceness Alain had never seen before. Alain shivered.

"Don't stop! Keep going! Be a good boy."

"No!" Bruno said. The fierceness vanished as quickly and mysteriously as it had arrived. A little boy was left in its place. Bruno folded his arms across his chest and pouted. "I *won't* do it!"

"What did you say?"

"I *won't* do it!"

"Oh, yes you will!"

"No I won't! I'm tired of you pushing me around, Alain! And I'm tired of you hurting people! I don't want people to hurt! And I'm sick of you calling me an idiot! I'm *not* an idiot! I'm smart!"

"What, are you going to stand there and throw a tantrum? Daddy's got a big pacifier for baby to suck on if that's what he wants," Alain said, and he stepped forward and held the gun within an inch of Bruno's lips.

"I could grab that from you *so* easy," Bruno said, radiating a confidence that was unusual, odd, eerie.

"That would be a very stupid thing to do, Bruno. Very stupid. You don't want to be stupid, do you? You're smart, like you said, right?"

"That's right!"

"So do the smart thing and turn around and walk."

Bruno's eyes suddenly widened. Alain wanted to believe that it was a look of compliance that he was seeing, that Bruno knew he was outmatched in every respect, and might as well acquiesce. But Bruno's next words challenged everything.

"Turn around quick, Alain! Look!" Bruno said, pointing over Alain's shoulder at something in the distance.

Alain didn't turn. "I'm not falling for that one, you idiot.

Get going!"

"No, look! He's coming!"

"That's the oldest one in the book, you—"

But before Alain could end his sentence with another insult, something came crashing down on the forearm of his gun hand, sending the weapon, followed by the camera, falling to the icy shoreline.

Two steely arms snaked under each of Alain's armpits, came across each side of his chest and then found their way to the back of his neck, where hands locked together to form an unbreakable full-nelson wrestling hold.

Alain could only gasp in horror as he watched Bruno quickly bend down and pick up the gun.

As Bruno stood up, Alain could see fierceness sliced into his face like a scary jack 'o' lantern carving. And burning behind it, Alain feared, was a searing hot desire for some painful payback.

Chapter 70

"How does it feel to be trapped and helpless, huh?" Dean shouted into the back of Alain's head. Rage surged through his body so strongly, he wanted to tear Alain's head from his body.

Alain grunted, but didn't give any sense that Dean was causing him great pain. This motivated Dean to push Alain's neck harder—but not so hard that Alain's head and body bent forward enough to make Dean an easy target for Bruno, who stood in front of them, pointing the Glock in their direction.

"*Descend-le!*"

"English! Speak English you sonofabitch!" Dean shouted. Although he knew it was ridiculous, he was overflowing with so much rage that even the French language, his difficulty in learning it, and the awkwardness that he'd suffered trying to fit in with its people seemed as much to blame for this night of horrors as anything else.

"*J'comprends pas.*"

"You understand. You gave it away more than once tonight. Speak it! Now! Or I'll break your fucking neck so fast! Understand *that*?" Dean wrenched Alain's neck far to the right, causing him finally to shout in pain.

"All right, all right!" Alain said, in English—a near flawless English. "Just don't hurt me."

"Not too bad for a sonofabitch that doesn't understand." Dean peeked over Alain's left shoulder to see Bruno. He didn't know what possessed him to say these next words, but they were the first ones to come out of his mouth. "You're free now, Bruno. Free of this sadistic bastard's control. You can put down the gun."

Bruno didn't budge from his ready-to-fire stance.

"What, are you two *friends*?" Alain said.

"Don't talk unless *I'm* talking to you!" Dean said. "I saw the way you talk to him, the way you treat him. I know about your type, how you live off others. Feed off their fear."

"I don't know what you're talking about. Bruno and I are best of friends. Aren't we, Bruno?"

Silence. Bruno's hands and arms trembled as he aimed the gun.

"You'll have to excuse him. He doesn't understand or speak English as well as I do."

"Yeah, well, you better hope that's his *only* problem because he looks like he's aiming that gun at you," Dean said.

"Don't be ridiculous! He's aiming it at *you*. He just doesn't have a clear shot. Yet. But when he does—"

Dean wrenched Alain's neck to the left. Alain shouted and cursed in French.

"Put down the gun, Bruno," Dean said.

Bruno didn't move.

"Bruno, put it down. Or I'll hurt your friend here."

Still, Bruno aimed the gun.

Dean slowly started to push Alain's head to the left again. "I'm not kidding. Put down the gun, Bruno, or I'll break your *best* friend's neck."

Alain grunted and groaned in ever-increasing pain.

Bruno arms swayed.

"Do it, Bruno! I'm not kidding!"

"Do what he says," Alain growled through grit teeth. "Put it down."

"But you hurt me, Alain."

"Sounds like he couldn't care *less* what happens to *you!*" Dean sneered in Alain's ear. 'Oh, I wish my brother was here to tear you apart!"

"Yeah? Your brother... That reminds me... I've got a funny... joke about that nervous little prick. Did you hear the one about your brother, Peter? He's dead! Shot to death by—"

"Alain, no!"

"Shut up, you sick fuck!" Dean said, twisting Alain's head so hard he was surprised it didn't pop off.

Alain screetched.

"Stop! Don't hurt him!" Bruno said.

Speaking in short, breathy phrases, Alain said, "Yeah... You heard my friend. Careful with the... the merchandise. Hey, Bruno. While our new friend is trying... to decapitate me... why don't you show him the video we made. The good part. When Peter... collected his grand prize... for the game show. Remember?"

Bruno's jaw began to tremble like his arms.

"Come on... Show him."

Bruno didn't budge.

"Show him! Now!"

"Go ahead. Show me the video," Dean said to Bruno,

motioning with his head for Bruno to pick up the camera from the ice.

"Rewind it to the... the good part," Alain said.

"*Quelle partie?*"

"The one with his shit-head little... brother, idiot!" Alain snarled.

Dean wrenched Alain's head to the side, making him yelp.

"But I don't want to, Alain!"

"Bruno! Do it, now! Or, so help me..."

Bruno played with the buttons on the top of the camera for a few seconds, rewinding, then checking where the tape was, then rewinding again. When he'd apparently gotten to the place on the tape that he'd wanted, he took a couple of steps closer and held the camera up above his head.

Dean could barely make out what was happening on the fold out, mini-screen viewer. He saw figures moving around in the dark—a lot of confusion—the fact that there was no sound didn't help either.

"I can't see anything," Dean said after several seconds. "Turn it off."

"Come closer Bruno."

"I said I can't see!"

"Let the nice man see who he should *really* be decapitating."

Bruno slowly slid forward. As if the timing had been choreographed well in advance, the muddy blobs moving about on the camera's viewer suddenly became sharpened. The star of the scene was a very cold, very scared-looking Peter.

"This is it," Alain said. "This is right near the good part."

"Shut it off," Dean said, looking away.

"No, no, keep it rolling, Bruno ol' boy. Clear my name."

"Shut it off, I said—I don't want to see." Dean twisted

Alain's neck to the left, then right.

"Keep it... rolling," Alain squeezed out of the back of his clenched throat.

"He doesn't want to see!" Bruno shouted at Alain.

"Oh, he wants to see! They *all* want to see!"

"No, he doesn't!" Bruno shouted again, but he seemed trapped in place with the camera held above his head, as if his body and mind were still in disagreement about the right course of action.

"Turn it off!" Dean yelled, bending Alain's neck so his ear crushed against his shoulder.

"But it's the best part! Look!"

"I said—"

"Look!"

"I'm stopping the tape, Alain!"

"No! Look! Look! It's happening!"

"No! I'm not going to look!" Dean screamed. But he did—for a fraction of a second.

It was a series of shaky, grainy images.

There was Bruno.

There was Peter on his hands and knees.

There was Bruno's arm with a gun in hand—

—aiming the gun at Peter.

—then at the camera, at Alain—

—then Peter.

All that was missing was the dramatic music building, building...

building...

There was a spark, followed by a popping sound.

Chaos.

Darkness.

Then death squeezing in from all four corners of the postcard-sized screen.

Dean fell silent.

"You should've heard him beg," Alain said.

"Alain!" Bruno shouted.

Alain laughed hysterically.

Dean's body went numb.

"You ruined it!" Bruno said.

"Ruined what? Your friendship? Oh, Bruno. But *I'm* your friend. You forget, I'm inside you like a virus."

Alain's laughing grew louder and more hysterical. More insane. Dean fixed his attention and rage on Alain, determined to make him pay a severe price before he thought about Bruno. He quickly pulled his arms away, out of their full-nelson hold and wrapped them around Alain's head and twisted—

"No!"

—turned—

"No, don't!"

—wrenched—

"Don't hurt him!"

—ravenous for the cracking sounds that would tell him the sick sonofabitch was dead.

But two shots from the gun knocked Dean off his feet before he could finish the job.

Chapter 71

Bruno knew he'd made a big mistake as soon as he pulled the trigger. He didn't want Dean to die; he seemed like a genuinely good, kind, caring person. And he'd seemed to trust Bruno and want to help him—although with what and why, Bruno wasn't sure.

But he'd been in the wrong place at the wrong time.

Bruno especially didn't want anything to happen to Alain, even though he was so angry at him only moments earlier for—for *everything*—and he thought maybe he could have at least *scared* some respect out of him, but even then, only in the erasable world of dreams where the consequences of all actions disappeared like the drawings on an etch-a-sketch once the body shook awake. But now look what happened.

The wrong place at the wrong time, too.

Dean and Alain lay in a heap on the ground, Alain positioned face up on top of Dean as if he were using him as a mattress. Neither one of them moved. Bruno felt guilt rumble through him like a freight train, making his knees buckle. He dropped the Glock and camera on the ground, afraid that by simply having either of them in his possession something terrible would happen again.

He was a bad boy, for sure. When Alain saw what he had done...

When Alain found out about...

When Alain...

Few of his thoughts didn't have Alain somehow connected to them. Alain had become something of a Siamese twin to every facet of Bruno's mental life, and to a lesser extent, his physical. To lose Alain was to lose a large part of himself. Alain's death would be very much his own.

Tears spilled from Bruno's eyes... only to quickly dry in a glow of hope.

He saw Alain move.

Alain wasn't dead. He was only injured, maybe even only slightly stunned by the gun blasts.

An arm... A leg... They jerked up and then fell back down. Then Alain's body started to rock back and forth. He looked as if he was trying to get up.

Bruno was so happy to see that his friend was all right. He moved forward to help Alain stand, and to tell him how sorry he was for what he'd done—but that it had been an accident—no, that he was trying whatever it took to protect Alain from being hurt—yeah, that was better.

"Alain! Alain!" Bruno shouted as he slipped and slid towards the writhing body. "Wait! Let me help you stand! Wait! Give me you hand. I'll pull you up."

Bruno held his arm out, reaching his hand down far enough so Alain could grab hold of it. Alain looked like he was still struggling to... to stand... to roll... to do *something*—

Bruno wasn't sure what his friend's intentions were now that he was up close.

"Alain, grab my hand."

Alain only shook and wiggled and rocked from side to side.

Maybe he was a little dazed and didn't see the helping hand, Bruno thought. I have to get closer.

He crouched beside his friend. He reached out, grabbed the front of Alain's coat and gave it a tug, all the while looking into Alain's open eyes for some sign of acknowledgment.

"Alain, come on. Snap out of it. I'm here. I'll help you stand."

He tugged another part of Alain's coat.

"Alain."

And then another part—tug, tug.

"Alain. Grab my—"

Bruno felt a hand lock around his ankle. He smiled. He looked down and saw both of Alain's hands—open.

Lifeless.

His smile fell as fast as a passing star of sleet.

Chapter 72

Dean had been trying to get Alain's body off himself for a couple of minutes, but the slippery surface made it difficult to push off against anything—even something so taken for granted as the ground beneath.

He tried pushing at the leg, the arm, tried rolling the body, but nothing seemed to work. And then he saw Bruno coming closer. Dean couldn't see if he had the gun and was coming to finish him off or if he knew he'd shot only Alain and was coming to help Dean get up.

Well, Dean didn't want the help. Not if that bastard—the one Dean *thought* had been a victim while in the sadistic, manipulative hands of Alain—had been the one who killed Peter, and possibly the others. Dean might have believed it was a lie. People like Alain were masters at twisting the truth, often in the most heated and trying of circumstances, to suit their needs. But he'd seen the video. Victim or no victim, Bruno had to pay for taking Peter away.

Dean didn't know what the best retribution would be, but he knew, at the very least, there was no way he was going to let Bruno escape. So when he saw Bruno come close and felt him push and pull at Alain and beg him to get up, even though Dean recognized the desperation and fear in Bruno's voice and actions and felt them pulling at some of the deepest strings in his own heart, he felt compelled to strike. His days of not being fully involved in the act of living and all the responsibility and trying times that came with it finally went up in flame and smoke like match heads.

By the way Bruno shouted joyfully when Dean grabbed his ankle, he obviously thought Alain was still alive. But by the way he tried to pull away from Dean, Bruno obviously had no intentions of being escorted calmly and quietly to the police.

Dean's hand slipped off Bruno's ankle as he tried to pull away, but quickly found it again. This time his fingers dug into the top of Bruno's boot, so as Bruno pulled away, he pulled Dean—and Alain—with him. The two bodies slid in the same direction as Bruno, who moved down from the slope they were on towards the more level edge of the shore where he'd been standing before. Because Dean didn't let go of Bruno's boot, he and Alain crashed into the back of Bruno's legs, cutting them out from underneath him, causing him to fall on top of the two bodies. The three-man pile slid to the shoreline where a rock jammed into Dean's side, abruptly stopping his slide. Bruno and Alain tumbled off him.

Dean quickly tried to stand, thinking that Bruno must already be aiming the gun at him. He immediately fell down. He tried to stand again, this time more carefully.

Bruno had already climbed off Alain and now stood on the shore about seven feet away, watching Dean. Not seeing any gun being aimed at him, Dean took a step forward as if he were going to rush Bruno. Bruno turned and took a step towards the river.

"Bruno! Wait!" Dean said, not liking how this was unfolding.

Bruno stopped and looked back over his shoulder, appearing more like a frightened animal than a killer.

"I want you to come with me."

"Are you crazy?" Bruno said, his Quebecois accent flavoring every word. "You'll kill me."

"I won't hurt you. I promise."

"But I killed your brother. You saw. You hate me."

He could have said anything else—*anything*—and it wouldn't have come within a galaxy's distance to affecting Dean the way those words, *I killed your brother*, did. Dean ground his back teeth and tried to swallow the rage that he felt blistering the back of his throat. Images of his brother begging for mercy at the feet of Bruno lashed the surface of his mind raw. At that very moment, he *was* going to hurt Bruno—horribly.

"Please, Bruno. Just... surrender," Dean said—so far, so good with keeping calm. But then the images of his brother being shot—images even worse, even bloodier, even more riddled with torture and pain than what he'd seen in an instant on that tiny viewer—sizzled Dean's inner eyes like a branding iron. His voice trembled now as he spoke—hardly a sign of calmness. "Because I'm telling you now, Bruno, there's no way you're going to get away from me. No matter what you do."

Bruno was scared; there was no doubt about it. His eyes, either one of which could have doubled as a full moon in a clear nighttime sky, said it all.

"You'll take me to the police if I give myself up to you?"

Dean had to push down the desire to say no, that he'd execute his own swift justice right then and there. "Yes," he said, holding out his arm and putting on his best poker face. "The police. We'll bring... We'll bring the video."

Bruno looked out at the river, then back over his shoulder at Alain lying at Dean's feet. He turned so he was facing Dean. He slowly raised his arms as if he were reaching for Dean's outstretched hand.

For a moment, Dean thought Bruno had concluded that he had no choice, that he would be much better off if he peacefully surrendered.

But then Dean saw something blacker than the night in Bruno's hand.

"Sorry. Maybe we could've been friends," Bruno said, and he fired two shots at Dean.

Chapter 73

Dean dove to the ground as both bullets ricocheted off a nearby rock.

He immediately jumped back up onto his feet. Bruno seemed shocked that he wasn't dead, as if by having simply pulled the gun's trigger, the intended deed would have been done. Bruno still held the gun at arm's length, pointing it in the general direction of Dean, but Dean was coming after him anyway, gun or no gun. He expected Bruno to fire another shot.

He didn't.

Instead, Bruno turned toward the river.

"Bruno, no!"

Bruno took a couple of steps forward and onto the ice-jammed Saint Laurent, his arms held out straight on either side, swaying up and down as he tried to keep his balance.

Dean shuffled to the shoreline and stopped. Did Bruno think he was going to cross the river and get away? It was a good three hundred yards across to the city; the most dangerous three hundred yards in the world that evening. Although Dean could see the city on the other side of the river, most of its width of the river was submerged in a heavy blackness.

Floating on the river were thick, broken pieces of ice that pushed against each other, overlapped each other, rose, sank, or split each other into a jammed and jumbled mess that resembled the jagged, broken, swept-into-a-pile remains of what was once a giant white ceramic bowl. Some of the pieces were six, seven, ten feet long; others less than a foot, but all were nearly ten inches thick and tipped in one direction or the other as the river's flow shoved them from the west side into the huge columns of the Jacques Cartier bridge less than a hundred yards to the east. They growled as they shifted, as if angry, rose and fell as if they were breathing.

The ice seemed alive.

Dean could see Bruno several feet out, stepping from one ice piece to another. He was getting away and there was nothing Dean could do about it.

Except...

Dean first told himself that since it was so dangerous out there, Bruno might very well take a wrong step and fall off or through one of the floating pieces of ice and drown.

But what if he didn't?

What if he made it to the other side?

Or what if he went only twenty feet out—far enough so it would be impossible to see him from the shore—then sneaked up or down river along the crusted margin before returning to shore?

Allowing Bruno to escape was not an option.

That left only one possibility.

Bruno was nearly ten feet away now, and not slowing

down.

Now was the time to decide, to act...

To slide...

I am now.

So much sliding this night—everything from sliding feet to sliding bodies to sliding vehicles to sliding states of mind to...

Dean raised his head from the Saint Laurent to the Cross still burning bright atop Mount Royal, and beside it, the lighted, orange CBC radio tower.

Orange tower... orange pilon...

Promises, shmomises...

It's your decision, boy. You've been given the play and the ball. Now what are you gonna do?

I am now.

He stretched his leg out to put his foot on the first piece of ice he could reach, all the while *being*, as opposed to merely thinking, *I am now*—fully aware, fully focused on his task at hand. The fear that he'd been wrapped up in only moments earlier dropped away from him and onto the ice, where it slithered through the cracks and into the river.

The first piece of ice was positioned relatively flat. Because it was crushed against the shore, it didn't move when Dean stepped on it—although he *thought* it had moved, causing him to lean to the left, then the right, trying to find a balance that he'd only imagined he'd lost.

I am now.

He stepped onto the second piece. This one dipped towards him, its far end rising up out of the water several inches. This time, though, he handled the real movement better than he had the imagined.

Dean could see the grayish/black murk of Bruno's shape moving off in the distance. He tried to take some solace in the fact that Bruno was moving fast; that might mean the going was easier there. Or it could mean...

I am now, I am now, I am now, Dean screamed at his mind, trying to distract it from scary thoughts.

He saw that he couldn't force his mind into submission; he had to let it happen on its own by staying fully aware of what he was doing—that's it—letting his naked awareness pass straight through the experience.

Another step onto a solid piece, then another, then another, all the pieces positioned relatively flat and stable and close to one another so Dean couldn't see the black water raging just inches below, threatening to pull his mind away from what he was doing and into a swirling vortex of fear.

Then the next step onto the next piece. It was smaller in size—only three feet in length—and positioned flatter than the ones that had come before. Dean didn't realize, though, that it was floating freely within its confines. He stepped on it with little concern for his safety, his mind already thinking of future steps. The ice tipped underneath his foot and then dipped below the water. Dean's foot and leg followed, plunging into water so cold it felt his leg was being rubbed against a cheese grater.

His heart stopped—

—and started again.

The sudden loss of balance threw Dean forward, his arms reaching out towards any object he could grab. His hands landed solidly on the far edge of the nearest piece. He strained to pull his body up and out of the water.

The ice Dean was clinging to began to tip slowly, the side he was pulling on lifting into the air as if he possessed superhuman strength and would any second fly off with it. Dean's left leg emerged out of the river as the ice slowly stood up on its end.

As it climbed towards a vertical position, Dean looked down past his feet and saw an open space filled with bubbling black water. It looked to Dean as if he were staring straight into the churning stomach of the river monster.

The piece continued flipping.

Dean's feet hit the water again. The river monster's digestive juices quickly bubbled up to his knees. Then thighs. Then hips.

So cold... Soooooooooooooooooo cold.

There was nothing he could do. His breath caught in his throat. The river was going to swallow him whole; he'd be lucky if he were found before spring.

The water moved quickly up past his stomach, burning his flesh like acid.

He screamed.

The water climbed past his chest, past his shoulders, past his neck...

He clung. He screamed. He didn't want to die.

The water filled his mouth. The piece of ice rumbled and growled and vibrated violently, as if it was trying to shake Dean off in an angry tantrum. It pitched slightly to the right, raising Dean up out of the river a couple of inches before coming to rest. There was a gap between the single piece and the rest of the ice flow. In this gap Dean's head and hands lay, still above the water. The same couldn't be said for his body, though, which was being pulled so hard by the river's current, his legs were pressed against the underside of the Saint Laurent's white crust.

Dean knew that if he loosened his grip, he'd be sucked under. But the current held his body in perfect position to slide out from under the ice through the slanted gap. Provided he had the strength in his arms.

How many pull-ups did you do that time during practice?

Forty? So what's one *when your life depends on it?*

He could feel his strength draining away in the cold current as quickly as his body heat. His entire body had been in the water less than thirty seconds, but he knew that every passing second decreased his chances of getting out... and back to shore... and through the park and over the bridge and back to the city and...

Maybe he should just let go.

The thought flashed in his mind like a camera bulb. He didn't know if it was an urban legend or what, but he thought he'd heard that drowning was one of the least painful ways to go. And that drowning in *extremely* cold water was even better because it was so quick. He had probably already experienced the worst of it, pain-wise, when he fell in.

So what was stopping him? Whom was he kidding with all this courageous crap? Could he really go back home and pack up Peter's things?

But as much as Dean had stared into the face of his own worst enemy that night—his mind—and had understood better how to let his thoughts slide through across his awareness rather than hold on to each and every one, he could also sense that that fluidity of being had to somehow be balanced with a certain amount of grounded effort, desire and motivation—the very places where his thoughts often got the best of him, imprisoning him in seemingly unbreakable chains of habitual emotions and actions. Part of him said, literally, to let go of the ice—and life—since this is where fate had put him. And, more profoundly, because he understood now that there really was no ultimate difference between life and death; they were merely two different waves in the same ocean. But another part of him, a primal part that wanted to live, *needed* to live, told himself to fight, to struggle, to try and overcome this cruel misfortune that had been dealt to him.

Form in emptiness; emptiness in form. The secret art of living seemed to lay somewhere in the heart of their union.

No time.

No thought.

Dean could only act with whatever intention surged strongest in his veins at the moment.

And that intention was to live.

He pulled with all his remaining strength. Because of the overhead position his arms were in, the first effort yielded disappointing results. His body slid only a few inches out of the gap, bringing his chest out of the water. He pulled again, his mind screaming for his muscles to give him more. They did, and he was able to pull his entire upper body forward until only his waist and legs were still submerged.

The air felt colder than the water he'd just come out from. As soon as it blew against him, it felt like rubbing alcohol being poured on a full-body abrasion.

Death might have been a welcome relief.

He had a hard time lugging the rest of his body out because he didn't have the use of the ice's edge to pull or push against. So instead, he had to lie back on the piece of ice and wiggle his way out. Each movement that helped him to escape, though, also brought him dangerously close to sliding back into the water.

But he didn't slide back in. And when he'd finally pulled his second foot out of the river and collapsed onto the ice, he felt happy he hadn't simply let go. He stared up at the sky, shielding his eyes from the sleet as best he could with one of his numb, trembling hands. He felt he could fall asleep right there, just close his eyes and dream he was in his home, in his warm bed, with Peter loudly snoring in the next room.

But shouldn't he try to stay *awaaaaaaaaaaaake*?

He let his eyes close. The fact that he'd freeze to death if he didn't get moving suddenly didn't matter so much. He couldn't feel most of his body anyway. Where could it possibly take him? What could it possibly do for him? He felt he was nothing but a head. Just separate him from his body and throw him in a large pickle jar and he'd be fine. Then he could just sleep...

He lay on the ice and listened to the sleet hissing all around him, felt a gentle rocking and rumbling... no concerns—let Bruno get away, he didn't care—no worries— if death was this peaceful feeling, let it come—no need to do or be anything but *sleeeeeeeeeeeeeeeeeeeeep*...

He began to sink into a thick, vigorous blackness that hummed and vibrated. His sense of self swirled and twisted and turned. He felt light as a feather. Then light as air. Then even lighter—

—then heavier—

—and heavier—

—and *very* heavy, until he was plummeting into himself, into oblivion.

Hurry!

But something caught him and quickly pulled him back to normalcy. It was an unusual sound, barely discernable above the growling ice, rushing river, and crackling sleet.

A voice.

Hurry!

A panicked cry.

Hurry!

Someone crying for help.

Chapter 74

Dean's eyes sprang open, only to be pricked by falling ice pellets.

The panicked cry once again rose above the cacophony of nature's sounds. It wasn't far away. Dean turned his head to the side, but could see only large floating chunks of ice. He had to collect all his energy to sit up, then stand.

He wobbled like a drunk from his numb, weakened muscles. Even though the hypothermia confused his thinking, he knew who was crying out.

Whether it was to see that the job was done or to finish the job or to perform a rescue, Dean didn't know. He simply felt that, having come this far, he couldn't turn and walk the other way.

Each piece of ice Dean stepped on was less steady than the ones he'd crossed over closer to shore, with many of them dipping and bobbing in one direction or another when touched. He carefully tried to step as close as possible to the middle of each of them. Some were canted as much as forty-five degrees, requiring Dean to either go around them or climb over the top.

His entire body ached like an exposed nerve. The wind acted as one giant, bullying thumb, constantly pushing everywhere it was sore, constantly reminding him that he was now a man more dead than alive.

Bruno continued to cry for help, which made it easier for Dean to locate him in the dark. What he was going to do *for* him—or *against* him—when he got there still hadn't taken form in his mind.

He felt an energy humming in his chest.

It suddenly occurred to Dean that Bruno was not yelling for help from just anyone; he was yelling for Alain.

Dean could finally see what was happening several yards ahead. Bruno had fallen into the river. Only his hands and arms were above the surface—his arms lying curved over a large piece of ice as if it were a floatation device. The ice piece was surrounded on three sides by the rest of the jam—up stream, down stream, and shore side. But on the far side, there was nothing but Bruno and the powerful river.

Not only was Bruno in danger of freezing and drowning, but the piece of ice he clung to looked as if it would just as soon pull out of its little lagoon and glide with the current. Bruno's feet kicking beneath the surface were probably enough to keep the ice piece where it was.

But soon Bruno's legs would grow so numb, they'd be useless.

Dean gave thought to what he should do. Should he just stand and watch, waiting for Bruno's legs to tire and his mini-iceberg to carry his down river to his death? Or should he try to help him?

The question, at first, seemed too easy to answer. But

then Bruno saw Dean standing there and started to shout for him instead of Alain.

"Help me! Please! Dean! Help me! I'm so sorry for all I did—help me, please!"

It seemed to Dean that Bruno's eyes glowed white; they were overflowing with panic. He wondered if his own eyes had looked like that when he had thought his life was over.

And Peter's? Had Bruno seen eyes like that looking at him when he pulled the trigger?

"Please, Dean! Please, help me, I beg you! Oh God, please help me! I beg you! Please!"

Perhaps if he'd had a mute button, he could have remained motionless and watched the images unfolding before him with little emotional involvement. But he couldn't mute the scene. Bruno's pleading penetrated his skin deeper than the cold river water and wind, making it impossible to simply standby and watch. Maybe yesterday—yes. Maybe tomorrow—yes. Maybe three or four hours ago even—yes. But now...

NOW...

"Help! Please! Help me!"

Dean worked his way over to Bruno. There was a three-foot gap filled with black river between Dean's postion and Bruno's floating ice piece.

"Hurry! I can't hold on much longer!"

"I'll do all I can. Just try and keep that piece of ice you're on as close to me as possible."

"Okay. Thank you. I'm so cold. Thank you, Dean. You've always been such a good friend," Bruno blubbered.

Dean didn't know if it was the hypothermia doing the talking or what.

"I'm going to throw you the end of my coat," Dean said, removing it. Because it was soaking wet, he didn't feel much of a difference in temperature when he took it off: He was slowly turning into a human popsicle either way.

He tied one of the coat sleeves around his wrist. He didn't trust his numb hands to be able to grip anything for too long or with much strength. When he was finished, from a half-crouched position on the edge of his piece of ice, he tossed as much of the coat as he could towards Bruno's hands. It fell several inches short. He collected the coat and tried again, but with the same results. He had to get closer.

"Quick! I can't hold much longer. I'm sliding off."

Dean got down on his hands and knees, leaned over the edge of his ice piece and tossed the coat. This time it hit Bruno's hand, but he had less than an inch of material to grab onto. He seemed unable to even pinch his fingers.

"Grab it!" Dean said, getting frustrated.

"I'm trying! My hands—they're frozen!"

"Dammit!"

Feeling he didn't have enough time to strip off one of his wet shirts to tie it to the sleeve with shaking hands and fingers he could barely feel, Dean attempted the only thing he thought possible at the moment. Still wanting to keep at least part of his body on his piece of ice, from his hands and knees, Dean carefully bridged the gap, so his upper body rested on Bruno's piece and his knees stayed on his own. He felt Bruno's piece bob up and down and suddenly start to pull away. For a moment, Dean thought he was going in the water again.

I am now.

Right mind became right action, effortlessly. Spontaneously.

Dean gained control over the wayward ice piece. He threw his coat out towards Bruno's hands again. The end of the sleeve landed in the water in front of Bruno's head. There was no way he couldn't grab it now.

"Wrap it around one of your hands so it doesn't slip."

"What? I don't understand?"

"Wrap it," Dean said, trying his best to demonstrate with his own hands.

Dean could see Bruno's hand shaking so much as he held it up and slowly twisted and wound the sleeve around it. His jaw, too, wouldn't stop. It would be a miracle if all his teeth weren't cracked to bits when this was done. It was then that Dean noticed his own jaw was also shaking uncontrollably. He tried to will it to stop, but it wouldn't. His body was operating under a different set of instructions now, doing what it had to do to keep itself alive.

When Bruno had the sleeve as secure around his hand as it ever was going to be, Dean pushed himself back onto his own piece of ice until he was on his knees. He pulled the coat. His arms and back and stomach hurt so much and were so tight and sore from the cold he thought they'd tear.

Bruno lifted up out of the water with Dean's first effort. He rested his chest on the edge of the ice while his lower body was still in the river. With a second pull, Bruno's entire body slid out of the water and onto his piece of ice, which wobbled from side to side, threatening to tip.

It was then that Bruno's piece set sail out of its mini-harbor.

It drifted into the open river.

Dean saw immediately what was happening and yelled to Bruno to get up and jump over to his piece. But Bruno lay on the ice exhausted.

The coat sleeve tied around Dean's hand pulled taut. He fumbled with it, trying to both untie and rip it from his wrist.

The ice caught in the river's swift current and took off like a dragster.

He had no choice; he had to act quickly. He stood up and jumped for Bruno's piece of ice. His feet immediately slipped out from underneath, causing him to crash hard on his rear-end. Before, he had wondered if it were possible to feel more pain than what he had been feeling. Now he knew. Stars-before-the-eyes kind of pain seared his nerve-endings.

He finally freed his wrist and hand from the binding coat sleeve. He turned over so he was on his hands and knees. The ice rose and dipped with each move, threatening to throw off its two hitchhikers. Dean quickly fell on top of Bruno, grabbed at his hands and searched his pockets, looking for a gun or other weapon. He found nothing.

Bruno, who seemed to be half-dazed, started to laugh maniacally. Dean, spooked by the look on his face, backed away as far as he could.

"I tried my best, Alain," Bruno said to Dean through the laughter. "I tried my best to get away, but I guess I messed up."

Dean stared, speechless. He felt like he was watching a man come apart at the seams.

"I know you're mad at me, but... please don't be. I'll be better next time. Please don't hate me, Alain. Please don't hurt me."

Dean didn't know if Bruno actually saw him as Alain or if he was simply talking to himself out loud.

"I'm sorry I made you hurt. I'm so sorry I made you hurt. I'm so sorry..." Bruno said over and over.

The words startled Dean because of their similarity to the ones he'd spoken to his dead father *that night* on the side of the Massachusetts Turnpike.

Again, because Dean could identify with Bruno at some level, he wanted to believe Bruno was someone he should feel badly for and take pity on.

Dean turned his attention away from Bruno and focused on what was happening around them. The river's current had taken full control of their frozen raft, carrying it swiftly towards the Jacques Cartier bridge towering above them just thirty yards ahead. The ice jam lay no more than seven feet to Dean's right and continued all the way up to the bridge's center column. Dean could see that they were going to pass very close to that center column; perhaps affording them their last chance to escape disaster.

"We've got to get off of this thing now," Dean said.

Bruno seemed to ignore Dean. He kept laughing and babbling.

"If we don't get off this thing, we're both gonna die," Dean said, more to himself than to Bruno. Bruno looked as good as dead anyway. As far as Dean was concerned, he'd done the right thing once in risking his own life to save Bruno's, but he wasn't about to do it again. If Bruno came with him, Dean would make sure he didn't get away this time. If Bruno stayed on the ice, that would be proof positive for Dean that the guy was a goner.

They briskly drifted toward the center column. Dean could tell they had maybe thirty seconds to make their move. If he jumped now, Dean knew he'd never make it, and the river's current would surely finish him off. But when he looked down river at the direction they were heading, he could see that their piece was going to come within a few feet of the ice jam up ahead.

"We've got to try and jump when we get closer up there," Dean said, pointing up ahead for Bruno's sake. "You see?" But Bruno remained sitting on the ice. His arms were pulling his knees up under his chin and he was rocking back and forth muttering something that Dean couldn't hear.

"Fine. You're on your own. I'm sure the river will take

care of you," Dean said, turning his attention away from Bruno and focusing on what he had to do. As he stood, Dean thought he was expecting the impossible of himself. His body literally felt frozen. The clothes he wore were stiff, but only half as stiff as the skin and muscles and bones they were supposed to be protecting.

The jumping point approached. He only hoped his knees held together.

"This is your last chance, Bruno. Are you coming?" Dean said, glancing over his shoulder. But Bruno hadn't moved from his seated fetal position. "Then I'd tell you to go burn in hell, but that would sounds like a vacation right about now."

Dean readied himself to leap. His timing would have to be perfect, his effort immense, to broad-jump it from a piece of ice with nearly zero traction and stability clear across the river. But it was the only choice he had. He crouched to test his knees. The numbness was so intense, any pain that he might feel from them was muted. But at least the knee cap held in place.

I am now.

It was the closest thing to a prayer or magic phrase that he knew.

He focused his concentration on the edge of the flow.

His timing had to be perfect.

He crouched down and cocked his arms behind his body, ready to spring.

Now! He had to jump now!

Just then a hand grabbed his shoulder and pushed it down, fusing his body to the ice. Dean saw a dark figure fly through the air beside him and land on the ice jam—a perfect jump. Dean lost his balance. He stumbled backwards a couple of feet. He saw Bruno turn and look back at him, grinning and waving.

Dean had no time to think. The distance between himself and the ice jam was growing quickly. He had to move immediately or risk being swept away down the river. He saw the bridge's center column towering before him. He had to leap for it and hope for the best—it was his last chance.

He stepped forward with force, trying to get a running start and enough momentum to clear the distance, but his foot slipped, causing him to stumble. He felt he was going to fall forward, straight into the river, head first, but at the last second, his foot stamped on the edge of the piece of ice; he was able to push off with an explosive energy born of desperation.

He landed face first on the main ice flow and slid.

The leap wasn't a complete success; it took its toll on one of Dean's knees, popping the kneecap out of position so it moved to the side of his leg. He dropped to the ground like a sack of potatoes.

The cold helped dull the agony, but Dean still gasped as he pushed the kneecap back into position.

He had no time to lick his wounds or pity himself. Bruno streaked by him and ran for the bridge's center column. Dean didn't know what his intentions were at first, but when he looked more closely at the column, he could see a set of U-shaped iron pieces had been set into its side to be used as a ladder. Dean followed the ladder with his eye. It disappeared into the darkness and precipitation halfway up the column, but Dean guessed it extended all the way up to the bridge's road surface.

Bruno shuffled to the ladder.

"Bruno, no! Stop!"

Bruno turned and looked at Dean, grinned again as he'd done before, and then said, "Come on, Alain. We're just starting to have fun." He started climbing.

Was this some kind of game for him? Dean thought. And why does he keep calling me Alain? He must have really lost it?

This coming from the guy who's heard his father's voice in his head for how many years?

Feeling sorry or ashamed for what happened before wasn't going to help him now. Climbing a ladder with his crabby knee was going to be difficult enough. Climbing a ladder that seemed to extend into the sky for eternity while enduring a crabby kneecap and the middle stages of hypothermia, all in order to catch a killer, might have been flirting with the impossible.

"Bruno!" Dean yelled again as he limped over to the ladder. "Bruno, stop! Don't do this!"

But Bruno kept climbing. And laughing.

Dean gripped the ladder's rungs and looked up.

If this isn't taking the fricking ball up the middle, I don't know what is.

He took a deep breath and started to climb. As his adrenaline rush wore off, each step, each pull, each rung brought increased agony to his body, but surprisingly little to his mind. His mind was focused only on each rung—never higher, never lower.

But then, a quarter of the way up, he made the mistake of looking down.

He suddenly felt how slippery the iron rungs were. His hands had trouble gripping them. With each step, the foot on his better leg slid backwards and forwards, side to side. His crabby knee seemed to be trying to sabotage his progress by giving out on him when he needed it most. His head started to spin, making left seem right and up seem down. He struggled to pull his attention back to the rungs he was gripping and standing on—and nothing else. This kept any deadly panic at bay.

Bruno seemed to be having his own problems—or it was just part of his game—because, by the time he'd reached the halfway point up the ladder, Dean had somehow closed the gap separating them.

Dean reached up and grabbed Bruno's ankle. Bruno shook his ankle free and kicked at Dean's head. Dean snapped his head away from the oncoming kick. His feet slipped to the side of the ladder's rung—and then off. Both his legs dangled in the air momentarily as his body twisted left and right in the gusting wind, his fingers and hands screaming for help.

He quickly found the rung, and started after Bruno. Again, Dean grabbed for his feet, this time getting a better grip on his ankle, and again Bruno tried to shake his leg free. But Dean wouldn't let go this time.

"Give up, before we *both* get killed!" Dean shouted, hoping there was at least a sliver of sense left in the guy. Bruno kept kicking and Dean continued pulling. Suddenly, Bruno's boot popped off, hit the top of Dean's head, and disappeared into the darkness below. It was then that Dean realized that pulling on Bruno's leg probably wasn't the best way to attack, since if Bruno fell, he'd undoubtedly take Dean with him.

Stupid decisions again! Stupid, stupid! Were you cursed to make stupid decisions for the rest of your life?

Dean took a moment to calm himself. He let Bruno advance while he stayed put and repeated *I am now* several times. The berating voice in his head quickly subsided, leaving only the vicious elements and the slippery rungs and his throbbing, numb body to deal with. When he felt better, he continued climbing after Bruno, focusing only on staying close to the killer rather than catching him.

The higher they got, the more the wind howled around them like an angry phantom. Over their left shoulder, the Durango could be seen hanging, its engine still running, its headlights still shining down—a mechanical monster breathing its last breaths as it dangled from the gallows pole.

Up ahead of Dean, Bruno seemed to have generated a burst of energy out of the only abundant resources around: frozen water and frozen air. Either that, or Dean's kneecap had fallen off and he hadn't noticed. Bruno moved as far ahead of Dean as in the beginning of the climb. He neared the top of the ladder looking light and nimble on his one booted-foot. Dean stopped and watched him push open a square doorway underneath the bridge and then disappear through it. He didn't bother to close the doorway behind himself. Dean continued on up the ladder, apprehensive that the open doorway might have been a prop in a set trap.

Dean prepared himself for an attack.

He quickly stuck his hand above the doorway and then pulled it back, waiting to see if someone was going to swat, kick, chop, stab, or shoot at it.

Nothing.

Didn't mean much, though. Even a delusional idiot could probably discern a hand from a head nine times out of ten. So Dean slowly moved his head through the doorway, just to the point that he could see above the sidewalk surface. Immediately in front of Dean lay the barrier and railing separating the sidewalk from the road. To his right, nothing but blackness. Behind himself, nothing but blackness. But to his left, Dean could see the back-end of the Durango stuck to the bridge, its red brake lights nearly snuffed out by a layer of semi-translucent ice and snow. To the right of the truck on the sidewalk lay the dead policeman. To the right of the dead police man, in the road, stood his twisted and torn patrol car.

But no Bruno.

Dean climbed through the doorway and lugged himself onto the sidewalk. He twisted from side to side because it was comfortable to move that way and because he could watch every direction. He shuffled toward the dead policeman, wondering where was the cop's backup. But then he remembered that there were a half-dozen or so other police cars wrecked about a paralyzed city to tend to. And who knew if this cop had even called for backup in the heat of the chase. Maybe he never imagined things would slide so far out of control as they did—who knew?

Dean wondered if the cop was another one of Bruno's victims, or if, as on Mount Royal, this had been Alain's doing. Looking down at the cop, Dean noticed how similar death looked in all cases, no matter what the dead person was like and no matter what the cause. There was a difference in the toll the dying took on the body, to be sure, whether it was through a long illness or by much quicker means, but a dead body had a certain stoic aloneness that was always the same; like a piece of scuffed and dusty luggage left behind on a seat at a busy airport terminal.

Dean searched the policeman for his gun, but didn't find one.

Although Dean couldn't see very far north or south along the Jacques Cartier bridge, he knew Bruno couldn't possibly have gone farther than he could see. He had to be nearby.

Like hiding behind the patrol car.

Dean slipped between the railings and limped in the direction of the wreck, watching for any signs of movement on its left or right side, or in the gaps between the twisted and torn pieces of metal.

No movement.

But that meant Bruno could be crouching down. Dean fearlessly approached the wreck from the nearest side and hobbled clear around it.

A bang.

Dean whirled around, ready for a confrontation, his kneecap popping out of position. He saw pieces of a burst icicle scatter across the road.

Dean thought he heard something coming from the patrol car wreck. He headed back in that direction, but nothing was there. It probably was just a piece of torn metal knocking against something in the gusting of wind.

He heard something else. Contained in the rumbling wind and sour situation was a sweet melody. For a moment, Dean thought he might be going nuts—another stage of hypothermia setting in before his demise. But no—

—it was real.

He was sure of it. But weren't the insane always sure of their demons?

Dean turned toward the Durango. The music seemed to be coming from there. If his ears were tricking him, his eyes couldn't very well join in on the same deception, could they? Dean limped towards the truck, trying to remember if the radio had been left on. He couldn't recall; everything had been so chaotic that night, like stirred-up mud, the details of which had yet to settle for closer scrutiny.

He told himself that the music wasn't anything important. But, nonetheless, he wanted to check it out in order that all sounds and sights were accounted for before continuing to search for Bruno.

As he got closer to the Durango, he was sure the music was coming from there. He leaned over the railing until he could peek through the frame of the busted-out back window.

He couldn't believe what he saw.

Curled up in the fetal position on the back of the driver's seat and deflated white airbag was Bruno. The music that Dean had heard was coming from the Durango's stereo. Christmas music. Bruno reached down to the dashboard below him and changed the song playing on the CD with a press of a button. It seemed he was trying to hear a bit of them all.

Dean heard him talking.

"Yeah, I like that one," he said. "That's one of my favorites, Alain." And then, when the next song started, "This one too, this is one of my favorites. I know you really liked this one. You like all those songs with a big choir. Me, I like... I like them, too."

Dean didn't know if he should say something. Why was Bruno down there? And why was he listening to Christmas music *now*? It didn't make any sense. But what did make sense was the loss Dean heard in Bruno's voice. He hadn't lost a friend that night—at least not a friend in the typical sense. Dean could tell that he'd lost himself. Bruno had already died that night, along with Alain. Although Bruno's heartbeat and his brain continued to function, everything Bruno was had been contained within Alain.

In some ways, it was as if Bruno had killed himself.

Now he was back here in the Durango, half off his rocker to be sure, listening to Christmas music—Alain's music. And Alain's music was his music. Alain's evil was his evil.

Dean understood what Bruno was feeling because he'd felt it himself after *that night*—albeit to a lesser extent. In the early years, Dean's entire sense of self was shaped by his father. After his father was gone, Dean's self was shaped by his memories—whether they were accurate or not. But tonight, Dean had begun to understand how one's sense of self is as volatile and fluid as the river one hundred feet below that nearly killed him.

I am now.

Dean looked up from the Durango and saw the Cross sitting atop Mont Royal. It glowed as eternally as Dean's need to transcend his old self. And part of that transcendence would involve the death of his old self and the birth of something new.

He looked down at Bruno and, this time, felt more disgust than pity for the man. Dean saw Bruno as a living exaggeration of everything he hated about himself, everything he wanted to die.

Without contemplation, Dean grabbed the back bumper of the Durango and lifted; strained with every ounce of remaining strength he possessed. The truck creaked forward, started to descend, then got hung up on another part of its bumper. Dean leaned over the railing, grabbed at the parts that were caught and pulled, trying to bend things just—

—enough—

—to—

It worked. The truck groaned and let go, slid free from the bridge's grasp.

But not before a hand grabbed Dean's wrist.

******

Bruno had somehow climbed up to the truck's back window. He'd leapt and grabbed Dean's hand as the Durango plunged down into the Saint Laurent.

Bruno held Dean's right arm with only his left arm, while the rest of his body dangled and waved frantically in the air. Dean held himself against the railing with his legs and left arm, but it was so icy they could have slipped at any second.

He felt his kneecap sliding.

"Help me, please!" Bruno cried to Dean, his eyes bulging out in terror. "Don't let me die! I don't want to die!"

Dean started to pull Bruno up, but he could feel his shoulder ready to pop out of its socket from the weight.

"Please! Don't drop me!" Bruno screamed.

Dean felt himself slipping. He didn't know what to do. He couldn't think straight. This was all so unexpected. Dean leaned forward over the railing, trying to lower his arm so Bruno could get a better grip. As he did so, though, Bruno's right arm rose. There was a gun in it—the dead cop's gun. He aimed it at Dean and grinned.

"Tag! You're it, Alain!" he shouted. He fired two shots at Dean. Both of the bullets pounded into Dean's left shoulder, their force throwing him back, breaking the bond with Bruno.

Dean could hear Bruno laughing as he fell, as death waited to catch him in its icy hands below.

Dean fell onto his back on the sidewalk and watched his white breath mix with the elements of the night, acutely aware of the constant flux of the universe . He closed his eyes and thought not of his brother, not of his employees, not of his good or bad decisions in life, not of his courage or fear, not of what had happened the last couple of hours or what might or might not happen in the future...

He listened to the howling wind and the hiss of the sleet and the sirens off in the distance heading his way, remaining perfectly in the center of waiting and not-waiting for whatever was to happen next, resting in the space between moments, letting himself slide into a blissful sense of the eternal and often ambiguous nature of being.

Note to the Reader

If you enjoyed this novel, please help the author by sharing your thoughts or the book itself with others. Word-of-mouth is invaluable in this business.

Don't forget that information on this and future novels by Matteson can be found on the author's web site, www.montrealstarvingartist.com.

Thank you.